The Rush for the Spoil

The Rush for the Spoil

Émile Zola

MINT EDITIONS

The Rush for the Spoil was first published in 1872.

This edition published by Mint Editions 2021.

ISBN 9781513282084 | E-ISBN 9781513287102

Published by Mint Editions®

MINT
EDITIONS

minteditionbooks.com

Publishing Director: Jennifer Newens
Design & Production: Rachel Lopez Metzger
Project Manager: Micaela Clark
Translated By: Ernest Vizetelly
Typesetting: Westchester Publishing Services

Contents

Preface

The public and the press have agreed that "L'Assommoir" is M. Zola's *chef d'œuvre*. Against this verdict I have no objection to offer. I believe it will meet with posterity's endorsement. But although "L'Assommoir" may lift its head the highest, there are many other volumes in the Rougon-Macquart series which stand on, and speak from equally lofty platforms of art. In my opinion, these are "La Faute de l'Abbé Mouret," "La Conquête de Plassans," and "La Curée."

I have spoken before of Zola as an epic poet: he is this more than he is anything, and as he is more epic in "La Curée" than elsewhere ("L'Assommoir" and "La Faute de l'Abbé Mouret" always excepted), it follows that it must be one of the best and most characteristic of his works. The qualities that endow a book with immortality exist independent of the artist's will, and the process of penetrating, of animating the whole with life, is accomplished as silently and unconsciously as the seed-grain germinates in the earth, as the child quickens with life in the womb. And, doubtless, Zola intended in the beginning to write merely the passionate love story of a woman who, oppressed and wearied of luxury, is forced to seek, in violent ways and fierce fancies, oblivion of golden idleness, of an aimless and satiated existence. This idea might have been worked out, and adequately worked out, in the analysis of the mind of a duke's daughter, who, after five years of husband hunting in London drawing-rooms, runs away and lives with her groom at Hampstead. And taken out of its setting, M. Zola's story is quite as simple. Renée is a young girl of the upper middle classes; she has been seduced; she is enceinte; it is necessary to find her a husband. Under such circumstances, it would be vain to be too particular, and an adventurer called Saccard is chosen. He is a genius who is waiting for a few pounds to make a million. Renée's fortune enables him to do this; he places her in a magnificent house in the Parc Monceaux; he gives her everything but an interest in life: to gain this she falls in love with her stepson, Maxime Saccard. The story of this incestuous passion becomes the theme of the book; and when Maxime deserts his stepmother to get married, she dies of consumption. That is all; but this slight outline soon began to grow, to take gigantic proportions in Zola's mind; and it was not long before he saw that his story was an allegory of the Second Empire. Renée became Paris; her dressmaker—Worms—became the Emperor; her dresses, the material of which costs sixty, the making-up of which, with the accumulated interest, costs six hundred, are the boulevards and buildings with which the city was adorned at ruinous expense. In the clamour of the fêtes in the Parc Monceaux, the demands of the creditors are silenced, and when Renée dies her debts are paid by her father—that is to say, by the Republic of M. Thiers.

Renée is a Venus, but not the Greek Venus—the white-breasted woman born of the sea foam and heralded by cupids and tritons; she is not even "the obscure Venus of the hollow Hill" that Baudelaire describes as having grown diabolic among ages that would not accept her as divine. Renée is the Venus of the counting house. Her hair is yellow as pale gold, her drawing-room is hung with yellow draperies, and her golden head, seen thereon as she leans back in her richly upholstered chairs, seems like a setting sun that sinks little by little, drowned in a bath of gold. But, unlike her earlier prototypes, she does not find the flesh sufficient; her sensualities are not the dark desire of the animal, but the nervous erethism of a human mind that, satiated with pleasure, longs and hungers for some strange and acute note to break the cloying sweetness—the monotonous melody of her life. Here there is no touch of pagan or mediæval thought. Maxime fears no god, he knows not remorse nor even desire; he is the son of the capitalist; he is the weed sprung from, but not the intelligence that has built up, the gold-heap, and he festers and rots like a weed in an overpoweringly rich soil. Saccard is Mammon. Nothing exists for him but gold. Thoughts, dreams, love, have long since disappeared; he is not even vicious: in the lust of speculation all other passions have been submerged, have sunk out of sight for ever. Men and things only suggest to him ideas for the accumulation of wealth; and from the heights of Montmartre he looks down upon Paris like a wolf upon its prey. His eyes flash with fierce light, his lips twitch with a wild mental hunger that manifests itself in physical actions: with his hand he divides Paris into sections, he sees how he will distribute it into boulevards, squares, and streets; and he hears in vision the cries of the huntsmen, and he longs to put himself at the head of the hounds, and to descend with open jaws upon the splendid quarry that even now run to death lies panting and bleeding before him.

The book is Paris—Paris as she feasted and flattered under the Second Empire—a Paris of adventurers, of courtezans—a Paris of debts—a Paris of women's shoulders, cotillons, champagne, of violins and pianos—a Paris of opera hats—a Paris of gold pieces, of fraud, of liars, of speculation, of supper tables—a Paris sonorous and empty as a wheel of fortune—a Paris of sweetmeats, rendezvous, bank-notes—a Paris of tresses of false hair forgotten in hackney carriages.

Yes, a Paris of this and of little else. There is the famous scene of the return from the Bois. Under the pale October sky, in which towards the Porte de la Muette, there still floats the dim light of an autumn sunset, the carriages are blocked; and the uncertain rays dance through the brightly painted wheels, touching with intense splendour the buckles of the harness, the large buttons on the liveries, and the burnished cockades. The artificial lake lies still, reflecting in its crystal clarity the innumerable graces of the poplars and pine trees that grow down to the very banks of the trim island. The walks are as bits of grey ribbon lost in the dark foliage. The scene looks like a newly varnished toy. All Paris is there—courtezans, diplomatists, and speculators. Renée is there; she is with Maxime, who is pointing out and telling her about his father's new mistress.

She is the celebrated Laure, to whose house Renée goes with Maxime, because she is anxious to know what a *cocotte's* ball is really like. Afterwards they sup, in a *cabinet particulier*, at the Café Riche. Renée is sipping a glass of chartreuse; the gas is hissing, the room has grown hot. They throw open the window. Paris rolls beneath them. The Boulevard is alive with the flashing lights of carriages, women go by in hundreds; they pass into the darkness of a traversing street; they reappear again like shadows thrown by a magic lantern. Groups of men sit round the tables at the door of the café; some are talking to women; some sit smoking vacantly, watching the interminable procession that passes and repasses before them. One woman wears a green silk; she sits with her legs crossed. Renée feels strangely interested. By-and-by, wearied of the Boulevard, she examines the looking-glass, scratched all over with diamond rings; and she asks Maxime questions concerning the women whose names are scrawled thereon. Maxime pleads ignorance: putting his cigar aside, he advances towards her; they look into each other's eyes; she falls into his arms.

There is the ball-room scene. Saccard is on the brink of ruin, but he gives a fête that costs him four thousand pounds. He is anxious that his son should marry a little hunchback, who has an immense fortune. The *tableaux vivants* are over, and the dancers, in the costumes of gods and goddesses, are dancing the cotillon. Renée, who is cognizant of her husband's projects, is wandering about mad with nervous rage and despair. She pursues Maxime, drags him with her into her bedroom, and tells him that he must fly with her to America, that she will never consent to give him up.

And I must not forget that requisite bit of description—ten lines, not more—which, for rapidity of observation and precision and delicacy of touch, seems to me unsurpassable; indeed, to find anything that might be set against it, I should have to turn to that supreme success, that final vindication of the divine power of words—Flaubert's "L'Éducation Sentimentale." The passage I allude to is when Renée goes to the great fête at the Tuileries. She wears a wonderful dress, composed entirely of white muslin and black velvet. The bodice is in black velvet, the skirt in white muslin, garnished with a million flounces, and all cut up and adorned with bows made out of black velvet: no ornament but one diamond in her fawn-coloured hair. Suddenly the people draw into lines, and the corpulent Emperor walks down the room on the arm of one of his generals. Renée shrinks back: but she cannot get away—she is in the front rank; and, when Napoleon fixes his, all eyes are fixed upon her. A heaven of lustres is above her head, a velvety carpet beneath her feet, and she hears the general whisper to the Emperor: "There's a carnation that would suit our button-holes uncommonly well." The rest of the fête is lost in this *moment d'âme*;—is an acute note that vibrates long in the monotonous melody of her life.

Whether "La Curée" is a faithful picture, true to the smallest detail, of life under the Second Empire, I cannot say. Nor do I care. I am content to take it for what it seems to me to be—a gorgeous, a golden poem, born of the author's contemplation of the scenes he describes. Although a tyrant, Napoleon the Third was a demagogue at heart. When he came into office Paris was starving. To govern, he saw that he would have to feed the people, and to do this the ingenious plan of creating an immense debt, living upon it and giving the city as security, was adopted. He appeased his enemies by calling new names to the front, he unchained, and he gave them unlimited means of gratifying their appetites. In a house of ill-fame politics do not occupy men's minds—why not turn Paris into a house of ill-fame? But what is true for individuals is true for nations: Sedan was the suicide of the prostituted city. This is the view M. Zola takes of the Second Empire. "La Curée" is but a corner of it, but I do not know any corner more beautifully finished, more perfectly proportioned. Of course faults may be urged: it may be said, and I admit with a certain show of reason, that the characters are more representative of the classes to which they belong than individual men and women. The same argument may be used, and with equal effect, against Hamlet, against Orestes, against every beautiful drawing of Hokousaï and Hokkeï: but when possible and impossible faults have been found, and all visible and invisible flaws taken note of, I believe it will be admitted by the blind, the dumb, and the lame that, when the last page of "La Curée" is read, the impression left upon the mind is one of intense artistic beauty.

GEORGE MOORE

I

O n the return home, the carriage could only move slowly along amidst the mass of vehicles winding round the lake of the Bois de Boulogne. At one moment, the block became such that the horses were even brought to a standstill.

The sun was setting in the faint grey October sky, streaked with slender clouds on the horizon. A last ray, which came from above the distant shrubbery of the cascade, streamed across the roadway, bathing the long line of now stationary carriages in a pale ruddy light. The golden glimmers, the bright flashes from the wheels, seemed to have become fixed to the straw-coloured fillets, whilst the dark blue panels of the carriage reflected portions of the surrounding landscape. And, higher up, full in the ruddy light which illumined them from behind, and which gave a sparkle to the brass buttons of their overcoats folded over the back of the box-seat, the coachman and the footman, dressed in a livery consisting of dull blue coats, putty-coloured breeches, and black and yellow-striped waistcoats, sat erect, grave and patient, like well-trained lackeys, whose temper is above being ruffled by a block of vehicles. Their hats, embellished with black cockades, gave them a most dignified appearance. The superb bay horses were alone snorting impatiently.

"Hallo!" said Maxime, "there's Laure d'Aurigny over there in that brougham. Look, Renée."

Renée raised herself slightly, and, blinking her eyes with that exquisite pout which was caused by the weakness of her sight, said:

"I thought she was travelling. She has changed the colour of her hair, has she not?"

"Yes," replied Maxime, with a laugh, "her new lover detests everything red."

Renée, bent forward, her hand resting on the low door of the carriage, continued looking, awakened from the sad dream which, for an hour past, had kept her silently reclining on the back seat, as though in an invalid's easy-chair. Over a mauve dress with an upper skirt and tunic, and trimmed with broad plaited flounces, she wore a little white cloth jacket with mauve velvet facings, which gave her a very dashing air. Her extraordinary pale fawn-coloured hair, the hue of which recalled that of the finest butter, was scarcely concealed beneath a slender bonnet adorned with a cluster of crimson roses. She continued to blink her eyes, in the style of an impertinent boy, her pure brow crossed by one long wrinkle, her upper lip protruding just like a sulky child's. Then, as she was unable to distinguish very well, she raised her double eye-glass, a regular man's eye-glass with a tortoise-shell frame, and holding it up in her hand without placing it on her nose, she examined stout Laure d'Aurigny at her ease, in a perfectly calm manner.

The block still continued. Amidst the uniform, dull-coloured patches caused by the long line of broughams—extremely numerous in the Bois on that autumn afternoon—the glass of a window, a horse's bit, a plated lamp-holder, or the gold or silver lace on the livery of some lackey seated up on high, sparkled in the sun. Here and there an open landau displayed a glimpse of a dress, some woman's costume in silk or velvet. Little by little a profound silence had succeeded the hubbub of the now stationary mass. In the depths of the carriages one could overhear the remarks of the pedestrians. There was an exchange of speechless glances from vehicle to vehicle; and all conversation ceased during this deadlock, the silence of which was only broken by the creaking of harness and the impatient pawing of some horse. The confused murmurs of the Bois were dying away in the distance.

In spite of the lateness of the season, all Paris was there: the Duchess de Sternich, in a chariot; Madame de Lauwerens, in a victoria, drawn by some very fine cattle; Baroness de Meinhold, in a delicious dark brown private cab; Countess Vanska, with her piebald ponies; Madame Daste and her famous black steppers; Madame de Guende and Madame Teissière, in a brougham; little Sylvia, in a deep blue landau; and Don Carlos, too, in mourning, with his ancient and solemn-looking livery; Selim Pasha, with his fez and without his tutor; the Duchess de Rozan, in her single-seated brougham, and with her powdered lackeys; Count de Chibray, in a dog-cart; Mr. Simpson, on a well-appointed mail-coach; the whole of the American colony. Finally, two members of the Academy in a cab.

The leading carriages were at length released, and the whole line was soon able to move slowly onwards. It was like an awakening. A thousand scintillations danced around, rapid flashes played to and fro amidst the wheels, whilst the harness shaken by the horses emitted a galaxy of sparks. Along the ground and on the trees were broad reflexions of fleeting glass. This glistening of harness and of wheels, this blaze of varnished panels all aglow with the red fire of the setting sun, the bright touches of the gorgeous liveries perched up on high, and of the rich costumes bursting from the confined space of the equipages, passed along in the midst of a hollow, continuous rumbling, timed by the pace of the thoroughbreds. And the procession continued, accompanied by the same sounds and the same scintillations, unceasingly and at one spurt, as though the leading vehicles had been dragging all the others after them.

Renée had yielded to the slight jolting of the carriage as it once more started off, and, dropping her eye-glass, she had resumed her half-reclining posture on the cushions. She shiveringly drew towards her a corner of the bearskin which filled the interior of the vehicle with a silky snow-white mass. Her gloved hands became lost amidst the long soft curly hairs. The north wind was beginning to blow. The warm October afternoon which, in giving to the Bois an appearance of spring, had brought out the most fashionable ladies in their open carriages, threatened to end in an evening of piercing chilliness.

For a while the young woman remained huddled up, enjoying the warmth of her corner, and abandoning herself to the voluptuous lullaby of all those wheels turning before her eyes. Then, raising her head towards Maxime, whose glances were quietly unrobing the women displayed in the adjoining broughams and landaus, she asked:

"Really now, do you think her pretty, that Laure d'Aurigny? You were praising her up so much the other day when some one spoke of the sale of her diamonds! By the way, you have not seen the necklace and the aigrette that your father bought me at the sale."

"Ah! he does everything well," said Maxime with a spiteful laugh, and without answering her question. "He manages to pay Laure's debts, and to make his wife presents of diamonds."

The young woman slightly shrugged her shoulders.

"Rascal!" murmured she with a smile.

But the young man had leant forward, following with his eyes a lady whose green dress interested him. Renée was resting her head, her eyes half closed, idly glancing at both sides of the avenue, but without seeing. On the right were copses and low bushes, with slender branches and reddened leaves; now and again, on the track reserved for riders, passed slim built gentlemen whose galloping steeds raised little clouds of dust. On the left, at the foot of the narrow sloping lawns, intersected by flower-beds and shrubberies, the lake, as clear as crystal, reposed without a ripple, as though neatly trimmed all round by the spades of the gardeners; and, on the opposite side of this limpid mirror, the two islands, with the connecting bridge forming a grey bar between them, displayed their pleasant shores, arraying against the pale sky the theatrical lines of their firs and of their evergreens, the dark foliage of which, similar to the fringe of curtains skilfully hung on the very edge of the horizon, was reflected in the still waters. This corner of nature, having the appearance of a piece of scenery freshly painted, was bathed in a slight shadow, in a bluey vapour which finished giving an exquisite charm to the background, an air of adorable falsity. On the other bank, the Châlet des Îles, looking freshly varnished, shone like a new toy; and those gravel contours, those narrow garden walks, which wind in and out of the lawns and border the lake, and are edged with cast-iron hoops imitating rustic woodwork, stood out more curiously from the soft green of the water and of the grass, at this last hour of daylight.

Used to the graces of these skilfully arranged points of view, Renée, again yielding to her feeling of weariness, had completely lowered her eyelids, no longer observing aught but her tapering fingers as she twined around them the long hairs of the bearskin. But there came a kind of jerk in the even trot of the line of carriages. And, raising her head, she bowed to two young women reclining side by side, with amorous languor, in a barouche which was noisily leaving the road that skirts the lane to turn down one of the lateral avenues. The Marchioness d'Espanet, whose husband, at that time one of the emperor's aides-de-camp, had just rallied with a good deal of fuss to the scandal of the sulking old nobility, was one of the most illustrious society queens of the Second Empire; the other, Madame Haffner, had married a famous manufacturer of Colmar, twenty times millionaire, and whom the Empire was turning into a political personage. Renée, who had known at school the two inseparables as they were slyly termed, always called them by their Christian names, Adeline and Suzanne. As, after greeting them with a smile, she was about to once more huddle herself up in her wraps, a laugh from Maxime caused her to turn round.

"No, really now, I feel sad, don't laugh, it's serious," said she on seeing the young man looking at her mockingly, making fun of her recumbent posture.

Maxime assumed a ludicrous tone of voice.

"We are very much to be pitied, we are jealous!"

She seemed quite astonished.

"I!" said she. "Jealous! whatever about?"

Then she added, with her disdainful pout, as though suddenly recollecting:

"Ah! yes, big Laure! She doesn't trouble me much, I can assure you. If Aristide, as you all wish to make me believe, has paid the creature's debts and thus saved her the necessity of taking a trip to foreign parts, it merely shows that he loves money less than I thought he did. This will make him quite a favourite with the ladies again. The dear fellow, I never interfere with him."

She smiled, she uttered "the dear fellow," in a tone of voice full of friendly indifference. And all on a sudden, becoming quite sad again, and casting around her that despairing glance of women who know not how to amuse themselves, she murmured:

"Oh! I should be only too delighted—But no, I'm not jealous, not in the least jealous."

She stopped, hesitating.

"You see, I feel bored," she at length said abruptly.

Then she relapsed into silence, her lips pressed firmly together. The line of vehicles still wended its way round the lake, with an uniform trot, and a noise greatly resembling that of some distant cataract. Now, on the left, between the water and the roadway, rose little clumps of evergreens with thin straight stems, forming curious clusters of tiny columns. On the right, the copses and low bushes had come to an end; the Bois had expanded into large lawns, immense carpets of turf, with groups of tall trees planted here and there; the greensward continued, with gentle undulations, as far as the Porte de la Muette, the low iron gates of which, looking like a piece of black lace drawn across the ground, could be seen far away in the distance; and, on the slopes, at the parts where the earth sank in, the grass had quite a bluey look. Renée gazed with fixed eyes, as though this enlargement of the horizon, these soft meads, all reeking with the night dew, had caused her to feel more keenly than ever the emptiness of her existence.

At the end of a pause she repeated, with the accents of subdued anger:

"Oh! I feel bored, I feel bored to death."

"You're not over lively, you know," said Maxime, quietly. "It's your nerves, I'm sure."

The young woman threw herself back again on her cushions.

"Yes, it's my nerves," retorted she, sharply.

Then she became quite maternal.

"I am growing old, my dear child; I shall soon be thirty. It's terrible. I take pleasure in nothing. At twenty, you cannot understand this."

"Did you ask me to come with you to listen to your confession?" interrupted the young man. "It will be terribly long."

She received this impertinent remark with a feeble smile, as though dealing with a spoilt child to whom everything is permitted.

"You're a nice one to complain," continued Maxime; "you spend more than a hundred thousand francs a year on your dress, you live in a splendid mansion, you possess some superb horses, your caprices become law, and the newspapers mention every new dress you wear as though they were relating something of the highest importance; all the women are jealous of you, every man would give ten years of his life just to kiss the tips of your fingers. Is it not so?"

She nodded her head affirmatively, but did not otherwise answer. With eyes cast down, she was again curling the hairs of the bearskin.

"Ah! do not be modest," resumed Maxime; "admit at once that you are one of the pillars of the Second Empire. Between ourselves, we can speak of these things. Everywhere, at the Tuileries, at the ministries, at the mansions of the mere millionaires, over the highest and the lowest, you reign with sovereign power. There is not a pleasure you have not partaken of, and if I dared, if the respect I owe you did not restrain me, I would say—"

He paused for a few seconds, laughing the while; then he cavalierly finished his sentence.

"I would say that you have tasted of every apple."

She did not wince.

"And yet you feel bored!" continued the young man with ludicrous vivacity. "But it's downright suicide! What is it you want? whatever is it you are dreaming of?"

She shrugged her shoulders, by way of saying she did not know. Though she held her head down, Maxime saw such a serious, such a gloomy look on her face, that he left off speaking. He watched the line of vehicles which, on reaching the end of the lake, spread out, and filled the vast carrefour. The carriages, no longer being so closely packed together, turned round with a superb grace; whilst the accelerated trot of the horses resounded loudly on the hard ground.

On going the round to rejoin the line, the carriage oscillated in a way which filled Maxime with a vague voluptuousness. Then, yielding to a desire to overwhelm Renée, he resumed:

"Ah! you deserve to never ride in anything better than a cab! It would serve you right! Why, just look at this crowd returning to Paris, this

ÉMILE ZOLA

crowd ready to fall down and worship you. You are hailed as a queen, and your dear friend Monsieur de Mussy can scarcely restrain himself from blowing kisses to you."

And indeed, a rider was at that moment bowing to Renée. Maxime had been speaking in a hypocritically mocking way. But Renée scarcely turned round, and contented herself by shrugging her shoulders. This time, the young man made a despairing gesture.

"Really," said he, "is it as bad as all that? But, good heavens! you have everything, what more do you want?"

Renée raised her head. Her eyes had a warm bright look, the ardent desire of unsatiated curiosity.

"I want something else," replied she in a low voice.

"But you have everything," resumed Maxime laughing, "something else is no answer. What is the something else you want?"

"Ah! what!" repeated she.

And she said nothing further. She had turned completely round, and was contemplating the strange picture which was disappearing behind her. It was now almost dark; dusk was gradually enveloping all like a fine dust. The lake, when looked at front ways, in the pale light which still hovered over it, seemed to become rounder, and had the appearance of an immense plate of brass; on either side, the plantations of evergreens, the slim straight stems of which looked as though they issued from the still water, assumed at this hour the aspect of violet tinted colonnades, describing with their regular architecture the elaborate curves of the shores; then, right at the back, rose groups of shrubs and trees, confused masses of foliage, broad black patches closing the horizon. Behind these patches there shone a bright glimmer, an expiring sunset which merely lit up a very small portion of the grey immensity. Above this motionless lake and these low copses, this point of view so peculiarly flat, the vault of heaven opened infinite, deeper and more expanded still. This great extent of sky over this tiny corner of nature caused a shudder, an undefinable sadness; and there descended from these pale altitudes such an autumnal melancholy, so sweet and yet so heartbreaking a darkness, that the Bois, enveloped little by little in a veil of obscurity, lost its worldly graces, and breaking its bounds became filled with all the powerful charm of a forest. The rumble of the vehicles, the bright colours of which became lost in the dim light, sounded like the distant murmurs of leaves and water-courses. Everything had an expiring air. In the centre of the lake, amidst the universal evanescence, the Latin sail of the large pleasure boat stood out, vigorously defined, against the last glow of the sunset. And one could no longer distinguish anything but this sail, this triangle of yellow canvas, inordinately enlarged.

In the midst of her satiety, Renée experienced a singular sensation of unavowable desires at the sight of this landscape she no longer recognised, of this bit of nature so artistically worldly, and which by its great shivering darkness seemed changed into some sacred wood, one of those ideal glades in whose recesses the gods of antiquity used to hide their giant loves, their divine adulteries and incests. And as the carriage drove away, it seemed to her that the twilight carried off behind her, hidden in its trembling veil, the land of her dreams, the shameful and unearthly alcove where she might at last have swaged her suffering heart, her wearied flesh.

When the lake and the copses, rapidly vanishing in the shades of night, merely appeared as a black bar against the sky, the young woman turned abruptly round, and, in a voice full of tears of vexation, she resumed her interrupted sentence:

"What? why something else, of course! I want something else. How can I tell what? If I only knew—But, you see, I'm sick of balls, of supper parties, of merry-makings. It's always the same thing over again. It's mortal. Men are unbearable, oh! yes, unbearable."

Maxime burst out laughing. Ardent desires pierced through the fashionable beauty's aristocratic bearing. She no longer blinked her eyes; the wrinkle on her forehead became more harshly accentuated; her lip, like a sulky child's, stood out, full of passion, in quest of those enjoyments for which she longed though unable to name them. She beheld her companion laughing, but she was too transported to stop; half reclining and swayed by the motion of the carriage, she continued in short jerky sentences:

"Yes, really, you are unbearable. I don't say that for you, Maxime; you are too young. But if I only told you how Aristide wearied me in the early days! And the others too! those who have loved me. You know, we are two good friends, I don't stand on ceremony with you; well! really, there are days when I am so tired of living my life of a rich, adored and honoured woman, that I should like to be a Laure d'Aurigny, one of those ladies who live like men."

And as Maxime laughed louder than ever, she laid more stress upon her words:

"Yes, a Laure d'Aurigny. It would surely be less insipid, not so much always the same thing."

She kept silent a few minutes, as though she were conjuring up the life she would lead, were she Laure. Then, she resumed in a tone of discouragement:

"After all, those ladies must have their troubles also. There is decidedly nothing really amusing. It's enough to make one sick of life. I was right when I said there was something else wanting; I can't guess what, you know; but something else, something which does not happen to every one, which one does not meet with every day, which would give a rare, an unknown enjoyment."

Her voice had softened. She uttered these last words as though she were seeking something, gradually falling into a deep reverie. The carriage was then ascending the avenue which leads to the way out of the Bois. The darkness increased; the undergrowth, on either side, flew past them like two grey walls; the yellow painted iron chairs, on which the holiday-making citizens lounge on fine evenings, sped along the side-walks, unoccupied, and wrapt in that black melancholy peculiar to garden furniture overtaken by winter; and the rumble, the dull and cadenced sound of the returning vehicles, was wafted over the deserted way like some sad wail.

No doubt Maxime felt all the bad form there was in finding life amusing. If he was still young enough to yield to an outburst of delighted admiration, he possessed an egotism too vast, an indifference too scoffing, he already felt too much real weariness, to do other than declare himself sick of everything, satiated, done for. He was usually in the habit of glorifying in this avowal.

He stretched himself out like Renée, and assumed a doleful tone of voice.

"Really now! you're right," said he; "it's enough to kill one. Ah! I don't amuse myself any more than you, you may be sure; I too have often dreamed of something else. Nothing is stupider than travelling. As for making money, I prefer far more to spend it, though that is not always as amusing as one would fancy at first. Then there's love-making, being loved, one soon has more than enough of it, is it not so? ah yes, one soon has more than enough of it!"

As the young woman did not answer, he continued, washing to astonish her by something grossly impious:

"I should like to be loved by a nun. Eh! perhaps there would be some amusement in that! Have you never dreamed of loving a man of whom you could never think without committing a crime?"

But she remained gloomy, and Maxime, seeing that she still kept silent, thought that she was not listening to him. With the nape of her neck leaning against the padded edge of the carriage, she seemed sleeping with her eyes open. She was wrapt in thought, inert, full of the dreams which kept her thus depressed, and, at times, a nervous twinge passed over her lips. She was softly overcome by the shadow of the twilight; all that this shadow contained of undefined sadness, of discreet voluptuousness, of unavowed hope, penetrated her, bathed her in a sort of languid and morbid atmosphere. Whilst looking fixedly at the round back of the footman on the box-seat, she was thinking no doubt of those joys of former days, of those parties she now found so dull, and for which she no longer cared; she looked back on her past life, the immediate satisfaction of every whim, the fulsomeness of luxury, the crushing monotony of similar affections and similar betrayals. Then, like a hope, there arose in her, as she quivered with desire, the thought of this "something else" which her overwrought mind was unable to fix upon. There, her reverie wandered. She made effort upon effort, but each time the sought-for word disappeared in the gathering night, became lost in the continuous rumble of the vehicles. The gentle motion of the carriage was a hesitation the more which prevented her formulating her desire. And an immense temptation ascended from out of this vagueness, from these copses slumbering in the shadows on either side of the avenue, from this noise of wheels and from this soft oscillation which filled her with a delicious torpor. A thousand little thrills passed over her flesh: unfinished dreams, nameless ecstasies, confused wishes, all the grace and monstrosity which a return from the Bois, at the hour when the heavens assume a pallid hue, can introduce into the wearied heart of a woman. She kept her hands buried in the bearskin, she felt quite hot in her white cloth jacket with mauve velvet facings. On thrusting out her foot as she stretched herself with bodily enjoyment her ankle rubbed against Maxime's warm leg, but he did not even notice the contact of her flesh. A jerk roused her from her lethargy. She raised her head, and her grey eyes looked in a bewildered sort of way at the young man who was seated in the most elegant attitude.

At this moment, the carriage left the Bois. The Avenue de l'Impératrice extended in a straight line in the twilight, with the two green borders of wooden fence which seemed to meet at the horizon. In the distance, a white horse, on the side-path reserved for riders, appeared like a bright speck in the midst of the grey shadow. Here and there, on the opposite side of the roadway, were groups of black dots, belated pedestrians, slowly wending their steps towards Paris. And, right at the top, at the end of the mixed and moving line of vehicles, the Arc-de-Triomphe, placed sideways, stood out all white against a vast stretch of sky the colour of soot.

Whilst the carriage ascended at a faster pace, Maxime, charmed with the English appearance of the landscape, examined the whimsically designed villas on either side of the avenue, with their lawns sloping down to the footpaths; Renée, still wrapt in reverie, amused herself by watching at the edge of the horizon the gas-lamps of the Place de l'Étoile as they were lighted up one by one; and as fast as their bright glimmers speckled the expiring light with little yellow flames, she fancied she could hear secret calls, it seemed to her that the flaring Paris of a winter's night was being illuminated on her account, and was preparing for her the unknown enjoyment after which her satiated body hankered.

The carriage turned down the Avenue de la Reine-Hortense, and drew up at the end of the Rue Monceaux, a few steps from the Boulevard Malesherbes, in front of a grand mansion situated between a courtyard and a garden. The two iron gates loaded with gilt ornaments, which gave admittance to the courtyard, were each flanked by a pair of lamps, shaped like urns and also covered with gilding, in which flared great flames of gas. Between the two gates, the doorkeeper occupied an elegant lodge which vaguely resembled a little Greek temple.

At the moment the carriage was about to enter the courtyard, Maxime jumped nimbly out.

"You know," said Renée, as she caught hold of his hand to detain him, "we dine at half-past seven. You have more than an hour to dress in. Don't keep us waiting."

And she added with a smile:

"We are expecting the Mareuils. Your father wishes you to be very attentive to Louise."

Maxime shrugged his shoulders.

"What a bore!" murmured he in a sullen tone of voice. "I don't mind marrying, but as for courting, it's too stupid. Ah! it would be so nice of you, Renée, if you would deliver me from Louise this evening."

He put on his most comical look, mimicking the grimace and the accent of the actor Lassouche, as he did every time he was about to make one of his funny remarks.

"Will you, my pretty darling mamma?"

Renée shook hands with him as with a comrade. And rapidly, with an audacity full of a nervous raillery, she answered:

"Ah! if I had not married your father, I really believe you would court me."

This idea must have struck the young man as highly comical, for he had turned the corner of the Boulevard Malesherbes before he had done laughing.

The carriage entered and drew up at the foot of the steps.

These steps, which were broad and low, were sheltered by a vast glass verandah edged with a scallop imitating golden fringe and tassels. The two storeys of the mansion rose above the domestic offices, the square windows of which, glazed with ground glass, appeared almost on a level with the soil. At the top of the steps, the hall-door stood out flanked by slender columns fixed in the wall, forming thus a kind of fore-part pierced at each floor by a round bay, and ascending as high as the roof where it terminated in a point. On either side, each storey had five windows, placed at regular intervals along the façade, and surrounded by a simple stone border. The roof, with its attic windows, was square shaped, with broad sides almost perpendicular.

But the façade on the garden side was far more sumptuous. A regal flight of steps led to a narrow terrace which extended the whole length of the ground floor; the balustrade of this terrace, in the style of the railings of the Parc Monceaux, was even more covered with gilt than the verandah and the lamps of the courtyard. Above this rose the mansion with a wing at either end, like two towers half inserted in the body of the building, and which contained rooms of circular shape. In the centre, another tower, even deeper inserted still, formed a slight curve. The windows, tall and narrow in the wings, wider apart and almost square on the flat portions of the façade, had stone balustrades on the ground floor, and gilded wrought-iron handrails at the upper storeys. It was a display, a profusion, a superabundance of riches. The mansion disappeared beneath the carvings. Around the windows, along the cornices, were scrolls of flowers and branches; there were balconies resembling masses of verdure supported by great nude women with strained hips and protruding breasts; then, here and there, were fantastical escutcheons, bunches of fruit, roses, every blossom it is possible to represent in stone or marble. As fast as one's glance ascended, the building seemed to bloom the more. Around the roof was a balustrade, bearing at equal distances urns on which burnt flames of stone. And there, between the oval windows of the attics, which opened amidst an incredible medley of fruits and foliage, expanded the crowning portions of this amazing ornamentation, the pediments of the two wings in the centre of which reappeared the great nude women, playing with apples and standing in every conceivable posture amongst sheaves of reeds. The roof, loaded with these ornaments, surmounted besides with galleries of carved lead, with two lightning conductors and with four enormous symmetrical chimney stacks sculptured like all the rest, seemed to be the final flare up of this architectural firework.

To the right was a vast conservatory, fixed to the side of the mansion, and communicating with the ground floor by means of a French window opening out of a little drawing-room. The garden, separated from the Parc Monceaux by a low iron railing hidden by a hedge, sloped rather sharply. Too small for the house, and so narrow that a lawn and a few clumps of evergreens occupied the entire space, it simply formed a kind of knoll, a verdant pedestal, on which the mansion was proudly planted decked out in its gayest attire. Seen from the park, towering above the bright grass and the shining foliage of the shrubs, this great building, looking still new and quite sickly, had the sallow complexion, the stupid and moneyed importance of some female upstart, with its heavy head-dress of slates, its gilded balustrades, and its flood of sculpture. It was a reproduction of the new Louvre on a smaller scale, one of the most characteristic specimens of the style of the Second Empire, that opulent bastard of every style. On summer evenings, when the last rays of the sun lit up the gilt of the balustrades against the white façade, the strollers in the park would stop to look at the red silk curtains hanging at the ground floor windows; and, through panes so large and clear that they seemed, like those of the great modern emporiums, placed there to display the interior wealth to the outer world, these families of modest citizens would catch glimpses of articles of furniture, of portions of hangings, and of corners of ceilings of dazzling splendour, the sight of which would root them to the spot with admiration and envy right in the centre of the pathways.

But, at this hour, the trees cast their shadows over the façade which was wrapt in gloom. In the courtyard on the other side, the footman had respectfully assisted Renée to alight from the carriage. The stables, with red brick dressings, opened on the right their wide doors of polished oak, at the end of a glass-roofed yard. On the left, as though to counterbalance, was a richly ornamented recess in the wall of the adjoining house, with a fountain of water perpetually flowing from a shell which two cupids supported in their outstretched arms. The young woman stood a moment at the foot of the steps, gently tapping her skirt to get it to hang right. The courtyard, through which the noise of the return had just passed, resumed its solitude, its aristocratic silence, broken by the eternal sing-song of the dripping water. And as yet, amidst the great black mass of the mansion—the chandeliers of which were so soon to be illuminated on the occasion of the first of the grand dinner parties of the autumn—only the lower windows were lighted up, all aglow and casting the bright reflection of a conflagration on the small paving-stones of the courtyard, as neat and regular as a draught-board.

As Renée pushed open the hall door, she found herself face to face with her husband's valet, who was on his way to the servants' quarters and carrying a silver kettle. Dressed all in black, tall, strong, pale-faced, this man looked superb, with the whiskers of an English diplomatist, and the grave and dignified air of a magistrate.

"Baptiste," inquired the young woman, "has your master come in?"

"Yes, madame, he is dressing," replied the valet with a bow worthy of a prince acknowledging the plaudits of the crowd.

Renée slowly ascended the staircase, withdrawing her gloves the while.

The hall was fitted up most luxuriously. On entering, one experienced a slightly suffocating sensation. The thick carpets, which covered the floor and the stairs, the broad red velvet hangings which hid the walls and the doors, made the atmosphere heavy with the silence and the warm fragrance of a chapel. The draperies hung from on high, and the lofty ceiling was ornamented with salient arabesques on a golden trellis. The staircase, with its double balustrade of white marble and handrail covered with red velvet, opened out into two slightly winding branches between which was placed the entrance to the grand drawing-room right at the back. An immense mirror covered the whole of the wall on the first landing. Down below, at the foot of the branching staircase, two bronze gilt female figures, on marble pedestals and nude down to the waist, supported gigantic lamp-posts carrying five burners, the brilliant light from which was softened by ground glass globes. And on either side was a row of splendid vases in majolica ware in which blossomed the rarest plants.

ÉMILE ZOLA

Renée ascended, and at each step she took her reflection in the mirror increased in size; she was asking herself, with that doubt entertained by the most popular actresses, whether she were really delicious, as every one told her.

Then, when she had reached her apartment, which was on the first floor, and overlooked the Parc Monceaux, she rang for Céleste, her maid, and had herself dressed for dinner. This operation lasted a good three quarters of an hour. When the last pin had been fixed, she opened the window as the room was very close, and leaning out remained there wrapt in thought. Behind her, Céleste was moving discreetly about, tidying the room.

Down below, the park was immersed in a sea of shadow. The inky coloured masses of the tall trees, shaken by sudden gusts of wind, swayed to and fro like the tide, with that rustling of dead leaves which recalls the breaking of the waves on a shingly strand. Piercing now and again this ebb and flow of darkness, the two yellow eyes of a carriage would appear and vanish between the shrubberies bordering the road which connects the Avenue de la Reine-Hortense with the Boulevard Malesherbes. In the face of all this autumnal melancholy Renée's sad thoughts returned. She fancied herself once more a child in her father's house, in that silent mansion of the Île Saint-Louis, where for two centuries past the Béraud Du Châtels had sheltered their gloomy magisterial gravity. Then her thoughts turned to her sudden marriage, to that widower who sold himself to become her husband, and who had trucked his name of Rougon for that of Saccard, the two sharp syllables of which had sounded in her ears, when first pronounced before her, with all the brutality of two rakes gathering up gold; he took her, and cast her into this life of turmoil amidst which her poor brain became a little more cracked every day. Then she set to dreaming with a childish joy of the happy games at battledore and shuttlecock she had played in the old times with her young sister Christine. And, some morning, she would awake from the dream of enjoyment she had been indulging for ten years past, crazy, and befouled by one of her husband's speculations, in which he himself would also sink. This passed before her like a rapid presentiment. The trees were lamenting in a louder tone. Troubled by these thoughts of shame and punishment, Renée yielded to the old and worthy middle-class instincts slumbering within her; she promised the black night she would reform, that she would no longer spend so much on her dress, and that she would seek some innocent occupation to amuse her, like in the happy school days, when she and her playmates sang beneath the plane-trees and danced in a ring.

At this moment, Céleste, who had been downstairs, returned and murmured in her mistress's ear:

"Master would be glad if madame would go down. There are already several persons in the drawing-room."

Renée started. She had not felt the chilly air which was freezing her shoulders. As she passed before her looking-glass, she stopped and glanced at herself mechanically. With an involuntary smile she went down.

And, indeed, most of the guests had arrived. There were her sister Christine, a young lady of twenty, very simply dressed in white muslin; her aunt Élisabeth, the widow of the notary Aubertot, in black satin, a little old woman of sixty, of most exquisite amiability; her husband's sister, Sidonie Rougon, a gentle, scraggy woman, of no particular age, with a face like soft wax, and whose dull-coloured dress effaced still further; then the Mareuils, the father, Monsieur de Mareuil, who had just gone out of mourning for his wife, a tall handsome man, empty-headed and serious, bearing a striking resemblance to the valet Baptiste; and the daughter, that poor Louise as people called her, a young girl of seventeen, puny and slightly hump-backed, who wore with a sickly grace a soft white silk dress with red spots; then quite a group of serious men, gentlemen wearing many decorations, official personages with pale and solemn faces; and, farther off, another group, young men with an air of vice about them, and wearing low cut waistcoats, surrounding five or six ladies of the greatest elegance, amongst whom throned the inseparables, the little Marchioness d'Espanet, in yellow, and the fair Madame Haffner, in violet. Monsieur de Mussy, the cavalier whose bow Renée had ignored, was also there, with the uneasy look of a lover expecting to receive his dismissal. And, in the midst of the long trains spread out over the carpet, two contractors, masons who had made their fortunes, named Mignon and Charrier, with whom Saccard had some business to settle on the morrow, were moving heavily about on their big feet, holding their hands behind their backs and feeling most uncomfortable in their dress suits.

Standing near the door, Aristide Saccard managed to greet each new arrival, whilst holding forth to the group of serious men with all his southern animation and snuffling. He shook the guest's hand and spoke a few amiable words. Short, and pitiful-looking, he bobbed up and down like a puppet; and of all his puny, dark and crafty person, the most prominent object was the red bow of his ribbon of the Legion of Honour which he wore very large.

When Renée entered, there rose a murmur of admiration. She was truly divine. Over a lower skirt of tulle, trimmed behind with a mass of flounces, she wore a tunic of pale green satin, edged with a broad border of English lace, and gathered up and fastened by large bunches of violets; a single flounce adorned the front of the skirt over which was a light muslin drapery kept in its place by more bunches of violets joined together by garlands of ivy. The gracefulness of the head and bust were adorable, above this skirt of royal amplitude and slightly overdone richness. Uncovered at the neck as low as the breast, her arms bare with tufts of violets on her shoulders, the young woman seemed to be emerging all naked from her sheath of tulle and satin, similar to one of those nymphs whose busts issue from the sacred oaks; and her white neck, her supple frame, appeared so delighted with this semi-freedom, that one expected at every moment to see the bodice and the skirts slip down like the costume of a bather in love with her flesh. Her tall head-dress, her fine yellow hair gathered up in the form of a helmet, and amidst which twined a sprig of ivy held in its place by a bunch of violets, increased still more her air of nudity by displaying the nape of her neck, slightly shaded by little downy hairs resembling threads of gold. Round her neck she wore a diamond necklace with pendants of the first water, and on her brow an aigrette formed of stems of silver set with the same precious stones. And she stood thus for a few seconds on the threshold of the room, erect in this magnificent costume, her shoulders shining in the warm glow. As she had come down quickly she was rather out of breath. Her eyes, which the darkness of the Parc Monceaux had filled with shadow, blinked in that sudden flood of light, and gave her that hesitating air of short-sighted people, which with her was full of gracefulness.

On perceiving her, the little marchioness rose hastily from her seat, and running up to her, seized hold of her hands; whilst examining her from her head down to her feet she murmured in a fluty tone of voice:

"Ah! pretty darling, pretty darling."

Then there was considerable commotion, all the guests came to pay their respects to the beautiful Madame Saccard, as Renée was called in society. She shook hands with nearly all the men. After which she embraced Christine, and inquired after her father who never visited the mansion in the Parc Monceaux. And she remained standing, smiling and still bowing, with her arms held indolently open, before the circle of ladies who were examining with curious eyes the diamond necklace and aigrette.

Fair Madame Haffner could not resist the temptation; she drew nearer, and after looking a long while at the jewels, said in a jealous tone of voice:

"They are the necklace and the aigrette, are they not?"

Renée nodded her head affirmatively. Then all the women gave vent to their praise; the jewels were enchanting, divine; then they began to speak, with an admiration full of envy, of Laure d'Aurigny's sale at which Saccard had bought them for his wife; they complained that those frail creatures always secured the best things, there would soon be no diamonds at all for virtuous women. And out of their complaints pierced the desire to feel on their bare skin one of those jewels which all Paris had beheld on the shoulders of some illustrious courtesan, and which would perhaps whisper in their ear the alcove scandals on which the thoughts of these grand ladies loved to linger. They knew the high prices realised, they quoted a superb cashmere, some magnificent lace. The aigrette had cost fifteen thousand francs, the necklace fifty thousand. Madame d'Espanet was quite enthusiastic about these figures. She called Saccard, exclaiming:

"Come and be congratulated! You are a good husband!"

Aristide Saccard went up to the ladies, bowed and did the modest. But his grimacing features betrayed a great delight. And out of the corner of his eye he watched the two contractors, the two masons who had made their fortunes, who were standing a few paces off listening with visible respect to the mention of such sums as fifteen thousand and fifty thousand francs.

At this moment, Maxime, who had just entered the room, looking adorable in his well-cut dress-coat, leant familiarly on his father's shoulder, and spoke to him in a low tone, as though to a comrade, calling his attention to the masons with a glance. Saccard smiled discreetly like an applauded actor.

A few more guests arrived. There were quite thirty persons in the drawing-room. The conversations were resumed; during the pauses, one could hear, on the other side of the wall, a jingling of crockery and plate. At length Baptiste opened the folding doors, and majestically uttered the sacramental phrase: "Madame is served."

Then, the procession slowly formed. Saccard gave his arm to the little marchioness; Renée took an old gentleman's, a senator, Baron

Gouraud, before whom everyone bowed down with great humility; as for Maxime, he was obliged to offer his arm to Louise de Mareuil; then followed the rest of the guests, in couples, and right at the end the two contractors swinging their arms.

The dining-room was a vast square apartment with a high dado all round of stained and varnished pear-tree ornamented with thin fillets of gold. The four large panels had probably been intended to be filled with paintings of inanimate objects; but they had remained empty, the owner of the mansion having no doubt hesitated before a purely artistical outlay. They had simply been covered over with dark green velvet. The furniture, the curtains and the door-hangings of the same material, gave to the room a grave and sober appearance calculated to concentrate on the table all the splendour of the illumination.

And indeed, at this hour, in the centre of the vast sombre Turkey carpet which deadened the sound of the footsteps, beneath the glaring light of the chandelier, the table, surrounded by chairs, the black backs of which relieved by fillets of gold framed it with a dark line, appeared like an altar, like some illuminated chapel, as the bright scintillations of the crystal glass and the silver plate sparkled on the dazzling whiteness of the cloth. In the floating shadow beyond the carved chair backs, one could just catch a glimpse of the wainscotting, of a large low sideboard, and of portions of velvet hangings trailing about. One's eyes forcibly returned to the table, and became filled with all this splendour. An admirable unpolished silver epergne glittering with chased work occupied the centre; it represented a troop of fauns bearing away some nymphs; and, issuing from an immense cornucopia above the group, an enormous bouquet of natural flowers hung down in clusters. At either end of the table were some vases also containing bunches of flowers; two candelabra matching the centre group, and each consisting of a satyr in full flight bearing on one arm a swooning woman, whilst with the other he grasped a ten-branched candelabrum, added the bright light of their candles to the radiance of the central chandelier. Between these principal objects the hot dishes, both large and small, bearing the first course, were symmetrically arranged in lines, flanked by shells filled with the *hors-d'œuvre*, and separated by china bowls, crystal vases, flat plates and tall comports, containing all of the dessert placed upon the table. Along the line of plates, the army of glasses, the water-bottles, the decanters, the tiny salt-cellars, in fact the whole of the glass was as thin and slender as muslin, uncut and so transparent that it did not cast the least shadow. And the epergne, and the other large ornaments looked like fountains of fire; the polished sides of the dishes sparkled; the forks, the spoons, and the knives with mother-of-pearl handles were so many bars of flame; rainbows illuminated the glasses; and, in the midst of this shower of sparks, of this incandescent mass, the decanters of wine cast a ruby glow over the cloth which seemed heated to a white heat.

On entering, an expression of discreet beatitude overspread the countenances of the gentlemen who were smiling to the ladies on their arms. The flowers gave a freshness to the warm atmosphere. Slight fumes from the dishes hung about and mingled with the perfume of the roses. And the tart smell of crawfish with the sourish odour of lemons dominated all.

Then, when everyone had found his name written on the backs of the bills of fare, there was a noise of chairs, a great rustling of silk dresses. The bare shoulders studded with diamonds, and flanked by black dress coats which set off their paleness, added their milky whiteness to the radiance of the table. The dinner commenced in the midst of smiles exchanged between neighbours, in a semi-silence as yet only broken by the gentle rattling of the spoons. Baptiste performed the duties of butler with the grave manners of a diplomatist; he had under his orders, besides the two footmen, four assistants whom he engaged only for the grand dinner parties. At each dish which he took to cut up on a side-table at the end of the room, three of the servants passed noiselessly behind the guests, dish in hand, and offering in a low voice the viands by name. The others poured out the wines, attended to the bread and the decanters. The *relevés* and the *entrées* were thus slowly discussed and removed, without the ladies' pearly laughter becoming a whit more shrill.

The guests were too numerous for the conversation to easily become general. Yet, at the second course, when the roasts and the side-dishes had replaced the *relevés* and the *entrées*, and the grand Burgundy wines, Pomard and Chambertin, had succeeded to the Léoville and Château-Lafitte, the sound of the voices swelled, and bursts of laughter caused the slender glasses to tinkle. Renée, seated at the middle of the table, had Baron Gouraud on her right, and on her left Monsieur Toutin-Laroche, a retired candle manufacturer, at that time a municipal councillor, a director of the Crédit Viticole and member of the board of supervision of the Société Générale of the ports of Morocco, a scraggy and important individual, whom Saccard, seated opposite between Madame d'Espanet and Madame Haffner, addressed at one moment in flattering tones as, "My dear colleague," and at another as, "Our great administrator." Then came the politicians: Monsieur Hupel de la Noue, a prefect who spent eight months of the year in Paris; three deputies, amongst whom Monsieur Haffner displayed his broad Alsatian countenance; then Monsieur de Saffré, a charming young man, secretary to a cabinet minister; and Monsieur Michelin, the head of the commission of public ways; and other heads of department besides. Monsieur de Mareuil, a perpetual candidate for the Chamber of Deputies, faced the prefect, at whom he kept casting sheep's-eyes. As for Monsieur d'Espanet, he never accompanied his wife into society. The ladies of the family were placed between the most distinguished of these personages. Saccard had however reserved his sister Sidonie, whom he had seated farther away, between the two contractors—Monsieur Charrier being on the right and Monsieur Mignon on the left—as though at a post of trust where it was a question of vanquishing. Madame Michelin, the wife of the head of the commission of public ways, a pretty plump brunette, found herself beside Monsieur de Saffré with whom she was carrying on an animated conversation in a low voice. Then, at either end of the table were the young people, auditors attached to the Council of State, the sons of influential fathers, little sprouting millionaires, Monsieur de Mussy who kept casting despairing glances in the direction of Renée, and Maxime who seemed fast succumbing to Louise de Mareuil seated on his right. Little by little, they had taken to laughing very loudly. It was from their corner that the first gay notes were heard.

Meanwhile Monsieur Hupel de la Noue was gallantly inquiring:

"Shall we have the pleasure of seeing his excellency this evening?"

"I'm afraid not," answered Saccard with an important air which hid a secret annoyance. "My brother is so busy! He has sent us his secretary to excuse him."

The young secretary, whom Madame Michelin was most decidedly monopolizing, raised his head on hearing his name uttered, and thinking some one had spoken to him, exclaimed:

"Yes, yes, there is to be a meeting of the cabinet this evening at nine o'clock at the residence of the keeper of the seals."

During this time, Monsieur Toutin-Laroche, who had been interrupted, was continuing gravely, as though he were delivering a speech amidst the attentive silence of the Municipal Council:

"The results are indeed superb. This city loan will remain as one of the finest financial operations of the epoch. Ah! gentlemen—"

But here again his voice was smothered by the laughter which suddenly broke out at one end of the table. In the midst of this outburst of mirth one could hear Maxime's voice as he concluded some anecdote:

"Wait a bit. I haven't finished yet. The poor rider was picked up by a road-labourer. It is said she is having him brilliantly educated as she intends to marry him later on. She will not allow that any other man than her husband can flatter himself that he has seen a certain brown mole situated somewhere above her knee."

The laughter redoubled; Louise laughed heartily, louder even than the men. And noiselessly in the midst of all this mirth, just as though deaf, a lackey at this moment thrust his pale grave face between the guests, offering some slices of wild duck in a low tone of voice.

Aristide Saccard was annoyed at the little attention paid to Monsieur Toutin-Laroche. To show him that he had been listening, he resumed:

"The city loan—"

But Monsieur Toutin-Laroche was not the man to lose the thread of an idea.

"Ah! gentlemen," continued he when the laughter had subsided, "yesterday was a great consolation to us whose administration is exposed to such vile attacks. The council is accused of bringing the city to ruin, and yet you see, the moment the city opens a loan, every one brings us their money, even those who cry out."

"You have performed miracles," said Saccard. "Paris has become the capital of the world."

"Yes, it is really prodigious," interrupted Monsieur Hupel de la Noue. "Just fancy that I, who am an old Parisian, can no longer find my way about Paris. I lost myself yesterday when going from the Hôtel de Ville to the Luxembourg. It is prodigious, prodigious!"

A short pause ensued. All the serious people were listening now.

"The transformation of Paris," continued Monsieur Toutin-Laroche, "will be the glory of the reign. The lower classes are ungrateful: they ought to kiss the emperor's feet. I was saying only this morning at the council, where the great success of the loan was being discussed: 'Gentlemen, let those brawlers of the opposition say what they like, to upset Paris is to fertilize it.'"

Saccard smiled and closed his eyes, as though the better to relish the smartness of the dictum. He leant behind Madame d'Espanet's back, and said to Monsieur Hupel de la Noue, loud enough to be heard:

"He is most adorably witty."

Now that the conversation had turned on the alterations being made in Paris, Monsieur Charrier was stretching his neck as though to take part in it. His partner Mignon was fully occupied with Madame Sidonie, who was giving him plenty to do. Ever since the beginning of the dinner, Saccard had been watching the two contractors from out of the corner of his eye.

"The administration," said he, "has met with so much devotion! Every one has wished to contribute to the great work. Without the rich companies which came to its assistance, the city would never have done so well nor so quickly."

He turned round, and added with a sort of brutal flattery:

"Messieurs Mignon and Charrier know something of this, they who have had their share of labour, and who will have their share of glory."

The two masons who had made their fortune received this compliment beatifically full in the chest. Mignon, to whom Madame Sidonie was saying in a lackadaisical manner, "Ah! sir, you flatter me; no, I am too old to wear pink—" interrupted her in the middle of her sentence, to reply to Saccard:

"You are too kind; we merely did our business."

But Charrier was more polished. He finished his glass of Pomard and found means to make an observation.

"The works about Paris," said he, "have enabled the workman to live."

"Say also," resumed Monsieur Toutin-Laroche, "that they have given a magnificent spurt to all financial and industrial undertakings."

"And don't forget the artistic side of the question; the new thoroughfares are majestic," added Monsieur Hupel de la Noue, who flattered himself on his good taste.

"Yes, yes, it is a fine piece of work," murmured Monsieur de Mareuil, for the sake of saying something.

"As for the cost," gravely declared the deputy Haffner, who only opened his mouth on grand occasions, "our children will pay it, and that is only justice."

And as, when saying that, he looked at Monsieur de Saffré, who had not seemed to be getting on so well with the pretty Madame Michelin for the last few minutes, the young secretary, wishing to appear thoroughly acquainted with what was being said, repeated:

"That is indeed only justice."

Every one had had his say in the group formed by the serious men at the middle of the table. Monsieur Michelin, the head of department, smiled and wagged his head; it was his usual way of joining in a conversation; he had smiles for greeting, for answering, for approving, for thanking, for wishing good-bye, quite a pretty collection of smiles which enabled him to dispense almost entirely with the use of his tongue, an arrangement he no doubt considered far more polite and more favourable to his own advancement.

Another personage also had remained silent—that was Baron Gouraud, who was slowly chewing like a drowsy ox. Up till then he had appeared absorbed in the contemplation of his plate. Renée, full of little attentions towards him, only obtained faint grunts of satisfaction. Therefore every one was surprised to see him raise his head and to hear him observe, as he wiped his greasy lips:

"I am a landlord, and when I do up and re-decorate any apartments, I raise the rent."

Monsieur Haffner's remark: "Our children will pay," had succeeded in awakening the senator. They all discreetly applauded, and Monsieur de Saffré exclaimed:

"Ah! charming, charming! I shall send that to-morrow to the newspapers."

"You are quite right, gentlemen, we live in good times," said the worthy Mignon by way of conclusion amidst the smiles and the praise which the baron's observation had called forth. "I know more than one who have nicely built up their fortunes. Everything is lovely, you see, when it enables one to make money."

These last words quite froze the grave men. The conversation stopped short, and each one seemed to avoid looking at his neighbour. The mason's remark unfortunately might have been applied to all these gentlemen. Michelin, who was just then looking at Saccard in a most agreeable manner, suddenly ceased smiling, greatly afraid of having appeared for a moment to apply the contractor's words to the master of the house. The latter glanced at Madame Sidonie, who once more monopolised Mignon, saying: "So you are fond of pink, sir?"—Then Saccard paid Madame d'Espanet a long compliment; his dark, mean-looking face almost touched the milky shoulders of the young woman as she leant back in her chair and laughed.

They had now arrived at the dessert. The lackeys turned more quickly round the table. There was a slight pause whilst the cloth was being covered with the rest of the fruit and the sweetmeats. At Maxime's end the laughter was becoming more silvery; one could hear Louise's shrill voice saying: "I assure you that Sylvia wore a blue satin dress in her part of Dindonnette;" and another childish voice added: "Yes, but the dress was trimmed with white lace." The air was laden with the warm fumes from the dishes. The faces of the guests had assumed a rosier hue, and seemed softened by an internal beatitude. Two lackeys made the round of the table, filling the glasses with Alicant and Tokay.

Ever since the commencement of the dinner, Renée had seemed absent-minded. She fulfilled her duties as mistress of the house with a mechanical sort of smile. At each burst of mirth which came from the end of the table where Maxime and Louise were sitting side-by-side joking like two comrades, she cast a glistening glance in their direction. She felt dreadfully bored. The serious men were too much for her. Madame d'Espanet and Madame Haffner looked at her in despair.

"And the coming elections, how do they promise to turn out?" suddenly inquired Saccard of Monsieur Hupel de la Noue.

"Very well indeed," replied the latter, smiling; "only as yet no candidates have been decided upon for my department. The minister is hesitating, it appears."

Monsieur de Mareuil, who had thanked Saccard with a glance for having introduced this subject, looked as though he were sitting on red-hot cinders. He blushed slightly and made a few awkward bows when the prefect, addressing him, continued:

"I have heard a great deal about you in the country, sir. Your vast estates have won you a great many friends there, and it is known how devoted you are to the Emperor. You have every chance in your favour."

"Papa, is it not true that little Sylvia sold cigarettes at Marseilles in 1849?" cried Maxime at this moment from his end of the table.

And as Aristide Saccard pretended not to hear, the young man continued in a lower tone of voice:

"My father knew her very intimately."

A few smothered laughs greeted this statement. Whilst Monsieur de Mareuil was still bowing, Monsieur Haffner had sententiously resumed:

"Devotion to the Emperor is the only virtue, the only patriotism, in these days of interested democracy. Whosoever loves the Emperor loves France. We would see Monsieur do Mareuil become our colleague with most sincere joy."

"You will succeed, sir," said Monsieur Toutin-Laroche in his turn. "All the great fortunes should gather round the throne."

Renée could stand it no longer. Opposite to her the marchioness was stifling a yawn. And as Saccard was again about to join in, his wife said to him with a delightful smile:

"For goodness sake, my dear, take compassion upon us. Do try and forget your horrid politics."

Then Monsieur Hupel de la Noue, gallant as a prefect should be, protested, saying that the ladies were right. And he forthwith commenced the story of a rather smutty affair which had occurred in the chief town of his department. The marchioness, Madame Haffner and the other ladies laughed immensely at some of the details. The prefect related in a very piquant style, interspersed with hints, reticences, and inflections of the voice, which gave a very naughty meaning to the most innocent expressions. Then they talked of the duchess's first Tuesday at home, of a burlesque that had been produced the night before, of the death of a poet, and of the last of the autumn races. Monsieur Toutin-Laroche, who at certain times could be very amiable, compared women to roses, and Monsieur de Mareuil, amidst the confusion in which his electoral hopes had plunged him, was able to make some profound remarks respecting the new shape for bonnets. Renée continued absent-minded.

The guests were no longer eating. A warm breath seemed to have passed over the cloth, clouding the glasses, scattering the bread, blackening the fruit parings in the plates, and upsetting all the beautiful symmetry of the table. The flowers were fading in the great chased silver cornucopia. And the guests lingered there a moment in presence of the remnants of the dessert, full of contentment, and lacking the courage to rise from their seats. One arm on the table, and bending slightly forward, they had a vacant look in their eyes, and showed the vague depression of that measured and decent inebriation of fashionable people who become intoxicated by degrees. The laughter had subsided and the conversation flagged. A great deal had been eaten and drank, and that gave a still deeper gravity to the group formed by the decorated men. In the close atmosphere of the apartment, the ladies felt a moisture about their necks and temples. They were awaiting the moment to adjourn to the drawing-room, looking serious and slightly pale, as though they felt a swimming in their heads. Madame d'Espanet was quite rosy, whilst Madame Haffner's shoulders had assumed a waxy whiteness. Monsieur Hupel de la Noue was examining the handle of a knife; Monsieur Toutin-Laroche was still addressing a few disconnected remarks to Monsieur Haffner who nodded his head in reply; Monsieur de Mareuil was musing as he looked at Monsieur Michelin, who was slyly smiling upon him. As for the pretty Madame Michelin, she had not been talking for a long while; she was very red in the face, whilst the cloth hung over one of her hands which Monsieur de Saffré was no doubt holding in his, for he was leaning awkwardly on the edge of the table, with his brows knit, and grimacing like a man trying to solve some problem in algebra. Madame Sidonie also had conquered; the Messieurs Mignon and Charrier, both turned towards her and with their elbows on the table, appeared delighted at being taken into her confidence; she was owning that she had a great liking for milky things, and that she was afraid of ghosts. And Aristide Saccard himself, with his eyes half closed, and plunged in that beatitude of the master of a house conscious of having honestly intoxicated his guests, had no thought of leaving the table; he was contemplating with respectful affection Baron Gouraud painfully digesting, with his right hand stretched over the white cloth, a sensual old man's hand, short and thick, studded with purple blotches and covered with reddish hairs.

Renée slowly drank up the few drops of Tokay which remained in her glass. Her face tingled; the little light hairs on her temples and at the nape of her neck were rebellious and would not remain in their places, as though moistened by some damp breath. Her lips and her nose were contracted nervously, her face bore the expression of a child who has drank pure wine. If good middle-class thoughts had come to her whilst in the presence of the shadows of the Parc Monceaux, these thoughts had now succumbed to the excitation of the viands, of the wines and of the lights, of these disturbing surroundings impregnated with noisy mirth and warm breaths. She was no longer exchanging quiet smiles with her sister Christine and her aunt Élisabeth, both of them modest and retiring, and scarcely uttering a word. With a harsh look she had forced poor Monsieur de Mussy to lower his eyes. In her apparent absent-mindedness, though, she was careful to avoid turning round and remained leaning against the back of her chair, whilst the satin of her dress body gently crackled, she allowed an almost imperceptible shudder of the shoulders to escape her each time a burst of laughter reached her from the corner where Maxime and Louise were joking, still as loudly as ever, in the expiring buzz of the conversations.

And behind her, just on the edge of the shadow—his tall person dominating the satiated guests and the disordered table—stood Baptiste, looking pale and grave, in the disdainful attitude of a lackey who has feasted his masters. He alone, in the atmosphere heavy with drunkenness, beneath the vivid light, now turning to a yellowish hue, of the chandelier, remained faultless, with his silver chain around his neck, his cold eyes in which the sight of the women's bare shoulders did not even kindle a spark, and his air of an eunuch waiting on some Parisians in the time of their decline and maintaining his dignity.

At length Renée rose with a nervous movement. Everyone followed her example. They adjourned to the drawing-room where coffee awaited them.

The principal drawing-room of the mansion was a vast oblong apartment, a sort of gallery going from one of the wings to the other, and occupying the whole of the façade on the garden side. A large French window opened on to the steps. This gallery was resplendent with gilding. The ceiling which was slightly arched was covered with fanciful scrolls winding about enormous gilded medallions, which glittered like shields. Arabesques and dazzling garlands formed the border; fillets of gold, like jets of molten metal, were scattered about the walls, framing the panels hung with red silk; clusters of roses crowned with tufts of full blown blossoms trailed down the sides of the mirrors. An Aubusson carpet displayed its purple flowers over the flooring. The furniture upholstered in red damask silk, the door hangings and the curtains of the same material, the enormous rock-work clock on the mantle, the China vases standing on the consoles, the legs of the two long tables ornamented with Florentine mosaics, even the flowerstands placed in the window recesses, were so to say reeking and dripping with gold. At the four corners were four great lamps standing on red marble pedestals to which they were attached by chains of gilded bronze which hung with symmetrical grace. And from the ceiling were suspended three crystal lustres streaming with pink and blue scintillations, and the ardent glare from which was dazzlingly reflected by all the gilding in the apartment.

The men soon withdrew to the smoking-room. Monsieur de Mussy, who, though six years older, had known Maxime at college, took him familiarly by the arm. He led him out on to the terrace, and, after they had lighted their cigars, he complained bitterly of Renée.

"But, tell me, whatever is the matter with her? When I saw her yesterday she was most charming. And now to-day she treats me as though all were over between us. What crime can I have been guilty of? It would be so kind of you, my dear Maxime, to ask her, and to tell her how she makes me suffer."

"Not if I know it!" replied Maxime laughing. "Renée's nerves are upset, I've no wish to receive the brunt of her ill-humour. Settle your differences between yourselves."

And after slowly puffing out the smoke of his havanna, he added:

"It's a pretty part you want me to play!"

Bat Monsieur de Mussy talked of his great friendship, and assured the young man he was only awaiting an opportunity to show him how devoted he was to him. He was very miserable, he loved Renée so!

"Very well! it's agreed," said Maxime at length, "I will speak to her; but, you know, I can promise nothing; she is pretty sure to send me about my business."

They re-entered the smoking-room, and stretched themselves out in two capacious easy-chairs. And during a good half hour Monsieur de Mussy related all his tribulations to Maxime; he told him for the tenth time how it was he had fallen in love with the young man's stepmother, and how she had been gracious enough to notice him; and whilst finishing his cigar Maxime gave him some advice, explaining Renée's nature to him, and showing him how he should set to work to overcome her.

Saccard having taken a seat a few steps away from the young men, Monsieur de Mussy lapsed into silence, and Maxime said in conclusion:

"Were I in your place, I would treat her very cavalierly. She likes it."

The smoking-room occupied, at one end of the principal drawing-room, one of the round apartments formed by the towers. It was fitted up in a style both very rich and very sober. Papered with a material imitating Cordovan leather, it had Algerian curtains and door hangings, and a Wilton carpet of Persian design. The furniture was upholstered with shagreen leather the colour of wood, and comprised settees, easy-chairs and a circular divan which went nearly all round the room. The little chandelier, the ornaments of the table and of the fire-place, were of pale green Florentine bronze.

There had only remained with the ladies a few young fellows, and some pale and flabby-faced old men, who held tobacco in horror. In the smoking-room, there was a great deal of laughing going on and some very broad jokes were being bandied about. Monsieur Hupel de la Noue diverted the gentlemen immensely by again relating the story he had told during dinner, but completing it this time by some most indecent details. He had a specialty for this sort of thing; he always had two versions of an anecdote, one for ladies, the other for men. Then, Aristide Saccard entered and was at once surrounded and complimented; and as he pretended not to understand what it was all about, Monsieur de Saffré told him, in a greatly applauded speech, that he had deserved well of his country for having prevented the beautiful Laure d'Aurigny from going over to the English.

"No, really, gentlemen, you are mistaken," stammered Saccard with false modesty.

"Oh! don't try to excuse yourself!" cried Maxime chaffingly. "It's very meritorious at your age."

The young man who had just thrown away the stump of his cigar returned to the drawing-room. A great number of visitors had arrived. The gallery was full of men in evening dress standing up and conversing in low tones, and of ladies in ample skirts which they spread out on the couches. Some lackeys were taking round some silver salvers bearing ices and glasses of punch.

Maxime, who wished to speak to Renée, passed right through the drawing-room, knowing very well where to find the ladies' favourite spot. At the opposite end to the smoking-room was another round apartment adorably fitted up as a boudoir. Its curtains and hangings of satin, the colour of buttercups, gave it a voluptuous charm, of quite an original and exquisite taste. The lights of the chandelier, which was of very delicate workmanship, appeared quite pale amidst all this sun-like splendour. The effect resembled a flood of the subdued rays from a sunset on a field of ripe corn. The light expired at one's feet on an Aubusson carpet strewn with dead leaves. An ebony piano inlaid with ivory, two little cabinets the glass doors of which displayed a host of nicknacks, a Louis XVI table, and a flowerstand holding an enormous sheaf of flowers, sufficed to furnish the room. The small couches, the easy-chairs and the settees, were covered with padded buttercup satin divided at intervals by broad black bands of the same material embroidered with gay coloured tulips. And there were also low seats, lounge-chairs, and every variety of stool, both elegant and fantastical. Not a glimpse of the woodwork of these articles was visible; the satin and the padding covered all. The backs were so curved as to be as comfortable as bolsters. They were like so many discreet beds on which one could sleep and love amidst the down, to the accompaniment of the sensual symphony of the pale yellow light.

Renée had an especial liking for this little room, one of the French windows of which opened into the magnificent conservatory fixed to the side of the mansion. During the day-time she spent most of her leisure hours there. Instead of softening her light hair, the yellow hangings gave it a strangely golden hue; her head stood out all pink and white in the midst of a dawn-like glimmer, like that of a fair Diana awakening at the break of day; and this was no doubt why she loved this little room which gave a heavenly setting to her beauty.

At this hour she was there with her intimate friends. Her sister and her aunt had just departed. There were none but madcaps in the sanctum. Leaning back in the depths of a sofa, Renée was listening to the secrets of her friend Adeline, who was whispering in her ear with feline playfulness and sudden bursts of laughter. Suzanne Haffner was in great request; she was holding her own against a group of young men who were pressing her closely, without losing any of her German languor, her provoking effrontery, as bare and cold as her shoulders. In a corner, Madame Sidonie was enlightening in a low voice a young woman with the eyes of a virgin. Farther off, Louise was standing talking with a big timid fellow who blushed violently; whilst Baron Gouraud was dozing in an easy-chair full in the light, displaying his flabby flesh, his pale elephantine form, in the midst of the frail graces and the silky daintiness of the ladies. And all about the room, on the stiff satin skirts shining like china, on the milky white shoulders studded with diamonds, a light of fairy-land fell in a golden dust. A soft voice, a laugh no louder than the cooing of a dove, had as limpid a ring as crystal. It was very warm in there. Fans were moving slowly to and fro like wings, disseminating at each breath in the sultry atmosphere the musked perfumes of the bodices.

When Maxime appeared in the doorway, Renée, who was listening to the marchioness in an absent-minded way, rose up hastily, pretending to have to play her part as mistress of the house. She passed into the principal drawing-room where the young man followed her. After smilingly taking a few steps there and shaking hands with different people, she drew Maxime aside.

"Well!" whispered she ironically, "the task seems an easy one; you don't appear to find courting as stupid as you imagined."

"I don't understand you," replied the young man, who was about to plead for Monsieur de Mussy.

"Why I think I did well not to deliver you from Louise. You don't waste any time, you two."

And she added with a sort of vexation:

"At table, too, it was quite indecent."

Maxime burst out laughing.

"Ah! yes, we were telling each other stories. I did not know her, the chit. She's very funny. She's just like a boy."

And as Renée's face still bore the irritated look of a prude, the young man, who had never known her so indignant before, resumed with smiling familiarity:

"Do you think, pretty mamma, that I pinched her legs under the table? Hang it all, one knows how to behave towards one's betrothed! I have something far more serious to tell you. Listen to me—you are listening, are you not?"

He lowered his voice still more.

"This is what's the matter. Monsieur de Mussy is very miserable; he has just told me so. You know it's not for me to bring you together again, if you've had a row. But, you understand, I was at college with him, and as he really seems to be in despair, I promised him I would speak to you."

He stopped. Renée was looking at him in a very strange manner.

"You don't answer?" continued he. "Anyhow, I have done what I promised. Settle the matter between you as you like. But, really now, I cannot help thinking you cruel. I quite feel for the poor fellow. In your place I would send him at least a kind message."

Then Renée, who had not taken the bright, fixed look of her eyes off Maxime, replied:

"Go and tell Monsieur de Mussy that he bores me."

And she resumed her slow walk amidst the groups, smiling, bowing, and shaking hands. Maxime stood for a moment lost in surprise; then he quietly laughed to himself.

Not at all desirous of delivering the message to Monsieur de Mussy, he took a turn round the principal drawing-room. The party was drawing to a close, marvellous and commonplace like most parties. It was close upon midnight; the guests were slowly departing. Not wishing to retire with a feeling of unpleasantness, he decided to seek Louise. He was passing before the hall door when he caught sight of the pretty Madame Michelin being wrapt up by her husband in a little pink and blue cloak.

"He was most charming, most charming," the young woman was saying. "We talked of you the whole of dinner. He will speak to the minister; only, it is not in his province—"

And as, close to them, a footman was assisting Baron Gouraud on with a big fur coat:

"That's the old fellow who could settle the matter!" added she in her husband's ear, whilst he was tying the string of her hood under her chin. "He does just as he likes at the ministry. At the Mareuils' to-morrow we must try—"

Monsieur Michelin smiled. He took his wife off with the greatest care, as though he had on his arm a most fragile and precious object. After assuring himself by a glance that Louise was not in the hall, Maxime went straight to the little drawing-room. She was still there, almost alone, and awaiting her father, who had probably spent the evening in the smoking-room with the politicians. The marchioness and Madame Haffner had taken their departure. There only remained Madame Sidonie telling the wives of some functionaries how much she loved animals.

"Ah! here's my little husband," exclaimed Louise. "Come and sit down and tell me in what chair my father can have fallen asleep. He must already be fancying himself in the Chamber."

Maxime answered her in a similar strain, and the two young people were soon again laughing as loud as during dinner. Seated on a very low chair at her feet, he ended by taking hold of her hands and by playing with her, just the same as with a comrade. And in truth, with her high-made dress of soft white silk studded with red spots, her flat chest, and her ugly and cunning little urchin's head, she resembled a boy disguised as a girl. But at times her puny arms, her crooked form, assumed negligent postures, and gleams of passion would appear in the depths of her eyes still full of childishness, without her blushing the least in the world at Maxime's playfulness. And they both laughed away, just as though they were by themselves, without even noticing Renée, who was standing half hidden in the centre of the conservatory watching them from a distance.

A moment ago, as she was crossing a path, the sight of Maxime and Louise had suddenly brought the young woman to a standstill behind a shrub. All about her, the warm conservatory, similar to the nave of a church, and the glass arched roof of which was supported on slender iron columns, displayed its fertile vegetation, its masses of gigantic leaves, its clumps of luxuriant verdure.

In the centre, in an oval tank on a level with the ground, lived, in the mysterious manner of water plants, all the aquatic flora of the land of the sun. A border of Cyclantheæ raising their tall green plumes, surrounded with a monumental belt the fountain which resembled the truncated capital of some Cyclopean column. Then, at either end, two enormous Tornelias reared their strange-looking bushes above the water, their dry, bare stems twisted like agonizing serpents, and emitting aerial roots which had an appearance of fishermen's nets hung up to dry. Close to the edge, a Pandanus from Java expanded its sheaf of greenish leaves streaked with white, as thin as swords, prickly and serrated like Malay daggers. And floating amid the warmth of the gently heated sheet of slumbering water, some Nymphæa opened their rosy stars, whilst some Euryale trailed their round and leprous-looking leaves over the surface, appearing like the backs of so many monstrous toads covered with pustules.

By way of carpeting, a broad edging of Selaginella surrounded the tank. This dwarf fern formed a thick moss-like sward of a tender green. And beyond the wide circular path, four enormous groups of exotic plants shot right up to the arched roof; the palms, slightly drooping in their gracefulness, spread out their fan-like leaves, displayed their rounded heads, hung down their branches like so many oars wearied by their eternal voyage in the azure of the air; the great bamboos from India ascended erect, slender and hard, with their fine shower of leaves falling from on high; a Ravenala, the traveller's tree, held up its bunch of immense Chinese screens; and, in a corner, a Banana tree loaded with fruit stretched out in all directions its long, horizontal leaves, on which two lovers might easily recline providing they kept pretty close to each other. In the corners were some Euphorbia from Abyssinia, those prickly, ill-shaped torch-thistles covered with horrid excrescences and reeking with poison. And the ground beneath the taller plants was carpeted by dwarf ferns, including the Adiantum and the Pteris, with fronds as delicate as the finest lace-work. A taller species, the Alsophilas, tapered upwards with their rows of symmetrical and sexangular foliage so regular that it had the appearance of enormous pieces of crockery intended to hold the fruits of some gigantic dessert. Then an edging of Begonias and Caladiums surrounded the beds; the Begonias with their twisted leaves superbly streaked with green and red; the Caladiums, the leaves of which, shaped like lance heads, white and veined with green, resemble the wings of some monstrous butterfly; bizarre plants which vegetate strangely with the sombre or palish glow of noisome flowers.

Behind the beds a second path, a narrower one, went right round the conservatory. And there, on stages, half hiding the pipes of the heating apparatus, bloomed Marantas, as soft to the touch as velvet, Gloxinias, with their purple bell-shaped flowers, Dracænas, resembling blades of old lacquer.

But one of the charms of this winter garden consisted in alcoves of verdure in the four corners, roomy arbours shut in by thick curtains of tropical creepers. Bits of virgin forests had weaved in these spots their walls of leaves, their impenetrable medley of stems, of supple shoots, clinging to the branches, traversing space by a bold leap, and hanging from the arched roof like the tassels of some rich drapery. A root of Vanilla, with its ripe pods exhaling a penetrating perfume, trailed about the arch of a moss-covered porch, whilst the Indian berry decked the little columns with its round leaves; Bauhinias, with their red bunches, and the Quisqualis, the flowers of which hung like necklets of glass beads, glided, twined and entangled themselves like slender snakes endlessly playing and stretching amidst the depths of the foliage.

And beneath the arches placed here and there between the beds, and held by wire chains, hung baskets filled with Orchids, those bizarre plants of the air, which spread in all directions their stunted and knotted shoots bent and twisted like crippled limbs. There were Lady's-slippers, the flowers of which resemble a marvellous shoe adorned on the heel with the wings of a dragon-fly; Ærides with their delicate perfume; and Stanhopeas, the pale streaked flowers of which, like the bitter mouth of some convalescent, exhale to a distance a strong and acrid breath.

But that which, from every point of view, was the most conspicuous object, was a great Hibiscus from China, its immense expanse of flowers and foliage covering the whole side of the mansion to which the conservatory was fixed. The large purple flowers of this gigantic mallow are ever being renewed, and live but a few hours. One could almost fancy them a woman's sensual, opening mouths, the red soft moist lips of some giant Messalina, bruised by kisses and yet ever reviving with their eager and bleeding smile.

Renée stood near the tank, and shivered in the midst of all these superb blossoms. Behind her, a great black marble sphinx, squatting on a block of granite, its head turned towards the water, wore on its features the wary and cruel smile of a cat; and it looked like the dark Idol with shining thighs of that land of fire. At this hour ground glass globes cast a milky light over the surrounding foliage. Statues, women's heads with the necks thrown back, and swelling with mirth, stood out white from the recesses of the groups of shrubs, with patches of shadow which contorted their mad laughter. Strange rays played about the deep still water of the tank, lighting up vague forms and glaucous masses resembling rough designs of monsters. Over the smooth leaves of the Ravenala, on the glossy fans of the Latanias, streamed a flood of white light; whilst from the lace-work of the ferns fell a gentle rain of sparks. Up above shone the reflections from the glass roof amongst the sombre heads of the tall palms. Then, all around, everything was wrapt in shadow; the arbours, with their drapery of tropical creepers, became lost in the darkness, like the nests of slumbering reptiles.

And Renée stood musing in the bright light, as she watched Louise and Maxime in the distance. It was no longer the floating fancies, the vague temptation of twilight, in the chilly avenues of the Bois. Her thoughts were no longer lulled and sent to sleep by the trot of her horses along the fashionable walks, and the glades in which middle-class families pic-nic on a Sunday. Now it was a definite, a keen desire which filled her whole being.

An immense love, a need of voluptuousness, floated about this close nave, full of the ardent sap of the tropics. The young woman was enveloped in these mighty bridals of the earth, engendering around her this dark verdure, these colossal stems; and the acrid confinement of this candent mother, this forest-like growth, this mass of vegetation all glowing with the entrails which nourished it, surrounded her with perturbing effluvia of most intoxicating power. At her feet, the tank, the mass of warm water, thickened by the juices of the floating roots, steamed and wrapt her shoulders in a mantle of heavy vapour, a mist which heated her skin like the contact of a hand moist with voluptuousness. On her head she felt a breath from the palms as the tall leaves sprinkled their aroma. And more than the close warmth of the atmosphere, than the bright lights, than the large dazzling flowers resembling faces laughing or grimacing amongst the foliage, the odours especially overpowered her. An undefinable perfume, powerful and exciting, hung about, composed of a thousand others: human perspiration, women's breaths, the scent of hair; and zephyrs sweet and insipid almost to faintness, were blended with coarse and pestilential smells loaded with poison. But amidst this strange amalgamation of odours, the one which dominated all, stifling the delicateness of the vanilla and the sharpness of the orchids, was that penetrating, sensual, human odour, that odour of love which escapes of a morning from the closed chamber of a young married couple.

Renée had slowly leant against the granite pedestal. In her green satin dress, with her face and shoulders of a rosy hue and sparkling with the pure scintillations of her diamonds, she resembled some great pink and green flower, one of the Nymphæa of the tank, swooning from the heat. At this hour of clear vision, all her good resolutions vanished for ever, the intoxication of the dinner regained possession of her faculties, imperious, triumphant, and rendered mightier than before by the flames of the conservatory. She no longer remembered the chill night air which had calmed her, nor those murmuring shadows of the park, the voices of which had counselled a happy peacefulness. Her ardent woman's senses, her satiated woman's capriciousness, were aroused. And, above her, the great black marble sphinx laughed a mysterious laugh, as though it had read the at length expressed desired which was galvanizing this dead heart, the desire which had remained so long elusive, the "something else" so vainly sought by Renée amidst the oscillating motion of her carriage, in the ashy gloom of the gathering night, and which had been so abruptly revealed to her beneath the glaring light of this garden of fire by the sight of Louise and Maxime, laughing and playing together, hand in hand.

At this moment a sound of voices issued from a neighbouring arbour, where Aristide Saccard had led the Messieurs Mignon and Charrier.

"No, really, Monsieur Saccard," the latter was saying in a thick voice, "we cannot take it back from you at more than two hundred francs the metre."

And Saccard retorted in his shrill tones:

"But in my share you valued it at two hundred and fifty francs."

"Well, listen! we will make it two hundred and twenty-five francs."

And the voices continued, harsh, and ringing strangely beneath the drooping palms. But they merely traversed Renée's dream like some vain noise, as there rose before her, conjured up by her delirium, an unknown enjoyment, hot with crime, and more vehement than all those she had already exhausted, the last that remained to her to partake of. She no longer felt weary.

The shrub behind which she remained half hidden was an accursed plant, a Tanghinia from Madagascar, with broad box-like leaves and whitish stems, the smallest veins of which distil a poisonous juice. And, at one moment, as Louise's and Maxime's mirth became louder, in the yellow reflection, in the sunset of the little drawing-room, Renée, her mind wandering, her mouth parched and irritated, took between her teeth a sprig of the Tanghinia, which was on a level with her lips, and closed them on one of the bitter leaves.

II

Aristide Rougon swooped down upon Paris on the morrow of the Coup d'État, with that scent of birds of prey which sniff the field of carnage from afar. He came from Plassans, a sub-prefecture of the South, where his father had at length netted in the troubled waters of events an office of tax collector for which he had long been angling. As for himself, still young, and having compromised his position like a fool, with neither glory nor profit, he could only feel very fortunate in issuing safe and sound from the squabble. He came, with a rush, enraged at his mistake, cursing the country, speaking of Paris with a wolf-like greed, and swearing "that he would never be caught napping again;" and the keen smile with which he accompanied these words assumed a terrible significance on his thin lips.

He arrived in the early days of 1852. He was accompanied by his wife Angèle, a fair and insignificant creature, whom he placed in a small lodging in the Rue Saint-Jacques, like some awkward piece of furniture he was anxious to be rid of. The young woman had been unwilling to be separated from her daughter, little Clotilde, a child four years old, whom the father would willingly have left behind to be taken care of by his relations. But he had only yielded to his wife's wish on condition that the college at Plassans should retain their son Maxime, a youngster of eleven, who would be looked after by the grandmother. Aristide wished to have his hands free; a woman and a child already seemed to him a crushing weight to encumber a man decided to overcome all obstacles, though he grovelled in the mud or perished in the attempt.

The very evening of his arrival, whilst Angèle was unpacking, he felt an eager longing to explore Paris, to hear his heavy countryman's boots striking that burning pavement from which he hoped to cause millions to spring forth. It was a regular taking of possession. He walked for the sake of walking, following the footpaths, just as though in a conquered country. He had a very clear conception of the battle he was about to offer, and it was not in the least repugnant to his feelings to compare himself to a skilful picklock who, by artifice or violence, was about to take his share of the common wealth which had been wickedly refused him until then. Had he felt the need of an excuse, he would have invoked his every desire denied him for ten years, his wretched country existence, his faults especially, for which he held society at large responsible. But at this moment, in that emotion of a gambler who at last places his eager hands on the green baize of the gaming-table, he was filled with joy, a joy of his own, in which blended the gratification of covetousness and the expectation of an unpunished rogue. The atmosphere of Paris intoxicated him, he fancied he could hear, in the rumbling of the vehicles, the voices from "Macbeth" calling to him: "You will be rich!" During close upon two hours he wandered thus from street to street, enjoying the voluptuousness of a man roaming amidst his own vice. He had not been back in Paris since the happy year he had passed there as a student. Night was falling; his dream grew in the bright lights which the shops and the cafés cast on the pavement; he lost himself.

When he raised his eyes, he found himself towards the middle of the Faubourg Saint-Honoré. One of his brothers, Eugène Rougon, lived in a street close by, the Rue de Penthièvre. In coming to Paris, Aristide had especially counted upon Eugène who, after having been one of the most active agents of the Coup d'État, had now become an occult power, a lawyer of no particular standing but who was shortly to blossom into a great political personage. But, superstitious as a gambler, he was unwilling to knock at his brother's door on that evening. He slowly retraced his steps to the Rue Saint-Jacques, inwardly envying Eugène's lot, glancing down at his own shabby clothes still covered with the dust of the journey, and seeking to console himself by resuming his dream of riches. Even this dream had become bitter to him. Having started out through a necessity for expansion, joyfully enlivened by the busy activity of Paris trade, he returned home irritated at the happiness which seemed to him to be rampant in the streets, feeling more ferocious than ever, imagining all kinds of desperate struggles in which he would take pleasure in defeating and duping that crowd which had jostled him on the pavement. Never before had he felt so keen and vast an appetite, so immediate and ardent a necessity for enjoying.

On the morrow he was at his brother's, almost at daybreak. Eugène occupied two large cold rooms, very barely furnished, and which quite chilled Aristide. He had expected to find his brother sprawling in the lap of luxury. The latter was seated working at a little black table. He merely said in his slow voice, accompanying his words with a smile:

"Ah! it's you, I was expecting your visit."

Aristide was very bitter. He accused Eugène of having left him to vegetate, of not even having bestowed upon him so much as a word of advice during the time he had been dabbling about in his native province. He would never be able to forgive himself for having remained Republican up to the very day of the Coup d'État; it caused him the most poignant regret, and filled him with eternal confusion. Eugène had quietly taken up his pen again. When the other had finished speaking, he observed:

"Bah! all mistakes can be rectified. You have a fine future before you."

He uttered these words in so clear a tone of voice, and with so penetrating a glance, that Aristide bowed his head, feeling that his brother was descending into the innermost depths of his being. The latter continued with a sort of friendly bluntness:

"You've come to me to get you something to do, have you not? I've already thought of you, but I've found nothing as yet. You see, I can't put you into the first position that offers. You need an occupation that will enable you to carry on your little game without danger either to yourself or to me. Don't protest, we're alone here, and can say anything to each other."

Aristide thought it best to laugh.

"Oh! I know that you're intelligent," continued Eugène, "and that you're not likely to do anything foolish again without you reap some benefit from it. So soon as a good opportunity offers, I will do something for you. Meanwhile, if you should happen to be in want of a twenty-franc piece, come to me for it."

They talked for a few minutes about the insurrection in the South, through which their father had gained his appointment of tax collector. Eugène dressed himself while talking. Just as he was parting from his brother outside in the street, he detained him a moment longer to say in a lower tone of voice:

"By-the-way, you'll oblige me by not loafing about, but by quietly waiting at home for the berth I promise you. It would annoy me to see my brother dancing attendance on any one."

Aristide had a high respect for Eugène, who seemed to him a wonderfully smart fellow. He did not however forgive him his mistrust, nor his rather rough frankness; nevertheless he obediently went and shut himself up in the Rue Saint-Jacques. He had arrived with five hundred francs which his wife's father had lent him. After paying the expenses of the journey, he made the three hundred francs that remained to him last a month. Angèle was a hearty eater; moreover she thought it necessary to retrim her best dress with some mauve ribbons. This month of waiting appeared interminable to Aristide. He was burning with impatience. Each time he leaned out of his window and felt the gigantic labour of Paris beneath him, he experienced a mad longing to throw himself into the furnace with one bound, so as to mould the gold with his quivering fingers, as though it had been wax. He inhaled those still vague vapours which rose from the great city, that breath of the nascent Empire, laden already with the odours of alcoves and financial hells, with the warm effluvia of every kind of enjoyment. The faint fumes that reached him seemed to tell him that he was on the right scent, that the quarry was scudding along before him, that the grand imperial hunt, the pursuit of adventures, of women, and of millions, was about to begin. His nostrils quivered, his instinct of a famished beast caught in a marvellous manner as they passed the slightest signs of that fierce division of spoil of which the city was to be the scene.

Twice he called on his brother to urge him to be more expeditious. Eugène received him rather ungraciously, repeating that he was not forgetting him, but that it was necessary to wait patiently. At length Aristide received a letter requesting him to call in the Rue de Penthièvre. He hastened thither, his heart beating violently, as though he were on his way to a lovers' meeting. He found Eugène seated before the same little black table, in the large cold room which he used as a study. On his appearance the lawyer held a document towards him, saying:

"There, I settled your matter yesterday. You are appointed deputy trustee of roads at the Hôtel de Ville. You will be in receipt of a salary of two thousand four hundred francs."

Aristide had remained standing. He turned ghastly pale, and did not take the document, thinking that his brother was poking fun at him. He had at least expected an appointment worth six thousand francs a year. Eugène, guessing what was passing within him, wheeled his chair round and folded his arms.

"Are you a fool after all?" he asked angrily. "You've been building castles in the air like a girl, have you not? You would wish to have a grand establishment with footmen, to live on the fat of the land, sleep in silk, gratify your desires at once in no matter whose arms, in a boudoir furnished in a couple of hours. You and those like you, if we allowed you to have your way, would empty the coffers even before they were full. Now, in the name of all that's good! do have a little patience! See how I live, and do at least take the trouble to stoop to pick up a fortune."

He spoke with profound contempt of his brother's schoolboy impatience. One could feel, in his rough speech, a loftier ambition, a longing for untarnished power; that naive appetite for money no doubt appeared to him both paltry and puerile. He continued in a gentler voice and with a crafty smile:

"No doubt your propensities are excellent, and I have not the least desire to thwart them. Men like you are precious. We have every intention of choosing our friends from among the most hungry. You may be quite easy, we shall keep open house, and the greatest appetites will be satisfied. And this is after all the easiest way of reigning. But, for goodness sake, wait till the cloth is laid, and, if you'll accept my advice, just go yourself and fetch your knife and fork from the kitchen."

Aristide continued to look very glum. His brother's pleasant comparisons were unable to bring a smile to his countenance. Then the latter again gave way to anger.

"Ah!" he exclaimed, "my first opinion was the right one: you're a fool! What on earth did you expect, whatever did you imagine I was going to do with your illustrious person? You didn't even have the courage to finish your reading for the bar, you went and buried yourself for ten years in the wretched berth of clerk at a sub-prefecture, and you come to me with the detestable reputation of a Republican whom the Coup d'État was alone able to convert. Do you think that with such a past there is the making of a cabinet minister in you? Oh! I know that you have in your favour a ferocious desire to reach the goal by any means possible. That is a great virtue, I admit, and it was precisely on that account that I obtained your admittance into the Hôtel de Ville."

And rising from his seat he placed the document containing the appointment in Aristide's hands.

"Take it," continued he, "you'll thank me some day. It's I who chose the berth, I know what you'll be able to get out of it. All you'll have to do will be to look about you and keep your ears open. If you are intelligent, you'll soon understand and know how to act. Now pay particular attention to what I am about to say to you. Make piles of money, I permit it; only do nothing foolish, no noisy scandal, otherwise I shall suppress you instantly."

This threat produced the effect his promises had been unable to obtain. All Aristide's ardour was rekindled at the thought of the fortune to which his brother alluded. It seemed to him that he was at last let loose in the thick of the fray, authorised to slaughter right and left, but legally, and without causing too much commotion. Eugène gave him two hundred francs to enable him to wait till the end of the month. Then he remained wrapt in thought.

"I'm thinking of changing my name," said he at length; "you ought to do the same. We should interfere with each other less."

"As you like," answered Aristide quietly.

"You need not trouble yourself about anything. I will attend to the necessary formalities. How would you like to call yourself by your wife's name Sicardot?"

Aristide glanced up at the ceiling, repeating the name, and listening to the sound of the syllables.

"Sicardot—Aristide Sicardot—no, on my word, it's clownish and has a suggestion of bankruptcy about it."

"Think of something better then," said Eugène.

"I would prefer Sicard without the ot," resumed the other after a pause; "Aristide Sicard—that isn't bad, is it? perhaps a bit jaunty—"

He stood thinking a few moments longer, and then triumphantly exclaimed:

"I've got it, I've found it at last! Saccard, Aristide Saccard! with a double c. Eh! there's money in such a name as that; it has a sound like the counting out of five franc pieces."

Eugène was rather brutal in his jokes. He dismissed his brother, saying to him with a smile:

"Yes, a name that will make you a convict or a millionaire."

A few days later Aristide Saccard found himself at the Hôtel de Ville. He there learnt that his brother must have commanded considerable influence to get him appointed without the customary examinations.

Then the couple began the monotonous life of the underpaid clerk. Aristide and his wife resumed their old Plassans ways. Only they fell from a dream of sudden fortune, and their poverty-stricken existence weighed heavier upon them, now that they looked upon it as a time of probation, the duration of which they were unable to fix. To be poor in Paris, is to be doubly poor. Angèle accepted the wretchedness of their position with all the listlessness of a chlorotic woman. She spent days in her kitchen, or else lying on the floor, playing with her daughter, and never lamenting except when she reached her last twenty-sou piece. But Aristide quivered with rage in the midst of this poverty, of this narrow existence, out of which he sought an issue like some caged beast. To him it was a period of ineffable suffering; his pride was wounded, his unsated cravings goaded him furiously. And he suffered all the more on learning that his brother had been elected to represent Plassans in Parliament. He felt too much Eugène's superiority to be foolishly jealous; but he accused him of not doing all that he might have done for him. On several occasions, absolute necessity forced him to knock at his door for the purpose of borrowing a trifle. Eugène lent the money, but at the same time roughly reproached him with being destitute of both courage and will. Then Aristide took the bull indeed by the horns. He swore to himself that he would never again borrow so much as a sou from any one, and he kept his oath. The last eight days of each month, Angèle would eat dry bread and sigh. This apprenticeship completed Saccard's terrible education. His thin lips became narrower still; he was no longer so stupid as to dream of millions out loud; his scraggy person became dumb, and no longer expressed but one will, one fixed idea nursed at every hour of the day. When he hurried along from the Rue Saint-Jacques to the Hôtel de Ville, his boots worn down at heel resounded harshly on the pavement, and he buttoned himself up in his shabby old overcoat as though in an asylum of hatred, while his weasel-like snout sniffed the air of the streets. He was an angular figure of the jealous misery that one sees roaming along the Paris side-walks, carrying with him his plan for conquering a fortune, and the dream of the eventual gratification of his appetite.

Early in 1853, Aristide Saccard was appointed trustee of roads. He now received a salary of four thousand five hundred francs. This rise came at an opportune moment; Angèle was slowly wasting away; little Clotilde was looking quite pale. He retained his small lodging of two rooms, the dining-room furnished in walnut, and the bedroom in mahogany, continuing to lead an austere life, carefully avoiding getting into debt, unwilling to touch other people's money until he could bury his arms into it to the elbows. He thus belied his instincts, disdaining the few extra sous he received, preferring to remain on the watch. Angèle felt completely happy. She bought herself some new clothes, and had a joint to roast every day of the week. She could no longer understand the reason of her husband's suppressed passion, his gloomy ways of a man working out the solution of some formidable problem.

Acting on Eugène's advice, Aristide was keeping his eyes and ears open. When he went to thank his brother for his promotion, the latter understood the revolution that had taken place within him; he complimented him on what he called his good appearance. The clerk, whom envy was inwardly rendering inflexible, had outwardly become pliant and insinuating. In a few months he was transformed into a marvellous comedian. All his southern animation had awakened, and he carried the art so far that his comrades at the Hôtel de Ville looked upon him as a jolly good fellow, whose near relationship to a deputy designed beforehand for some grand appointment. This relationship also secured him the good will of his chiefs. He thus enjoyed a kind of authority superior to his position, which enabled him to open certain doors, and to poke his nose into certain portfolios, without his indiscretion appearing in the least culpable. For two years he was seen roaming about all the passages, lingering in all the rooms, getting up from his seat twenty times a day to talk to a comrade, carry an order, or take a stroll through the different departments, endless wanderings which caused his colleagues to say:

"That devil of a Southerner! he can't keep still a minute; he must indeed have quicksilver in his legs."

His own particular friends took him for a lazy fellow, and the worthy man laughed when they accused him of seeking to rob the service of a few minutes. He never committed the mistake of listening at key-holes; but he had a bold way of opening doors, and crossing rooms, apparently deeply intent upon some document or other in his hand, and with so slow and regular a walk that he never lost a word of whatever was being said. They were the tactics of a genius; people ended by no longer interrupting their conversation when this energetic clerk passed by, gliding so to say in the shadow of the offices, and seemingly so wrapt in his own business. He had yet another method; he was extremely obliging, and would offer to assist his comrades, whenever they were behindhand with their work; and then he would study the registers and the documents that passed through his hands with quite a meditative tenderness. But one of his favourite peccadilloes was to form acquaintance with the messengers. He would even shake hands with them. For hours together he would keep them talking in doorways, stifling little bursts of laughter, telling them stories, and drawing them out. These worthy fellows quite worshipped him, and were in the habit of saying:

"There's a gentleman who isn't a bit proud!"

The moment there was the least scandal, he knew of it before any one. It was thus that at the end of two years the Hôtel de Ville held no mysteries for him. He knew everybody employed there, even to the lamp cleaners, and was acquainted with every paper the place contained, not omitting the washing books.

At this time, Paris formed, for a man like Aristide Saccard, a most interesting spectacle. The Empire had just been proclaimed, after that famous journey during which the Prince President had succeeded in arousing the enthusiasm of some Bonapartist departments. Silence reigned both at the tribune and in the press. Society, saved once more, was congratulating itself and indolently resting, now that a strong government was protecting it and relieving it even of the trouble of thinking and of attending to its own business. The great preoccupation of society was to know in what way it should kill time. As Eugène Rougon so happily expressed it, Paris was dining and anticipating no end of pleasure at dessert. Politics produced an universal scare, like some dangerous drug. The wearied minds turned to pleasure and money-making. Those who had any of the latter brought it out, and those who had none sought in all the out-of-the-way places for forgotten treasures. A secret quiver seemed to run through the multitude, accompanied by a nascent jingling of five-franc pieces, by the rippling laughter of women, and the yet faint clatter of crockery and murmur of kisses. Amidst the great silence of the reign of order, the profound peacefulness brought by the change of government, there arose all sorts of pleasant rumours, gilded and voluptuous promises. It was as though one were passing in front of one of those little houses, the carefully drawn curtains of which reveal no more than the shadows of women, and where one can overhear the jingling of gold on the marble mantelpieces. The Empire was about to turn Paris into the bagnio of Europe. The handful of adventurers who had just stolen a throne needed a reign of adventure, of shadowy business transactions, of consciences sold, of women bought, of furious and universal intoxication. And, in the city where the blood of December was scarcely wiped away, there slowly uprose, timidly as yet, that mad desire for enjoyment which was destined to bring the country to the lowest dregs of corrupt and dishonoured nations.

From the very first days Aristide Saccard had felt the approach of this rising tide of speculation, the foam of which was soon to envelop the whole of Paris. He watched its progress with profound attention. He found himself right in the very midst of the warm downpour of silver crowns falling thick and fast on to the roofs of the city. In his constant wanderings through the Hôtel de Ville, he had obtained an inkling of the vast project for the transformation of Paris, of the plan of the demolitions and of the new thoroughfares and the altered districts, of the formidable jobbery with respect to the sale of the land and the buildings, which was kindling all over the town the battle of interests and the flare-up of unbridled luxury. From that moment his activity had an object. It was at this epoch that he became quite a jolly good fellow. He even grew a trifle stout, he no longer hurried about the streets like a half starved cat in search of something to devour. At his office he was more talkative, more obliging than ever. His brother, to whom he paid occasional visits, in some measure official, congratulated him on so happily putting his counsels into practice. In the early days of 1854, Saccard confided to him that he had several affairs in view, but that he would require some rather large advances in the way of money.

"You should look about," said Eugène.

"You are right, I will look about," he replied without the least trace of ill-humour, and without appearing to notice that his brother declined to furnish him with the necessary funds.

How to procure this money had now become his constant thought. His plan was formed; it grew maturer every day. But he was as far as ever from obtaining the first few thousands of francs he required. His faculties became keener; he began to look at people in a profound and nervous manner, as though he were seeking a lender in every passer-by. Angèle continued to lead at home her secluded and happy existence. He was for ever watching for an opportunity, and his laugh of a jolly good fellow became more bitter as this opportunity delayed in presenting itself.

Aristide had a sister living in Paris. Sidonie Rougon had married a solicitor's clerk at Plassans, who had come with her to the Rue Saint-Honoré to start business as a dealer in Southern commodities. When her brother came across her, the husband had disappeared, and the business had long ago gone to the dogs. She occupied in the Rue du Faubourg-Poissonnière, a small mezzanine floor consisting of three rooms. She also leased the shop beneath, a narrow and mysterious shop in which she pretended to carry on the business of a dealer in lace. True enough, there was a display of Valenciennes and Maltese lace suspended from gilt rods in the window; but inside, the place had more the look of an ante-room, with its polished wainscotting, and a total absence of goods of any description. Light curtains hung before the glazed door and the window, intercepting the glances of the passers-by, and helping to give the shop the veiled and discreet appearance of a waiting-room at the entrance to some strange temple. It was very seldom that any customer was seen to call at Madame Sidonie's; the handle was even generally removed from the door. She spread a report in the neighbourhood that she went personally to offer her wares to ladies of fortune. The convenient arrangement of the place, she would say, had alone caused her to rent the shop and the floor above which communicated by a staircase hidden in the wall. And indeed the lace-dealer was constantly out of doors; she might be seen hurrying in or out at least ten times a day.

The lace trade, however, was not her only business; she utilised her upper floor—cramming it full of merchandise of one sort or another, bought up no one knew where. At different times she had dealt there in gutta-percha goods, such as waterproof coats, shoes, braces, &c; then had followed a new oil to promote the growth of the hair, various orthopedic instruments, and an automatic coffee-pot, a patented invention, the working of which gave her a great deal of trouble. The first time her brother came to see her, she had gone in for pianos, to such an extent that her apartments were full of them; they were even in her bedroom, a very daintily decorated room, which contrasted violently with the commercial untidiness of the two others. She carried on her two businesses with perfect method; the customers who came for the goods on the mezzanine floor, entered and departed by means of a carriage entrance which gave admittance to the house from the Rue Papillon; only those acquainted with the mysterious little staircase were able to form an idea of the lace-dealer's underhand trading. Up in her apartments she was known as Madame Touche, which was the name of her husband, whilst she had had only her Christian name painted on the shop-door, which was the reason for her being generally addressed as Madame Sidonie.

Madame Sidonie was thirty-five years of age, but she dressed so carelessly, she had so little of the woman in her appearance, that one would have taken her to be much older. In truth, she was a person whose age it would have been difficult to tell. She was always seen in the same black dress, frayed at the edges, rumpled and discoloured by constant wear, reminding one of a lawyer's old gown become threadbare through years of daily attendance in court. With a black bonnet which came as low as her forehead and hid all her hair, and a pair of thick heavy shoes, she scurried along the streets, carrying on her arm a little basket the handles of which had been mended with pieces of string. This basket, which never left her, was quite a little world in itself. Whenever she raised the lid, samples of all sorts issued forth, diaries, pocket books, and especially bundles of stamped documents, the almost illegible writing of which she deciphered with extraordinary dexterity. She comprised in her person something of the broker and of the man of law.

She lived amidst protests, writs, and orders of the court; when she had secured an order for ten francs' worth of pomatum or lace, she would insinuate herself into the good graces of her customer, and become her man of business, calling in her stead on solicitors, barristers and judges.

She would thus carry for weeks together at the bottom of her basket all the documents relating to a case, taking no end of trouble about it, going from one end of Paris to the other, with the same regular little trot-trot, never for a moment thinking of riding to save her legs. It would have been difficult to say what profit she obtained from such a business; in the first place she engaged in it through an instinctive taste for questionable matters, a love for cavilling; besides this, however, it enabled her to secure a host of little profits; invitations to dinner in every direction, innumerable franc pieces pocketed here and there. But her clearest gain was undoubtedly the numerous secrets confided to her wherever she went, which showed her where a good stroke of business was to be done or a handsome windfall to be obtained. Living in the homes of others and wrapt up in their affairs, she had become a veritable repertory existing on offers and demands. She knew where there was a daughter ready to be married at once, a family in need of three thousand francs, an old gentleman willing to lend the three thousand francs, but on substantial security and at a high rate of interest. She knew of matters more delicate still: the sadness of a fair lady whose husband did not understand her, and who longed to be understood; the secret desires of a good mother who dreamed of settling her daughter advantageously; the taste of a certain baron for little supper-parties and very young girls. And smiling faintly, she went about hawking these offers and these demands, she would walk a couple of leagues to bring her clients together; she sent the baron to the good mother, prevailed upon the old gentleman to lend the three thousand francs to the needy family, obtained the necessary consolation for the fair lady and a not over-scrupulous husband for the young girl in a hurry to marry.

She was also engaged in some very important business, business that there was no occasion to keep secret, and with which she pestered whoever went near her: an interminable law-suit that a noble but ruined family had intrusted her with, and a debt owing by the English to the French nation since the time of the Stuarts, and which amounted with the compound interest to nearly three milliards of francs. This debt of three milliards was her hobby-horse; she would explain the case with no end of particulars, launching out into quite a course of history, and a flush of enthusiasm would rush to her cheeks, usually yellow and flabby like wax. At times, between a call on a lawyer and a visit paid to a lady friend, she would secure an order for a coffee-pot, a mackintosh, a piece of lace, or a piano on hire. These were matters arranged in a moment. Then she would hurry back to her shop, where a lady customer had an appointment with her to see a piece of Chantilly. The customer arrived and glided like a shadow into the discreet and veiled shop. And it often happened that a gentleman, entering by way of the carriage entrance in the Rue Papillon, called at the same time to see Madame Touche's pianos on the floor above.

If Madame Sidonie had not made a fortune, it was because she often worked for love of the thing. With a great hankering after legal business, forgetting her own affairs for those of others, she allowed herself to be fleeced by the lawyers, which procured her, however, an enjoyment unknown to any but litigious persons. There was scarcely anything womanly left about her; she had become nothing more nor less than a man of business, an agent ever bustling about the four corners of Paris, carrying in her legendary basket articles of the most equivocal description, selling every thing, dreaming of milliards, and even going to the court-house for a favourite client to plead in a case of a disputed ten francs. Short, skinny and pale, dressed in that thin black garment which looked as though it had been cut out of a barrister's gown, she seemed to have shrivelled up, and to see her scuttling along close to the houses, one would have taken her for an errand-boy disguised as a girl. Her complexion had the mournful wanness of stamped paper. Her lips parted in a dim smile, whilst her eyes seemed to be wandering amidst the hubbub of business, matters of every description with which she loaded her brain. Of discreet and timid ways, moreover, combined with a vague odour of the confessional and a midwife's sanctum, she always appeared as gentle and maternal as a nun who, having renounced all the affections of this world, takes pity on the sufferings of the heart. She never mentioned her husband, neither did she allude to her childhood, her family, or her affairs. There was only one thing she did not deal in, and that was herself; not that she had any scruples about the matter, but because the idea of such a bargain could never occur to her. She was as dry as an invoice, as cold as a protest, and at heart as brutal and indifferent as a bumbailiff.

Saccard, all fresh from his province, could not at first fathom the delicate depths of Madame Sidonie's numerous callings. As he had during twelve months studied for the bar, she one day spoke to him of the three milliards with a very grave air, which gave him but a poor opinion of her intelligence. She came and rummaged in all the corners of the lodging in the Rue Saint-Jacques, weighed Angèle at a glance, and never again put in an appearance excepting when her own affairs brought her into the neighbourhood, and when she felt a desire to again discuss the question of the three milliards. Angèle had swallowed the bait of the story of the English debt. The woman of business mounted her hobby, and made it rain gold for an hour or more. It was the crack in this shrewd intellect, the gentle myth with which she deluded her life wasted in a wretched traffic, the magical lure that intoxicated not only herself but the more credulous of her clients. Thoroughly convinced, moreover, she ended by speaking of the three milliards as of some private fortune, which the judges would have to restore to her sooner or later, and this shed a marvellous aureola around her shabby black bonnet on which hung a few faded violets attached to brass-wire stems bare of all covering. Angèle would open her eyes wide with amazement. On several occasions, she spoke to her husband of her sister-in-law with great respect, saying that Madame Sidonie would perhaps make them all rich one day. Saccard merely shrugged his shoulders; he had gone and inspected the shop and floor above in the Rue du Faubourg-Poissonnière, and the only impression he had taken away with him was that of an approaching bankruptcy. He wished to know Eugène's opinion of their sister; but his brother became grave and merely replied that he never saw her, that he knew she was very intelligent, though perhaps rather compromising.

However as Saccard was returning to the Rue de Penthièvre some little while afterwards, he fancied he saw Madame Sidonie's black dress leave his brother's abode and glide rapidly along the houses. He hastened forward, but lost all trace of the black garment. The woman of business had one of those spare figures which so easily lose themselves in a crowd. This set him thinking, and it was from this moment that he commenced to study his sister more attentively. It was not long before he began to understand the immense task performed by that pale and shadowy little body, whose entire face seemed to squint and melt away. He came to look upon her with respect. She had the true Rougon blood in her veins. He recognised that appetite for money, that longing for every kind of intrigue which was characteristic of the family; only, in her case, thanks to the surroundings amidst which she had grown old, thanks to that Paris where every morning she had been obliged to set forth to seek her evening meal, the common temperament had deviated from its usual course to produce this extraordinary hermaphrodism of a woman changed into a being without a gender, both man of business and procuress at the same time.

When Saccard, after having fixed upon his plan, was seeking for the means for putting it into execution, he naturally bethought him of his sister. She shook her head, and with a sigh alluded to the three milliards. But the civil servant would not humour her whim, he pulled her up rather roughly each time she mentioned the debt connected with the Stuarts; such a chimera seemed to him to dishonour so practical an intelligence. Madame Sidonie, who quietly swallowed the most cutting irony without in any way allowing her convictions to be shaken, next explained to him in a very lucid manner that he would never raise a sou, having no security to offer. This conversation took place opposite the Bourse, where she no doubt dabbled with her savings. Towards three o'clock one was sure to find her leaning against the railing to the left, near the post-office; it was there that she gave audience to individuals as fishy and shadowy as herself. Her brother was on the point of leaving her, when she murmured regretfully: "Ah! if only you were not married!" This reticence, the full and exact sense of which he was unwilling to ask, made Saccard singularly thoughtful.

Months passed by, the Crimean war had just been declared. Paris, quite unaffected by a war so far away, was launching with more ardour than ever into speculation and women; whilst Saccard stood by gnawing his fists as he assisted at this ever increasing mania which he had long before foreseen. The hammers in the gigantic forge beating the gold upon the anvil made him quiver with rage and impatience. His intelligence and his will were worked up to such a pitch that he lived as in a dream, like a somnambulist walking along the edge of a roof a prey to some fixed idea. He was therefore surprised and annoyed one evening to find Angèle ill and in bed. His home-life, regulated like a clock, was getting out of order, and this exasperated him like some intentional spitefulness of destiny. Poor Angèle complained in a gentle voice; she had taken a severe chill. When the doctor arrived, he appeared very anxious; he told the husband, outside on the landing, that his wife was suffering from inflammation of the lungs and that he could not answer for her life. From that moment the civil servant tended the invalid without a vestige of anger; he no longer went to his office, he remained beside her, watching her with an indefinable expression as she lay sleeping, flushed and panting with fever.

Madame Sidonie, in spite of the overwhelming business which claimed her attention, found time to call each evening to make diet drinks which she pretended were sovereign remedies. To all her other trades she could add that of a sick-nurse by vocation, taking an interest in suffering, in medicaments, and in the heart-rending conversations which go on at the bedsides of those about to depart this life. Besides this, she seemed to be full of a tender friendship for Angèle; she loved women of amorous natures, showing her affection by a thousand little caressing ways, no doubt because of the pleasure they gave mankind; she treated them with the delicate attentions which dealers show towards the more precious of their wares, calling them "My beauty, my darling," cooing and almost swooning before them, like a lover in the presence of his mistress. Though Angèle was one of those from whom she expected nothing, she petted her up like the others, just by way of principle. When the young woman took to her bed, Madame Sidonie's effusions became quite pathetic, she filled the silent chamber with demonstrations of her devotion. Her brother watched her moving about, his teeth tightly set, and looking as though utterly wrapt up in a silent grief.

The disease took a turn for the worse. One evening the doctor informed them that the patient would not live through the night. Madame Sidonie had called early, with a preoccupied air, and she kept looking at Aristide and Angèle out of her watery eyes, lighted up every now and then by sudden flashes of fire. When the doctor had taken his departure, she turned down the lamp, and a great silence enveloped all. Death was slowly entering into this warm and dampish room, where the irregular breathing of the dying woman resembled the spasmodic ticking of a clock about to stop. Madame Sidonie had given up the diet drinks, and now allowed the disease to go its course. She had seated herself before the fire-place, at the side of her brother, who was stirring the coals with a feverish hand, and casting now and again an involuntary glance at the bed. Then, as though enervated by the close atmosphere, and by the sad spectacle, he withdrew into the adjoining room. Little Clotilde had been shut in there, and was playing very quietly with her doll on the edge of the rug. His daughter was smiling up at him when Madame Sidonie, creeping to where he stood, drew him into a corner, and commenced to speak in a hushed voice. The door had remained ajar. One could hear the faint rattle in Angèle's throat.

"Your poor wife," sobbed the business woman. "I fear the end is at hand. You heard what the doctor said?"

For all answer Saccard mournfully bowed his head.

"She was a good creature," continued the other, speaking as though Angèle were already dead and buried. "You may find many richer women, and ones more used to the world, but you will never meet with another heart like hers."

And as she stopped, and set to mopping her eyes, as though seeking a means of bringing the conversation to the subject she was driving at.

"You have something to tell me?" asked Saccard, without any beating about the bush.

"Yes, I have been busying myself about you, in reference to the matter you spoke of, and I think I have found something—but at such a moment—you see, my heart is bursting."

She mopped her eyes again. Saccard let her have her way, and did not utter a word. Then she made up her mind to speak.

"It's a young girl, her relations wish to see her married at once," said she. "The dear child has met with a misfortune. There is an aunt who will be willing to make any sacrifice—"

She interrupted herself, she was continuing to moan, drawling out her words as though she were still pitying poor Angèle. She did this with a view of making her brother lose patience and forcing him to question her, so as not to have the whole responsibility of the offer she was about to make him. And, indeed, an inward feeling of irritation began to work upon the civil servant.

"Come, say what you have to say!" said he. "Why do they wish to see this young girl married?"

"She had just left school," resumed the woman of business in a doleful voice, "and a man seduced her, down in the country, at the home of one of her schoolfellows where she was staying. The father has just discovered her condition. He wished to kill her. The aunt, to save the dear child, made herself her accomplice, and they have both of them told the father a story, to the effect that the seducer was a worthy fellow who was longing to redeem his momentary error."

"Therefore," said Saccard in a tone of surprise and as though annoyed, "the man in the country is going to marry the young girl?"

"No, he cannot, he is already married."

A pause ensued. The rattle in Angèle's throat resounded more painfully in the quivering atmosphere. Little Clotilde had ceased playing; she was now looking at Madame Sidonie and her father, with her great eyes of a thoughtful child, as though she had understood their words. Saccard began to put a few brief questions.

"How old is the young girl?"

"Nineteen."

"How long has she been in her present condition?"

"Three months. There will no doubt be a miscarriage."

"And the family is a wealthy and honourable one?"

"An old middle-class family. The father was a judge. A very handsome fortune."

"What is the aunt prepared to give?"

"A hundred thousand francs."

Another pause ensued. Madame Sidonie was no longer blubbering; she was on business, her voice assumed the metallic jingle of a second-hand dealer trying to drive a bargain. Her brother took a covert glance at her, and added with some slight hesitation:

"And you, what will you want?"

"We'll talk of that later on," replied she. "You can do me a service in your turn."

She waited a few seconds, and as he remained silent, she asked him plainly:

"Well, what have you decided? These poor women are in despair; they wish to prevent a scandal. They have promised the father to tell him to-morrow the name of the seducer. If you accept, I will send them one of your cards by a commissionaire."

Saccard seemed to awaken from a dream; he started, and turned with a frightened air towards the adjoining room, where he fancied he had heard a slight noise.

"But I cannot," said he with anguish; "you know very well that I cannot."

Madame Sidonie looked at him fixedly, with a cold and disdainful gaze. All the Rougon blood, all his ardent longings came rushing back to his throat. He took a card from his pocket-book and gave it to his sister, who, after carefully scratching out the address, placed it in an envelope. She then went out. It was barely nine o'clock.

Left alone, Saccard went and pressed his forehead against the icy cold window panes. He forgot himself so far as to beat the tattoo on the glass with the tips of his fingers. But the night was so black, the darkness outside hung about in such strange masses, that he could not help experiencing a feeling of uneasiness, and he mechanically returned to the room in which Angèle was dying. He had quite forgotten her, and received a terrible shock on finding her half raised up in bed on her pillows; her eyes were wide open, a flush of life seemed to have returned to her lips and cheeks. Little Clotilde, still holding her doll, was seated on the edge of the bed; the moment her father had turned his back she had quickly glided into that chamber from which she had so long been kept, and to which her gladsome childish curiosity attracted her. His head full of what his sister had been saying to him, Saccard suddenly beheld his dream dashed to pieces. A frightful thought must have glared from out his eyes. Seized with terror, Angèle tried to bury herself in the bedclothes right up against the wall; but death was nigh, this awakening in the midst of the last agony was the supreme flicker of the lamp going out. The dying woman was unable to move, and as her last remnant of strength left her, she continued to keep her wide open eyes fixed on her husband, as though to watch his every movement.

Saccard, who for a moment had believed in some diabolical resurrection, invented by destiny to keep him in poverty, became reassured on seeing that the wretched woman had scarcely another hour to live. His other feelings gave way to one of intolerable uneasiness. Angèle's eyes said plainly enough that she had overheard the conversation between her husband and Madame Sidonie, and that she feared he would strangle her if she did not die quick enough. And her eyes were also full of the horrible amazement of a gentle and inoffensive nature which learns at the last moment the infamies of this world, and shudders at the thought of having passed years side by side with a bandit. By degrees her look became more kind; she was no longer frightened, she no doubt found excuses for the wretch as she recollected the desperate struggle he had been maintaining so long against fate. Followed by the dying woman's gaze, in which he read such bitter reproach, Saccard clung to the furniture for support, and sought the darkest corner of the room. Then, feeling on the point of fainting, he tried to drive away this nightmare which was maddening him, and advanced into the light of the lamp. But Angèle motioned him not to speak, and she continued looking at him with that air of terror-stricken anguish, to which was now joined a promise of pardon. Then he stooped to take up Clotilde in his arms and carry her into the other room. She again forbade him with a movement of her lips. She insisted upon his remaining where he was. She slowly passed away, not once removing her gaze from him, and as he paled beneath it, this gaze grew more and more benign. She forgave with her last sigh. She died as she had lived, tamely; her diffidence in life attending her till death.

ÉMILE ZOLA

Saccard stood shivering before the dead woman's eyes, which remained wide open, and transfixed him by their very immobility. Little Clotilde nursed her doll on the edge of the sheet, very gently though, so as not to wake her mother.

When Madame Sidonie got back it was all over. Like a woman in the habit of performing such operations, she deftly closed Angèle's eyes with a touch of her fingers, and this was an immense relief to Saccard. Then, after putting the little girl to bed, she quickly arranged the room as befits the chamber of death. When she had lighted two candles on the chest of drawers, and carefully drawn the sheet up to the chin of the corpse, she cast a satisfied glance around her, and ensconced herself in an easy-chair, where she dozed till daybreak. Saccard passed the night in the adjoining room, writing letters announcing his wife's death. He interrupted himself now and again, musing and adding up columns of figures on odd bits of paper.

On the evening of the day of the funeral, Madame Sidonie took Saccard to her apartment on the mezzanine floor, and grand resolutions were formed there. The civil servant decided that he would send little Clotilde to one of his brothers, Pascal Rougon, a doctor at Plassans, who led a bachelor life, wrapt up in the love of science, and who had often offered to take his niece to live with him to enliven his silent home. Madame Sidonie then made Saccard understand that he could no longer sojourn in the Rue Saint-Jacques. She would take an elegantly furnished apartment for him for a month, somewhere in the neighbourhood of the Hôtel de Ville; she would try to find this apartment in a private house, so that the furniture should appear to belong to him. As to the chattels in the Rue Saint-Jacques, they should all be sold, so as to efface every trace of the past. He could use the money in buying himself a trousseau and some decent clothes.

Three days later, Clotilde was handed over to an old lady who it so happened was just starting for the South. And Aristide Saccard, triumphant and rosy-cheeked, looking fattened up in three days by the first smiles of fortune, occupied in a quiet and respectable house in the Rue Payenne, situated in the Marais quarter, a charming floor of five rooms through which he wandered with embroidered slippers on his feet. They were the apartments of a young abbé who had been suddenly called to Italy, and who had instructed his servant to let the rooms during his absence. This servant was a friend of Madame Sidonie's, who rather fancied the cloth; she loved priests with the same love that she showered on women, through instinct, no doubt establishing a certain nervous relationship between cassocks and silk skirts. From that time Saccard was ready; he arranged the part he was to play with exquisite art; he awaited without betraying the least emotion the difficulties and niceties of the situation which he had accepted.

On the dreadful evening when Angèle died, Madame Sidonie had faithfully told in a few words the misfortune which had overtaken the Bérauds. The father, Monsieur Béraud Du Châtel, a fine old man of sixty, was the last representative of an ancient middle-class family, who could trace their origin much farther back than many a noble house. One of his ancestors was a companion of Étienne Marcel. In 1793 his father perished on the scaffold, after saluting the Republic with all the enthusiasm of a Paris citizen, in whose veins flowed the revolutionary blood of the city. He himself was one of those Spartan republicans who dream of a government of full justice and wise liberty. Grown old in the magistracy, where he had contracted quite a professional stiffness and severity, he resigned his post of presiding judge in 1851, at the time of the Coup d'État, after refusing to be a member of one of those mixed commissions which dishonoured French justice.

Since that time he had been living, solitary and retired, in his mansion on the Île Saint-Louis, situated at the extremity of the island, almost opposite the mansion of the Lamberts. His wife had died young. Some secret drama, the wound from which still remained unhealed, probably added to the gloom of the judge's grave countenance. He was already the father of a girl of eight, Renée, when his wife expired on giving birth to a second daughter. This latter, who was named Christine, was taken care of by a sister of Monsieur Béraud Du Châtel's, the wife of Aubertot the notary. Renée was sent to a convent. Madame Aubertot, who had no child of her own, was filled with quite a maternal affection for Christine, whom she brought up herself. Her husband dying, she took the little one back to her father, and remained between the silent old man and his smiling fair-haired daughter. Renée was forgotten at her school. During the holidays she filled the house with such an uproar that her aunt heaved a great sigh of relief when she at length escorted her back to the ladies of the Visitation, where the child had been a boarder since she was eight years old. She did not leave the convent for good until she was nineteen, and then she went to pass the summer at the home of her friend Adeline, whose parents owned a beautiful estate in the Nivernais. When she came back in October, her Aunt

Élisabeth was surprised to find her very grave and profoundly sad. One evening she discovered her stifling her sobs in the pillow, writhing on her bed in an attack of mad grief. In the misery of her despair the child told her a most heart-rending story: a man of forty, rich, married, and whose wife, a young and charming person, was also staying at the house, had violated her during her visit in the country, without her daring or knowing how to defend herself.

This confession terrified Aunt Élisabeth; she accused herself, as though she had felt she were an accomplice; she regretted her preference for Christine, and could not help thinking that, if she had also kept Renée beside her, the poor child would not have succumbed. Henceforward, to drive away that bitter remorse which her tender nature still further exaggerated, she did her best to sustain the erring one; she bore the brunt of the father's anger when they both apprised him of the horrible truth by the very excess of their precautions; in the bewilderment of her solicitude she invented that strange project of marriage which to her idea was to arrange everything, appease the father and rehabilitate Renée, and the shamefulness and fatal consequences of which she was unwilling to see.

It was never known how Madame Sidonie had got wind of this magnificent piece of business. The honour of the Bérauds had been dragged about in her basket amongst the protested bills of every dollymop of Paris. When she learned the story, she almost forced them to accept her brother, whose wife lay at death's door. Aunt Élisabeth ended by thinking that she was under an obligation to this lady, so gentle and humble, and who was so devoted to poor Renée, that she even found her a husband in her own family. The first interview between Saccard and the aunt took place in the little apartment on the upper floor of the Rue du Faubourg-Poissonnière. The civil servant, who had gained admittance through the carriage entrance in the Rue Papillon, understood, on beholding Madame Aubertot arrive by way of the shop and little staircase, all the ingenious mechanism of the two entrances. He was full of tact and good manners. He treated the marriage as a matter of business, but like a man of the world about to settle his gambling debts. Aunt Élisabeth was by far the more trembling of the two; she stammered, not daring to mention the hundred thousand francs which she had promised. It was he who first brought forward the money question, in the manner of a solicitor discussing a client's case. According to him, a hundred thousand francs was a ridiculous fortune for Mademoiselle

Renée's husband to start housekeeping upon. And he laid a gentle stress on the word "Mademoiselle." Monsieur Béraud Du Châtel would despise still more a poor son-in-law; he would accuse him of having seduced his daughter for the sake of her money; perhaps, it might even occur to him to make some secret inquiries. Madame Aubertot, greatly frightened, and scared by Saccard's calm and polite way of talking, lost her head and consented to double the sum when he declared that he would not dare to ask for Renée's hand for less than two hundred thousand francs, not wishing to be considered an infamous fortune-hunter. The worthy lady departed quite confused, scarcely knowing what to think of a fellow who could be so indignant and yet enter into such an arrangement.

This first interview was followed by an official visit which Aunt Élisabeth paid Saccard at his apartments in the Rue Payenne. This time, she came in the name of Monsieur Béraud. The retired judge had refused to see "that man," as he called his daughter's seducer, so long as he was not married to Renée, to whom he had also closed his door. Madame Aubertot had full powers to arrange everything. She appeared delighted with the civil servant's luxurious surroundings; she had feared that the brother of that Madame Sidonie, with the draggled skirts, might be a blackguard. He received her, arrayed in a delicious dressing-gown. It was at the time, when the adventurers of the 2nd of December, after having paid their debts, were pitching their worn-out boots and frayed coats into the sewers, having their dirty chins shaved, and becoming respectable members of society. Saccard was at length joining the band; he took to cleaning his nails and using at his toilet the most invaluable powder and perfume. He was quite gallant; he changed his tactics and showed himself most prodigiously disinterested. When the old lady broached the subject of the marriage contract, he made a gesture as though to say that it was a matter of indifference to him. For a week past he had been studying the Code, considering this grave question upon which his future liberty of action in his underhand dealings would depend.

"For goodness' sake," said he, "let's say no more about this disagreeable money question. My opinion is that Mademoiselle Renée should remain mistress of her fortune and I master of mine. The notary will settle all that."

Aunt Élisabeth approved this arrangement; she trembled for fear this fellow, whose iron grip she could vaguely feel, should wish to thrust his fingers into her niece's dowry. She next gave the particulars of this dowry.

"My brother," said she, "possesses a fortune consisting mainly of landed property and houses. He is not the man to punish his daughter by reducing the share he intended for her. He gives her an estate in Sologne, valued at three hundred thousand francs, as well as a house in Paris said to be worth about two hundred thousand francs."

Saccard was quite dazzled, he had not expected such an amount; he slightly turned away his head so as to hide the rush of blood which dyed his face.

"That makes five hundred thousand francs," continued the aunt; "but I must not hide from you that the Sologne property only yields two per cent."

He smiled and repeated his disinterested gesture, wishing to imply that that could not affect him as he declined to meddle with his wife's fortune. He was seated in his easy-chair in an attitude of adorable indifference, with an absent-minded air, his foot playing with his slipper, and he appeared to be listening purely out of politeness. Madame Aubertot, with the good nature of a worthy old soul, spoke with difficulty, choosing her words so as not to wound him.

"Besides that, however, I wish to make Renée a present," she resumed. "I have no child of my own, my fortune will one day devolve to my nieces, and it is not because one of them is in grief that I would now close my hand. The wedding presents for both of them have been long ready. Renée's consists in some vast plots of ground near Charonne, which I have reason to believe are worth two hundred thousand francs. Only—"

At the word ground, Saccard slightly started. In spite of his pretended indifference he was listening with profound attention. Aunt Élisabeth became confused, at a loss for words to express what she wished to say. Turning very red, she at length continued:

"Only I wish that the ownership of this ground should be settled on Renée's first child. You no doubt understand my reason: I do not desire that this child should one day be an expense to you. Should it die, the property will become solely Renée's."

He did not display the least sign of disappointment, but his knit brow showed how deeply he was thinking. The plots of ground at Charonne had awakened a host of ideas within him. Madame Aubertot feared she had offended him by speaking of Renée's child, and she remained abashed and quite unable to continue the conversation.

"You have not told me in what street the house property valued at two hundred thousand francs is situated," said he, resuming his pleasant air.

"In the Rue de la Pépinière," she replied, "almost at the corner of the Rue d'Astorg."

This simple answer produced a decisive effect upon him. He could no longer conceal his delight; he drew his easy-chair nearer the lady, and with his southern volubility, and in coaxing tones said:

"Dear madame, have we not said enough, must we still continue to discuss this horrid money question? Listen, I wish to speak to you with all frankness, for I should be in despair did I not merit your esteem. I lost my wife lately, I have two children to look after, I am practical and sensible. By marrying your niece I shall be doing every one a good turn. If you have still any prejudice against me you will lose it later on, when I shall have dried all your tears and made the fortunes of all my descendants. Success is a golden flame which purifies everything. I will force Monsieur Béraud himself to hold out his hand to me and thank me."

He went rattling on, speaking for a long while in the same strain with mocking impudence which showed at times beneath his pleasant air. He talked of his brother the deputy, and of his father the receiver of taxes at Plassans. He ended by completely ingratiating himself with Aunt Élisabeth, who beheld with involuntary joy the drama through which she had been suffering for a month past terminate almost in a merry comedy in the hands of this clever man. It was settled that they should see the notary on the morrow.

As soon as Madame Aubertot took her departure he went to the Hôtel de Ville, and spent the day there examining certain documents with which he was acquainted. At the meeting at the notary's he raised a difficulty, he said that as Renée's dowry consisted solely in landed property he feared it would give her no end of trouble, and he thought it would be wise to sell at least the house in the Rue de la Pépinière and to invest the money for her in the funds. Madame Aubertot wished to refer the matter to Monsieur Béraud Du Châtel, who continued to shut himself up in his room. Saccard went out again until the evening. He visited the Rue de la Pépinière, he hurried about Paris with the thoughtful air of a general on the eve of a decisive battle. The next morning Madame Aubertot stated that Monsieur Béraud Du Châtel left everything to her. The marriage contract was drawn up on the basis already discussed. Saccard brought two hundred thousand francs, Renée's dowry consisted of the Sologne property and the house in the Rue de la Pépinière, which latter she undertook to sell; besides this, she would, in the event of her first child dying, be sole owner of the plots of ground at Charonne given by her aunt. The contract was in accordance with the system of separate estates which preserves to the husband and wife the entire administration of their respective fortunes. Aunt Élisabeth, who was listening attentively to the notary, appeared to be satisfied with this arrangement which seemed to insure her niece's independence by placing her fortune beyond the reach of any attempts that might be made upon it. A vague smile played upon Saccard's countenance as he saw the worthy lady approve each clause with a nod. The marriage was fixed to take place at the shortest possible date.

When everything was settled, Saccard went and paid a ceremonious visit to his brother Eugène to announce to him his union with Mademoiselle Renée Béraud Du Châtel. This master stroke astonished the deputy. As he did not attempt to conceal his surprise, the civil servant said:

"You told me to look about; I did so and I have found what I wanted."

Eugène, quite at sea at first, then began to see the truth. And in a charming tone of voice he observed:

"Come now, you're a clever fellow. You've called to ask me to be your best man, have you not? You may count upon me. If necessary I will bring all the members of the right of the Corps Législatif to your wedding; that would be a famous thing for you."

Then as he had opened the door, he lowered his voice to add:

"But tell me? I must not compromise myself too much just now, for we have a very difficult law to pass—The lady's condition is not too apparent, is it?"

Saccard gave him such a bitter look, that Eugène said to himself as he closed the door:

"That is a joke that would cost me dear, were I not a Rougon."

The marriage was performed at the church of Saint-Louis-en-l'Île. Saccard and Renée did not see each other until the eve of the great day. The interview took place in the evening, just at nightfall, in a low room of the Béraud mansion. They examined each other with curiosity. Since arrangements had been entered into for her marriage, Renée had regained her giddy ways, her light-heartedness. She was a tall girl of an exquisite though turbulent beauty, who had grown up at random amidst her school-girl caprices. She found Saccard little and ugly, but of a restless and intelligent ugliness which did not displease her; he was, moreover, perfect both in manners and conversation. He made a slight grimace on first seeing her; she no doubt appeared to him too tall, taller than he was himself. They exchanged a few words without embarrassment. Had the father been present, he might indeed have thought that they had known each other a long while, that they had committed some grievous fault together. Aunt Élisabeth assisted at the interview and blushed for them.

On the day after the wedding, which was quite an event in the Île Saint-Louis thanks to the presence of Eugène Rougon, whom a recent speech had brought to the fore, the newly married couple were at length admitted to the presence of Monsieur Béraud Du Châtel. Renée wept on finding her father looking older, graver and more mournful. Saccard, whom nothing had put out of countenance till then, was frozen by the chilliness and the dim light of the apartment, by the sad austerity of the tall old man, whose piercing eye seemed to him to search into the very depths of his conscience. The retired judge slowly kissed his daughter on the forehead, as though to tell her that he forgave her, and then turning to his son-in-law:

"Sir," said he simply, "we have suffered much. I count upon you to make us forget the wrong you have done us."

He held out his hand to him. But Saccard stood shivering. He was thinking that if Monsieur Béraud Du Châtel had not been bent low by the tragic grief of Renée's shame, he would at a glance, and without an effort, have seen through Madame Sidonie's machinations. The latter, after having brought her brother and Aunt Élisabeth together, had prudently made herself scarce. She had not even gone to the wedding. He made a point of being very frank with the old man, having read in his look his surprise at finding his daughter's seducer to be a little ugly fellow forty years old. The newly married couple were obliged to pass the first nights at the Béraud mansion. A month before, Christine had been sent away, so that the child of fourteen should have no suspicion of the drama that was being enacted in that house as serene and undisturbed as a cloister. When she returned home, she gazed with astonishment at her sister's husband, whom she also thought old and ugly. Renée was the only one who did not seem to notice either her husband's age or his sorry appearance. She treated him without contempt as without affection, with an absolute tranquillity through which occasionally gleamed a touch of ironical disdain. Saccard strutted about and made himself at home, and really, thanks to his frankness and good spirits, he little by little won the friendship of one and all. When they took their departure to occupy a superb suite of apartments in a new house in the

Rue de Rivoli, Monsieur Béraud Du Châtel's look no longer displayed any astonishment, and little Christine romped with her brother-in-law as with an old friend. Renée was at that time four months gone in the family way; her husband was on the point of sending her into the country, when, in accordance with Madame Sidonie's prophecy, she had a miscarriage. She had laced herself up so tightly to hide her condition, which, moreover, disappeared beneath the fulness of her skirts, that she was obliged to keep her bed for several weeks. He was delighted with the adventure; fortune was at length smiling upon him; he had made a golden bargain, a magnificent dowry, a wife lovely enough to have him decorated in six months, and not the least encumbrance. He had been paid two hundred thousand francs to give his name to a fœtus which the mother would not even look at. From that moment his thoughts lovingly lingered on the plots of ground at Charonne. But for the time being he was giving all his attention to a speculation which was to form the basis of his fortune.

Notwithstanding the high position of his wife's family, he did not at once resign his post at the Hôtel de Ville. He talked of work on hand to be finished, and of some other occupation to be sought for. The truth was he wished to remain till the end on the battle-field where he was playing his first cards. He was so to say at home, and could cheat more at his ease.

His plan for making his fortune was simple and practical. Now that he possessed more money than he had ever hoped for to commence his operations, he intended to put his designs into execution on a grand scale. He knew Paris by heart; he knew that the shower of gold which was already beating against the walls would fall heavier every day. Clever people had only to open their pockets. He had placed himself among the clever ones by reading the future in the offices of the Hôtel de Ville. His duties had taught him what can be stolen in the buying and selling of houses and ground. He was fully acquainted with all the classic swindles: he knew how to sell for a million that which only cost five hundred thousand francs; how to pay the right to ransack the cash boxes of the State, which smiles and shuts its eyes; how, by making a Boulevard pass over the entrails of some old neighbourhood, to juggle with six storeyed houses, amidst the applause of all the dupes. And that which in those still clouded days, when the chancre of speculation was not beyond the period of incubation, made him a terrible gambler was that he foresaw more than his chiefs themselves respecting the future of stone and plaster reserved to Paris. He had ferreted about so much, collected together so many clues, that he might have prophesied the spectacle the new districts would offer in 1870. At times, as he walked along the streets, he would look at certain houses in a singular manner, as though they were old friends whose destiny, known to him alone, affected him deeply.

Two months previous to Angèle's death, he had taken her one Sunday to the Buttes Montmartre. The poor woman delighted in eating at restaurants; she was never more pleased than when, after a long walk, he would take her to dine at some suburban eating-house. That day they had their dinner right at the top of the hill, in a restaurant, with windows overlooking Paris, that ocean of houses with bluey roofs, looking like surging billows filling the immense horizon. Their table was placed before one of the windows. The sight of the Paris roofs enlivened Saccard. At dessert he called for a bottle of Burgundy. He smiled at space, he was most unusually gallant. And his look kept lovingly returning to that living, swarming sea, from which issued the deep voice of the crowd. It was autumn; beneath the vast pale sky the city lay languishing, a soft and tender grey in hue, studded here and there with dark green foliage, which resembled great leaves of nenuphars floating on a lake; the sun was setting behind a red cloud, and, whilst the background was filled with a slight haze, a golden dust, an auriferous dew was falling upon the city on the right bank of the river, in the neighbourhood of the Madeleine and the Tuileries. It was like the enchanted corner of some city of the "Arabian Nights," with trees formed of emeralds, roofs of sapphires, and weather-cocks of rubies. There came a moment when a ray of sunshine, gliding between two clouds, was so resplendent that the houses seemed to flare up and melt away like an ingot of gold in a crucible.

"Oh! look," said Saccard, with a childish laugh, "a shower of twenty-franc pieces has burst over Paris!"

Angèle began to laugh too, accusing these pieces of not being easy to gather up. But her husband had risen from his seat, and leaning against the handrail of the window, he continued:

"That's the Vendôme column shining over there, isn't it? There, more to the right, is the Madeleine—a fine neighbourhood, where there's plenty to be done. Ah! this time, it'll all be ablaze! Do you see? One could almost fancy that the whole neighbourhood was boiling in some chemist's still."

His voice was becoming grave and agitated. The comparison he had drawn seemed to strike him immensely, he had drank a few glasses of

Burgundy and was musing; and he went on, stretching out his arm to show the different sights of Paris to Angèle, who was also leaning over the handrail on her side of the window.

"Yes, yes, what I said was right enough, more than one district will be melted down, and gold will stick to the fingers of those who heat and stir the copper. That great noodle Paris! see how immense he is and how innocently he slumbers! Such great towns are always fools! He has no idea of the army of picks that will attack him one of these fine mornings, and some of the mansions in the Rue d'Anjou would not shine so brightly beneath the setting sun if they knew they had no more than three or four years to live."

Angèle fancied her husband was joking. He had at times a taste for immense and disquieting jokes. She laughed, but with a vague fear, at seeing the little man tower above the giant crouched at his feet, and shake his fist at him while ironically pursing his lips.

"It's already begun," continued he; "but nothing to speak of as yet. Look over there, beside the Halles, Paris has been cut into four."

And with his extended hand, open and sharp edged like a cutlass, he made a motion as though separating the city into four portions.

"You're alluding to the Rue de Rivoli and the new Boulevard they are making aren't you?" asked his wife.

"Yes, the great window of Paris as it's called. They're clearing away the buildings that hide the Louvre and the Hôtel de Ville. But that's mere child's play! It's only good to rouse the public's appetite. When the first improvements are completed the grand work will begin. The city will be pierced in every direction to unite the suburbs to the main artery. The houses will fall amidst clouds of plaster. Look, follow the direction of my hand a minute. From the Boulevard du Temple to the Barrière du Trône will be one gap; then, more this way, from the Madeleine to the Plaine Monceaux will be another; and a third in this direction, another along here, another over there, and still another farther away, in fact gaps everywhere, Paris hacked about as with a sabre, its veins opened, feeding a hundred thousand navvies and masons, traversed right and left by splendid strategical ways which will bring the very forts right into the heart of the old quarters of the city."

Night was coming on. His dry and nervous hand kept hacking about in space. Angèle slightly shuddered before this living knife, these iron fingers mercilessly chopping up the boundless mass of dusky roofs. For some little while past the haze of the horizon had been slowly descending from the heights, and she fancied she could hear, beneath the gloom that was gathering in the hollows, a distant and prolonged sound of cracking, as though her husband's hand had really made the openings he had been speaking of, opening up Paris from one end to the other, severing beams, crushing masonry, leaving in its wake long and frightful wounds of demolished walls. The diminutiveness of this hand, implacably hovering over a giant prey, ended by becoming alarming, and whilst it tore open the entrails of the enormous city without an effort, it seemed to assume a strange shimmer of steel in the bluey twilight.

"There will be a third artery," continued Saccard, at the end of a pause, as though speaking to himself; "but that one is too distant, I see it less plainly. I have come across only a few signs of it. But it will be pure madness, the infernal gallop of millions, Paris intoxicated and overwhelmed!"

He again relapsed into silence, his eyes ardently fixed on the city, where the shadows were gathering deeper and deeper. He was probably interrogating that too distant future which escaped him. Then night enveloped all, the city became lost in a confused mass, one could hear it breathing plentifully, like some sea, the crest of the pale waves of which is all the eye can distinguish. Here and there, a few walls still preserved a whitish hue; and the yellow flames of the gas-jets pierced the gloom one by one, similar to stars shining amidst the darkness of a stormy sky.

Angèle shook off her feeling of uneasiness and continued the jest her husband had commenced at dessert.

"Ah! well," said she with a smile, "there's been a good shower of those twenty-franc pieces! The Parisians are counting them now. Look at the fine piles they're making at our feet!"

She pointed to the streets which descend from the Buttes Montmartre, with their double rows of lighted gas-lamps looking like piles of gold.

"And over there," cried she, indicating a galaxy of lights, "that is surely the treasury!"

The remark made Saccard laugh. They remained a few minutes longer at the window, delighted with this flood of "twenty-franc pieces," which was ending by covering the whole of Paris. On returning from Montmartre, the civil servant no doubt regretted having gossiped so much. He put it down to the Burgundy, and requested his wife not to repeat the "nonsense" he had been saying; he wished, said he, to be considered a serious person.

ÉMILE ZOLA

For a long time past, Saccard had been studying these three lines of streets and Boulevards, the pretty correct plan of which he had so far forgotten himself as to place before Angèle. When the latter died, he in nowise regretted that she carried with her into the tomb the recollection of all he had said up on the Buttes Montmartre. It was there that his fortune lay, in those famous gaps which his hand had, so to say, opened in the very heart of Paris, and he had made up his mind to share his idea with no one, knowing well enough that on the day of the sharing of the spoil there would be plenty of crows hovering over the gutted city.

His original plan had been to purchase, on low terms, some building or other which he knew beforehand was condemned to shortly come down, and to realize an immense profit by obtaining a substantial indemnity. He would, perhaps, have decided to make the attempt without a sou, to buy the building on credit and merely to pocket the difference afterwards, like people do on the Bourse, when his second marriage, bringing him in a premium of two hundred thousand francs, fixed and developed his plan. He had now made his calculations: under the name of an intermediary, and without appearing personally in the matter, he would purchase the house in the Rue de la Pépinière from his wife, and treble his outlay, thanks to the knowledge he had acquired in his perambulations through the Hôtel de Ville, and to his friendly relations with certain influential personages.

The reason he started when Aunt Élisabeth told him where the house was situated, was because it happened to be in the line of a contemplated thoroughfare, the piercing of which was at that time kept secret outside the sanctum of the prefect of the Seine. This thoroughfare, the Boulevard Malesherbes, would necessitate the clearance of the entire house. It was one of the first Napoleon's old projects which it was proposed to put into execution, "to give a normal outlet," so said serious people, "to districts lost behind a labyrinth of narrow streets, on the slopes of the hills which hem in Paris." This official phrase did not, of course, admit the interest the Empire had in the turning over of money, in those vast alterations about the city which left the working classes no time to think. One day at the prefect's, Saccard had ventured to consult that famous plan of Paris on which "an august hand" had marked, in red ink, the principal thoroughfares of the second network of streets. These gory-looking strokes from a pen cut deeper into Paris even than did the civil servant's hand.

The Boulevard Malesherbes, which razed to the ground some superb mansions in the Rue d'Anjou and the Rue de la Ville-l'Évêque, and which necessitated some very considerable levelling works, was to be laid out one of the first. When Saccard went to inspect the building in the Rue de la Pépinière, his thoughts reverted to that autumn evening, to that dinner he had eaten with Angèle up on the Buttes Montmartre, and during which, while the sun was setting, so thick a shower of gold had seemed to fall about the neighbourhood of the Madeleine. He smiled; he fancied that the dazzling cloud had burst right over his own courtyard, and that all he had to do was to go and gather up the twenty-franc pieces.

Whilst Renée, luxuriously installed in the apartments in the Rue de Rivoli, in the very midst of that new Paris of which she was about to become one of the queens, was meditating on her future toilettes, and trying her hand at leading the life of a great lady of fashion, her husband was devoutly nursing his first great scheme. He first of all purchased of his wife the house in the Rue de la Pépinière, thanks to the intermediary of a certain Larsonneau, whom he had come across prying like himself into the secrets of the Hôtel de Ville, but who had been foolish enough to get caught one day that he was examining the contents of the prefect's drawers. Larsonneau had set up in business as an agent at the end of a dark and dank courtyard, at the foot of the Rue Saint-Jacques. His pride and his covetousness suffered cruelly there. He found himself in the same position as Saccard before his marriage; he had, he would say, also invented "a machine for coining five franc pieces;" only he was minus the funds necessary to take advantage of his invention. It needed only a few words for him to come to an understanding with his former colleague, and he set to work with so good a will that he obtained the house for a hundred and fifty thousand francs. Renée was already, at the end of a few months, in need of considerable sums of money. The husband did not appear in the matter except to authorise his wife to sell. When everything was settled she asked him to invest a hundred thousand francs for her in the funds, and confidently handed him the money, no doubt as an appeal to his feelings and to shut his eyes regarding the fifty thousand francs she retained. He smiled in a knowing manner; it formed part of his calculations that she should squander her money; these fifty thousand francs which were about to disappear in jewellery and lace were to bring him in cent per cent. He carried his honesty so far, for he was so well satisfied with his first affair, as to really invest Renée's hundred thousand francs and to hand her the certificates. His wife could not realize upon them; he was certain of finding them in the nest if ever he happened to want them.

"My dear, this will do for your dress," said he gallantly.

When he was in possession of the house, he was skilful enough to sell it twice in a month to fictitious persons, increasing each time the amount paid. The last purchaser gave no less than three hundred thousand francs. Meanwhile, Larsonneau, who alone appeared as representative of the successive landlords, worked upon the tenants. He pitilessly declined to renew the leases, unless they consented to a formidable increase of rent. The tenants, who had an inkling of the approaching dispossession, were in despair; they ended by agreeing to the increase, especially when Larsonneau added in a conciliatory manner that this increase should remain a fictitious one during the first five years. As for the tenants who continued nasty, they were replaced by persons to whom the apartments were let for nothing and who signed everything they were asked to; there was thus a double profit: the rent was raised, and the indemnity reserved to the tenant for his lease was to go to Saccard. Madame Sidonie was willing to assist her brother by starting a piano-dealer's in one of the shops. It was then that Saccard and Larsonneau were carried away by their greed for gain and rather overreached themselves: they concocted the books of a regular business, they falsified accounts, so as to establish a sale of pianos on an enormous footing. During several nights they sat scribbling away together. Worked in this skilful manner the house increased in value threefold. Thanks to the last sale, to the raising of the rent, to the false tenants, and to Madame Sidonie's piano business, it might be considered worth five hundred thousand francs when the indemnity commission came to inquire into the matter.

The mechanism of the instrument of dispossession, of that powerful machine which during fifteen years turned Paris topsy-turvy, breathing fortune and ruin the while, is of the simplest. Directly a new thoroughfare is decided upon, the road inspectors draw up the plan in separate portions and appraise the various buildings to be removed. They generally, after making inquiries, arrive at the total amount of the rents and can thus fix upon the approximate value. The indemnity commission, consisting of members of the municipal council, always offers something beneath this sum, knowing that the interested parties will be sure to demand more, and that there will be a mutual concession. When they are unable to come to terms, the matter is brought before a jury which decides without appeal between the offer of the municipality and the claims of the dispossessed landlord or tenant.

Saccard, who had remained at the Hôtel de Ville for the decisive moment, had at one time the impudence to wish to be appointed to appraise his own house when the Boulevard Malesherbes was commenced. But he feared by so doing to paralyse his influence with the members of the indemnity commission. He caused one of his colleagues to be chosen, a gentle and smiling young man named Michelin, whose wife, an adorably beautiful creature, came at times to offer her husband's excuses to his chiefs when he absented himself through indisposition. Saccard had noticed that pretty Madame Michelin, who glided so humbly through the half closed doorways, was all-powerful; Michelin gained some advancement at each illness, he made his way by taking to his bed. During one of his absences, when his wife was calling nearly every morning at the office to say how he was getting on, Saccard came across him twice on the outer Boulevards, smoking his cigar with the tender and delighted air which never left him. This filled Saccard with sympathy for the good young man, for the happy couple so ingenious and so practical. He had a great admiration for all money-making machines cleverly worked. When he had got Michelin appointed he called on his charming wife, insisted on introducing her to Renée, and talked before her of his brother the deputy, the illustrious orator. Madame Michelin understood. From that day her husband kept his most select smiles for his colleague. The latter, who had no intention of taking the worthy fellow into his confidence, contented himself by being present as if by chance on the day when the other proceeded to appraise the house in the Rue de la Pépinière. He assisted him. Michelin, who had the stupidest and emptiest head it is possible to imagine, followed his wife's instructions, which were to satisfy Monsieur Saccard in all things. Moreover, he had not the slightest suspicion of anything; he imagined that his friend was in a hurry to see him finish his work so as to take him off to a café. The leases, the receipts for rent, Madame Sidonie's famous books passed through his colleague's hands beneath his eyes, without his even having time to check the figures which the other read out. Larsonneau was there also, treating his accomplice as a perfect stranger.

"Come, put down five hundred thousand francs," Saccard ended by saying. "The house is worth more. Hurry up, I think there is going to be a change in the staff of the Hôtel de Ville, and I want to talk to you about it so that you may let your wife know."

The business was thus carried through. But he still had other fears. He was afraid that the sum of five hundred thousand francs would appear rather excessive to the indemnity commission, for a house which was notoriously only worth two hundred thousand. The formidable rise in the value of buildings had not then taken place. An inquiry would have caused him to run the risk of serious unpleasantness. He recalled his brother's words: "No noisy scandal or I shall suppress you;" and he knew that Eugène was the man to put his threat into execution. It was necessary to blindfold the gentlemen forming the commission and to ensure their good will. He cast his eyes on two influential men whom he had made his friends by the way in which he saluted them in the passages whenever he met them. The thirty-six members of the municipal council were carefully selected by the Emperor himself from a list drawn up by the prefect comprising the senators, deputies, lawyers, doctors, and great manufacturers who prostrated themselves the most devotedly before the power that was; but amongst them all Baron Gouraud and Monsieur Toutin-Laroche especially deserved the good will of the Tuileries by their fervour.

All Baron Gouraud's history is contained in this short biography: made a baron by Napoleon I for supplying bad biscuits to the grand army, he had successively been a peer under Louis XVIII, Charles X, and Louis-Philippe, and he was now a senator under Napoleon III. He was a worshipper of the throne, of the four gilded boards covered with velvet; it mattered little to him who the man was that sat upon it. With his enormous stomach, his ox-like countenance, his elephantine manner, he boasted a delightful rascality; he would sell himself majestically and commit the greatest infamies in the name of duty and conscience. But this man surprised one still more by his vices. Stories were told of him which could only be whispered from ear to ear. His seventy-eight years flourished amidst the most monstrous debauchery. On two occasions it had been necessary to hush up some filthy adventures so that his embroidered senator's coat should not be dragged through the dock of the assize court.

Monsieur Toutin-Laroche, who was tall and thin, and the inventor of a mixture of suet and stearin for the manufacture of candles, had a hankering to enter the senate. He stuck to Baron Gouraud like a leech; he rubbed up against him with the vague idea that his doing so would bring him luck. In reality he was thoroughly practical, and had he come across a senator's chair to be sold he would have fiercely higgled over the price. The Empire was about to bring out this greedy nonentity, this narrow mind which had a genius for dabbling in industrial affairs. He was the first to sell his name to a bogus company, one of those associations which sprouted up like poisonous toadstools on the dunghill of imperial speculations. At that time one could have seen on all the walls a poster bearing the following words in bold black letters:—"Société générale of the ports of Morocco," and beneath which the name of Monsieur Toutin-Laroche, with his title of municipal councillor, appeared at the head of the list of directors, all more or less unknown personages. This proceeding, which has become far more popular since, succeeded wonderfully; the shares were snapped up, though the question of the ports of Morocco was not very clear, and the worthy people who brought their money were themselves unable to explain to what purpose it was to be put. The poster announced in a superb manner the project of establishing commercial stations along the Mediterranean coast. For two years past certain newspapers had been celebrating this magnificent undertaking, which they declared to be more and more prosperous every three months. Amongst the municipal council Monsieur Toutin-Laroche had the reputation of being a first-class administrator; he was one of the strong minds of the neighbourhood, and his acrimonious tyranny over his colleagues was only equalled by his devout platitude in the presence of the prefect. He was already engaged in founding a great financial company, the Crédit Viticole, a sort of loan office for vine growers, and to which he would allude in a grave and reticent manner which aroused the covetousness of the fools around him.

Saccard secured the protection of these two personages by rendering them certain services, of the importance of which he cleverly pretended to be ignorant. He brought his sister and the baron together, the latter being then compromised in a very objectionable affair. He took her to him, under the pretence of soliciting his support in the favour of the dear woman who had been petitioning for a long time to obtain an order for the supply of curtains to the Tuileries. But it so happened that, when the road inspector left them together, it was Madame Sidonie who promised the baron to enter into negotiations with certain people who were stupid enough not to have felt honoured by the attention that a senator had deigned to bestow on their daughter, a little girl ten years old. Saccard took Monsieur Toutin-Laroche in hand himself; he manœuvred so as to obtain an interview with him in a corridor, and then brought the conversation round to the famous Crédit Viticole. At the end of five minutes, the great administrator, dazed and astounded by the amazing things told him, took the civil service clerk familiarly by the arm and detained him a full hour in the passage. Saccard whispered in his ear some financial deals which were prodigiously ingenious.

When Monsieur Toutin-Laroche took his departure, he shook his hand in an expressive manner, and gave him the glance of a freemason.

"You shall belong to it," murmured he, "you must really belong to it."

Saccard surpassed himself throughout this affair. He carried his prudence so far as not to make Baron Gouraud and Monsieur Toutin-Laroche accomplices. He visited them separately, letting drop a word or two in their ear in favour of one of his friends who was about to be dispossessed of his house in the Rue de la Pépinière; he was careful to tell each of his confederates that he would mention the matter to no other member of the commission, that it was all very uncertain, but that he counted on his friendliness.

The road inspector had done right to fear and to take his precautions. When the documents relating to his house came before the indemnity commission, it so happened that one of the members lived in the Rue d'Astorg, and knew the house. This member protested against the sum of five hundred thousand francs, which, according to him, should have been reduced to less than half. Aristide had had the impudence to have a claim sent in for seven hundred thousand francs. On that day Monsieur Toutin-Laroche, who was usually very disagreeable towards his colleagues, was even of a more detestable temper still. He became quite angry, and took the part of the landlords.

"We're all of us landlords, gentlemen," cried he. "The Emperor wishes to do grand things, don't let us stick at trifles. This house is no doubt worth the five hundred thousand francs; it's one of our own people, a city inspector, who fixed this price. Really, one would almost fancy we were living amongst thieves; you'll see, we shall end by suspecting one another."

Baron Gouraud, sitting heavily on his chair, watched in a surprised manner, from out of the corner of his eye, Monsieur Toutin-Laroche storming away in favour of the owner of the house in the Rue de la Pépinière. He had a suspicion. But, after all, as this violent outburst saved him the trouble of speaking, he set to slowly nodding his head as a sign of his complete approval. The member hailing from the Rue d'Astorg indignantly resisted, determined not to yield to the two tyrants of the commission in a matter in which he felt himself to be more competent than they. It was then that Monsieur Toutin-Laroche, noticing the baron's marks of approval, hastily pounced upon the documents relating to the case, and said curtly:

"Very well. We'll dispel your doubts. If you will allow it, I'll take the matter in hand, and Baron Gouraud shall join me in the inquiry."

"Yes, yes," said the baron gravely, "there must be no underhand dealings to sully our decisions."

The documents had already disappeared inside Monsieur Toutin-Laroche's capacious pockets. The commission had no choice but to accept the arrangement. As they stood outside upon the quay on leaving the meeting, the two cronies looked at each other without smiling. They felt themselves to be confederates, and this added to their assurance. Two vulgar minds would have sought an explanation; they continued to plead the case of the landlords, as though they could still be overheard, and to deplore the spirit of mistrust which was insinuating itself everywhere. Just as they were about to separate, the baron observed, with a smile:

"Ah! I was forgetting, my dear colleague, I am just about to leave for the country. You would be very kind to make this little inquiry without me. And, above all, don't peach; our colleagues are already complaining that I take too many holidays."

"Be easy," replied Monsieur Toutin-Laroche, "I will go at once to the Rue de la Pépinière."

He went quietly home, with a certain feeling of admiration for the baron, who so cleverly got out of the most ticklish positions. He kept the documents in his pocket, and at the next sitting of the commission he declared, in a peremptory tone of voice, both in his own name and in the baron's, that between the offer of five hundred thousand francs and the claim of seven hundred thousand, they should take a medium course, and award six hundred thousand francs. There was not the slightest opposition. The member hailing from the Rue d'Astorg, having no doubt reflected, said, with great simplicity, that he had been mistaken: he had thought it was the next house.

It was thus that Aristide Saccard won his first victory. He quadrupled his outlay, and secured two accomplices. One thing alone made him uneasy; when he wished to destroy Madame Sidonie's famous books, he was unable to find them. He hastened to Larsonneau, who boldly avowed that he had them, and that he meant to stick to them. The other did not lose his temper; he inferred that he had only been anxious on his dear friend's account, who was far more compromised than he by these entries, which were almost entirely in his handwriting, but that he was quite easy now that he knew they were safe. In reality, he would willingly have strangled "his dear friend;" he remembered a very compromising document, a bogus inventory, which he had been foolish enough to draw up, and which must have been left in one of the ledgers.

Handsomely remunerated, Larsonneau started a business agency in the Rue de Rivoli, where he had offices furnished as luxuriously as any courtesan's apartments. On leaving the Hôtel de Ville, Saccard, having a considerable amount of funds at his disposal, launched madly into speculation, whilst Renée, carried away by her intoxication, filled Paris with the clatter of her equipages, the sparkle of her diamonds, and the whirl of her noisy and adorable existence.

Now and again, the husband and wife, those two enthusiasts of money and pleasure, penetrated into the chilly mists of the Île Saint-Louis. They felt as though they were entering a dead city.

The Béraud mansion, built in the early part of the seventeenth century, was one of those square buildings, gloomy and severe-looking, with tall narrow windows, so numerous in the Marais district, and which are let to schoolmasters, manufacturers of seltzer water, and bonders of wines and spirits. The building, however, was in an admirable state of preservation. On the Rue Saint-Louis-en-l'Île side it consisted of only three storeys, storeys fifteen and twenty feet high. The ground floor, not near so lofty, had its windows protected by enormous iron bars, windows which sunk dismally into the dreary thickness of the walls, whilst the arched door, almost as broad as high, and bearing a cast-iron knocker, was painted a deep green and strengthened with enormous nails, forming stars and lozenges on either panel. This door was typical, with blocks of granite on each flank, half buried in the soil and protected by broad bands of iron. One could see that formerly a gutter had run under the centre of this door, the pavement of the porch sloping gently down on either side: but Monsieur Béraud had decided to close up this gutter by having the entrance laid with bitumen; this was, moreover, the only sacrifice he was ever willing to make to modern architecture. The windows of the upper floors were ornamented with slender handrails of wrought iron, which allowed a full view of the colossal sashes of substantial brown wood frames and little greenish panes of glass. Right at the top, opposite the attics, the roof came to an end, and the gutter alone continued on its way to discharge the rain water into the pipes placed for the purpose. And what tended to increase still further the austere bareness of the frontage was the total absence of any blind or shutter, for at no season of the year did the sun ever shine on these pale and melancholy stones. This frontage, with its venerable air, its middle-class severity, slumbered solemnly amid the peacefulness of the neighbourhood, the silence of the street, seldom disturbed by the passage of vehicles.

In the interior of the mansion was a square courtyard surrounded by arcades, a kind of Place Royale on a reduced scale, paved with enormous flags, which finished giving to this lifeless abode the appearance of a cloister. Facing the porch a fountain, a lion's head half worn away, the gaping jaws of which were alone distinguishable, discharged from an iron tube a thick and monotonous water into a trough all green with moss, its edges polished by wear. This water was icy cold. Tufts of grass sprouted up between the flagstones. In summer-time a narrow ray of sunshine entered the courtyard, and this occasional visit had whitened a corner of the frontage on the south side, whilst the three other walls, morose and blackish, were streaked with mildew. There, in the depths of this courtyard as chilly and silent as a well, lighted with the white glimmer of a wintry day, one could have thought oneself a thousand leagues away from that new Paris wherein was flaring every passionate enjoyment, amidst the hubbub of the millions. The apartments of the mansion possessed the sad calm, the cold solemnity of the courtyard. Reached by a broad staircase with an iron handrail, where the footsteps and the coughing of visitors resounded as in the aisle of a church, they extended in long suites of vast and lofty rooms, in which the ancient furniture of dark woodwork and squat design seemed lost; and the pale light was only peopled by the figures on the tapestries, whose great colourless bodies were just vaguely distinguishable. All the luxury pertaining to the old Parisian middle classes was there, a stiff and wear-resisting luxury, chairs the oak seats of which are scarcely covered with a handful of tow, beds of inflexible material, linen chests in which the roughness of the boards would peculiarly compromise the slender existence of modern dresses. Monsieur Béraud Du Châtel had selected his apartments in the darkest portion of the mansion, on the first floor, between the street and the courtyard. He was there in a marvellous surrounding of peacefulness, silence and shade. When he pushed open the doors, traversing the solemnity of the rooms with his slow and serious step, one could have fancied him one of those members of the old parliaments, whose portraits adorned the walls, returning home wrapt in reverie after discussing and refusing to sign an edict of the king's.

But in this still house, in this cloister, there existed a warm nest full of life, a corner of sunshine and gaiety, an abode of adorable childhood, fresh air, and bright light. One had to ascend a host of little staircases, pass along ten or twelve corridors, go down and come up again; in fact, make quite a journey, and then one at last reached a vast chamber, a kind of belvedere built up on the roof, at the back of the mansion, right above the Quai de Béthune. It was in a full southern aspect. The window opened so wide that the heavens, with all their rays, fresh air, and azure blue, seemed to enter there. Perched aloft like a pigeon-house, the apartment contained long boxes full of flowers, an immense aviary, but not a single article of furniture. There was simply some matting spread over the floor. It was the "children's room." Throughout the mansion it was known and called by this name. The house was so cold, the courtyard so damp, that aunt Élisabeth had dreaded some harm might come to Christine and Renée from this chill breath which hung about the walls; more than once had she scolded the children for running about the arcades, and taking a delight in dipping their little arms in the icy water of the fountain. Then she had the idea to turn this out-of-the-way garret to account for them, the only nook wherein the sunshine had been entering and rejoicing, all by itself, for two centuries past, in the midst of the cobwebs. She gave them some matting, some birds, and some flowers. The little girls were delighted. During the holidays Renée lived there, bathing in the yellow sunshine, which seemed pleased with the embellishments made to its retreat, and with the two fair heads sent to keep it company. The room became a paradise, ever resounding with the chirping of the birds and the chatter of the children. It had been given up to them entirely. They called it "our room;" it was their domain; they even went so far as to lock themselves in to prove to their satisfaction that they were the sole mistresses of it. What an abode of happiness! A massacre of playthings lay expiring on the matting in the midst of the bright sunshine.

And the great delight of the children's room was, after all, the vast horizon. From the other windows of the mansion there was nothing to gaze upon but black walls a few feet off. But from this one, one could see all that portion of the Seine, all that district of Paris which extends from the Cité to the Pont de Bercy, flat and immense, and which resembles some primitive city in Holland. Down below, on the Quai de Béthune, were some tumble-down wooden sheds, accumulations of beams and fallen roofs, amidst which the children often amused themselves by watching enormous rats scamper about, with a vague dread of seeing them crawl up the high walls. But it was beyond this that the real delight of the view began. The boom, with its tiers of timbers, its buttresses resembling those of some Gothic cathedral, and the slender Pont de Constantine swaying like a piece of lace beneath the footsteps of passengers, crossed each other at right angles, and seemed to dam up and keep in check the enormous mass of water. Right in front, the trees of the Halle aux Vins, and further away, the shrubberies of the Jardin des Plantes were a mass of green, and spread out as far as the horizon; whilst, on the other side of the river, the Quai Henri IV and the Quai de la Rapée extended their low and irregular buildings, their row of houses which, looked at from above, resembled the tiny wood and cardboard houses the little girls kept in boxes. In the background, to the right, the slate roof of the Salpêtrière rose with a bluish tinge above the trees. Then, in the centre, descending right down to the Seine, the broad paved banks formed two long grey tracks, streaked here and there by a row of casks, a horse and cart, or an empty coal or wood barge lying stranded high and dry. But the soul of all this, the soul which filled the landscape, was the Seine, the living river; it came from afar, from the vague and trembling border of the horizon, it emerged from over there, as from a dream, to flow straight to the children, in the midst of its tranquil majesty, its mighty expansion which spread and became a flood of water at their feet, at the extremity of the island. The two bridges which crossed it, the Pont de Bercy and the Pont d'Austerlitz, seemed like necessary bonds placed there to keep it in check, and prevent it rising to the room. The little ones loved the giant, they filled their eyes with its colossal flow, with that ever murmuring flood which rolled towards them, as though to reach to where they were, and which they could feel rive and disappear to the right and left into the unknown, with the docility of a conquered Titan. On fine days, mornings with a blue sky overhead, they were charmed with the beautiful dresses the Seine assumed; varying dresses which changed from blue to green, with a thousand infinitely delicate tints; one could have fancied them of silk, spotted with white flames, and trimmed with frills of satin; whilst the boats drawn up at either bank formed an edging of black velvet ribbon. In the distance, especially, the material became quite admirable and precious, like some fairy's tunic of enchanted gauze; beyond the strip of dark green satin, with which the shadow of the bridges girdled the Seine, were plastrons of gold and skirts of some plaited material the colour of the sun. The immense sky formed a vaulted roof above this water, these low rows of houses, this foliage of the two parks.

Weary at times of this boundless horizon, Renée, already a big girl, and full of a carnal curiosity picked up at school, would take a peep at

Petit's floating swimming-baths moored to the extremity of the island. She sought to catch a glimpse, between the waving linen clothes hung up on lines in place of a roof, of the men in their bathing drawers, and with their chests all bare.

III

Maxime remained at the college of Plassans until the holidays of 1854. He was thirteen years and a few months old and had just passed through the fifth class. It was then that his father decided that he should come to Paris, reflecting that a son of Maxime's age would consolidate his position and establish him for good in the part he played as a rich and serious re-married widower. When he mentioned his plan to Renée, towards whom he prided himself upon being extremely gallant, she negligently answered:

"Quite so, let the little fellow come. He will amuse us a bit. One is bored to death of a morning."

The little fellow arrived a week afterwards. He was already a tall, spare urchin with an effeminate face, a delicate, wide-awake look, and pale flaxen hair. But how he was rigged out; good heavens! Cropped to the ears, with his hair so short that the whiteness of his skull was barely covered with a slight shadow, he moreover wore a pair of trousers too short for his legs, carter's shoes, and a frightfully threadbare tunic which was much too full and made him almost look hunchbacked. Thus accoutred, surprised by the new things he saw, he looked around him, not at all timidly but with the savage, cunning air of a precocious child who hesitates about trusting himself to anyone at once.

A servant had just brought him from the railway station, and he was in the large drawing-room, delighted with the gilding of the furniture and the ceiling, completely happy at sight of this luxury amid which he was going to live, when Renée, returning from her tailor's, swept in like a gust of wind. She threw off her hat and the white burnous which she had placed upon her shoulders to shield her from the cold, which was already keen; and she appeared before Maxime—stupefied with admiration—in all the glow of her marvellous costume.

The child thought she was disguised. Over a delicious skirt of blue faille with deep flounces, she wore a kind of *garde française* habit in pale grey silk. The lappets of the habit, lined with blue satin of a deeper shade than the faille of the skirt, were coquettishly caught up and secured with bows of ribbon; the cuffs of the tight sleeves, the broad facings of the bodice expanded on either side trimmed with the same satin. And, as a supreme seasoning, as a bold stroke of eccentricity, large buttons imitating sapphires, and fastened on blue rosettes, adorned the front of the habit in a double row. It was at once ugly and adorable.

As soon as Renée perceived Maxime, "It's the little fellow, isn't it?" she asked of the servant; she was surprised to find him as tall as herself.

The child was eating her with his eyes. This lady, with so white a skin, whose bosom could be seen through a gap of her plaited chemisette, this sudden and charming apparition with her hair raised high on her head, her gloved slender hands and her little masculine boots with pointed heels, delighted him; she seemed to be the good fairy of this warm gilded room. He began to smile, and he was just awkward enough in manner to retain his urchin-like gracefulness.

"Why, he is funny!" exclaimed Renée. "But how horrible! How they have cut his hair! Listen, my little fellow, your father will probably only come home for dinner and I shall be obliged to settle you here. I'm your stepmamma, sir. Will you kiss me?"

"Willingly," answered Maxime without any fuss; and he kissed the young wife on both cheeks, taking hold of her by the shoulders, whereby the *garde française* habit was a trifle crumpled.

She freed herself, laughing, and saying: "Dear me! how funny he is, the little shearling!" Then again approaching him and more serious: "We shall be friends sha'n't we? I want to be a mother to you. I reflected about it while I was waiting for my tailor, who was engaged, and I said to myself that I ought to be very kind and bring you up quite properly. I will be very nice!"

Maxime continued looking at her, with his blue, minx-like eyes, and suddenly: "How old are you?" he asked.

"But that is a question one never asks!" she exclaimed, clasping her hands together. "He doesn't know it, poor little fellow! It will be necessary to teach him everything. Fortunately I can still confess my age. I am twenty-one."

"I shall soon be fourteen. You might be my sister—"

He did not finish his sentence, but his eyes added that he had expected to find his father's second wife much older. He was very near her and looked at her neck so attentively that she almost finished by blushing. Besides, her giddy head was turning, it could never dwell for long on the same subject; and she began to walk about and talk of her tailor, forgetting that she was addressing a child.

"I ought to have been here to receive you. But, just fancy, Worms brought me this costume this morning. I tried it on and found it rather successful. It is very stylish, isn't it?"

She had placed herself before a mirror. Maxime was coming and going behind her to examine her on all sides.

"However as I put on the coat," she added, "I noticed there was a large fold there on the left shoulder, do you see? That fold is very ugly, it makes me look as if I had one shoulder higher than the other."

He had approached and passed his finger over the fold as if to smooth it down, and his vicious schoolboy hand seemed to tarry on the spot with a certain amount of satisfaction.

"Well," she continued, "I couldn't wait. I had the horses harnessed and I went to tell Worms what I thought of his inconceivable carelessness. He promised me he would set it right."

Then she remained in front of the mirror still looking at herself, lost as it were in a sudden reverie. She ended by placing a finger on her lips with an air of thoughtful impatience. And in a low voice as if talking to herself she said: "There is something wanting—yes, really, there is something wanting—"

Then, with quick motion, she turned and stationed herself in front of Maxime and asked him:

"Is it really the thing? Don't you think there is something wanting, a trifle, a bow somewhere?" The schoolboy, reassured by the young woman's familiarity, had regained all the assurance of his forward nature. He drew back, drew near, blinked his eyes and muttered:

"No, no, nothing's wanting, it's very pretty, very pretty—I rather think that there is something too much."

He slightly blushed despite his audacity, drew still nearer, and tracing with his finger-tip an acute angle on Renée's breast: "In your place," he continued, "I should round that lace like that and put on a necklace with a large cross."

She clapped her hands and looked radiant. "That's it, that's it," she cried, "I had the large cross on the tip of my tongue."

She folded back her chemisette, disappeared for a couple of minutes, and then returned with the necklace and the cross, and placing herself again in front of the mirror with an air of triumph:

"Oh! that's the ticket, quite the ticket," she muttered. "The little shearling isn't at all a fool. Did you dress women in the country then? I see that we shall really be good friends. But you must listen to me. To begin with, you must let your hair grow and you mustn't wear that frightful tunic any more. Besides, you must pay proper attention to my lessons in good manners. I want you to be a nice young man."

ÉMILE ZOLA

"Why, of course," said the child naively, "as papa is rich at present and as you are his wife."

She smiled and with her usual vivacity:

"Then let us begin by thee-and-thouing one another. I say thou and you in the same breath. It's stupid. You will love me a great deal?"

"I will love thee with all my heart," he answered with the effusive manner of an urchin towards his sweetheart.

Such was Maxime and Renée's first interview. The lad did not go to school till a month later. During the earlier days his stepmother played with him as with a doll. She polished off his countryfied air, and it must be added that he seconded her with extreme willingness. When he appeared, dressed from head to foot in new clothes supplied by his father's tailor, she gave a cry of joyous surprise. He was as pretty as a heart, such was her expression. The only thing was that his hair grew with most annoying sluggishness. The young woman frequently said that all one's face was in one's hair. She tended her own devoutly. For a long while she had been greatly worried by its colour, that particular pale yellow tint, which reminded one of the best butter. But when the fashion of wearing yellow hair set in she was delighted, and to make people believe that she did not follow the fashion by compulsion she declared that she dyed her hair every month.

Maxime was already terribly knowing for his thirteen years. His was one of those frail precocious natures in which the senses assert themselves early. He practised vice even before he knew desire. On two occasions he had all but been expelled from the college. Had Renée's eyes been accustomed to provincial graces she would have noticed that, despite his ill-fitting clothes, the little shearling, as she called him, smiled, turned his neck and extended his arms in a pretty way, with the feminine air of those who serve as schoolboys' girls. He was very careful about his hands, which were slight and long; and although his hair remained cropped short by order of the principal, an ex-colonel of engineers, he possessed a little looking-glass which he pulled out of his pocket during lesson time, which he placed between the pages of his book, and into which he gazed for whole hours, examining his eyes, his gums, making pretty faces at himself, and learning various kinds of coquetry. His schoolfellows hung round his blouse as round a skirt, and he buckled his belt so tightly that he had a grown woman's slim waist and undulation of the hips. To tell the truth, he received as many blows as caresses. The college of Plassans, a den of little bandits, like most provincial colleges, thus proved to be a hotbed of contamination in which Maxime's neutral temperament and childhood fraught with evil owing to some mysterious hereditary cause, were singularly developed. Fortunately age was about to alter him. But the trace of his childish abandonments, the effemination of his whole being, the time when he had thought himself a girl, were destined to remain in him and strike him for ever in his virility.

Renée called him "Mademoiselle," without knowing that six months earlier she would have spoken the truth. To her he seemed very obedient, very loving, and indeed his caresses often made her ill-at-ease. He had a manner of kissing that heated her skin. But what delighted her was his artfulness; he was exceedingly funny and bold, already speaking of women with a smile and holding his own against Renée's friends, dear Adeline who had just married M. d'Espanet, and fat Suzanne, married quite recently to the great manufacturer Haffner. When he was fourteen he had a passion for the latter. He had taken his stepmother into his confidence and she was greatly amused.

"For myself I should have preferred Adeline," she said, "she's prettier."

"Perhaps so," replied the urchin, "but Suzanne is ever so much fatter. I like fine women. It would be very kind of you to speak to her for me."

Renée laughed. Her doll—this tall urchin with a girl's manners—seemed to her more amusing than ever since he was in love. The time came when Madame Haffner seriously had to defend herself. Moreover the ladies encouraged Maxime with their stifled laughter, their unfinished sentences, and the coquettish attitudes which they assumed in his presence. There was a touch of very aristocratic debauchery in all this. The three of them, scorched by passion amid their tumultuous life, lingered over the urchin's delightful depravity as over a novel harmless spice which tickled their palates. They let him touch their dresses, and pass his fingers over their shoulders when he followed them into the ante-room to help them on with their wrappers; they passed him along from hand to hand, laughing like lunatics when he kissed their wrists near the veins, on the spot where the skin is so soft; then they became maternal and learnedly taught him the art of being a fine gentleman and pleasing women. He was their toy, a little fellow of ingenious mechanism who kissed and courted, who had the most delightful vices in the world, but who remained a plaything, a little cardboard puppet whom they did not much fear, though just enough to quiver very agreeably at the touch of his childish hand.

After the holidays, Maxime went to the Lycée Bonaparte. It was the college of fashionable society, the one that Saccard was bound to choose for his son. However soft and light headed the little fellow might be, he still had a keen intelligence; but he applied it to something very different to classical studies. However he was a tolerably efficient pupil who never fell to the Bohemian level of dunces, but remained among the well dressed and properly conducted young gentlemen of whom nothing was ever said. All that remained to him of his early youth was a perfect worship for dress. Paris opened his eyes, made him a swell young man, tightly buttoned up in his clothes and following the fashions. He was the Brummel of his class. He presented himself there as he would have presented himself in a drawing-room, daintily booted, tightly gloved, with prodigious neckties and ineffable hats. There were some twenty pupils of the kind who formed a sort of aristocracy, who in leaving school for the day offered each other Havannah cigars contained in cases with gold mountings, and who were followed by servants in livery carrying their packets of books. Maxime had persuaded his father to buy him a tilbury and a little black horse which were the admiration of his school fellows. He himself drove, while on the seat behind sat a footman with folded arms, who carried on his knees the collegian's copy book case, a perfect ministerial portfolio in brown leather. And you should have seen how lightly, scientifically and correctly Maxime came in ten minutes from the Rue de Rivoli to the Rue du Havre, drew his horse up sharp before the college door and said to the footman, "At half past four, Jacques, eh?" The neighbouring shopkeepers were delighted with the grace of this fair haired youngster whom twice a day at regular hours they saw arrive and start off in his trap. On returning home he sometimes gave a lift to a friend, whom he set down at his door. The two children smoked, looked at the women and splashed the passers-by as if they were returning from the races. 'Twas an astonishing little world, a conceited foolish brood, that could be seen each day in the Rue du Havre, correctly attired in masher's jackets, aping rich and wearied men, whilst the Bohemian contingent of the college, the real schoolboys, arrived shouting and shoving, stamping on the pavement with their heavy shoes, and with their hooks hanging at the end of a strap over their backs.

Renée, who wished to consider the part she played as a mother and a schoolmistress a serious one, was delighted with her pupil. It is true that she neglected nothing to perfect his education. She was then passing through a period full of mortification and tears; a lover had abandoned her, in scandalous style in sight of all Paris, to attach himself to the Duchess de Sternich. She dreamt that Maxime would be her consolation, she made herself older, she endeavoured to be maternal, and became the most eccentric mentor that can be imagined. Maxime's tilbury often remained at home; it was Renée who came to fetch the collegian with her roomy carriage. They hid the brown portfolio under the cushion, and went to the Bois de Boulogne then in its freshness. She there gave him a course of lectures on high elegance. She pointed out to him the upper ten of imperial Paris, fat and happy, still ecstasied by the warm touch which changed the starvelings and pigs of the day before into great lords and millionaires puffing and fainting under the weight of their cash boxes. But the youngster particularly questioned her about women, and as she was very familiar with him, she gave him precise particulars: Madame de Guende was stupid but admirably formed; the wealthy Countess Vanska had been a street singer before she married a Pole who was said to beat her; as for the Marchioness d'Espanet and Suzanne Haffner they were inseparable; and although they were Renée's intimate friends, she added—compressing her lips as if to prevent herself from saying any more—that some very nasty stories were told about them; beautiful Madame de Lauwerens was also a very compromising woman, but she had such pretty eyes, and after all everyone knew that she herself was irreproachable, although somewhat too much mixed up in the intrigues of the poor little women who frequented her, Madame Daste, Madame Teissière and the Baroness de Meinhold. Maxime wished to have the ladies' portraits; and with them he adorned an album which remained on the drawing-room table. With that vicious artfulness which was his predominant characteristic he tried to embarrass his stepmother by asking her for particulars concerning the fast women, at the same time pretending to take them for women of society. Renée, becoming moral and serious, said that they were frightful creatures and that he ought to carefully avoid them; then forgetting herself she talked about them as if they were people whom she had known intimately. One of the youngster's great delights was to set her talking about the Duchess de Sternich. Each time that her carriage passed theirs in the Bois, he never missed naming the duchess with cruel artfulness and an under glance which proved that he was acquainted with Renée's last adventure. Then she in a harsh voice tore her rival to pieces; how old she was looking, poor woman, she painted her face, she had lovers hidden in all her cupboards, she had given herself to a chamberlain so as to be in the imperial bed. And Renée ran on and on, while Maxime, to exasperate her, declared that he thought Madame de Sternich charming. Such lessons singularly developed the collegian's intelligence, and this, all the more, as his young teacher repeated them every where, in the Bois, at the theatre, and in the drawing-rooms. The pupil thus became very proficient.

Maxime adored living amid women's skirts, finery and rice powder. He always remained somewhat girlish with his tapering hands, his beardless face, and his white, fleshy neck. Renée gravely consulted him about her dresses. He knew the good costumiers of Paris and pronounced judgment upon each of them in a word, he talked about the "savour" of such a one's bonnets and the "logic" of such a one's dresses. At seventeen there was not a milliner whom he had not proved, not a bootmaker whose heart he had not penetrated and studied. This strange abortion who during the English lessons at college, read the prospectuses that his perfumer sent him every Friday, would have delivered a complete discourse on Parisian society, customers and tradespeople included, at an age when country youngsters don't dare look a housemaid in the face. On his way home he often brought a bonnet, a box of soap or an article of jewellery that his stepmother had ordered the day before. Some strip of musk-scented lace always lingered in his pockets.

However his great affair was to accompany Renée when she called on the illustrious Worms, the tailor of genius, before whom the queens of the Second Empire fell on their knees. The great man's waiting room was vast, square and furnished with roomy divans. Maxime entered it with a feeling of religious emotion. Dresses certainly have a special perfume; silk, satin, velvet, lace had there mingled their light aroma with that of women's hair and amber-shaded shoulders; and the atmosphere of the room retained an oderiferous warmth, an incense of flesh and luxury which transformed the apartment into a chapel consecrated to some secret divinity. It was often necessary for Renée and Maxime to dance attendance during hours; a series of feminine solicitors were there, waiting their turn, dipping biscuits into glasses of Madeira, taking a snack on the large central table covered with bottles and plates full of little cakes. The ladies were at home, they talked freely, and when they ensconced themselves around the room you would have thought that a flight of Lesbian nymphs had alighted on the divans of a Parisian drawing-room. Maxime, whom they put up with and even liked on account of his girlish air, was the only man admitted into the circle.

He there tasted divine delight: he glided along the divans like a supple snake; he was discovered under a skirt, behind a bodice, or between two dresses, where he made himself as small as possible and kept very quiet, inhaling the perfumed warmth of his feminine neighbours.

"That youngster pokes himself everywhere," said the Baroness de Meinhold tapping him on the cheeks.

He was so slightly built that the ladies did not think him more than fourteen. They amused themselves by intoxicating him with the illustrious Worms's Madeira, whereupon he said some astounding things which made them laugh till they cried. However it was the Marchioness d'Espanet who hit upon the right remark for the circumstance. As Maxime was discovered one day, in a corner of the divan, behind her back—

"That boy ought to have been a girl," she murmured, seeing him so rosy and blushing, so penetrated with the delight he had experienced at being close to her.

Then when the great Worms finally received Renée, Maxime followed her into the study. He had ventured to speak two or three times whilst the master became absorbed in contemplating his customer, just like Leonardo da Vinci in presence of the Joconde, according to the pontiffs of art. The master had deigned to smile at the appropriateness of Maxime's remarks; he made Renée stand upright before a mirror, rising from the parquetry to the ceiling, and he pondered with a contraction of the eyebrows, whilst the young woman, affected, caught her breath so as not to stir. And after a few minutes the master, as if seized and shaken by inspiration, roughly and jerkily described the work of art he had just conceived, exclaiming in curt phrases:

"Montespan dress in ash tinted silk—the train describing a rounded skirt in front—large bow of grey satin catching it up on the hips—finally an apron composed of puffs of pearl grey tulle, the puffs separated by bands of grey satin."

He again reflected, seemed to dive to the very depths of his genius, and with the triumphant grimace of a python seated upon the tripod he concluded:

"In the hair, upon this smiling head, we will place the dreamy butterfly of Psyche with wings of changeful blue."

But on other occasions, inspiration was sluggish. The illustrious Worms summoned it in vain and concentrated his faculties to no purpose. He tortured his eyebrows, turned livid, took his poor head, which he wagged in despair, between his hands, and conquered, throwing himself into an arm-chair:

"No," he would mutter in a sorrowful voice, "no, not to-day—it isn't possible—These ladies presume too much. The source is dried up."

And he would turn Renée out of doors, repeating:

"Impossible, impossible, dear madame, you must call again another day. I'm not in the vein to deal with your style this morning."

The fine education that Maxime received had a first result. At seventeen the youngster seduced his stepmother's maid. The worst of the affair was that the girl found herself in the family way. It was necessary to send her into the country with the kid and make her a small allowance. Renée was terribly vexed by this adventure. Saccard occupied himself about it merely to settle the pecuniary side of the question; but the young woman roundly scolded her pupil. To think he should compromise himself with such a girl when she wanted to make a gentleman of him! What a ridiculous, shameful beginning, what a disgraceful prank! If he had at least only launched forth with one of those ladies!

"Oh! quite so," he answered quietly, "if your dear friend Suzanne had only chosen she could have gone into the country instead of the maid."

"Oh! you naughty fellow," muttered Renée, disarmed and enlivened by the idea of seeing Suzanne retire into the country with an allowance of twelve hundred francs a year.

Then a funnier thought occurred to her, and forgetting her part as an irritated mother, bursting into pearly laughter which she restrained with her fingers, she stammered, glancing at him out of the corner of her eyes:

"I say, how angry Adeline would have been with you, and what a scene she would have had with her—"

She did not finish. Maxime was laughing with her. Such was the fine ending of Renée's lecture on this occasion.

Meanwhile Saccard troubled himself but little concerning the two children, as he called his son and his second wife. He left them complete liberty, feeling happy at seeing them such good friends, whereby the flat was filled with noisy gaiety. It was a singular flat, this first floor in the Rue de Rivoli. The doors were opening and shutting all day long, the servants talked aloud; through the fresh bright luxury of the place there constantly swept a flight of huge skirts, and processions of tradespeople; and in addition there was all the disorder occasioned by Renée's friends, Maxime's chums, and Saccard's visitors. From nine till eleven a.m. the last named received the strangest throng one could find, senators and lawyers' clerks, duchesses and old clothes-dealers, all the scum that the tempests of Paris landed of a morning at his door; silk dresses, dirty skirts, blouses, dress coats, all of which he received with the same hasty language and the same impatient nervous gestures. He settled a business affair in a couple of minutes, dealt with twenty difficulties at once and furnished solutions on the run. One would have thought that this restless little man, whose voice was very loud, was fighting in his study with his visitors, with the furniture, turning somersaults, knocking his head against the ceiling to make ideas flash forth from it, and always falling victorious on his feet again. Then at eleven o'clock he went out and was not seen again for the day; he lunched, and indeed, he often dined away from home. Then the house belonged to Renée and Maxime. They took possession of the father's study, they unpacked the tradespeoples' cardboard boxes there, and articles of finery lay about among the business papers. At times serious people waited for an hour at the door of the study whilst the collegian and the young woman seated at either end of Saccard's writing table, discussed a bow of ribbon. Renée had the horses put to ten times a day. They seldom shared a meal together; two of the three were ever on the wing, forgetting time, and only returning home at midnight. It was a dwelling of noise, business and pleasure, into which modern life swept like a gust of wind, with a sound of chinking gold and rustling dresses.

Aristide Saccard had found his vein at last. He had revealed himself as a great speculator and juggled with millions. After the masterly stroke of the Rue de la Pépinière he boldly threw himself into the struggle, which was beginning to scatter flashing triumphs and shameful wrecks through Paris. At first he executed safe strokes, repeating his first success, buying up houses which he knew to be threatened with the pickaxe, and utilising his friends so as to obtain heavy indemnities. There came a moment when he had five or six houses, those houses that he had looked at so strangely in former times, as acquaintances of his when he was merely a poor road inspector. But all that was the mere infancy of art, it did not require much cunning to run out leases, to plot with tenants, and to rob the State and private people; and he considered that the game was not sufficiently remunerative. For that reason he soon placed his genius at the service of more complicated affairs.

Saccard at first invented the dodge of buying houses secretly on behalf of the city of Paris. The latter's situation had become a difficult one owing to a decision of the Council of State. The city authorities had purchased, by private contract, a large number of houses in the hope of running out the leases and getting rid of the tenants without the payment of an indemnity. But these purchases were considered by the Council of State to be real expropriations and the city had to pay. It was then that Saccard offered to lend his name to the city; he bought houses, ran out the leases, and for a consideration handed the property over to the authorities at the date agreed upon. Indeed he finished by playing a double game; he bought property both for the city and for the prefect. When the affair was too tempting he stuck to the house himself. The State paid. In reward for his services he obtained the right to cut bits of streets and open spaces which had been planned, a right which he sold again to some one else before the new thoroughfare was even commenced. It was a hot game; people gambled with the new streets just as with stocks and shares. Certain ladies, pretty prostitutes, intimate with high functionaries, were in the swing; one of them, whose white teeth are famous, nibbled whole streets on various occasions. Saccard grew more hungry than ever, feeling his desires increase at the sight of the flood of gold which glided between his fingers. It seemed to him as if a sea of twenty-franc pieces expanded around him, swelling from a lake to an ocean, filling the vast horizon with a strange wave-like noise, a metallic music which tickled his heart; and he grew adventurous, becoming each day a bolder swimmer, diving, rising again to the surface, now on his back, now on his belly, crossing this immensity in fair and foul weather alike, and relying on his strength and skill to prevent him from ever sinking to the bottom.

Paris was then disappearing in a cloud of plaster dust. The times that Saccard had predicted on the heights of Montmartre had come. The city was being slashed to pieces with sabre strokes and he had a finger in every slash, in every wound. He had piles of building materials derived from demolished houses in the four corners of the city. In the Rue de Rome he was mixed up in that astonishing story of a pit which a company dug to carry off five or six thousand cubic metres of soil and create a belief in a gigantic enterprise, and which had to be filled up again by bringing soil from Saint-Ouen when the company had failed. Saccard got out of the affair with his conscience at ease and his pockets full, thanks to his brother Eugène, who was kind enough to intervene. At Chaillot he assisted in cutting through the heights and throwing them into a hollow to make way for the boulevard running from the Arc-de-Triomphe to the Alma bridge. In the direction of Passy it was he who had the idea of scattering the refuse cleared away from the Trocadéro, upon the plateau, so that the good soil is now-a-days two yards below the surface, and even weeds refuse to grow amid the broken plaster. He might have been found in twenty directions at once, at every spot where there was some insurmountable obstacle, a mass of clearings which no one knew what to do with, a hollow which it was difficult to fill up, a pile of soil mingled with plaster over which the engineers in their feverish haste grew impatient, but which he sifted with his own hands and in which he always finished by finding some sop or other, or a speculation in his own peculiar line. On the same day he ran from the works round about the Arc-de-Triomphe to those of the Boulevard St. Michel, from the clearings of the Boulevard Malesherbes to the embankments of Chaillot, dragging with him an army of workmen, lawyers, shareholders, dupes, and scamps.

But his purest glory was the Crédit Viticole, which he had established in conjunction with Toutin-Laroche. The latter was the official director, he himself only figured as a member of the board. In this circumstance Eugène had again done his brother a good turn. Thanks to him the government authorized the establishment of the company and watched its operations with great indulgence. On one difficult occasion, when an evil-minded newspaper ventured to criticise one of the company's operations, the "Moniteur" went so far as to publish a note forbidding any discussion concerning so honourable an undertaking, which the State deigned to patronize. The Crédit Viticole was based on an excellent financial system; it lent farmers half of the estimated value of their property, obtained a mortgage as guarantee for the loan, and received interest from the borrowers as well as an annual instalment of the principal. No financial system was ever more dignified or proper. Eugène had informed his brother with a sly smile that the Tuileries wished people to be honest. M. Toutin-Laroche interpreted this wish by letting the farmers' loan-machine work quietly, and by annexing to it a banking-house which attracted capital and gambled feverishly, launching forth into all sorts of adventurous enterprises. The Crédit Viticole thanks to the formidable impulsion it received from its director, soon enjoyed a well-established reputation of solidity and prosperity. At the outset, in view of offering at the Bourse, at one go, a mass of shares freshly detached from their counterfoils, and to give them the aspect of having long been in circulation, Saccard ingeniously had them trodden on and beaten, during a whole night, by the bank collectors provided with birch brooms. The headquarters of the Crédit Viticole might have been taken for a branch of the Bank of France. The house where the offices were located seemed to be the grave and dignified temple of Mammon, with its courtyard full of equipages, its solemn iron railings, its broad flight of steps and its monumental staircase, its suites of luxurious private rooms, and its world of clerks and liveried lackeys; and nothing could fill the public with more religious emotion than the sanctuary, the cashier's office, reached by a passage of sacred bareness, and where one perceived the safe, the god, crouching, embedded in the wall, squat and somniferous with its three locks, its massive flanks, and its air of divine brutishness.

Saccard jobbed a big affair with the city of Paris. The latter, hard-up, crushed by its debt, dragged into this dance of millions which it had started to please the Emperor and fill certain people's pockets, was now reduced to borrowing covertly, not caring to own its violent fever, its stone-and-pickaxe madness. It had just begun to issue what it called delegation bonds, real bills of exchange at a distant date, so as to pay the contractors on the very days that the agreements were signed, and thus enable them to obtain money by having these bonds discounted. The Crédit Viticole had graciously accepted this paper from the contractors; and one day when the city was in need of money Saccard went to tempt it. A considerable sum was lent it on the security of delegation bonds which M. Toutin-Laroche swore he had obtained from contracting companies, and which he had dragged through all the gutters of speculation. After that the Crédit Viticole was above attack; it held Paris by the throat. The director now only talked with a smile about the famous Société Générale of the Ports of Morocco; and yet it still existed, and the newspapers continued regularly extolling the great commercial stations. One day when M. Toutin-Laroche tried to persuade Saccard to take some shares in this enterprise, the latter laughed in his face, asking him if he thought him fool enough to invest his money in the "General Company of the Arabian Nights."

Saccard had so far speculated successfully, with safe profits, cheating, selling himself, making money by contracts, deriving some sort of gain from each of his operations. Soon, however, this jobbing did not suffice him, he disdained gleaning, picking up the gold which folks like Toutin-Laroche and Baron Gouraud dropped behind them. He plunged his arms into the bag, up to the shoulders. He went into partnership with Mignon, Charrier & Co., the famous contractors, who were then just starting, and who were destined to make colossal fortunes. The city of Paris had already decided not to execute the works itself, but to have the boulevards laid out by contract. The contracting companies agreed to deliver a thoroughfare complete, with its trees planted, its benches and lamp-posts duly placed, in exchange for a specified indemnity; at times they even delivered the thoroughfare for nothing, finding themselves amply remunerated by retaining the bordering building ground, for which they asked a greatly enhanced price. The fever of speculation in land, the furious rise in the value of house property date from this period. Saccard, thanks to his connections, obtained a grant to lay out three lots of boulevard. He was the ardent and somewhat muddling soul of the partnership. Messieurs Mignon & Charrier, his dependents at the outset, were fat, artful fellows, master masons, who knew the value of money. They laughed slyly at sight of Saccard's equipages; they generally retained their blouses, never refused to shake hands with a workman, and returned home covered with plaster dust. They came from Langres both of them, and into this burning, never satisfied Paris they brought their Champagnese prudence, their calm brains, somewhat obtuse and deficient in intelligence, but very quick in profiting of opportunities for filling their pockets, free to enjoy themselves later on. If Saccard promoted the affair and infused life into it with his fire and rageous appetite, Messieurs Mignon & Charrier by their plodding habits, their narrow methodical management, prevented it a score of times from being capsized by the astonishing imagination of their partner. They would never consent to have superb offices in a mansion which he wanted to build to astonish Paris. They also refused to entertain the secondary speculations which sprouted in his brain every morning, such as the erection of concert halls and vast bathing establishments on the building ground bordering their thoroughfare; of covered galleries, which would have doubled the rent of the shops and have allowed people to circulate through Paris without getting wet. To put a stop to these plans, which frightened them, the contractors decided that the building ground should be divided between the three partners, and that each should do what he pleased with his share. They themselves wisely continued selling their lots while he built upon his. His brain boiled. He would, in all seriousness, have proposed placing Paris under a huge bell-glass to change it into a conservatory and grow pine apples and sugar cane there.

Turning over money by the shovelful he soon had eight houses on the new boulevards. He had four that were completely finished, two in the Rue de Marignan, and two on the Boulevard Haussmann; the four others, situated on the Boulevard Malesherbes, remained in progress, and indeed one of them, a vast enclosure of planks where a magnificent mansion was to rise, had only the flooring of the first floor laid. At this period his affairs became so complicated, he had so many strings attached to each of his fingers, so many interests to watch over and puppets to set in motion, that he slept barely three hours a night and read his correspondence in his carriage. The marvellous thing was that his cash-box seemed inexhaustible. He was a shareholder in every company, built houses with a kind of fury, turned himself to every trade and threatened to inundate Paris like a rising tide, without once being seen to realise a clear profit or pocket a large sum shining in the sunlight. The river of gold, of unknown source, which seemed to flow from his study in quickly recurring waves, astonished the Parisian cockneys, and at one moment made him the prominent man to whom the newspapers ascribed all the witticisms of the Bourse.

With such a husband Renée was about as little married as she could be. She remained for whole weeks almost without seeing him. On the other hand he was perfect; he threw his cash-box wide open for her. In point of fact, she liked him as she would have liked an obliging banker. When she went to the Béraud mansion she praised him highly before her father, whose severity and coldness did not abate on account of his son-in-law's fortune. Her contempt had fled; this man seemed so convinced that life is a mere business affair, he was so plainly born to coin money out of whatever fell into his hands, women, children, paving-stones, sacks of mortar, and consciences, that she could not reproach him for having made their marriage a bargain. Since that bargain he in a measure looked upon her as upon one of those fine houses which honoured him and from which he expected to derive large profits. He liked to see her well dressed, noisy, making all Paris turn the head. It consolidated his position, doubled the probable figure of his fortune. By his wife he seemed handsome, young, amorous, and giddy. She was a partner, an accomplice without knowing it. A new pair of horses, a dress costing two thousand crowns, a weakness for a lover, facilitated, often ensured the success of his most remunerative transactions. Moreover, he frequently pretended to be worn-out, and sent her to a minister's, or some functionary's, to solicit an authorisation or receive a reply. "And be good!" he said to her in a tone, at once jesting and coaxing, which only belonged to himself. And when she returned, when she had succeeded, he rubbed his hands, repeating his famous phrase, "And you were good?" Renée laughed. He was too active to wish his wife to be a Madame Michelin. He simply liked coarse witticisms and indecent suppositions. Besides, if Renée had "not been good" he would only have experienced the mortification of having really paid for the minister's or functionary's compliance. To dupe people, to give them less than their money's worth, was a feast for him. He often said: "If I were a woman I should perhaps sell myself, but I should never deliver the merchandise; it's too stupid."

This madcap Renée, who had appeared one night in the Parisian firmament like the eccentric fairy of fashionable sensuality, was the least analyzable of women. No doubt if she had been brought up at home she would by means of religion or some other satisfaction for the nerves have attenuated the desires by which she was at times really maddened. She belonged to the middle classes by her mind; she was perfectly upright, with a love for logical things, a fear of heaven and hell and a huge dose of prejudices; she belonged to her father's side, to the calm and prudent race among which fireside virtues flourish. And yet it was in this nature of hers that prodigious fancies, ever reviving inquisitiveness and desires not to be confessed, sprouted and grew. While she was with the ladies of the Visitation, free, her mind wandering amid the mystical voluptuousness of the chapel and the carnal attachment of her young friends, she had framed for herself a fantastic education, learning vice, throwing all the frankness of her nature into it, unsettling her young brain to such a point that she singularly embarrassed her confessor by owning to him that she had felt a most unreasonable longing to get up and kiss him one day during mass. Then she struck her breast, she turned pale at the thought of the devil and his cauldrons. The fault which, later on, had brought about her marriage with Saccard, that brutal rape which she had experienced with a kind of frightened expectation, made her despise herself and in a great measure caused the abandonment of her whole life. She thought that she no longer had to struggle against evil that it was in her, that logic authorized her to follow the bad science to the end. With her there was yet more curiosity than appetite. Thrown into the society of the Second Empire, abandoned to her imagination, provided with money, encouraged in her loudest eccentricities, she gave herself, regretted it, and finally succeeded in killing her expiring principles, always lashed, always urged onward by her insatiable longing to learn and feel.

Besides she was as yet only at the earlier pages. She willingly talked in a low tone, and laughing, about the extraordinary circumstances of the tender attachment between Suzanne Haffner and Adeline d'Espanet, of the questionable calling of Madame de Lauwerens, and of the kisses which the Countess Vanska gave at a fixed price; but she still contemplated these things from afar off, with a vague notion of perhaps tasting them, and this indeterminate desire which at evil moments rose within her, increased her turbulent anxiety still more and urged her on in her mad search for an unique exquisite enjoyment of which she alone would partake. Her first lovers had not spoiled her; she had on three occasions fancied herself seized with a great passion; love burst forth in her brain like a cracker, the sparks of which did not reach her heart. She was mad for a month, showed herself throughout Paris with her dear lord; and then one morning, amid all the racket of her love, she became conscious of depressing silence and immense vacuity. The first, the young Duke de Rozan, was barely more than a breakfast of sunshine; Renée who had noticed him on account of his gentleness and excellent manners, found him altogether superficial, washed out, and plaguy when they were alone together. Mr. Simpson, an attaché of the American embassy, who came next, almost beat her, and for that reason remained with her for nearly a year. Then she smiled on an aide-de-camp of the Emperor, the Count de Chibray, a vain handsome man who was beginning to tire her when the Duchess de Sternich took it into her head to fall in love with him and carry him off from her; thereupon she wept for him and let her friends understand that her heart was crushed, and that she should never love again. She thus progressed to the most insignificant being in the world, Monsieur de Mussy, a young man who was making his way in the diplomatic career by conducting cotillons with especial gracefulness; she never exactly knew why she had given herself to him but she retained him for a long time, feeling lazy, disgusted with an unknown land which one discovers in half an hour, and deferring the worry attendant upon a change until she had met with some extraordinary adventure. At twenty-eight years of age she already felt terribly wearied. Ennui appeared to her all the more insupportable, as her middle-class virtues profited by the hours when she was bored to complain and worry her. She closed her door, she had frightful headaches. Then when the door opened again it was a flood of silk and lace that swept forth with a great racket, a being of luxury and joy without a care or a flush upon the brow.

Still she had had a romance in her commonplace fashionable life. One day, at sunset, after going on foot to see her father, who did not like to hear the noise of carriages at his door, she noticed, while passing along the Quai Saint-Paul on her way home, that she was being followed by a young man. It was warm and the daylight was waning with amorous softness. She, who was usually only followed on horseback in the pathways of the Bois de Boulogne, found the adventure spicy and was flattered by it as by a new homage, somewhat brutal no doubt, but the very coarseness of which titillated her. Instead of returning home she took the Rue du Temple and promenaded her gallant along the Boulevards. The man however grew bolder and became so pressing that Renée, somewhat intimidated, lost her head, followed the Rue du Faubourg-Poissonnière, and took refuge in the shop kept by her husband's sister. The man came in behind her. Madame Sidonie smiled, seemed to understand, and left them alone. And when Renée wished to follow her sister-in-law the stranger retained her, spoke to her with feeling politeness and won her forgiveness. He was a clerk called Georges whose surname she never asked. She went to see him twice, going in by the shop while he arrived by the Rue Papillon. This chance love affair, found and accepted in the street, proved one of her keenest pleasures. She always thought of it with a little shame, but with a singular smile of regret. Madame Sidonie's profit in the affair was that she at last became the accomplice of her brother's second wife, a part which she had been anxious to play ever since the wedding-day.

Poor Madame Sidonie had experienced a deception. While she was promoting the marriage she had hoped in a degree to espouse Renée herself, make her a customer and derive a number of little profits by her. She judged women at a glance like connoisseurs judge horses. And so, after allowing the couple a month to settle themselves, her consternation was great when, on perceiving Madame de Lauwerens enthroned in the centre of the drawing-room, she realised that she came too late. Madame de Lauwerens, a handsome woman of twenty-six, occupied herself with launching newcomers into the swing. She belonged to a very old family and was married to a man of the upper financial world, who had the fault of refusing to settle tailors' and milliners' bills. His wife, a very intelligent person, coined money and kept herself. She held men in horror, she said; but she supplied all her female friends with them; there was always a full stock to choose from in the flat which she occupied in the Rue de Provence, over her husband's offices. Little collations took place there; and one met one another in an unforeseen charming manner. There was no harm in a girl going to see her dear Madame de Lauwerens, and if chance brought men there who were at all events very respectful and belonged to the best society—why so much the worse. The lady of the house was charming in her long lace wrappers. A visitor would very often have chosen her in preference to her collection of blondes and brunettes. But report asserted that she was altogether well conducted. The whole secret of the affair lay in that. She still held her high situation in society, had all the men for her friends, retained her pride as a virtuous woman, and experienced a secret joy in lowering the others and deriving a profit by their fall. When Madame Sidonie had enlightened herself as to the mechanism of the new invention she was sorely distressed. It was the classical school, the woman in an old black dress, carrying love letters at the bottom of her basket, set in front of the modern school, the lady of high degree, who sells her friends in her boudoir while sipping a cup of tea. The modern school triumphed. Madame de Lauwerens glanced coldly at the shabby dress of Madame Sidonie in whom she scented a rival; and it was from her hand that Renée received her first worry, the young Duke de Rozan, whom the beautiful financier found it difficult to dispose of. It was only later on that the classical school won the day, when Madame Sidonie lent her lodging to her sister-in-law so that she might gratify her fancy for the stranger of the Quai Saint-Paul. She remained her confidante.

Maxime however was one of Madame Sidonie's boon friends. When only fifteen years old he went on the prowl to his aunt's, smelling the forgotten gloves which he found lying on the furniture. She, who hated clear situations and never owned her little services, ended by lending him the keys of her rooms, on certain days, saying that she would remain in the country until the morrow. Maxime talked about some friends whom he wished to entertain and whom he did not like to take to his father's. It was in the rooms of the Rue du Faubourg-Poissonnière that he spent several nights with the poor girl whom one was afterwards obliged to send into the country. Madame Sidonie borrowed money from her nephew, and went into ecstacies before him, murmuring in a soft voice that he was "without a hair, as rosy as a Cupid."

Maxime had grown however. He was now a pretty, slightly built young man who had retained the rosy cheeks and blue eyes of childhood. His curly hair completed that girlish appearance, which so delighted the ladies. He resembled poor Angèle with his soft eyes and blonde pallor. But he was not even the equal of that indolent shallow woman. In him the race of the Rougons had a tendency to refinement and became delicate and vicious. The offspring of too young a mother, constituting a strange, jumbled, and so to say unmingled combination of his father's furious appetites and his mother's self-abandonment and weakness, he was a defective offspring in whom the parental failings were completed and aggravated. This family of the Rougons lived too fast; it was dying out already in the person of this frail creature whose sex must have remained in suspense during formation, and who no longer represented a will, eager for gain and enjoyment like Saccard, but a species of cowardice, devouring fortunes already made; a strange hermaphrodite ushered at the right time into a society that was rottening. When Maxime went to the Bois de Boulogne, with his waist tightly compressed like a woman's, lightly dancing in the saddle on which he was swayed by the canter of his horse, he was the god of the age, with his strongly developed hips, his long slender hands, his sickly lascivious air, his correct elegance, and his slang learnt at petty theatres. At twenty years of age he placed himself above all surprises and all disgusts. He had certainly dreamt of the most unusual beastliness. But with him vice was not an abyss, as it is with certain old men, but a natural external bloom. It curled upon his fair hair, smiled upon his lips, and dressed him like his clothes. However his great characteristic was especially his eyes, two clear and smiling blue apertures, true mirrors for a coquette, but behind which one perceived all the emptiness of his brain. Those harlot eyes were never lowered; they courted pleasure, a pleasure without fatigue which one summons and receives.

The everlasting gust of wind which swept into the rooms in the Rue de Rivoli and banged their doors, blew stronger and stronger while Maxime grew up, while Saccard enlarged the sphere of his transactions, and Renée threw more fever into her search for unknown enjoyment. These three beings ended by leading an astonishing life of liberty and folly. It was the ripe and prodigious fruit of a period. The street invaded the flat with its rumble of vehicles, its elbowing of strangers, and its licence of language. The father, the stepmother, the stepson, acted, talked, and set themselves at ease just as if they had each been alone living a bachelor life. Three boon friends, three students sharing the same furnished room, would not have disposed of that room more unceremoniously to install therein their hobbledehoy vices, loves, and noisy pleasures. The Saccards met with hand-shakes, did not seem to suspect the reasons which united them under the same roof, and behaved cavalierly and joyously towards each other, each thus assuming absolute independence. They replaced family ties by a kind of partnership, the profits of which are divided in equal shares; each one drew his share of pleasure to himself, and it was tacitly understood that each should dispose of that share as he thought fit. They went so far as to take their enjoyment in presence of one another, to display it, and describe it without awakening aught but a little envy and curiosity.

Maxime now instructed Renée. When he went to the Bois with her he told her stories about prostitutes which greatly enlivened her. A new woman could not appear near the lake without his setting forth on a campaign to ascertain the name of her protector, the allowance he made her, and the style in which she lived. He was acquainted with these ladies' homes, and with the particulars of their private life; indeed he was a perfect living catalogue in which all the harlots were numbered, with a complete description of each of them. This gazette of scandal was Renée's delight. On race-days at Longchamps, when she passed by in her carriage, she listened eagerly, albeit retaining her haughtiness as a woman of good society, to the story of how Blanche Müller deceived her embassy attaché with a hair-dresser; or how the little baron had found the count in his drawers in the alcove of a skinny, red-haired notoriety who was called the Crawfish. Each day brought its tattle. When the story was rather too stiff Maxime lowered his voice, but he nevertheless went on to the end. Renée opened her eyes wide, like a child to whom a good trick is related, restrained her laughter, and then stifled it in her embroidered handkerchief, which she gently pressed to her lips. Maxime also brought these women's photographs. He had portraits of actresses in all his pockets and even in his cigar case. At times he had a clearing out and placed these women in the album which was always trailing over the furniture in the drawing-room, and which already contained the portraits of Renée's female friends. There was also some men's photographs in it, Messieurs de Rozan, Simpson, De Chibray, and De Mussy, as well as actors, writers, and deputies who had come to swell the collection no one knew how. It was a strangely mixed society, the prototype of the jumble of ideas and personages that crossed Renée's and Maxime's lives. Whenever it rained, or whenever one was bored, this album proved a great subject of conversation. It always ended by falling under one's hand. The young woman opened it with a sigh for the hundredth time perhaps. By-and-by, however, her curiosity was awakened and the young fellow came and leant behind her. Then long discussions began about the Crawfish's hair, Madame de Meinhold's double chin, Madame de Lauwerens's eyes, and Blanche Müller's bosom; about the Marchioness's nose, which was a trifle on one side, and about the mouth of little Sylvia, who was notorious for her thick lips. They compared the women with each other.

"For myself, if I were a man," said Renée, "I should choose Adeline."

"That's because you don't know Sylvia," answered Maxime, "she has such a funny style. For myself, I prefer Sylvia."

The pages were turned over; at times the Duke de Rozan or Mr. Simpson, or the Count de Chibray appeared, and Maxime added, sneering:

"Besides, your taste is perverted, everyone knows it. Can you see anything more stupid than these gentlemen's faces? Rozan and Chibray look like Gustave, my barber."

Renée shrugged her shoulders as if to say that this irony did not affect her. She still forgot herself in contemplating the wan, smiling, or stern faces which the album contained; she tarried longer over the portraits of the fast women, and inquisitively studied the exact microscopical details of the photographs, the little wrinkles and the little hairs. One day she even procured a strong magnifying glass, fancying she had perceived a hair on the Crawfish's nose. And, indeed, the glass revealed a slight golden thread which had strayed from the eyebrows down to the middle of the nose. This hair amused them for a long time. For a whole week the ladies who called had to assure themselves in person of the presence of this hair. Thenceforth the magnifying glass served to scrutinize the women's faces. Renée made some astonishing discoveries; she found some unknown wrinkles, rough skins, cavities imperfectly filled up with rice powder. And Maxime ended by hiding the magnifying glass, declaring that one ought not to disgust oneself with the human face like that. The truth was that she scrutinized too closely the thick lips of Sylvia, for whom he had a particular affection. They then invented a new game. They asked this question: "With whom would I willingly spend a night?" and they opened the album, which was entrusted with the duty of replying. This gave rise to some strange couplings. Renée's female friends played at the game during several evenings, and Renée herself was successively married to the Archbishop of Paris, to Baron Gouraud, to M. de Chibray, at which she greatly laughed, and to her husband in person, at which she was greatly distressed. As for Maxime,

ÉMILE ZOLA

either by chance, or by the maliciousness of Renée, who opened the album, he always fell upon the Marchioness. But there was never so much laughter as when luck coupled two men or two women together.

The familiarity of Renée and Maxime went so far that she told him her private sorrows. He consoled her and gave her advice. It seemed as if his father did not exist. Then later on they began to tell each other about their childhood. It was especially during their drives in the Bois de Boulogne that they felt a vague languor, a longing to relate things which are difficult to tell and are not told. The delight that children take in whispering about forbidden things, the attraction that exists for a young man and young woman to lower themselves to sin, be it only in words, unceasingly brought them back to suggestive subjects. They partook deeply of voluptuousness, for which they did not reproach one another, but which they tasted together, lazily reclining in the two corners of their carriage, like two comrades who recall their past freaks. They ended by becoming perfect braggarts of immorality. Renée owned that the little girls at her school were very immodest. Maxime improved upon that and made so bold as to relate some of the shameful doings of the college of Plassans.

"Ah! I can't tell—" murmured Renée.

Then she leant forward close to his ear, as if the sound of her voice alone would have made her blush, and confided to him one of those convent stories which appear in disgusting songs. He, on his side, had too rich a collection of anecdotes of this kind to remain behindhand. He hummed in her ear some very indecent verses. And by degrees they found themselves in an especial state of beatitude, rocked by all the carnal fancies that they stirred, titillated by little desires which were not expressed. The carriage rolled gently on, and they returned home deliciously fatigued, more tired indeed than after a night of love. They had sinned, like two young fellows who, wandering along the country lanes without any mistresses, might content themselves with their mutual recollections.

Even greater familiarity and licence existed between the father and the son. Saccard had realised that a great financier ought to love women and do some foolish things for them. He was a rough lover and preferred money; but it formed part of his programme to hang about alcoves, scatter bank-notes on certain mantelshelves, and from time to time use some notorious wench as a gilded signboard for his speculations. When Maxime had left college he and his father met in the same women's rooms and laughed over it. They were even rivals in a degree. At times when the young fellow dined at the Maison-d'Or with some noisy party, he would overhear Saccard's voice in a neighbouring private room.

"Hallo, papa's next door," he would exclaim with a grimace which he borrowed from the actors then in favour.

And he would go and knock at the door of the private room, anxious to see his father's conquest.

"Ah! it's you?" Saccard would say in a gay tone, "come in. You make enough noise to prevent one from hearing oneself eat. Who are you with then?"

"Why, there's Laure d'Aurigny, Sylvia, the Crawfish, and two others, I fancy. They are awfully funny. They poke their fingers in the dishes and chuck handfuls of salad at our heads. My coat is all greasy with oil."

The father would laugh, thinking this very funny.

"Ah! young folks, young folks," he would mutter. "That isn't like us, is it, my little kitten? We have dined very quietly and now we are going to by-by."

And he would chuck the chin of the woman whom he had beside him, and coo with his Provençal snuffle, which produced strange music for a lover.

"Oh! the old noodle!" the woman would cry. "Good-day, Maxime. Mustn't I love you, eh! to consent to dine with your scamp of a father— One never sees you now. Come early on the day after to-morrow morning. No, really, I've something to tell you."

Saccard would finish eating an ice or some fruit, beatifically, taking small mouthfuls. Then he would kiss the woman's shoulder, saying humorously:

"You know, my ducks, if I'm in the way, I'll leave the room. You can ring the bell when you are ready for me to come in again."

Then he would take the woman off, or, at times, go with her to join in the racket in the neighbouring room. Maxime and he shared the same shoulders; their hands met round the same waists. They called to one another on the divans, and repeated to each other, aloud, the confidential statements which the women had whispered in their ears. And they carried their good fellowship so far as to conspire together to carry off from the gathering the blonde or brunette which one or the other of them had chosen.

They were well known at Mabille. They went there arm in arm, after some dainty dinner, strolled round the garden, nodding to the women, and tossing them a remark as they passed by. They laughed aloud, without unlocking their arms, and came to each other's assistance whenever business was discussed. The father, who was very expert on this point, negotiated his son's love affairs advantageously. At times they sat down and drank with a party of girls. Then they changed their table or resumed their stroll. And they were seen till midnight with their arms always linked like a couple of chums, following the skirts along the yellow pathways under the glaring flame of the gas jets.

When they returned home they brought with them, from out-of-doors, in their coats, a dash of the women they had just left. Their loose attitudes, and the after-part of certain suggestive remarks and low gestures, made the flat in the Rue de Rivoli seem like a fast woman's lodging. The gentle wanton way in which the father gave his hand to his son, of itself proclaimed whence they came. It was in this atmosphere that Renée inhaled her sensual caprices and longings. She chaffed them nervously:

"Where can you have come from?" she would say to them. "You smell of tobacco and musk. It's certain that I shall have a headache."

And indeed, the strange smell profoundly disturbed her. It was the regular perfume of this singular domestic hearth.

However, Maxime was smitten with a fine passion for little Sylvia. He bored his stepmother with this girl during several months. Renée soon knew her from one end to the other, from the soles of her feet to the tip of her hair. She had a bluish mark on the hip; nothing could be more adorable than her knees; and there was this peculiarity about her shoulders, that only the left one was dimpled. Maxime evinced some maliciousness in devoting his drives with Renée to the description of his mistress's perfections. One evening, on returning from the Bois, Renée's carriage and Sylvia's were caught in a block, and had to draw up, side by side, in the Champs-Elysées. The two women eyed each other with acute curiosity, while Maxime, whom this critical situation delighted, tittered on the quiet. As his stepmother preserved gloomy silence when the carriage began to roll on again he thought she was in the sulks, and expected one of those maternal scenes, one of those strange scoldings with which she still, at times, occupied her moments of lassitude.

"Do you know that person's jeweller?" she abruptly asked him, at the moment when they reached the Place de la Concorde.

"Alas, yes!" he answered with a smile; "I owe him ten thousand francs—Why do you ask me that?"

"For nothing."

Then after a fresh silence:

"She had a very pretty bracelet, the one on the left wrist. I should have liked to see it close to."

They reached home. She said no more on the matter then. Only on the following day, just as Maxime and his father were going out together, she took the young fellow aside, and spoke to him in an undertone, with an embarrassed air, and a pretty smile which courted indulgence. He seemed surprised and went off, laughing in his wicked way. In the evening he brought Sylvia's bracelet which his stepmother had begged him to show her.

"There's what you wanted," said he. "One would thieve for your sake, pretty mamma."

"She didn't see you take it?" asked Renée who was eagerly examining the bracelet.

"I don't think so—She wore it yesterday, so she certainly wouldn't put it on to-day."

Meantime the young woman approached the window. She had put the bracelet on and she held her wrist somewhat raised slowly turning it round, delighted and repeating:

"Oh! very pretty, very pretty. There are only the emeralds that don't quite please me."

At this moment Saccard came in, and as she still held her wrist up in the white light from the window:

"Hallo!" he cried in astonishment, "Sylvia's bracelet!"

"You know this jewel?" said she, more embarrassed than he was and not knowing what to do with her arm.

He had recovered himself, and he threatened his son with his finger, muttering:

"That scamp always has some forbidden fruit in his pockets! One of these days he will bring us the lady's arm as well as her bracelet."

"Why! it isn't my doing," replied Maxime with cunning cowardice. "It's Renée who wanted to see it."

The husband contented himself with saying, "Ah!" And he looked at the bracelet in his turn, repeating like his wife, "It is very pretty, very pretty."

Then he quietly went off and Renée scolded Maxime for having betrayed her like that. But he declared that his father did not care a fig about the matter! Whereupon she returned him the bracelet, adding:

"You must call on the jeweller, and order one exactly like it for me; only, you must have the emeralds replaced by sapphires."

Saccard could not keep any living or inanimate object near him for any length of time without trying to sell it, or derive some profit by it. His son was not twenty when he already thought of utilising him. A handsome fellow, the nephew of a minister and the son of a great financier, ought to be invested well. He was certainly rather young, still one could always seek a wife and a dowry for him, and, afterwards, one could have the wedding deferred or hastened according to the financial position of the establishment. Saccard proved lucky. On a board of directors, to which he belonged, he found a tall handsome man, M. de Mareuil, who in a couple of days belonged to him. M. de Mareuil, rightly named Bonnet, was an ex-sugar refiner of Le Havre. After amassing a large fortune he had married a young girl of noble birth and also very rich, who was looking out for a fool of stylish appearance. Bonnet obtained permission to assume his wife's name, which was a first satisfaction for his pride; but his marriage had made him madly ambitious, and he dreamt of remunerating Hélène for this noble name by acquiring a high political position. From that time forward he invested money in new newspapers, bought a large estate in the depths of the Nièvre, and by all known means prepared for himself a candidature to the Corps Législatif. So far he had failed but without losing aught of his solemnity. His was the most incredibly empty brain that could be met with. He was of superb stature, with the white pensive face of a great statesman; and as he listened marvellously well, with a deep look, and majestic calmness of face, people could readily imagine that a prodigious work of comprehension and deduction was going on in his mind. In reality he was thinking about nothing. But he succeeded in disturbing people, who no longer knew whether they had to deal with a man of superior attainments or a fool. M. de Mareuil attached himself to Saccard as to a raft that might save him. He was aware that an official candidature would be vacant in the Nièvre, and he ardently hoped that the minister would select him; it was his last card. So he handed himself up, bound hand and foot, to the minister's brother. Saccard, who scented a remunerative transaction, gradually set him thinking of a marriage between his daughter Louise and Maxime. De Mareuil then became most effusive, thought that he himself had initiated this idea of a marriage, and considered himself very fortunate to enter a minister's family and give Louise to a young man who seemed to have such fine prospects.

Louise, said her father, would have a dowry of a million francs. Deformed, ugly, and yet adorable, she was condemned to die young; a chest complaint was stealthily undermining her, lending her nervous gaiety and caressing grace. Young girls who are ailing quickly grow old, and become women before their time. She was sensually ingenuous, she seemed to have been born at fifteen years of age in full puberty. When her father, a healthy brutified colossus, looked at her he could not believe that she was his daughter. Her mother, during her lifetime, had also been a strong well-built woman; but stories were told about her which explained this child's stuntedness, her manners of a millionaire Bohemian, and her vicious and charming ugliness. People said that Hélène de Mareuil had died from the most shameful profligacy. Pleasure had eaten into her like an ulcer, without her husband realising her lucid madness, though he ought to have had her shut up in a private asylum. Developed in this diseased form, Louise had left it with impoverished blood and crooked limbs, with her brain attacked and her memory already full of a dirty life. She thought at times that she could confusedly remember another existence, she saw strange scenes unfolded before her in a vague dimness, men and women kissing one another, quite a carnal drama with which her childish curiosity was amused. It was her mother that spoke within her. This vice remained in her throughout her childhood. As she gradually grew up, nothing astonished her, she recollected everything, or rather she knew everything, and she went to forbidden things, with a sureness of hand that made her, in life, seem like a person returning home after a long absence, and only having to stretch out his hand to set himself at ease and partake of the comforts of his abode. This singular girl, whose evil instincts flattered Maxime, and who, moreover—in this second life which she lived as a virgin with all the science and shame of a grown woman—possessed an ingenuous effrontery, a spicy mixture of childishness and boldness, was bound in the result to please the young fellow, and seem to him very much funnier even than Sylvia, who, the daughter of a worthy stationer, possessed a usurer's heart and was horribly middle-class at bottom.

The marriage was arranged with a laugh, and it was decided that "the youngsters" should be allowed to grow up. The two families lived on a footing of close friendship. M. de Mareuil promoted his candidature. Saccard watched his prey. It was understood that Maxime should place his nomination as an auditor of the Council of State among the marriage presents.

Meanwhile the Saccards' fortune seemed to have reached its culminating point. It blazed in the midst of Paris like a colossal bonfire. It was the moment when the ardent sharing of the hounds' fees fills a corner of the forest with the barking of dogs, the clacking of whips and the blazing of torches. The appetites let loose were at last satisfied in the impudence of triumph, amid the racket of falling houses and of fortunes built up in six months. The city was now but a great saturnalia of millions and women. Vice, coming from above, flowed along the gutters, spread itself out in the sheets of ornamental water, reascended in the fountains of the public gardens to fall again on to the roofs in a fine penetrating rain. And at night time, when one passed over the bridges, it seemed as if the Seine drew along with it, amid the sleeping metropolis, all the refuse of the city—crumbs fallen from tables, bows of lace left on divans, false hair forgotten in cabs, bank notes that had slipped out of bodices, everything that the brutality of desire, and the immediate satisfaction of instinct fling into the street broken and soiled. Then amid the feverish sleep of Paris, and better still amid its breathless hankering in the broad daylight, one realised the unsettling of the brain, the golden and voluptuous nightmare of a city, madly enamoured of its gold and its flesh. The violins sounded till midnight: then the windows became dark and shadows descended over the city. It was like a colossal alcove in which the last candle had been blown out, the last virtue extinguished. In the depths of the shade there was nothing left save a great rattle of furious, wearied love; while the Tuileries, on the river bank, stretched their arms out into the night as if for a huge embrace.

Saccard had just had his mansion of the Parc Monceaux built on some ground stolen from the city. He had reserved for himself on the first floor, a superb private room, all violet ebony and gold, with lofty glass doors to the book-cases, which were full of business papers but where not a book was to be seen; the safe, embedded in the wall, had the depths of an iron alcove large enough to accommodate the amours of a milliard. It was here that his fortune bloomed, impudently displayed itself. Everything seemed to succeed with him. When he left the Rue de Rivoli, increasing his household, doubling his expenditure, he talked to his friends about some considerable winnings. According to his account his partnership with Mignon and Charrier brought him enormous profits; his speculations on house property were more remunerative still; and as for the Crédit Viticole, it was an inexhaustible milch cow. He had a way of enumerating his riches that bewildered his listeners and prevented them from clearly seeing the truth. His Provençal snuffling increased, and, with his curt phrases and nervous gestures, he let off fireworks, in which millions rose like rockets, and which finished by dazzling even the most incredulous. The reputation which he had acquired as a lucky gamester was mainly due to this turbulent pantomimic action. To tell the truth, no one knew him to be possessed of a clear solid capital. His different partners, who perforce were acquainted with his situation as regarded themselves, explained his colossal fortune by believing him to be invariably fortunate in other speculations, those which they were not acquainted with. He spent a deal of money: the effluence of his cash-box continued, without the sources of this golden river having so far been discovered. It was pure madness, a frenzy for scattering money, handfuls of louis flung out of window, the safe emptied every evening to its last copper, but filling itself again during the night, no one knew how, and never supplying such large sums as when Saccard pretended he had lost the keys.

Renée's dowry was shaken, carried off and drowned in this fortune which clamoured and overflowed like a winter-torrent. The young wife, who had been distrustful in earlier days and desirous of managing her fortune herself, soon grew tired of business matters; besides, she felt herself poor beside her husband, and crushed by her debts, she was obliged to have recourse to him, to borrow money from him, and place herself at his discretion. At each fresh bill, which he paid with the smile of a man who is indulgent towards human weakness, she surrendered herself a little more, confided State bonds to him, and authorized him to sell this or that. When they went to live in the mansion in the Parc Monceaux she already found herself almost completely stripped. He had taken the place of the State and served her the interest of the hundred thousand francs coming from the Rue de la Pépinière; on the other hand, he had induced her to sell the estate in La Sologne to place the proceeds in a great affair, a superb investment, he said. She therefore had nothing left her excepting the property at Charonne, which she obstinately refused to part with so as not to sadden that excellent Aunt Élisabeth. And, in this respect again, he was preparing a stroke of genius with the assistance of his former accomplice Larsonneau. She certainly remained under obligations to him; if he had taken her fortune, he paid her the income it would have furnished, five or six times over. The interest on the hundred thousand francs, with the revenue of the Sologne money, scarcely amounted to nine or ten thousand francs, just enough to pay for her linen and boots. He gave her or paid away for her fifteen and twenty times that paltry sum. He would have worked for a week to rob her of a hundred francs, but he kept her in regal style. And thus like everybody she held her husband's monumental safe in respect without trying to penetrate the nihility of the river of gold which passed under her eyes and into which she threw herself every morning.

At the Parc Monceaux there was a mad crisis, a flashing triumph. The Saccards doubled the number of their carriages and horses; they had an army of servants, whom they dressed in a dark-blue livery with putty-coloured breeches, and waistcoats striped black and yellow—somewhat quiet colours that the financier had selected so as to seem altogether serious-minded, which was one of the dreams he had most caressed. They displayed their luxury on the house top, and drew back the curtains when they gave grand dinners. The breeze of contemporary life, which had banged the doors of the first floor in the Rue de Rivoli, became in the mansion a perfect whirlwind that threatened to carry off the very partitions. In the midst of these princely rooms, along the gilded balustrades, over the fine woollen carpets, in this fairy palace of the parvenu, there trailed the smell of Mabille; the fashionable quadrilles were danced there with all their wriggling jactitance, the whole period passed with its mad stupid laugh, its eternal hunger and its eternal thirst. It was the suspicious abode of fashionable pleasure, the pleasure which widens the windows so that passers-by may see what is transpiring in the alcoves. The husband and the wife lived there, freely, under the eyes of their servants. They had divided the house between them, and they camped in it, scarcely looking as though they were at home, but rather as if tossed, at the end of a tumultuous bewildering journey, into some regal hotel, where they had merely taken the time to open their trunks, so as to hasten the more speedily to the delights of a fresh city. They lodged there by the night, only remaining at home on the days when grand dinners were given, ever carried away by a ceaseless peregrination through Paris, but returning at times for an hour, as one returns into a room at an inn between two excursions. Renée felt herself become more anxious, more nervous there; her silken skirts glided with snake-like hisses over the thick carpets, past the satin of the couches; she was irritated by the stupid gilding which surrounded her, by the high empty ceilings where after fête nights there only lingered the laughter of young fools and the remarks of old scoundrels; and to fill this luxury, to abide amidst this effulgence, she longed for a supreme amusement which her curiosity vainly sought for in all the corners of the mansion, in the little sun-tinted drawing-room, in the conservatory full of luxuriant vegetation. As for Saccard he began to realise his dream; he received great financiers, Monsieur Toutin-Laroche and Monsieur de Lauwerens; and great politicians also, Baron Gouraud and Deputy Haffner; his brother the minister had even condescended to come two or three times to consolidate his position by his presence. And yet like his wife he experienced nervous anxiety, a disquietude which lent a strange sound of broken window panes to his laughter. He became so ungovernable, so scared, that his acquaintances remarked, "That devil of a Saccard! he makes too much money, it will end by driving him mad!" In 1860 he had been decorated with the Legion of Honour, after rendering a mysterious service to the prefect, by lending his name to a lady for the sale of some land.

It was about the time when they went to live near the Parc Monceaux that an apparition crossed Renée's life, leaving her an ineffaceable impression. The minister had so far resisted the supplications of his sister-in-law, who was dying with a longing to be invited to the court balls. However, he gave way at last, believing that his brother's position was definitely established on a sound basis. For a month Renée did not sleep for thinking of it. But the great evening arrived at last, and she sat trembling all over, in the carriage which was taking her to the Tuileries.

She wore a costume of prodigious grace and originality, a real gem which she had lighted upon during a night of sleeplessness, and which three of Worms's workpeople had come to her house to make up under her eyes. It was a simple dress of white gauze, trimmed however with a multitude of little scalloped flounces edged with bands of black velvet. The black velvet tunic was cut square, very low to show her bosom, framed with some narrow lace, barely a finger broad. There was not a flower, not a bit of ribbon; but round her wrists, some bracelets without the least chasing, and on her head a narrow diadem of gold, a plain circlet which seemed to be an aureola.

When she reached the reception rooms, and her husband had left her for Baron Gouraud, she experienced a momentary embarrassment. But the mirrors, in which she saw herself look adorable, soon reassured her, and she was accustoming herself to the warm atmosphere, to the murmur of voices, to the crush of dress coats and white shoulders, when the Emperor appeared. He slowly crossed the room on the arm of a short, fat general, who puffed as if he were troubled with a bad digestion. The bare shoulders ranged themselves in two lines, whilst the dress coats, with a discreet air, instinctively drew back a step. Renée found herself pushed to the end of the line of shoulders near the second door, the one that the Emperor was approaching with a faltering, unsteady step. She thus saw him come towards her from one door to the other.

He wore a dress coat, with the red ribbon of the Grand Cordon. Renée, again seized with emotion, retained but imperfect vision, and to her this bleeding stain seemed to cast splashes over the whole of the sovereign's breast. As a rule, she thought him little, with swaying loins, and legs too short for the trunk of his body; but now she was delighted, and, as she saw him, he looked handsome, despite his pale face and the heavy leaden lids which fell over his lifeless eyes. Under his moustaches, his lips were languidly parted, and his nose alone remained bony amid the whole of his puffy face.

With a worn-out air, and vaguely smiling, the Emperor and the old general continued to advance with short steps, seemingly sustaining each other. They looked at the ladies bending forward, and their glances, cast to the right and to the left, glided into the bodices. The general leant on one side, said a word to his master, and pressed his arm in the manner of a gay companion. And the Emperor, supine and nebulous, duller even than usual, still approached with his lagging step.

They were in the middle of the room, when Renée felt their glances fall upon her. The general gazed at her with a look of surprise, while the Emperor, half raising his eyelids, let a sensual gleam shoot from his grey, hesitating, bleared eyes. Renée, losing countenance, lowered her head, bowed, and saw nothing more but the pattern of the carpet. Still, she watched their shadows, and she understood that they were pausing for a few seconds before her. And she fancied that she heard the Emperor, that licentious dreamer, murmur, as he gazed at her, immersed in her muslin skirt striped with velvet:

"Look there, general, a flower to be culled, a mysterious pink, variegated white and black."

And the general answered in a more brutal voice:

"That pink would look awfully well in our button-holes, sire."

Renée raised her head. The apparition had disappeared, the crowd was thronging round about the doorway. After that evening she often returned to the Tuileries, she even had the honour of being complimented by his majesty aloud, and of becoming a little bit his friend; but she always remembered the sovereign's slow, heavy walk along the centre of the reception-room between the two rows of shoulders; and whenever she experienced any new joy amid her husband's growing prosperity, she again saw the Emperor overtopping the bowing bosoms, coming towards her, and comparing her to a pink which the general advised him to place in his button-hole. For her this was the high note of her life.

IV

The well-defined, galling desire which had risen to Renée's heart amid the troublous perfumes of the conservatory, while Maxime and Louise laughed on a couch of the little buttercup room, seemed to die away like a nightmare of which naught remains save a slight shudder. The young woman had retained the bitterness of the Tanghinia on her lips all night; and it had seemed to her, on feeling the burning of the cursed leaf, that a mouth of flame was pressing itself to hers, blowing her a devouring love. Then this mouth escaped her, and her dream was immersed in vast waves of shade which rolled around her.

In the morning she slept a little, and when she awoke she thought she was ill. She had the curtains drawn, spoke to her doctor of nausea and headache, and for a couple of days actually refused to go out. And as she pretended that she was being besieged, she forbade her door. Maxime came and knocked at it fruitlessly. He did not sleep in the house, as he preferred to be able to dispose freely of his rooms; indeed, he led the most nomadic life in the world, lodging in his father's new houses, selecting whatever floor suited him, and moving every month, often out of sheer caprice, and at times to make room for serious tenants. He dried the walls in the company of some mistress. Accustomed to his stepmother's whims, he feigned great compassion for her, and went upstairs four times a-day to inquire after her, with a most distressed look, though, in point of fact, he merely wished to tease her. On the third day he found her in the little drawing-room, rosy and smiling, and with a calm and rested look.

"Well, did you amuse yourself very much with Céleste?" he asked her, alluding to the long tête-à-tête she had had with her maid.

"Yes," she answered, "she is a very useful girl. She always has such cold hands; she placed them on my forehead, and soothed my poor head a little."

"But that girl's a remedy then!" cried the young fellow. "If I ever have the misfortune to fall in love, you'll lend her to me, eh? so that she may place her two hands on my heart."

They joked, and went for their usual drive to the Bois. A fortnight passed by. Renée had thrown herself more madly than ever into her life of visits and balls; her head seemed to have turned once more, she no longer complained of lassitude and disgust. Still, one might have thought that she had committed some secret sin, which she did not speak of, but which she confessed by a more strongly marked contempt for herself and by increased depravity in her whims as a fashionable woman. One evening she confessed to Maxime that she longed to go to a ball which Blanche Müller, an actress in vogue, meant to give to the princesses of the footlights and the queens of the fast world. This avowal surprised and embarrassed even the young man, and yet he was not particularly scrupulous. He tried to catechise his stepmother: really, that wasn't her place; besides, she would see nothing very funny there; and then, if she were recognised, it would cause a scandal. She answered all these good reasons with clasped hands, supplicating, and smiling.

"Come, my little Maxime, be kind. I'm determined on it. I will put on a very dark domino; we will only pass through the rooms."

Maxime always ended by giving way, and would have taken his stepmother to all the disreputable places in Paris had she but begged him ever so little to do so. So he consented to escort her to Blanche Müller's ball, whereupon she clapped her hands like a child to whom an unhoped-for holiday is granted.

"Ah! you are a dear fellow," said she. "It's for to-morrow, isn't it? Come and fetch me very early. I want to see those women arrive. You will name them to me, and we shall amuse ourselves awfully well."

She reflected, and then added:

"No, don't come. Wait for me in a cab on the Boulevard Malesherbes. I will go out by the garden."

This mysterious way of proceeding was a spice which she added to her escapade, a simple refinement of pleasure, for had she left the house at midnight by the front door, her husband would not even have put his head out of window.

On the morrow, after telling Céleste to sit up for her, she crossed the dark shadows of the Parc Monceaux with shudders of exquisite fear. Saccard had profited by his good understanding with the Hôtel de Ville authorities to obtain a key to a little gate of the park, and Renée had wished to have one for herself as well. She almost lost her way, however, and only found the cab, thanks to the two yellow eyes of the lamps. At that period the Boulevard Malesherbes, scarcely finished, was still a perfect solitude at night-time. The young woman glided into the vehicle in great emotion, her heart beating as delightfully as if she were going to some love meeting. Maxime was philosophically smoking, half asleep, in one corner of the cab. He wished to throw away his cigar, but she prevented him from doing so, and, as she tried to restrain his arm in the darkness, she placed her hand full on his face, which greatly amused them both.

"I tell you that I like the smell of tobacco!" she exclaimed. "Keep your cigar. Besides, we're going on the spree to-night. I'm a man, I am!"

The Boulevard was not yet lighted up, and while the cab rolled down it towards the Madeleine, it was so dark inside that they could not see each other. Every now and then, when the young fellow carried his cigar to his lips, a red point stood out amid the dense obscurity. This red point interested Renée. Maxime, who was half covered by the folds of her black satin domino, which filled the inside of the vehicle, continued smoking in silence, with a bored air. The truth was, that his stepmother's whim had prevented him from following to the Café Anglais a party of women who had determined to begin and finish Blanche Müller's ball there. He was crusty, and she discerned his sulkiness in the darkness.

"Are you ill?" she asked him.

"No, I am cold," he answered.

"Dear me. Why, I'm burning. I feel quite stifled here. Take part of my skirts on your knees."

"Oh! your skirts," he muttered, bad-humouredly. "I already have them up to my eyes."

But this remark made him laugh himself, and by degrees he grew lively. She told him of the fright she had had in the Parc Monceaux. And then she confessed another of her longings: she would like one night to go for a row in the boat which she could see from her windows, moored at the edge of a pathway. On hearing this, he considered that she was becoming sentimental. The cab still rolled on, the darkness remained, profound, and they leaned towards one another to hear each other amid the noise of the wheels, touching each other when they moved their arms, and at times, when they approached too closely, inhaling each other's warm breath. And at equal intervals Maxime's cigar was revivified, setting a red blur on the darkness, and casting a pale rosy flash on Renée's face. She looked adorable, seen by this fleeting glimmer; so much so that the young man was struck by it.

"Oh! oh!" said he. "We seem to be very pretty this evening, stepmamma. Let's see a bit."

He brought his cigar nearer, and precipitately drew a few puffs. Renée, in her corner was illumined by a warm and seemingly panting light. She had slightly raised her hood. Her bare head, covered with a mass of little curls, with a simple blue ribbon, looked like that of a real urchin peering above the large blouse of black satin which rose to her neck. She thought it very funny to be thus looked at and admired by the light of a cigar, and she threw herself back with little bursts of laughter, while he added with an air of comic gravity:

"The deuce! I shall have to watch over you, if I am to take you back safe and sound to my father."

Meanwhile the cab turned round the Madeleine and went up the Boulevards. Here it became filled with a leaping light, with the reflection of the shops, the fronts of which were flaming. Blanche Müller resided two steps off, in one of the new houses which have been built on the raised ground of the Rue-Basse-du-Rempart. As yet there were only a few vehicles at the door, it was barely more than ten o'clock. Maxime wanted to take a turn on the Boulevards and wait an hour, but Renée, whose curiosity was becoming more acute, straightway declared to him that she should go upstairs alone if he did not accompany her. He followed her therefore, and felt glad on finding that there was more company upstairs than he had expected. The young woman had put on her mask, and leaning on the arm of Maxime, to whom she gave peremptory orders in a low voice, and who submissively obeyed her, she ferreted about the rooms, raised the corners of the door-hangings, examined the furniture, and would perhaps have searched the drawers had she not feared being seen. Although the rooms were richly upholstered, there were corners suggestive of a Bohemian life, and in which one scented the mummer. It was particularly in these spots that Renée's nostrils dilated, and that she compelled her companion to walk slowly so as to lose nothing of the sight or the smell. She especially forgot herself in a dressing-room, the door of which had been left wide open by Blanche Müller, who, when she entertained company, gave everything up to her guests, even to her alcove in which the bed was pushed back to make room for card tables. But the dressing-room did not satisfy Renée: it seemed to her common, and even rather dirty, with its carpet which incandescent cigar ash had pitted with little round burns, and its blue silk hangings stained with pomatum and splashed with soap-suds. When she had fully inspected the rooms, and set every feature of the abode in her memory, so as to be able to describe it, later on, to her intimate friends, she passed on to the people who were present. As for the men she knew them; they were, for the most part, the same financiers, the same politicians, the same young fellows about town who came to her Thursday at-homes. She fancied herself in her own drawing-room at certain moments, when she found herself in front of a group of smiling dress coats, who, on the previous evening, had worn the same smile in speaking to the Marchioness d'Espanet, or to the fair Madame Haffner at her house. And even when she looked at the women her illusion was not completely dispelled. Laure d'Aurigny was in bright yellow like Suzanne Haffner, and Blanche Müller, like Adeline d'Espanet, wore a white dress which left her bare down to the middle of her back. At last Maxime implored mercy, and she consented to sit down on a couch beside him. They remained there for a moment, the young fellow yawning, the young woman asking him these ladies' names, undressing them with a glance and counting the yards of lace that they wore around their skirts. Seeing her absorbed in this serious study he ended by slipping away in compliance with a sign which Laure d'Aurigny made him with her hand. She joked him about the lady whom he had on his arm, and then made him swear to come and join her party at the Café Anglais, at one o'clock.

"Your father will be there," she shouted to him at the moment when he joined Renée again.

The latter found herself surrounded by a group of women who were laughing very loudly, while Monsieur de Saffré had profited by Maxime leaving his seat vacant to glide beside her and make gallant proposals in the style of a cab driver. Then Monsieur de Saffré and the women all began to shout and smack their hips to such a degree that Renée, fairly deafened, and yawning in her turn, rose up, saying to her companion—

"Let us go, they are too stupid."

As they were leaving the room, Monsieur de Mussy came in. He seemed delighted to meet Maxime, and without paying any attention to the masked woman who was with him.

"Ah, my dear fellow," he murmured with a love-sick air, "she will cause my death. I know that she is better, but she still forbids me her door. Tell her you have seen me with tears in my eyes."

"Be easy, your message shall be delivered," said the young fellow, with a strange laugh.

And on the way downstairs—

"Well, pretty mamma, didn't that poor fellow touch you?" She shrugged her shoulders without replying. Outside, on the pavement, she paused before getting into the cab which had brought them, looking hesitatingly in the direction of the Madeleine, and in the direction of the Boulevard des Italiens. It was scarcely half-past eleven, and the Boulevard was still very animated.

"So we are going home," she murmured regretfully.

"Unless you would like to take a drive along the Boulevards," answered Maxime.

She assented. She had been disappointed in her feast of feminine curiosity, and she was distressed at having to go home like that, with an illusion the less, and a headache setting in. She had long fancied that an actresses' ball was the height of fun.

As often happens during the last days of October, it seemed as if the spring had returned; the night air had a May-like warmth, and the occasional cold gusts that passed by lent an additional zest to the atmosphere. Renée, with her head at the window, remained silent, looking at the crowd, the cafés and the restaurants, the interminable line of which stretched away before her. She had become quite serious, absorbed in the depth of the vague wishes which fill the reveries of women. This broad side-walk, which was swept by the dresses of harlots, and on which the men's boots rung with peculiar familiarity, the grey asphalte over which, it seemed to her, the gallop of facile love and pleasure was passing, awoke her slumbering desires, and made her forget the idiotic ball that she had just left to allow her to espy other delights of enhanced spiciness. At the windows of Brébant's private rooms she perceived women's shadows against the whiteness of the curtains. And Maxime thereupon told her a very indecent story of a deceived husband who had thus detected, on a curtain, the shadow of his wife embracing the shadow of a lover. She scarcely listened to him, but he, growing lively, ended by taking hold of her hands and teasing her by talking about that poor Monsieur de Mussy.

As they drove back and again passed in front of Brébant's—

"Do you know," she said abruptly, "that Monsieur de Saffré invited me to supper this evening?"

"Oh! you would have fared badly," replied Maxime laughing. "Saffré doesn't possess the least culinary imagination. He hasn't got beyond lobster salad."

"No, no, he talked of oysters and cold partridge. But he thee-and-thou'd me, and that disturbed me."

She stopped short, looked again at the Boulevard, and, after a moment's silence, added with a distressed air—

"The worst of it is that I'm awfully hungry."

"What! you're hungry!" exclaimed the young man. "It's very simple, we'll sup together—Shall we?"

He spoke quietly, but she refused at first, declaring that Céleste had prepared her a collation at home. However, Maxime, who did not wish to go to the Café Anglais, had stopped the cab at the corner of the Rue Le Pelletier, in front of the restaurant of the Café Riche; he had even alighted, and as his stepmother still hesitated.

"After all," said he, "if you're afraid that I shall compromise you, say so. I'll get up beside the driver and take you back to your husband."

She smiled and alighted from the cab with the manners of a bird which is afraid of wetting its claws. She was radiant. The side-walk which she felt under her feet warmed her heels, and imparted to the surface of her skin a delightful quiver of fear and contented caprice. Ever since the cab had been rolling along she had had a mad longing to spring out upon this side-walk. She crossed it with short steps, and furtively, as if she derived a greater pleasure from the fear that she might be seen. Her escapade was decidedly turning into an adventure. She certainly did not regret having declined Monsieur de Saffré's coarse invitation. But she would have gone home terribly out of sorts if Maxime had not had the idea of letting her taste forbidden fruit. He went quickly up the stairs as if he had been at home. She followed him, rather short of breath. A slight fume of game and fish was wafted about, and the carpet, secured to the stairs with brass rods, had a smell of dust which increased her emotion.

Just as they were reaching the first landing they met a dignified looking waiter who drew back to the wall to let them pass him.

"Charles," said Maxime, "you'll serve us, eh? Give us the white room."

Charles bowed, reascended to the landing and opened the door of a private room. The gas was lowered, and it seemed to Renée as if she were penetrating into the twilight of a suspicious and charming spot.

A continuous rumble swept in through the window which was wide open, and in the reflection cast on the ceiling by the café below, the shadows of promenaders passed swiftly by. But with a touch of the thumb the waiter turned on the gas. The shadows on the ceiling vanished, and the room was filled with a glaring light which fell full upon the young woman's head. She had already thrown her hood back. The little curls had become slightly disordered in the cab, but the blue ribbon had not stirred. She began to walk about, abashed by the manner in which Charles looked at her; he blinked his eyes and screwed up their lids the better to see her, in a way which plainly signified, "I don't know this one yet."

"What shall I serve you, sir?" he asked aloud.

Maxime turned towards Renée.

"Monsieur de Saffré's supper, eh?" said he, "some oysters, a partridge—"

And seeing the young man smile, Charles discreetly imitated him, murmuring—

"Then the same supper as last Wednesday, if that will suit?"

"The supper of last Wednesday—" repeated Maxime. Then suddenly remembering: "Yes, it's all the same to me, give us Wednesday's supper."

When the waiter had retired Renée took her eye-glasses and went inquisitively round the little room. It was a square apartment all white and gold and furnished with boudoir-like coquetry. In addition to the table and the chairs, there was a low dinner waggon and a large divan, a perfect bed, placed between the chimney-piece and the window. A Louis XVI clock and candlesticks adorned the white marble mantelshelf. But the curiosity of the room was the looking-glass, a handsome squat looking-glass which women's diamonds had covered with names, dates, murdered verses, prodigious sentiments and astounding avowals. Renée fancied she espied something beastly but she lacked the courage to satisfy her curiosity. She looked at the divan, experienced fresh embarrassment at the sight, and to give herself a countenance began gazing at the ceiling and the chandelier of gilt copper with five gas jets. However the uneasiness she felt was delightful. While she raised her brow, as if to study the cornice, looking grave and holding her eye-glasses in her hand, she derived profound enjoyment from the presence of the equivocal furniture, which she knew to be around her; that clear cynical looking glass, the purity of which, being wrinkled by those dirty scrawls, had proved useful in adjusting so many false chignons; that divan which shocked her by its breadth; the table and the carpet itself in which she found the same smell she had detected upon the stairs, a vague, penetrating and almost religious smell of dust.

Then, when it was at last necessary for her to lower her eyes:

"What is this Wednesday supper?" she asked of Maxime.

"Nothing," he answered, "a bet that one of my friends lost."

In any other spot, he would without any hesitation have told her that he had supped there on Wednesday with a lady whom he had met on the Boulevard. But since he had entered the private room he had instinctively treated her like a woman whom one has to please, and whose jealousy ought to be spared. However she did not insist on the point, but went and leaned on the rail of the window, where he soon

ÉMILE ZOLA

joined her. Charles came in and went out behind them amid a noise of crockery and plate.

It was not yet midnight. On the Boulevard below, Paris was thundering and prolonging the ardent day before making up its mind to go to bed. The rows of trees separated in a confused line the whiteness of the foot walk from the vague darkness of the roadway along which passed the rumble and the fleet lamps of the vehicles. On either edge of this dim strip of ground, the kiosks of the newspaper vendors shed their light here and there, like great Venetian lanterns, tall and strangely variegated, which had been set at regular intervals on the ground for some colossal illumination. But at this time of night their subdued brilliancy was lost in the glare of the neighbouring shop fronts. Not a shutter was up, the foot walks stretched away without a line of shadow under a stream of rays which lighted them with a golden dust, with the warm brilliant glare of full daylight. Maxime pointed out to Renée the Café Anglais, the windows of which were shining in front of them. The lofty branches of the trees somewhat prevented them, however, from seeing the houses and the footway across the Boulevard. They leaned forward and looked below them. There was a continual coming and going: promenaders passed by in groups, harlots in couples trailed their skirts which they raised from time to time with a languid gesture, casting wearied yet smiling glances around them. Under the window itself the tables of the Café Riche were spread out in the blaze of the gas-jets, the brilliancy of which penetrated half across the thoroughfare; and it was especially in the centre of this ardent focus that they saw the wan faces and pale smiles of the passers by. Around the little tables men and women were mingled together drinking. The girls were in showy dresses with their hair down their necks; they lounged about on their chairs and made loud remarks which the noise of the traffic prevented one from hearing. Renée especially noticed one woman who was dressed in a blue costume trimmed with white Maltese lace, and who sat alone at a table, leaning back with her hands on her stomach; she was waiting with a gloomy resigned look and leisurely sipping a glass of beer. Those who were walking, slowly disappeared among the crowd, and the young woman, who took an interest in their doings, let her eyes follow them, and gazed from one end of the Boulevard to the other, into the noisy confused depths of the thoroughfare full of the black swarm of promenaders and where the lights became mere sparks. And the endless procession, a strangely mingled crowd always the same, passed by with fatiguing regularity amid the bright colours and the dark depths, in the airy-like confusion of the thousand leaping flames which swept like waves out of the shops, lending colour to the transparencies of the windows and the kiosks, tracing fillets, letters and fiery designs over the house fronts, studding the darkness with stars and gliding along the roadway continually. Amid the deafening noise which rose on high was a clamour, a prolonged monotonous rumble like an organ note accompanying an eternal procession of little automatic dolls. At one moment Renée thought that an accident had taken place. There was a stream of people in motion on the left, a little beyond the Passage de l'Opéra. But on taking her glasses she recognised the omnibus office; there were a great many people on the side-walk standing waiting, and rushing forwards as soon as a vehicle arrived. She could hear the rough voice of the official calling out the numbers, and then the tinkle of the registering bell was wafted to her like a crystalline ringing. Her eyes next lighted upon an advertisement on a kiosk glaringly coloured like an Épinal print. On the pane of glass, in a green and yellow frame, there was a sneering devil's head, with hair on end, a hatter's advertisement which she did not understand. Every five minutes the Batignolles omnibus with its red lamps and yellow body passed by, turning round the corner of the Rue Le Pelletier and shaking the house with its din; and she saw the men riding on the knife-board, fellows with weary faces who rose up to look at them, Maxime and herself, with the inquisitive glances of hungry people peeping through a keyhole.

"Ah!" said she, "the Parc Monceaux is quietly asleep by this time."

It was the only remark she made. They remained there for nearly twenty minutes, silent, and surrendering themselves to the intoxication of the noise and illumination. Then, the table being laid, they went and sat down, and as she seemed inconvenienced by the waiter's presence Maxime dismissed him.

"Leave us—I will ring for dessert."

Renée had little flushes on her cheeks, and her eyes shone; one would have thought she had just been running. She brought with her from the window some of the din and animation of the Boulevard. She would not let her companion close the sashes.

"Why! it's the orchestra," said she, when he complained of the noise. "Don't you think it a funny music? It will be a fine accompaniment to our oysters and partridge."

The escapade lent youth to her thirty years. She had quick movements and a dash of fever, and this private room, this tête-à-tête with a young man amid the din of the street, gave her the look of a fast girl. She attacked the oysters with resolution. Maxime was not hungry and he watched her with a smile while she devoured.

"The deuce!" he muttered, "you would have made a good supper companion."

She stopped short, annoyed that she had eaten so quickly. "You think that I'm too hungry. What would you? It's the hour we spent at that idiotic ball which emptied me. Ah! my poor fellow, I pity you for living in such society as that!"

"But you know very well," said he, "that I have promised you to send Sylvia and Laure d'Aurigny to the right about on the day that your friends consent to come and sup with me."

With a superb gesture she answered, "Of course! I quite believe it. We are a good deal more amusing than those women, confess it now— if one of us bored her lover like your Sylvia and your Laure d'Aurigny must bore you, why the poor little woman would not keep her lover a week! You will never listen to me, but try it one of these days."

To avoid summoning the waiter Maxime rose, removed the oyster shells and brought the partridge which had been placed on the dinner waggon. The table had the luxurious aspect customary in the fashionable restaurants. A breath of adorable debauchery sped over the damask cloth, and it was with little quivers of contentment that Renée let her slender hands stroll from her fork to her knife, from her plate to her glass. She who usually drank water barely tinged with wine, now drank white wine neat. As Maxime, standing with his napkin on his arm, waited on her with comical complaisance, he resumed:

"What can Monsieur de Saffré have said to you to make you so furious? Did he find you ugly?"

"Oh! he," she answered, "he is a nasty man. I should never have thought that a gentleman of such distinguished bearing, and so polite when he calls on me, could talk such language. But I forgive him. It was the women who irritated me. One might have thought they were apple-stall keepers. There was one who complained of a boil on her hip, and, a little bit more, I believe she would have turned up her skirt to shew her sore to everyone."

Maxime was splitting with laughter.

"No, really now," she continued, growing more animated, "I don't understand you men, those women are dirty and stupid. And to think that when I saw you go to Sylvia's I imagined prodigious things, banquets in the ancient style, like one sees in paintings, with creatures crowned with roses, gold cups and extraordinary voluptuousness. What a sell! You showed me a dirty dressing-room and some women who swore like carters. Under such conditions it really isn't worth while to do wrong."

He wanted to protest, but she silenced him, and holding between her finger-tips a partridge bone which she was daintily nibbling, she added in a lower tone:

"Sin ought to be something exquisite, my dear fellow. I, who am a respectable woman, when I feel bored and commit the sin of dreaming of impossibilities, I am sure that I devise much nicer things than such as Blanche Müller could think of."

And with a grave air she concluded by a profound remark of naive cynicism:

"It is a question of how one is brought up, do you see?"

She gently laid the little bone on her plate. The rumble of the vehicles continued without any louder sound rising above it. She was obliged however to raise her voice so that he might hear her; and her cheeks became still redder. On the dinner waggon there were still some truffles, a sweet entremets; and some asparagus, a curiosity for that time of the year. He set everything on the table, so as to avoid having to disturb himself again; and as the table was rather narrow he placed on the floor, between them, a silver pail containing a bottle of champagne surrounded by ice. The young woman's appetite had ended by overtaking him too. They tasted all the dishes, and emptied the bottle of champagne with brusque gaiety, launching out into suggestive theories, with their elbows on the table like two friends who ease their hearts after a drinking bout. The noise on the Boulevard was diminishing; but to Renée's ears it increased, and at times all those wheels seemed to be revolving in her head.

When he spoke of ringing for dessert she rose up and shook her long satin blouse to make the crumbs fall off, saying:

"That's it—You know you can light a cigar."

She felt somewhat giddy. Attracted by a peculiar noise which she could not explain to herself, she went to the window. The shops were being shut up.

"Dear me," said she, turning towards Maxime, "the orchestra is clearing off."

Then she leant out again. In the centre of the thoroughfare the coloured eyes of the cabs and omnibuses, fewer and moving faster, were still passing one another. Large pits of darkness seemed to have opened in front of the closed shops—along the footpaths on either side. The cafés alone were still flaming, striping the asphalte with sheets of light. From the Rue Drouot to the Rue du Helder she thus perceived a long row of white and black squares, amid which the last promenaders sprang up and vanished again strangely. The harlots, with the trains of their dresses, by turns glaringly illuminated and immersed in darkness, seemed like apparitions, like pale marionettes crossing the limelight of some extravaganza. Renée amused herself for a moment with the sight. There was no longer a full-shed light; the gas was being turned off; the variegated kiosks stood out more defined amid the darkness. From time to time a rush of people who had just left some theatre, passed by. But soon there was vacancy again, and then under the window there lingered two or three men together whom a woman accosted. They stood in a group and discussed terms. Some of their remarks rose audibly in the subsiding din, and then it generally happened that the woman went off with one of the men. Other girls wandered from café to café, strolled round the tables, pocketed the forgotten lumps of sugar, laughed with the waiters, and gazed fixedly at the belated customers, with a silent, questioning, proffering look. And then, just after Renée had let her eyes follow the all but unoccupied knife-board of a Batignolles omnibus, she recognised, at the corner of the foot-pavement, the woman in the blue dress and white lace, who stood glancing about her, still in search of a man.

When Maxime came to fetch Renée at the window, where she was forgetting herself, he smiled as he looked at one of the partly opened casements of the Café Anglais. The idea that his father was there supping on his side seemed comical to him; but that evening a peculiar pudicity restrained his customary banter. Renée only left the window-rail regretfully. An intoxication and languor rose from the vague depths of the Boulevard. There was a coaxing summons to self-indulgent sleep in the attenuated rumble of the vehicles, and the obliteration of the bright lights. The whispers that sped by, the groups assembled in shadowy corners, transformed the side-walk into the passage of some large inn, at the hour when travellers repair to their chance beds. The gleam and the noise became fainter and fainter, the city was falling asleep, and a breath of love swept over the housetops.

When the young woman turned her head the light of the little chandelier made her blink her eyes. She was now somewhat pale and felt slight quivers at the corners of her mouth. Charles was setting out the dessert; he left the room, came in again, swinging the door, slowly and phlegmatically like a well-bred man.

"But I'm no longer hungry!" exclaimed Renée, "take away all those plates and bring us the coffee."

The waiter, accustomed to the whims of the women he served, cleared the dessert away and poured out the coffee. He filled the whole room with his importance.

"Pray do send him away," said the young woman—half sickened by the sight of him—to Maxime.

Maxime dismissed him; but scarcely had he disappeared, than he returned once more to draw the large curtains of the window closely together with a discreet air. When he had at last retired, the young fellow, who, on his side, was beginning to feel annoyed, rose from his seat and going to the door:

"Wait a bit," he said, "I have the means of getting rid of him."

And he pushed the bolt.

"That's it," she rejoined, "we shall at least be by ourselves."

Their confidential, friendly chatting began again. Maxime had lighted a cigar. Renée sipped her coffee and even allowed herself a glass of chartreuse. The room grew warmer and became filled with bluish smoke. She ended by setting her elbows on the table and by resting her chin between her two half-closed fists. Under this slight pressure her mouth grew smaller, her cheeks were slightly raised, and her narrow eyes shone more brightly. Thus unsettled, her little face looked adorable, under the stream of golden curls which now fell down upon her eyebrows. Maxime gazed at her through the smoke of his cigar. He found she had an original look. At certain moments he was no longer quite sure as to her sex; the long wrinkle which crossed her forehead, the pouting forwardness of her lips, the undecided air imparted by her shortsightedness, made a tall young man of her; the more so, as her long black satin blouse rose so high that one barely espied a white fatty strip of neck under her chin. She let herself be looked at with a smile, no longer moving her head, but with her eyes lost in vacancy and her lips closed.

Then suddenly she woke up, and went to look at the mirror, towards which her dreamy eyes had turned since a few moments. She raised herself on tip-toe, and leant her hands on the edge of the mantelshelf to read the signatures, the coarse remarks which had shocked her before supper. She spelt the syllables with some little difficulty, laughed, and

　　　　　　　　　　　　　　　　　ÉMILE ZOLA

then still read on like a schoolboy who is turning over some pages of Piron in his desk.

"'Ernest and Clara'," said she, "and there is a heart underneath, which looks like a funnel. Ah! this is better, 'I love men because I like truffles.' Signed, 'Laure.' I say, Maxime, was it that woman d'Aurigny who wrote that?—Then here are the arms of one of these women, I fancy: a hen smoking a big pipe. And more names, a perfect calendar of saints: 'Victor, Amélie, Alexandre, Édouard, Marguerite, Paquita, Louise, Renée'—Ah, so there's one who is named like me—"

Maxime could see her ardent face in the looking-glass. She raised herself up still more, and her domino, drawn more closely behind, outlined the curve of her figure, the development of her hips. The young fellow's eyes followed the line of the satin which moulded her form like a chemise. He rose up in his turn and threw away his cigar. He was ill at ease and nervous. Something usual and accustomed was lacking about him.

"Ah, here's your name, Maxime," exclaimed Renée. "Listen—'I love—'"

But he had seated himself on a corner of the divan, almost at the young woman's feet. And after succeeding in taking hold of her hands with a prompt movement, and making her turn away from the looking-glass, he said in a strange voice:

"Pray don't read that."

She struggled, laughing nervously.

"Why not? Am I not your confidante?"

But he insisted in a more husky tone.

"No, no, not this evening."

He was still holding her, and she tried to free herself with little jerks of the wrists. Their eyes had an expression they were not acquainted with; there was a touch of shame in their long, constrained smile. She fell upon her knees at the edge of the divan. They continued struggling although she no longer made an effort to return to the mirror, and was already surrendering herself. And as the young fellow caught her round the body, she said with an embarrassed dying laugh:

"Come, leave me. You are hurting me—"

It was the sole murmur that came from her lips. Amid the profound silence of the room where the gas seemed to shoot up higher, she felt the ground tremble and heard the crash of a Batignolles omnibus which must have been turning the corner of the Boulevard. And it was all over.

When they again found themselves, seated side-by-side on the divan, he stammered out, amid their mutual embarrassment:

"Bah! it was bound to happen one day or other."

She said nothing. With an overwhelmed air, she looked at the pattern of the carpet.

"Were you thinking of it?" continued Maxime, stammering more and more. "I wasn't, not at all. I ought to have mistrusted the private room."

But in a deep voice, as if all the middle-class uprightness of the Bérauds Du Châtel had been awakened by this supreme sin:

"What we have just done is infamous," she murmured, sobered, her face aged and very grave.

She was stifling. She went to the window, drew back the curtains, and leant over the rail. The orchestra was hushed; the sin had been committed amid the last quiver of the basses and the distant chant of the violins, the vague soft music of the Boulevard now sleeping and dreaming of love. The road and the side-walks stretched away below in grey solitude. All the rumbling cab wheels seemed to have gone off, taking the lights and the crowd away with them. Below the window, the Café Riche was closed, not a ray of light glided from between the shutters. Across the way, brazen-like gleams alone appeared upon the façade of the Café Anglais, especially lighting up one window which was partly open and whence a faint sound of laughter escaped. And all along this ribbon of darkness, from the turn at the Rue Drouot to the other end, as far as her eyes could reach, she no longer saw aught save the symmetrical blurs of the kiosks tinging the night with red and green, without illuminating it, and looking like night-lights spaced along some giant dormitory. She raised her head. The high branches of the trees stood out against a clear sky, while the irregular outline of the house roofs died away till it seemed like a clustering heap of rocks on the shore of a bluish sea. But this strip of sky saddened her all the more, and it was in the darkness of the Boulevard alone that she found some consolation. What lingered of the noise and vice of the evening on the surface of the deserted thoroughfare excused her. She thought she could feel the heat of all these men and women's footsteps ascend from the cooling footway. The shames that had trailed there, the desires of a minute, the whispered offers, the weddings of a night paid for in advance, were evaporating, floating about in a heavy mist rolled away by the breath of morning. Leaning out into the darkness she inhaled this quivering silence, this alcove-like smell, as an encouragement which came to her from below, as an assurance that her shame was shared and accepted by a colluding city. And when her eyes had grown accustomed to the obscurity she perceived the woman in the blue dress trimmed with lace, standing in the same place, alone in the grey solitude, waiting and offering herself to the deserted darkness.

On turning, the young woman beheld Charles who was looking around him, scenting like a dog. He ended by perceiving Renée's blue ribbon, lying rumpled and forgotten on a corner of the divan. And with his polite air, he hastened to take it to her. Then she realised all her shame. Standing in front of the looking-glass she tried with clumsy hands to tie the ribbon again. But her chignon had fallen, the little curls were flattened on her temples, and she was unable to tie the bow. Charles came to her help, saying, as if he were offering some usual thing, a finger glass or some toothpicks:

"If madame would like the comb?"

"Oh! no, there's no need," interrupted Maxime, giving the waiter an impatient look. "Go and fetch us a cab."

Renée made up her mind to pull the hood of her domino over her head. And as she was about to leave the looking-glass, she lightly raised herself in search of the words which Maxime's grasp had prevented her from reading. Slanting upwards towards the ceiling, and written in a large, abominable hand there was this declaration signed Sylvia: "I love Maxime." On reading it Renée bit her lip and drew her hood rather lower.

They experienced a horrible constraint in the vehicle. They had seated themselves one in front of the other as when they left the Parc Monceaux. They could not think of a word to say to each other. The cab was full of opaque darkness, and Maxime's cigar didn't even dot it with a red speck, a pink charcoal-like glimmer. The young fellow, again hidden among the skirts, "which he had up to his eyes," felt ill at ease amid this darkness and silence, near this speechless woman, whom he felt beside him, and whose eyes he imagined he could see gazing wide open into the night. To seem less foolish he ended by seeking her hand, and when he held it in his own he felt relieved and found the situation tolerable. Renée abandoned this hand of hers, languidly and dreamily.

The cab crossed over the Place de la Madeleine. Renée was reflecting that she was not guilty. She had not been bent on incest. And the more she descended into herself, the more innocent she considered she had been, at the outset of her escapade, at her furtive departure from the Parc Monceaux, at Blanche Müller's, on the Boulevard, and even in the private room at the restaurant. Why had she fallen on her knees at the edge of that divan? She no longer knew. She had certainly not thought of *that* for a moment. She would have angrily refused. She had made this excursion as a joke, she had been bent on amusing herself, nothing more. Thus did she ponder, and in the rumbling of the cab she seemed again to find the deafening orchestra of the Boulevard, that coming and going of men and women, while bars of fire burned her tired eyes.

Maxime was also musing, with some sense of worry, in his corner. The adventure annoyed him. He laid the blame on the black satin domino. Had one ever seen a woman rig herself out in that style? You couldn't even see her neck. He had taken her for a boy, he had played with her, and it wasn't his fault if the game had become something serious. He certainly wouldn't have touched her with the tips of his fingers, had she only shown her shoulders a bit. He would then have remembered that she was his father's wife. Then, as he did not care for disagreeable reflections, he forgave himself. So much the worse, after all! he would try not to begin again. It was folly.

The cab stopped, and Maxime alighted the first, to help Renée out. But at the little gate of the park he did not dare to kiss her. They shook hands according to their wont. She was already on the other side of the railing, when, in view of saying something, and at the same time unwittingly confessing a preoccupation which had vaguely crossed her reveries since leaving the restaurant:

"What was that comb," she asked, "which the waiter spoke about?"

"That comb," repeated Maxime, embarrassed, "I'm sure I don't know."

But Renée abruptly realised the truth. The room, no doubt, had a comb which formed part of its appurtenances like the curtains, the bolt, and the divan. And without waiting an explanation, which did not come, she plunged into the darkness of the Parc Monceaux, hastening her steps, and thinking she could see behind her the tortoise-shell teeth in which Laure d'Aurigny and Sylvia had left some of their fair and their dark hairs. Renée was very feverish, and it became necessary for Céleste to put her to bed and watch her till the morning. On the sidewalk of the Boulevard Malesherbes, Maxime consulted himself for a moment as to whether he should go and join the joyous party at the Café Anglais; then, with the idea that he was punishing himself, he decided that he ought to go home to bed.

On the morrow, Renée awoke at a late hour from a heavy dreamless sleep. She had a large fire lighted, and said that she should spend the day in her room. This was her refuge in serious moments. Towards noon, as her husband did not see her come down to lunch, he asked her permission to speak with her a moment. She was already refusing the request, with a tinge of nervousness, when she decided otherwise. On the day before she had sent Saccard Worms's bill, amounting to a hundred and thirty-six thousand francs, a rather high figure, and, no doubt, he wished to indulge in the gallantry of giving her a receipt in person.

A thought came to her of the little curls of the day before; and she mechanically looked in the glass at her hair, which Céleste had knotted in large tresses. Then she ensconced herself in a corner by the fire-place, burying herself in the lace of her dressing-gown. Saccard, whose rooms also were on the first floor, corresponding with his wife's, came to see her in his slippers, in the true style of a husband. He barely set foot in Renée's room once a month, and then only for some delicate pecuniary matter. That morning he had red eyes, and the wan complexion of a man who has not slept. He kissed the young woman's hand gallantly.

"You are not well, my dear?" he said, as he sat down on the other side of the chimney-piece. "A little headache, isn't it? Excuse my coming to worry you with my business rigmaroles, but the matter is somewhat serious."

From one of the pockets of his dressing-gown he drew forth Worms's bill, the glazed paper of which Renée recognised.

"I found this bill on my table, yesterday," he continued, "and I'm very sorry, but I really can't pay it just now."

Out of the corner of his eye he watched the effect that his words produced on his wife, who seemed to be deeply astonished. He resumed with a smile:

"As you know, my dear, I'm not in the habit of looking into your expenses. I don't say that certain items in this bill haven't surprised me a little. For instance, on the second page, I find this: 'Ball dress: material, 70 francs; making up, 600 francs; money lent, 5000 francs; perfumery, 6 francs.' That seventy franc dress comes to rather a stiff figure. But you know very well that I understand all kinds of weaknesses. Your bill amounts to a hundred and thirty-six thousand francs, and you have been almost moderate, relatively speaking, I mean—Only, I must repeat it, I can't pay, I'm hard up."

She stretched out her hand with a gesture of restrained mortification.

"Very well," she said curtly, "hand me back the bill. I will attend to it."

"I see that you don't believe me," muttered Saccard, enjoying his wife's incredulity respecting his financial embarrassment, as much as if it had been a triumph. "I don't say that my position is threatened, but business is very queer for the moment. I worry you, no doubt, but let me explain our position to you. You confided your dowry to me, and I owe you complete frankness."

He laid the bill on the mantelshelf, took up the tongs, and began to poke the fire. This mania for raking the cinders, while he was talking about business matters, was a system which had become a habit with him. Whenever he reached a figure or a remark, which it bothered him to enunciate, he brought about some downfall of the logs, which he began repairing laboriously, bringing the logs closer together, collecting and piling the little splinters of wood, one above the other. On other occasions he almost disappeared into the fire-place in search of some straying embers. He spoke in a lower tone, you grew impatient, you became interested in his skilful edification of incandescent firewood, you no longer listened to him, and, as a rule, you left his presence defeated but content. Even at other people's houses he despotically took possession of the tongs. In the summer he toyed with a pen-holder, a paper or a pen-knife.

"My dear," said he, giving a blow which sent the fire flying, "I must once again ask your forgiveness for entering into all these details. I have punctually paid you the interest of the funds which you placed in my hands. I can even say, without wishing to hurt your feelings, that I merely looked upon that interest as your pocket-money, paying your expenses, and never asking you to contribute your share of the household disbursements."

He paused. Renée suffered as she looked at him, while he made a large hole in the cinders to bring the end of a log among them. He was approaching a delicate matter.

"As you will understand, I was obliged to make your money yield a high interest. The funds are in safe hands, be assured of that. As for the amount coming from your property in Sologne, it partly served to pay for the house we live in, the remainder is invested in an excellent affair, the Société Générale of the Ports of Morocco. We are not settling accounts, are we? but I want to prove to you that very often we poor husbands are not judged at our worth."

A powerful motive must have impelled him to lie a little less than usual. The truth was that Renée's dowry had for a long time ceased to exist; it had simply become a fictitious asset in Saccard's safe. Although he paid the interest at the rate of two or three hundred per cent, he could not have produced a single security, or have found the smallest solid particle of the original capital. As he half confessed, the five hundred thousand francs derived from the Sologne property had served to give something on account for the house and the furniture, which between them had cost nearly two millions of francs. Saccard still owed a million to the upholsterer and the builder.

"I don't claim anything from you," said Renée at last, "I know that I owe you a deal of money."

"Oh! my dear," he exclaimed, taking hold of his wife's hand, but without relinquishing the tongs, "what a bad idea you have of me! In two words, now, I have been unlucky at the Bourse, Toutin-Laroche has been playing some foolish pranks, and Mignon and Charrier are a couple of brutes who have swindled me. And that is why I can't pay your bill. You will forgive me, won't you?"

He seemed really moved. He thrust the tongs between the logs and made the sparks dart forth like rockets. Renée remembered how nervous he had seemed for some time past. But she was unable to penetrate the astonishing truth. Saccard had reached the point that he had to accomplish a miracle every day. He resided in a house which had cost two millions of francs, he lived on the footing of a prince's civil list, and yet on certain mornings he had not a thousand francs in his safe. His expenditure did not seem to diminish, however. He lived upon debt among a people of creditors who swallowed up, day by day, the scandalous profits which he realised by certain transactions. In the meantime, at the same moment indeed, companies crumbled around; before him yawned fresh and deeper pits, over which he had to spring, being unable to fill them up. He thus went on over mined ground, amid a continuous crisis, settling bills of fifty thousand francs, and not paying his coachman's wages, still marching on with an assurance which became more and more regal, and emptying over Paris, more ragefully than ever, his empty safe, whence the golden river of legendary source still continued to flow.

The times were momentarily bad for speculation. Saccard was the worthy offspring of the Hôtel de Ville. Like Paris, he had been eager for transformation, feverishly bent upon enjoyment, and blindly lavish in expenditure. And at this moment, like the city itself, he found himself in the presence of a formidable deficit which it was necessary he should make good secretly; for he would not hear speak of sobriety, economy, calm, and simple life. He preferred to retain the useless luxury and real misery of these new thoroughfares, whence he had derived that colossal fortune ushered each morning into being, but always swallowed up when evening came. Passing from adventure to adventure, he now only possessed the gilded façade of an absent capital. In that time of fierce madness, Paris herself did not engage her future with less self-restraint, or march more straightly towards every folly and every financial trickery. The liquidation threatened to be a terrible one.

The finest speculations fell through in Saccard's hands. As he confessed, he had just experienced considerable losses on the Bourse. M. Toutin-Laroche had almost capsized the Crédit Viticole by a "bulling" game which had suddenly turned against him; fortunately the government, intervening secretly, had reset the famous farmers' loan machine on its legs. Saccard—already badly shaken by this double blow, warmly rated by his brother the minister on account of the danger which had threatened the delegation bonds of the city of Paris, compromised at the same time at the Crédit Viticole—was yet even unluckier in his speculations in house property. Mignon and Charrier had altogether ceased dealing with him. If he accused them it was because he was secretly enraged to think that he had blundered by building on his share of the land, whilst they prudently sold theirs. While they were netting a fortune, he remained hampered by his houses which he was often only able to dispose of at a loss. Among others he sold a mansion in the Rue de Marignan, on which he still owed three hundred and eighty thousand francs, for three hundred thousand. He had certainly invented a dodge worthy of him, which consisted in demanding ten thousand francs for a flat worth eight thousand at the most. The frightened tenant only signed a lease when the landlord consented to make him a present of the first two years' rent; the apartment was thus brought down to its real value, but the lease enunciated the figure of ten thousand francs, and when Saccard found a purchaser and capitalized the income of the property the valuation proved most fantastic. He could not apply this swindle on a large scale as his houses did not let; indeed he had built them too soon; the clearings, amid which they were so to say lost, in the mud and the winter cold, isolated them and lowered their value considerably. The affair, which affected Saccard the most, was the vulgar swindle of Messieurs Mignon and Charrier, who bought back from him the mansion which he had been compelled to give up building on the Boulevard Malesherbes. The contractors were at last smitten with the desire of residing on "their Boulevard." As they had sold their share of the building plots at a profit, and scented the embarrassed circumstances of their ex-partner, they offered to rid him of the enclosure in the centre of which the mansion rose to the flooring of the first storey, where the iron girders were partly placed. Only they talked of the solid foundations in cut stone as "useless rubbish," saying that they would have preferred the soil to be bare so as to build upon it according to their taste. Saccard had to sell, without taking the hundred and odd thousand francs which he had already expended into account. And what exasperated him the more was that the contractors would never agree to take the ground back at the rate of two hundred and fifty francs the metre, at which figure it had been valued when the plots were shared. They knocked off twenty-five francs per metre, like those second-hand dealers who will only give four francs for an object which they sold for five the day before. Forty-eight hours later, Saccard had the grief of seeing an army of masons invade the enclosure and continue building upon the so called "useless rubbish."

He thus played the impecunious all the better before his wife, as his affairs were becoming more and more muddled. He was not the man to confess himself for the simple love of truth.

"But if you find yourself embarrassed," said Renée with an air of doubt, "why did you buy me that aigrette and necklace which cost you, I believe, sixty-five thousand francs? I have no use for those jewels and I shall be obliged to ask your permission to dispose of them so as to give Worms something on account."

"Never do that!" he exclaimed nervously. "If you were not seen wearing those jewels at the ball at the ministry to-morrow people would gossip about my position."

He was good-natured that morning, so he ended by smiling and muttering with a wink:

"We speculators, my dear, are like pretty women, we have our little trickeries. Pray keep your aigrette and your necklace for love of me."

He could not tell the story, for although a very amusing one, it was in somewhat questionable taste. Saccard and Laure d'Aurigny had entered into an alliance one night after supper. Laure was head over heels in debt, and was trying to find some nice young man who would kindly elope with her and take her to London. Saccard on his side felt the ground giving way beneath him; his failing imagination sought for an expedient which would show him to the public wallowing on a bed of gold and bank notes. The harlot and the speculator came to an understanding amid the semi-intoxication of dessert. He hit upon the idea of that sale of diamonds which attracted all Paris, and where amid a great fuss he purchased some jewels for his wife. Then with the product of the sale, some four hundred thousand francs, he succeeded in satisfying Laure's creditors who were owed about twice that amount. It may even be believed that he recouped a part of his sixty-five thousand francs. When he was seen liquidating the d'Aurigny's affairs, he was supposed to be her protector, people thought that he had paid her debts in full, and that he was doing all sorts of foolish things for her. Every hand was stretched out to him, and his credit returned, formidable. At the Bourse he was joked about his passion with smiles and allusions which delighted him. Meanwhile, Laure d'Aurigny, brought into notoriety by all this fuss, and with whom he did not even spend a single night, pretended she was deceiving him with eight or ten fools allured by the idea of stealing her from a man of such colossal wealth. In one month she obtained two sets of furniture and more diamonds than she had sold. Saccard had fallen into the habit of going to smoke a cigar at her place of an afternoon on leaving the Bourse; and he often perceived coat tails flying off in terror through the doorways. When he and Laure were alone they could not look at each other without laughing. He kissed her on the forehead as if she were a perverse girl whose knavery delighted him. He did not give her a copper; on the contrary, she once lent him some money to pay a gambling debt.

Renée wished to insist, and spoke of at least pawning the jewels; but her husband made her understand that it was not possible, that all Paris expected to see her wearing them on the morrow. Thereupon the young woman who was greatly worried about Worms's bill tried to devise another expedient.

"But my Charonne affair," she suddenly exclaimed, "it is progressing well, isn't it? You told me only the other day that the profits would be superb. Perhaps Larsonneau would advance me the hundred and thirty-six thousand francs?"

For a minute Saccard had forgotten the tongs between his legs. He now hastily took hold of them again, leant forward and almost disappeared into the fire-place, whence the young woman heard his voice huskily muttering:

"Yes, yes, Larsonneau might perhaps—"

She was at last coming of her own accord to the point to which he had gently tried to lead her since the outset of the conversation. For two years already he had been preparing his masterly stroke in the direction of Charonne. His wife had never consented to part with Aunt Élisabeth's property; she had sworn to the latter that she would keep it intact to bequeath it to her children, should she become a mother. In presence of this obstinacy, the speculator's imagination had set to work and had ended by constructing something poetical—a design of exquisite knavery, a colossal piece of trickery by which the city of Paris, the State, his wife, and even Larsonneau would be victimized. He no longer talked about selling the ground; only he every day deplored the folly of leaving it unproductive, of contenting oneself with an income of two per cent. Renée, always pressed for money, had ended by entertaining the idea of a speculation. Saccard based his operation on the certainty of an approaching expropriation for the cutting of the Boulevard du Prince Eugène, the line of which was not yet clearly decided upon. And then it was that he brought forward his old accomplice Larsonneau, as a partner who made an agreement with his wife on the following basis. She on her side brought the ground representing a value of five hundred thousand francs; and Larsonneau, on his side, undertook to expend a similar sum in building upon this ground a popular music-hall with a large garden where games of all kinds, swings, skittles, and bowls should be installed. The profits were naturally to be divided, just as the losses were to be equally shared. In the event of one of the partners wishing to retire, he might do so by claiming his share, according to the valuation which would be made. Renée seemed surprised by this high figure of five hundred thousand francs, when the ground was worth three hundred thousand at the most. But Saccard made her understand that it was a skilful plan for tying Larsonneau's hands later on, for his buildings would never represent such an amount.

Larsonneau had become an elegant man about town, well gloved, with dazzling linen and astounding neckties. To go about he had a tilbury as light as a piece of clock-work, with a very high seat, and which he drove himself. His offices in the Rue de Rivoli were a set of sumptuous rooms in which one never saw the least portfolio or business paper lying about. His clerks wrote on tables of blackened pear-wood adorned with marquetry and ornaments of chased brass. He had assumed the style and title of an expropriation agent, a new calling which the works of Paris had brought into being. By his connection with the Hôtel de Ville he was informed in advance of the cutting of any new thoroughfares. When he had induced a road inspector to show him the proposed line of route of a new Boulevard, he went to offer his services to the threatened householders. And he brought forward his little plan for increasing the indemnity by acting before the decree of public utility was issued. As soon as a householder accepted his proposals, he took all the expense on himself, drew a plan of the property, brought the affair before the courts and paid an advocate, the whole for a percentage on the difference between the offer made by the city and the indemnity awarded by the jury. To this calling, which after all might be avowed, he annexed several others. He especially practised usury. He was not the usurer of the old school, ragged and dirty, with white expressionless eyes like five franc pieces, and pale lips tightly drawn together like the strings of a purse. He smiled, gave charming glances, had himself dressed by Dusautoy, and went to lunch at Brébant's with his victim, whom he called "My dear fellow" when he offered him an havannah at dessert. At bottom, despite his waistcoats tightly buckled round his waist, Larsonneau was a terrible fellow who, without losing aught of his amiability, would have prosecuted a debtor for payment of a bill until the unfortunate man was reduced to commit suicide.

Saccard would willingly have chosen another partner. But he still entertained anxiety respecting the false inventory which Larsonneau preciously preserved. So he preferred to interest him in the affair, hoping that he would be able to profit by some circumstance to regain possession of this compromising document. Larsonneau built the music-hall, an edifice in planks and plaster, surmounted by little tin belfries which he painted red and yellow. The garden and the games proved successful in the populous district of Charonne. At the end of a couple of years the speculation seemed a prosperous one, although the profits were in reality very small. So far, Saccard had always spoken enthusiastically to his wife concerning the prospects of such a fine idea.

On seeing that her husband did not make up his mind to come out of the fire-place, where his voice was becoming more and more indistinct, Renée exclaimed:

"I shall go to see Larsonneau to-day. It is my only resource."

Thereupon he abandoned the log with which he was struggling.

"The errand's done, my dear," he said smiling. "Don't I forestall all your desires? I saw Larsonneau last night."

"And he promised you the hundred and thirty-six thousand francs?" she asked anxiously.

Between the two flaming logs he was building a mountain of live cinders, delicately taking up the smallest fragments with the tongs, and looking with a satisfied air at the elevation which he raised with infinite art.

"Oh! how fast you go!" he muttered. "A hundred and thirty-six thousand francs make a large sum. Larsonneau is a good fellow, but his means are still limited. He is quite ready to oblige you—"

He paused, blinking his eyes and rebuilding a corner of the elevation which had fallen through. The pastime began to confuse the young woman's ideas. Despite herself she watched the work of her husband whose clumsiness increased. She felt inclined to give him advice. Forgetting Worms, the bill, and her need of money, she ended by exclaiming:

"But place that large bit, there, underneath; the others will then keep up."

Her husband submissively obeyed her, and added:

"He can only find fifty thousand francs. It will always make a nice instalment. Only, he won't mix this affair up with the Charonne one. He is but an intermediary, do you understand, my dear? The person who really lends the money demands enormous interest. He wants a note of hand for eighty thousand francs at six months' date."

And having crowned the height with a pointed cinder he crossed his hands over the tongs and looked fixedly at his wife.

"Eighty thousand francs!" she cried. "But that's robbery! Do you advise me to do anything so foolish?"

"No," he answered plainly. "But, if you are in absolute need of money, I won't forbid it."

He rose up as if he meant to leave the room. Renée, in a state of cruel indecision, looked at her husband, and at the bill which he laid upon the mantelshelf. She ended by taking her poor head in her hands and murmuring:

"Oh! these business matters! My head is splitting, this morning. Well, I shall sign this bill for eighty thousand francs. If I didn't, I should become altogether ill. I know myself, I should spend the day in frightful tortures—I prefer to be foolish at once. It will relieve me."

And she spoke of ringing to have a bill stamp fetched. But he insisted upon rendering her this service in person. No doubt he had the bill stamp in his pocket, for his absence scarcely lasted a couple of minutes. While she was writing at a little table which he had drawn to the fireside, he examined her and an astonished feeling of desire lighted up his eyes. It was very warm in the room, which was still full of the young woman's rising and the scent of her first toilet. Whilst speaking, she had let the folds of the dressing-gown in which she had swathed herself, fall down, and the eyes of her husband, who stood in front of her, glided over her bent head from amid the gold of her hair far down to the whiteness of her neck and bosom. He smiled with a singular air; this ardent fire which had burnt his face, this closed room, the heavy atmosphere of which was impregnated with a scent of love, this yellow hair and this white skin which tempted him with a kind of conjugal disdain, made him dreamy, enlarged the scope of the drama in which he had just played a scene, and prompted some secret voluptuous design in his brutal jobber's flesh.

When his wife held him out the bill, begging him to finish the affair for her, he took it, still looking at her.

"You are bewitchingly beautiful," he murmured.

And as she leant forward to push the table aside, he roughly kissed her on the neck. She gave a little cry. Then she rose up, quivering, trying to laugh, thinking despite of herself of the other's kisses the night before. But he regretted having given her this cabman's kiss, and on leaving he simply pressed her hand in a friendly manner and promised her that she should have the fifty thousand francs that same evening.

Renée dozed all day in front of the fire. At hours of crisis she experienced a creole-like languor; all her turbulent nature became lazy, chilly, benumbed. She shivered, she needed blazing fires, a suffocating heat, which brought little drops of perspiration to her forehead, and tranquillized her. In this burning atmosphere, in this bath of flames, she scarcely suffered; her pain became like a light dream, a vague oppression, the very ambiguity of which ended by becoming voluptuous. It was thus that, until the evening, she lulled her remorse of the night before, in the red glow of the hearth, opposite a terrible fire, which made the furniture around her crack, and at moments deprived her of the consciousness of being. She was able to dream of Maxime as of an inflamed enjoyment, the rays of which burnt her. She had a nightmare of strange amours, amid flaring logs, on beds heated white-hot. Céleste went to and fro about the room with the calm face of a servant with icy blood. She had orders not to admit anyone; and she even kept the door shut to those inseparables, Adeline d'Espanet and Suzanne Haffner, when they called on returning from lunching together at a villa which they had rented at Saint-Germain. However, towards the evening, when Céleste came to inform her mistress that her master's sister, Madame Sidonie, wished to see her, she received orders to show her in.

As a rule Madame Sidonie only called at dusk. And yet her brother had prevailed upon her to wear silk dresses. But no one knew how it happened, although the silk she wore came fresh from the shop, it never looked new; it was shabby, destitute of sheen, and seemed to be in tatters. She had also consented not to bring her basket to Saccard's house, but by way of compensation her pocket always overflowed with papers. She was interested in Renée, whom she was unable to transform into a reasonable customer resigned to the necessities of life. She visited her regularly, wearing the discreet smile of a doctor who does not like to frighten his patient by telling her the name of her disease. She commiserated her little worries, as if they had been petty ailments which she could cure immediately if the young woman only chose. The latter, who was in one of those moments when one feels the need of being pitied, simply received her to tell her that she had intolerable pains in her head.

"Why, my beauty," muttered Madame Sidonie, as she glided through the shade of the room, "why, you are stifling here! Still your neuralgic pains, eh? It's worry. You take life too much to heart."

"Yes, I have a great deal of worry," replied Renée.

Night was coming on. She had not allowed Céleste to light the lamp. The fire alone shed a grand red glow which fully illuminated her, as she reclined in her white dressing-gown, the lace of which had a pinkish tinge. At the edge of the shade one could just see an end of Madame Sidonie's black dress, and her two crossed hands encased in grey cotton gloves. Her soft voice emerged out of the darkness.

"Still worry about money?" she said, in a tone full of gentleness and pity, just as if she had spoken of the worries of the heart.

Renée lowered her eyelids, and made a gesture of avowal.

"Ah! if my brothers listened to me!" said Madame Sidonie, "we should all be rich. But they shrug their shoulders whenever I speak to them about that debt of three milliards, you know. Still I have good hopes. For the last ten years I have been wanting to make a journey to England, but I have so little time for myself. Anyhow I recently made up my mind to write to London, and I am waiting for the answer."

And as the young woman smiled:

"I know you are incredulous as well. Still you would be very pleased if I made you a present of a pretty million one of these days. Oh! the story is simple enough: it was a Paris banker who lent the money to the son of the King of England, and as the banker died without leaving any direct heirs, the State can now-a-days claim the reimbursement of the debt with compound interest. I have calculated it—it amounts to two milliards nine hundred and forty-three millions two hundred and ten thousand francs. It will come, it will come; never fear!"

"In the meantime," said the young woman with a dash of irony, "you ought to obtain me a hundred thousand francs. I could then pay my tailor, who is greatly worrying me!"

"A hundred thousand francs can be found," replied Madame Sidonie, quietly. "It is only a question of paying for them."

The fire was glowing. Renée, feeling more and more languid, stretched out her legs, and showed the tips of her slippers at the edge of her dressing-gown, while the woman of business resumed in her commiserating voice:

"Poor dear, you are really not reasonable. I know a great many women, but I have never seen a single one so careless about her health as you are. For instance, that little Michelin, there's one who knows how to manage. In spite of myself I think of you when I see her so happy and well. Do you know that Monsieur de Saffré is madly in love with her, and that he has already given her presents worth nearly ten thousand francs? I believe that her dream is to have a country house."

Madame Sidonie was growing more animated, and fumbled in her pocket.

"I still have about me a letter from a poor young woman. If we had a light I would let you read it. Just fancy, her husband doesn't provide for her. She had accepted some bills, and she has been obliged to borrow from a gentleman I know. It was I who rescued the promissory notes from the lawyer's clutches, and it wasn't an easy matter. The poor children, do you think they are wrong? I receive them at my place as if they were my son and daughter."

"You know a money-lender?" asked Renée negligently.

"I know ten. Between women one can say a number of things, can't one? and it isn't because your husband is my brother that I excuse his conduct in running after strumpets and leaving a beautiful woman like you to mope at the fireside. That Laure d'Aurigny costs him a fortune. It wouldn't astonish me if he had refused you money. He *has* refused you, hasn't he? Oh, the wretch!"

Renée listened complacently to this voice which emerged out of the shade like the vague echo of her own dreams. With her eyelids half lowered, almost recumbent in her arm-chair, she no longer realised that Madame Sidonie was there; she fancied she dreamt that evil thoughts had come to her and tempted her with infinite gentleness; meanwhile the other spoke on at length, and her voice was like a monotonous flow of lukewarm water.

"It was Madame de Lauwerens who spoilt your life," she said. "You wouldn't believe me. Oh! you wouldn't be reduced to cry by your fireside if you hadn't mistrusted me; and I love you like my eyes, my beauty. You have a bewitching foot. You will no doubt laugh at me, but I must tell you my folly. When I haven't seen you for three days I am absolutely impelled to come and admire you. Yes, I lack something; I feel the need of feasting my eyes on your beautiful hair, your face which is so white and delicate, and your slim waist. Really I have never seen anyone else with such a figure."

Renée ended by smiling. Her lovers themselves had not shown such warmth, such pious ecstasy in speaking to her of her beauty. Madame Sidonie observed her smile.

"Come, it's agreed," she said, rising hastily. "I run on and on and forget that I make your head split. You will come to-morrow, won't you? We will talk over money matters; we will find a lender. You hear me? I'm determined that you shall be happy."

The young woman, still motionless and enervated by the heat, answered after a pause, as if she had had to make a laborious effort to understand what was being said around her:—

"Yes, yes, it's agreed, and we will have a chat; but not to-morrow. Worms will be satisfied with something on account. When he worries me again, we will see. Don't talk to me about all that now. Business has made my head split."

Madame Sidonie seemed greatly vexed. She was on the point of sitting down again and resuming her coaxing monologue, but Renée's weary attitude decided her to defer the attack till another occasion. She drew a handful of papers out of her pocket, searched among them, and ended by finding an object enclosed in a kind of pink box.

"I came to recommend you a new soap," she said, resuming her business voice. "I take a great interest in the inventor, who is a charming young man. It is a very soft soap, very good for the skin. You will try it, won't you! And you will speak of it to your friends—I will leave it there on your mantelshelf."

She had gone to the door when she returned again, and standing upright amid the rosy glow of the fire which lighted up her waxen face, she began to praise an elastic belt, an invention intended to take the place of stays.

"It gives you a perfectly round waist, a true wasp's waist," she said. "I saved it from bankruptcy. When you come, you will try the specimens, won't you? I had to run about among solicitors during a whole week. The documents are in my pocket and I am now going to my lawyer to have the last attachment raised—Good-bye for the present, pretty one. Remember that I am waiting for you and that I want to dry your beautiful eyes."

She glided away and disappeared. Renée did not even hear her close the door. She remained there, before the dying fire, continuing her dream of the whole day, with her head full of dancing cyphers, while in the distance she heard the voices of Saccard and Madame Sidonie who offered her considerable sums in the tone with which an auctioneer invites bids for a lot of furniture. She felt her husband's rough kiss on her neck, and when she turned round she fancied the other was there at her feet, with her black dress and her flabby face, making passionate speeches to her, praising her perfections, and begging for an appointment with the attitude of a lover past resignation. This made her smile. The heat became more and more stifling in the room. And the young woman's torpor, the strange dreams she made, were but a light, an artificial sleep, amid which she always beheld the little private room on the Boulevard, and the broad divan against which she had fallen on her knees. She no longer suffered at all. When she raised her eyelids again Maxime's image passed through the rosy mass of fire.

At the ministers' ball, on the morrow, beautiful Madame Saccard looked marvellous. Worms had accepted the fifty thousand francs on account, and she emerged from this pecuniary worry with the laughter of convalescence. When she crossed the reception rooms in her robe of pink faille with a long Louis XIV train, edged with deep white lace, there was a murmur, and the men shoved one another aside to see her. Her intimate friends bent low with a discreet, knowing smile, rendering homage to those beautiful shoulders with which all official Paris was so well acquainted, and which were, indeed the firm columns of the Empire. She had bared her bosom with such a contempt for other people's looks, she walked by so tender and so gentle in her nudity, that it was almost not indecent. Eugène Rougon, the great politician, who felt that his sister-in-law's bare bosom was even more eloquent than his speeches in the chamber, softer and more persuasive in making people appreciate the charms of the reign and converting sceptics, went to compliment her on her happy audacity in lowering her dress-body a couple of finger-breadths. Almost all the Corps Législatif was there, and by the way that the deputies looked at the young woman, the minister made up his mind that he should have a fine success on the morrow in the delicate question of the loans of the city of Paris. People could not vote against a power which, on the hotbed of millions, reared such a flower as this Renée, so strange a flower of voluptuousness, with silken flesh and statuesque nudity, a living enjoyment that left a scent of tepid pleasure behind. But what made the whole ball whisper were the necklace and the aigrette. The men recognised the jewels and the women furtively called each other's attention to them with their eyes. These diamonds were the one subject of talk throughout the evening. And in the white light of the chandeliers, the reception rooms stretched away, filled with a resplendent throng which looked like a jumble of stars huddled into too small a corner of space.

At about one o'clock Saccard disappeared. He had enjoyed his wife's success like a man whose clap-trap succeeds. He had again consolidated his credit. A business matter required his presence at Laure d'Aurigny's so he went off, begging Maxime to take Renée home after the ball.

Maxime spent the evening soberly beside Louise de Mareuil, both of them very much occupied in saying frightful things about the women who passed by. And when they had said something rather stronger than usual, they stifled their laughter in their pocket handkerchiefs. Renée had to come to ask the young fellow for his arm when she wished to leave. She was nervously gay in the carriage; she still quivered with all the intoxication of the light, the perfumes, and the noise that she had just left. She moreover seemed to have forgotten their "nonsense" of the Boulevard as Maxime called it. She only asked him in a strange tone of voice:

"Is that little hunchback Louise so very funny then?"

"Oh! very funny," replied the young man, beginning to laugh again. "You saw the Duchess de Sternich with a yellow bird in her hair, didn't you? Well, Louise pretends that it is an automatic bird which flaps its wings every hour and cries: 'Cuckoo! Cuckoo!' to the poor duke."

This jest coming from a girl who had just left school seemed very comical to Renée. When they reached the house, as Maxime was about to take his leave, she said to him:

"Aren't you coming up? Céleste has no doubt prepared me something to eat."

He ascended in his usual easy manner. Upstairs however there was nothing to eat and Céleste had gone to bed. Renée had to light the tapers in a little candelabrum. Her hand slightly trembled.

"That foolish girl," she said, speaking of her maid. "She must have misunderstood my orders—I shall never be able to undress myself unhelped."

She passed into the dressing room. Maxime followed her to relate another remark of Louise's which had just recurred to his mind. He was as much at his ease as if he had stayed late at a friend's and was looking for his cigar-case to light an havannah. But when Renée had set the candelabrum down she turned round and fell, speechless and portentous, into the young man's arms, pressing her mouth upon his own.

Renée's private suite of rooms was a nest of silk and lace, a marvel of coquettish luxury. A tiny boudoir preceded the bedroom. The two apartments formed but one, or rather the boudoir was scarcely more than the threshold of the bedroom, a large alcove, furnished with couches and having a pair of curtains instead of a door. The walls in both apartments were hung with flax-tinted silken stuff, embroidered with huge bouquets of roses, white lilac and buttercups. The curtains and door-hangings were of Venetian lace over a silken lining formed alternately of grey and pink bands. In the bedroom the white marble chimney piece, a real jewel, displayed like a flower bed its incrustations of lapis lazuli and precious mosaics repeating the roses, white lilac and buttercups of the hangings. A large grey and pink bed, the padded and upholstered woodwork of which was not seen, and the head of which stood against the wall, filled quite one-half of the room with its flow of drapery, lace and silk, brocaded with bouquets and falling from the ceiling to the carpet. You would have taken it for a woman's dress, rounded, scalloped, decked with puffs, bows, and flounces; and the large curtain swelling out like a skirt made you dream of some tall love-sick wench, leaning back, fainting away, and almost sinking upon the pillows. Under the curtains it was quite a sanctuary—plaited cambric, a snowy mass of lace, all sorts of delicate transparent things, enveloped in a church-like dimness. Beside the bedstead, this monument the devout amplitude of which suggested a chapel adorned for some festival, the other articles of furniture, some low seats, a cheval glass six feet high, and chiffoniers provided with a multitude of drawers, subsided into nothingness. On the floor the bluish-grey carpet was studded with pale full-blown roses. And on either side of the bed lay two large black bearskins, edged with pink velvet, having silver claws, and with their heads turned towards the window, gazing fixedly at the empty sky through their glass eyes.

Soft harmony, muffled silence reigned in this room. No high note, no metallic reflection or bright gilding broke into the dreamy scale of pink and grey. Even the chimney ornaments, the frame of the mirror, the clock, the little candelabra, were of old Sèvres, and their mountings of gilt copper were barely visible. These ornaments were marvels, the clock especially, with its circle of podgy cupids, who descended and leaned around the dial like a band of naked urchins careless to the rapid flight of time. This discreet luxury, these colours and objects which Renée's taste had chosen soft and smiling, lent a crepuscular appearance to the room, the dimness of an alcove with the curtains drawn. It seemed as if the bed stretched afar, as if the whole room, indeed, were one huge bed with its carpets, bearskins, stuffed seats and padded hangings, prolonging the softness of the floor up the walls to the ceiling. And, as in a bed, the young woman left the imprint, the warmth and the perfume of her body upon all the things. When one drew aside the double hangings screening the room from the boudoir it seemed as if one raised some silken counterpane, and entered some vast couch still warm and moist, where one found on the fine linen the adorable figure, the slumber and dreams of a Parisian woman of thirty.

An adjoining spacious apartment, hung with old chintz, was simply furnished all round with lofty wardrobes containing Renée's army of dresses. Céleste, who was very methodical, classified the dresses according to their age, ticketed them and introduced arithmetic amid all her mistress's yellow or blue caprices, and kept the apartment in a state of vestry-like impressiveness and stable-like cleanliness. Beyond the wardrobes, there was not an article of furniture, and no finery was left lying about. The wardrobe doors shone cold and clean like the varnished panels of a brougham.

The marvel of the suite, however, the apartment that all Paris talked about, was the dressing-room. Folks said: "Beautiful Madame Saccard's dressing room," as one says; "The Gallery of Mirrors at Versailles." This apartment was situated in one of the towers of the mansion, just over the little buttercup drawing-room. On entering it one fancied oneself in a large circular tent, a fairy-like tent, pitched in full phantasy by some love-sick amazone. In the centre of the ceiling a crown of chased silver held up the drapery of the tent, which extended cupola-like to the walls, and then fell straight to the floor. This drapery, these rich hangings, were formed of pink silk covered with a muslin of a very open texture, which was caught in plaits at intervals. A band of lace separated the plaits, and silver fillets descended from the crown and glided along the hangings on either side of each of these bands. Here the pinkish grey of the bedroom grew brighter, became a pinkish white, like naked flesh. And in this bower of lace, beneath these curtains which hid all the ceiling save a bluish cavity inside the small circle described by the crown, where Chaplin had painted a laughing cupid, looking down and preparing his dart, one could have fancied oneself at the bottom of a sweetmeat box, or in some precious jewel-case, enlarged and made to display the nudity of a woman instead of the brilliancy of a diamond. The carpet of snowy whiteness stretched around without the least flowery design. A wardrobe with plate glass doors, and the two panels of which were mounted with silver; a couch, two arm-chairs, some white satin stools; a large toilet table, with a slab of pink marble, and the legs of which where screened by flounces of muslin and lace, furnished the room. The glasses, the vases, and the basin on the toilet table, were of old Bohemian crystal, streaked pink and white. And there was yet another table, incrusted with silver like the wardrobe, and on which all the implements, the toilet utensils, were ranged; it was like a strange surgical case, displaying a large number of little instruments, the purpose of which was not readily guessed—back scrapers, shining brushes, files of every dimension and every shape, straight and curved scissors, every variety of pincers and pins. Each one of these objects in silver and ivory was marked with Renée's monogram.

But the dressing-room had one delightful corner, and to that corner especially did it owe its fame. In front of the window the folds of the tent parted, and in a kind of alcove, of considerable length but limited breadth, one espied a bath, a tank of pink marble, embedded in the flooring and with its sides—chamfered like those of a large shell— rising to a level with the carpet. One descended into the bath by marble steps. Above the silver taps, shaped like swans' heads, a Venetian mirror, frameless, but with curved edges and a design ground in the crystal, filled the back of the alcove. Renée took a bath of a few minutes' duration every morning, and this bath filled the dressing-room with moisture, with a perfume of fresh, wet flesh for the whole day. At times an open scent bottle, a piece of soap left out of its dish, lent a dash of something stronger to this rather insipid smell. The young woman liked to remain there, almost in a state of nudity, until noon. The round tent itself was also naked. The pink bath, the pink tables and basins, the muslin of the ceiling and the walls, beneath which one seemed to see pink blood coursing, acquired the roundness of flesh, the curves of bare shoulders and bosoms; and, according to the hour of the day, one would liken the apartment to the snowy skin of a child or to the warm skin of a woman. It was one vast nudity. When Renée left her bath her fair form lent but a little more pink to all the rosy flesh of the room.

It was Maxime who undressed her. He understood that kind of thing, and his nimble hands divined pins, and glided round her waist with innate science. He let down her locks, took off her diamonds, and then dressed her hair for the night. And as he mingled jokes and caresses with his duties of chambermaid and hair-dresser, Renée laughed with a greasy stifled laugh, while the silk of her dress-body rustled and her petticoats were loosened one by one. When she saw herself naked, she blew out the tapers of the candelabrum, caught hold of Maxime round the body and all but carried him into the bedroom. The ball had completed her intoxication, and in her fever she was conscious of the previous day which she had spent by the fireside, of that day of ardent torpor and vague and smiling dreams. She still heard Saccard's and Madame Sidonie's voices talking, calling out figures through their noses like lawyers. It was these people who bored her, who drove her to crime. And even now, when in the depths of the vast dark bed she sought for Maxime's lips, she still saw him amid the fire of the day before looking at her with scorching eyes.

The young fellow only went off at six o'clock in the morning. She gave him the key of the little gate of the Parc Monceaux and made him swear to come back every night. The dressing-room communicated with the buttercup drawing-room by a little staircase hidden in the wall, and connecting all the apartments of the tower. From the buttercup room it was easy to pass into the conservatory and thence reach the park.

On going out at dawn, amid a thick fog, Maxime was somewhat stupefied by his good fortune. He accepted it, however, with his usual complaisance as a neutral being.

"So much the worse!" thought he, "it's she who wishes it, after all. She's deucedly well formed; and she was quite right, she's twice as funny in bed as Sylvia is."

They had glided to incest from the day when Maxime, in his threadbare collegian's tunic, had hung on Renée's neck, creasing her *garde française* habit. From that time forward there had been a prolonged perversion of every minute between them. The strange education which the young woman gave the child; the familiarities which made them boon comrades; later on the smiling audacity of their confidential chats; all this perilous promiscuity had ended by linking them together with a strange bond, the joys of friendship almost becoming carnal satisfactions. They had surrendered themselves to each other for years; the brutish act was but the acute crisis of this unconscionable malady of passion. Amid the maddened society in which they lived, their crime had sprouted as upon a rich dung-heap full of impure juices; it had developed itself with a strange refinement amid a particular kind of debauchery.

When the roomy carriage conveyed them to the Bois, and rolled them gently along the pathways, whispering smutty things into each other's ears, diving back into their childhood in search of the dirty practices of instinct—it was but a deviation, but an unconfessed mode of satisfying their desires. They felt themselves to be vaguely guilty, as if they had just slightly touched one another; and this original sin, this languor born of dirty conversation, though it wearied them with voluptuous fatigue, titillated them even more softly than plain positive kisses. Their familiarity was thus a slow lover's march which was fatally destined to lead them some day or other to the private room at the Café Riche and to Renée's large grey and pink bed. When they found themselves in each other's arms they did not even feel the shock of sin. One would have said that they were lovers of long standing whose kisses were full of recollections. And they had spent so much time in a contact of their whole beings, that despite themselves they talked of the past which was so full of their ignorant tenderness.

"Do you recollect the day when I came to Paris?" said Maxime; "you wore a funny costume; and I traced an angle on your bosom with my finger, and I advised you to open your dress, in a point. I felt your skin under your chemisette, and my finger embedded itself a little. It was very nice."

Renée laughed, kissing him and murmuring:

"You were already awfully vicious. How you did amuse us at Worms's—do you recollect? We used to call you 'our little man.' I always believed that fat Suzanne would have readily yielded to you, if the marchioness hadn't watched her with such furious eyes."

"Ah! yes, we had some good laughs," muttered the young fellow. "The photographic album, eh? And all the rest, our rambles through Paris, our snacks at the pastry cook's on the Boulevard; those little strawberry tarts which you liked so much, you know? For myself I shall always remember the afternoon when you related to me Adeline's adventure at the convent when she wrote letters to Suzanne, signing herself 'Arthur d'Espanet,' like a man, and proposing to carry her off."

The lovers again grew merry over this good story, and then Maxime continued in his coaxing voice:

"When you came to fetch me at the college in your carriage, we must have looked funny both of us. I was so small that I disappeared under your skirts."

"Yes, yes," she stammered, quivering, and drawing the young fellow towards her, "it was very nice, as you say. We loved each other without knowing it, eh? I realised it before you did. The other day, on returning from the Bois, my leg rubbed against yours, and I started. But you didn't notice anything, eh? You didn't think of me?"

"Oh, yes, I did," he replied, a little embarrassed. "Only I didn't know, you understand—I didn't dare—"

He lied. The idea of possessing Renée had never plainly occurred to him. He had rubbed up against her with all his vice, without really desiring her. He was too feeble for such an effort. He accepted Renée because she imposed herself upon him, and he had glided to her couch without willing or foreseeing it. When he had rolled there, however, he remained there, because it was warm, and because he habitually forgot himself at the bottom of all the holes into which he fell. At the outset he even tasted some satisfactions of self-love. She was the first married woman that he had possessed. He did not reflect that her husband was his father.

But Renée brought with her, in sinning, all the ardour of a heart which has lost caste. She also had slided down the slope. Only she had not rolled as far as the bottom like a mass of inert flesh. Desire had been kindled within her when it was too late to resist it and when the fall had become inevitable. This fall abruptly appeared to her as one of the necessities of her boredom, as a rare extreme enjoyment which alone could rouse her tired senses, her wounded heart. It was during that autumnal promenade, in the twilight, when the Bois was falling asleep, that the vague idea of incest came to her, like a titillation which lent an unknown quiver to her skin; and in the evening, in the semi-intoxication of the dinner, this idea, lashed by jealousy, became precise, rose up ardently before her, amid the flames of the conservatory, as she watched Maxime and Louise. At that hour she desired sin, the sin which no one commits, the sin which would fill her empty life, and finally set her in that hell of which she was still afraid, just as she had been when she was a little girl. Then on the morrow, by a strange sentiment of remorse and lassitude, she no longer wished it. It seemed to her as if she had already sinned, that it was not so nice as she had fancied, and that it would really be too dirty. The crisis was bound to be fatal, to come from herself, apart from those two beings, those comrades who were destined to deceive each other one fine evening, and to couple themselves, thinking they were merely exchanging a hand-shake. However, after this stupid fall, she returned to her dream of a nameless pleasure, and then she took Maxime in her arms again, inquisitive about him, inquisitive as to the cruel delights of a love which she regarded as a crime. Her volition accepted incest, required it, decided upon tasting it to the end, even to remorse should that ever come. She was active, and conscious of her doings. She loved with the fury of a great fashionable lady, with the nervous prejudices she possessed as an offspring of the middle classes, with all the struggles, joys, and disgusts of a woman who drowns herself in self-disdain.

Maxime returned every night. He came by way of the garden at about one o'clock. Renée usually awaited him in the conservatory, which he had to cross to reach the little drawing-room. They, moreover, displayed perfect audacity, barely concealing themselves, and forgetting the most classical precautions of adultery. It is true that this corner of the house belonged to them. Baptiste, the husband's valet, alone had a right to enter it; and Baptiste, like a serious man, took himself off as soon as his duties were over. Maxime even pretended with a laugh that he withdrew to go and write his memoirs. One night, however, when the young fellow had just arrived, Renée shewed him Baptiste, who was solemnly crossing the drawing-room with a candlestick in his hand. The tall valet, with his minister-like figure, lighted by the yellow glow of the wax, had a more dignified and severe physiognomy than usual. As the lovers leaned forward, they saw him blow out his candle and go towards the stables, where the horses and ostlers were asleep.

"He is going his round," said Maxime.

Renée remained quivering. Baptiste usually alarmed her. It often happened to her to say that, with his coldness and his clear glances which never fell upon women's shoulders, he was the only honest man in the house.

They then evinced some prudence in seeing each other. They closed the doors of the little drawing-room, and were able to dispose of this room, with the conservatory and Renée's apartments, in all tranquillity. It was a little world. And during the earlier months they there tasted the most refined, the most delicately sought-for delights. They promenaded their amours from the large grey and pink bed of the sleeping-room, to the white and rosy nudity of the dressing-room, and to the pale yellow symphony of the little drawing-room. Each chamber, with its particular scent, its hangings, its special life, lent them a different form of tenderness, and made Renée a different lover. She was delicate and pretty on her padded great lady's couch, in the warm aristocratic bedroom where love underwent a tasteful attenuation; she showed herself a capricious, carnal female under the flesh-coloured tent, amid the perfume and damp languor of the bath, on leaving which she surrendered herself to Maxime, who preferred her thus; then downstairs, in the bright sunrise of the little drawing-room, amid the yellow aurora which gilded her hair, she became a goddess with her fair Diana-like head, her bare arms which assumed chaste postures, her beauteous form which reclined on the couches in attitudes revealing noble outlines of antique gracefulness. But there was a spot which Maxime was almost frightened of, and where Renée only led him on evil days, the days when she felt the need of more bitter intoxication. Then they loved in the conservatory. It was there that they tasted incest.

One night, in an hour of anguish, the young woman had compelled her lover to go and fetch one of the black bearskins. Then they had stretched themselves on this inky fur, at the edge of an ornamental basin in the large circular pathway. Out of doors it was freezing terribly amid the limpid moonlight. Maxime had arrived shivering, with frozen ears and fingers, and the conservatory was heated to such a point that he fainted on the bearskin. Coming from the dry biting cold, he entered into so heavy a flame that he felt a smarting as if he had been whipped with a rod. When he recovered himself, he saw Renée kneeling, leaning over him with fixed eyes and a brutish attitude which frightened him. With her hair down and her shoulders bare, she was resting herself on her fists, with her figure stretched out, and looking like a huge cat with phosphorescent eyes. Above the shoulders of this adorable, amorous animal gazing at him, the young fellow, lying on his back, perceived the marble sphinx, with her glistening hips lighted by the moon. Renée had the attitude and the smile of the feminine-headed monster, and in her loosened skirts, she looked like the white sister of this black deity.

Maxime remained supine. The heat was suffocating; it was a dull heat, which did not fall from the sky in a rain of fire, but trailed on the ground, like some unhealthy exhalation, and its steam ascended like a storm-charged cloud. A warm humidity covered the lovers with a kind of dew, an ardent sweat. For a long time they remained motionless and speechless in this bath of flame, Maxime flat and inert, Renée quivering on her wrists as on supple nervous hams. Outside, through the little panes of the conservatory, one caught glimpses of the Parc Monceaux, of the clumps of trees with fine black outlines, of the grass lawns as white as frozen lakes—quite a dead landscape, the delicate light tints of which reminded one of bits of Japanese engravings. And this spot of burning soil, this inflamed couch on which the lovers were stretched, boiled strangely amid the great mute cold.

They passed a night of mad love. Renée was the man, the passionate acting will. Maxime submitted. What with his lank limbs, his graceful slimness, like that of a Roman youth, this neutral, fair-haired pretty being, stricken in his virility since childhood, became a big girl in the young woman's inquisitive arms. He seemed to have been born and to have grown up for a perversion of love. Renée enjoyed her domination, and with her passion she bent this creature, whose sexuality always seemed indeterminate. For her it was a constant astonishment of desire, a surprise of the senses, a strange sensation of uncomfortableness and acute pleasure. She no longer knew what he was; and she thought doubtingly of his fine skin, his fleshy neck, his abandonment and fainting fits. She then enjoyed an hour of repletion. By revealing to her an unknown ecstasy, Maxime completed her foolish toilets, her prodigious luxury, her mad life. He set in her flesh the high note which she already heard singing around her. He was the lover who matched the fashions and follies of the period. This pretty young fellow whose puny figure was revealed by his attire, this man who ought to have been a girl, who strolled on the Boulevards, his hair parted in the middle, with little bursts of laughter and bored smiles, became in Renée's hands the instrument of one of those debaucheries suited to days of decline, and which among rotten nations, at certain periods, use up flesh and unsettle intelligence.

And it was especially in the conservatory that Renée was the man. That ardent night they spent there was followed by several others. The conservatory loved and burnt with them. Amid the heavy atmosphere, in the whitish moonlight, they saw the strange world of plants around them, moving confusedly and exchanging embraces. The black bearskin stretched right across the pathway. At their feet the basin steamed full of a swarming, a thick entanglement, of roots, while the rosy stars of the Nymphæa opened on the surface of the water like virgin bodices, and the bushy Tornelias drooped like the hair of languishing water nymphs. Then around them, the palms and the lofty Indian bamboos rose up towards the arched roof, near which they leaned and mingled their leaves together, assuming the unsteady attitudes of tired lovers. Lower down the ferns, the Pteris, the Alsophilas looked like green ladies with ample skirts trimmed with symmetrical flounces, and who, mute and motionless at the edge, of the pathway, awaited love. Beside them the twisted red-spotted foliage of the Begonias, and the white leaves shaped like lance heads of the Caladiums, furnished a vague suite of bruises and pallidities, which the lovers could not explain to themselves, but amid which they at times discerned roundnesses like those of hips and knees wallowing on the ground, beneath the brutality of bleeding caresses. And the Bananas, bending with the weight of their bunches of fruit, spoke to them of the rich fertility of the soil, while the Abyssinian Euphorbia, the prickly, deformed, tapering stems of which—covered with horrid excrescences—they could espy in the darkness, seemed to perspire with sap, with the overflowing flux of their fiery growth. But by degrees as the lovers' glances dived into the corners of the conservatory, the darkness was filled with a more furious debauchery of leaves and stems; they could not distinguish on the stages the Marantas, soft like velvet, the Gloxinias with violet bells, the Dracænas resembling blades of old varnished lacquer; it was a round dance of living plants pursuing each other with unquenched tenderness. At the four corners, at the point where the curtains of tropical creepers formed arbours, their carnal fancy grew madder again, and the supple shoots of the Vanillas, the Indian berries, the Quisqualis and the Bauhinias seemed to be the interminable arms of lovers who could not be seen, but who distractedly lengthened their embrace to draw all scattered delights towards them. These endless arms drooped with lassitude, locked together in a spasm of love, sought for each other, entwined together like a crowd bent on copulation. It was, indeed, the immense copulation of the conservatory, of this bit of virgin forest ablaze with the foliage and the flowers of the tropics.

Maxime and Renée, with their senses perverted, felt themselves carried away amid these mighty nuptials of nature. The soil burnt their backs through the bearskin, and drops of heat fell upon them from the lofty palms. The sap which arose in the tree trunks penetrated them as well, and imparted to them mad desires of immediate growth, of gigantic procreation. They took part in the copulation of the conservatory. It was then, in the pale glimmer, that visions stupefied them, nightmares amid which, during long intervals, they beheld the amours of the palms and ferns; the foliage assumed a confused, equivocal aspect, which their desires transformed into something sensual; murmurs, whispers were wafted to them from the clumps of shrubs, faint voices, sighs of ecstasy, stifled cries of pain, distant laughter, all that was noisy in their own kisses and that echo sent them back. At times they thought themselves shaken by an earthquake, as if the earth itself, in a crisis of satisfied desire, had burst forth into voluptuous sobs.

If they had closed their eyes, if the suffocating heat and the pale light had not imparted to them a depravation of every sense, the aromas alone would have sufficed to throw them into an extraordinary state of nervous erethism. The basin enveloped them in a deep pungent aroma, amid which passed the thousand perfumes of the flowers and the foliage. At times the Vanilla sang with dove-like cooings; then came the rough notes of the Stanhopeas whose streaked mouths had the same strong-smelling bitter breath as a convalescent. The orchids, in their baskets secured by wire chains, also breathed like animated incense burners. But the odour that predominated, the odour in which all these vague breaths were mingled, was a human odour, an odour of love, which Maxime recognised when he kissed Renée on the nape of her neck, when he plunged his head into her flowing hair. And they remained intoxicated by this scent, the scent of an amorous woman, which trailed through the conservatory as in an alcove where earth might be engaged in procreation.

As a rule, the lovers lay down under the Tanghinia from Madagascar, under the poisoned shrub, a leaf of which the young woman once had bitten. Around them the white statues laughed, gazing at the mighty coupling of foliage. The moon, as it turned, displaced the groups, and animated the drama with its changing light. They were a thousand leagues from Paris, far from the easy life of the Bois de Boulogne and official drawing-rooms, in a corner of some Indian forest, of some monstrous temple, of which the black marble sphinx became the deity.

ÉMILE ZOLA

They felt themselves rolling to crime, to accursed love, to wild-beast tenderness. All the pullulation which surrounded them, the swarming of the basin, the naked immodesty of the foliage, threw them fully into the Dantesque hell of passion. It was then, in the depths of this glass cage, boiling over with the flames of summer, lost amid the clear coldness of December, that they tasted incest, as though it had been the criminal fruit of some over-heated soil, feeling the while a dim fear of their terrifying couch.

And in the centre of the black bearskin Renée's body seemed whiter, as she crouched like a huge cat with her back stretched out, and her wrists extended like supple nervous shins. She was all swollen with voluptuousness, and the light outlines of her shoulders and loins stood out with feline angularity against the inky stain which blackened the yellow sand of the pathway with its fur. She watched Maxime, this prey extended beneath her, who abandoned himself, and whom she possessed completely. And from time to time, she abruptly leant forward and kissed him with her irritated mouth. Her lips then parted with the greedy bleeding brilliancy of the Chinese Hibiscus, the expanse of which covered the side of the mansion. She was then nothing but a burning daughter of the conservatory. Her kisses bloomed and faded like those red flowers of the gigantic mallow which last barely a few hours, and which ever spring to life again, like the bruised insatiable lips of a giant Messalina.

V

The kiss which Saccard had imprinted on his wife's neck preoccupied him. He had not availed himself of his marital rights for a long time. The rupture had come quite naturally, neither the one nor the other caring for a connection which interfered with their habits. For Saccard to think of returning to Renée's room, some good stroke of business must necessarily be the object of his conjugal tenderness.

The Charonne affair, from which he hoped to derive a fortune, was progressing favourably, though he had some anxiety as to its termination. Larsonneau, with his dazzling shirt-front, smiled in a manner that displeased him. The expropriation agent was a simple go-between—a man of straw, whom he intended to remunerate for his obligingness with a commission of ten per cent on the ultimate profits. However, although the agent had not invested a copper in the enterprise, and although Saccard had taken every precaution—such as a deed of retrocession, letters, the dates of which had been left in blank, and receipts given in advance—he nevertheless experienced an inward fear, a presentiment of some treachery. He scented that his accomplice intended to blackmail him with the help of that false inventory which he preciously preserved, and to which alone he was indebted for his share in the enterprise.

However, the two accomplices shook hands vigorously. Larsonneau styled Saccard his "dear master." He had, at the bottom of his heart, a real admiration for this equilibrist, and watched his performances on the tight rope of speculation like a connoisseur. The idea of duping him titillated him like some rare and spicy voluptuousness. He caressed a plan which was still vague, however, for he did not very well know how to employ the weapon he possessed, and he feared wounding himself with it. Besides, he felt that he was at the mercy of his ex-colleague. The ground and the buildings, which carefully prepared inventories already valued at nearly two millions of francs, though they were not worth a quarter of that amount, must end by being swallowed up in a colossal bankruptcy, if the fairy of expropriation did not touch them with her golden wand. According to the original plans which the two confederates had been able to consult, the new Boulevard, opened in view of connecting the artillery depôt of Vincennes with the Prince Eugène barracks, and of bringing the guns and ammunition into the heart of Paris without passing through the Faubourg Saint-Antoine, would cross a part of the ground; but it was still to be feared that only a corner of the latter might be cut off, and that the ingenious speculation of the music hall would fall through by reason of its very impudence. In that case Larsonneau would remain with a delicate matter to deal with. Still this peril did not prevent him, despite the secondary part which he played perforce, from feeling soul-sick when he thought of the paltry ten per cent which he would pocket in this colossal robbery of millions. And at those moments he could not resist the furious longing he felt to extend his hand and carve out a larger share for himself.

Saccard had not even allowed him to lend money to his wife, he had preferred to amuse himself with this big piece of theatrical trickery, which delighted his partiality for complicated transactions.

"No, no, my dear fellow," he said, with his Provençal accent, which he exaggerated whenever he wished to impart additional salt to a joke, "don't let us mix up our accounts. You are the only man in Paris to whom I have sworn never to owe a copper."

Larsonneau contented himself with insinuating that his colleague's wife was a gulf. He advised him not to give her another sou, so that she would then be compelled to transfer her property to them immediately. He would have preferred to have to deal with Saccard alone. He probed him at times, and carried things so far as to say, with the weary indifferent air of a man about town:

"All the same, I must put my papers in a little order. Your wife frightens me, my good fellow. I don't want justice to place the seals on certain documents at my office."

Saccard was not the man to submit to such allusions patiently, especially as he was well acquainted with the frigid meticulous order which prevailed in the agent's offices. The whole of his cunning, active little person revolted against the terror with which this coxcomb of a usurer in yellow kid gloves tried to inspire him. The worst was that he felt himself seized with shudders when he thought of a possible scandal; and he beheld himself brutally exiled by his brother, and living in Belgium by some avocation not to be acknowledged. One day he grew angry and said to Larsonneau:

"Listen, my boy, you are a nice fellow, but it would be as well for you to return me the document you know of. You'll see, that scrap of paper will end by making us quarrel."

The agent feigned astonishment, pressed his "dear master's" hand, and assured him of his devotion. Saccard regretted his momentary hastiness. It was at this period that he began to think seriously of drawing nearer to his wife. He might yet have need of her against his accomplice, and he moreover said to himself that business matters are discussed marvellously well between man and wife in bed. That kiss on his wife's neck gradually revealed to him quite a new system of tactics.

Besides, he was not in a hurry, he husbanded his resources. He devoted the whole winter to ripening his plan, though worried by a hundred different affairs, each of which was more muddled than the other. It was a terrible winter for him, full of shocks, a prodigious campaign during which he had to conquer bankruptcy daily. However, far from cutting down his expenses at home, he gave fête after fête. But if he succeeded in meeting every difficulty, he had to neglect Renée, whom he reserved for a triumphal blow, when the Charonne transaction became ripe. He contented himself with preparing the finish, by continuing not to give her any money, save through the intermediary of Larsonneau. When he was able to dispose of a few thousand francs, and she complained of her poverty, he took them to her, saying that Larsonneau's people required a note of hand for double the amount. This comedy vastly amused him, the stories connected with these promissory notes delighted him by the touch of romance which they imparted to the affair. Even at the period of his clearest profits he had served his wife her income in the most irregular manner, at one time making her princely presents, abandoning handfuls of bank notes to her, and then leaving her in the lurch for a paltry amount during weeks together. Now that he found himself seriously embarrassed, he talked about the expenses of the household, and treated her like a creditor to whom one is unwilling to confess one's ruin, and whom one disposes to patience by means of cock-and-bull stories. She scarcely listened to him, however; she signed whatever he chose, and only pitied herself for not being able to sign more.

Already, however, there were two hundred thousand francs' worth of promissory notes signed by her which barely cost him one hundred and ten thousand. After having these bills endorsed by Larsonneau to whose order they were made payable, he placed them in circulation in a prudent manner, intending to employ them as decisive weapons later on. He would never have been able to hold out to the end of that terrible winter, to lend his wife money usuriously and keep up his style of living, but for the sale of his ground on the Boulevard Malesherbes, which Messieurs Mignon and Charrier paid him for in hard cash, retaining, however, a formidable discount.

For Renée this same winter was one long joy. Lack of money was her only suffering. Maxime cost her very dear; he still treated her as a stepmother, and allowed her to pay everywhere. But this hidden poverty was an additional delight for her. She exercised her wits and racked her brain, so that her dear child should want for nothing; and when she had prevailed upon her husband to find her a few thousand francs, she and her lover expended them in some costly folly, like two schoolboys let loose on their first escapade. When they were hard up they remained at home and derived their enjoyment from this large building of such new and insolently stupid luxury. The father was never there. The lovers sat by the fireside more frequently than formerly. The fact was, that Renée had filled the icy emptiness of the gilded ceilings with a warm enjoyment. The suspicious abode of worldly pleasure had become a chapel in which she secretly practised a new religion. Maxime did not merely lend to her nature that high note which harmonized with her mad dresses. He was the very lover fitted to this mansion, with broad windows like shop fronts, and which a flood of sculpture inundated from garret to cellar. He animated all this plaster, from the two podgy Cupids who let a stream of water flow from their shell in the courtyard, to the tall, naked women supporting the balconies, and playing with apples and ears of corn, amid the pediments. He explained the unduly ornate hall, the tiny dimensions of the garden, the dazzling rooms in which one saw too many arm-chairs, and not one work of art. The young woman who had formerly felt bored to death in the house, suddenly began to amuse herself there, and availed herself of it, just as she might have done with something, the use of which she had not understood at first. And it was not only through her own apartments, through the buttercup drawing-room, and the conservatory that she promenaded her love, but through the entire mansion. She even ended by finding an enjoyment in lying on the divan of the smoking-room. She forgot herself there, and declared that the vague smell of tobacco pervading the apartment was very agreeable.

She appointed two reception days instead of one. On Thursdays all the mere acquaintances called. But Mondays were reserved to intimate female friends. Men were not admitted. Maxime alone was present at those choice gatherings, which took place in the buttercup drawing-room. One evening she had the astounding idea, of dressing him up as a woman, and of presenting him as one of her cousins. Adeline, Suzanne, the Baroness de Meinhold, and the other friends who were there, rose up and bowed, astonished by the sight of this face which they vaguely recognised. Then when they realized the truth, they laughed a great deal, and absolutely refused to let the young man go and change his clothes. They kept him with them in his skirts, teasing him, and lending themselves to equivocal jokes. When he had seen these ladies off by the main gate he went round the park and returned into the house by way of the conservatory. Renée's dear friends never had the slightest suspicion of the truth. Indeed the lovers could not behave together more familiarly than they had previously done, when they declared themselves to be boon comrades. And if it happened that a servant saw them rather close together behind a door, he expressed no surprise at it, being used to the pleasantries of his mistress, and his master's son.

This complete liberty, this impunity emboldened them still more. If they slipped the bolts at night-time, in the daylight they kissed each other in every room of the house. They invented a thousand little games on rainy days. But Renée's great delight was still to pile up a terrible fire, and doze in front of the grate. Her linen was marvellously luxurious that winter. She wore the most costly chemises and wrappers, the cambric and inserted embroidery of which barely covered her with a white cloud. And in the red glow of the fire she looked naked, with rosy lace and skin, the heat penetrating through the thin stuff to her flesh. Maxime, squatting at her feet, kissed her knees, without even feeling the garment which had the same warmth and colour as her lovely form. In the dull cloudy weather a kind of twilight penetrated the bedroom hung with grey silk, whilst Céleste went backwards and forwards behind them, with a quiet step. She had naturally become their accomplice. One morning when they had forgotten themselves in the bed, she found them there, and retained all the coolness of a servant with icy blood. They then ceased restraining themselves, she came in at all hours without the sound of their kisses making her turn her head. They relied upon her to warn them in the case of alarm. They did not purchase her silence. She was a very economical, very honest girl, and was not known to have a single lover.

Renée, however, was not cloistered. Taking Maxime in her train, like a fair-haired page in a dress-coat, she frequented society, where she tasted even more acute pleasures. The season was one long triumph for her. Never had her imagination been bolder as regards toilets and head-dresses. It was then that she risked wearing that famous bush-tinted robe, on which a complete stag hunt was embroidered with such attributes as powder flasks, hunting horns, and broad bladed knives. It was then, also, that she set the fashion of wearing the hair in the antique style; Maxime having to go and sketch patterns for her at the Campana Museum which had recently been opened. She grew younger, she was in all the plenitude of her turbulent beauty. Incest lent her a fire which glowed in the depths of her eyes and heated her laughter. Her eye-glasses looked superbly insolent on the tip of her nose, and she gazed at the other women, at the dear friends who basked in the enormity of some vice, with the air of a bragging hobbledehoy, and with a fixed smile which signified "I also have my crime."

Maxime, on his side, declared that society was wearisome. It was not merely for show that he pretended to be bored in it, for he really did not amuse himself anywhere. At the Tuileries, at the ministers' residences, he disappeared amid Renée's skirts. But he became the master again as soon as some freak was in question. Renée wished to see the private room on the Boulevard again, and the breadth of the divan made her smile. Then he took her a little bit everywhere, to harlots' houses, to the opera ball, to the stage boxes of petty theatres, to all the equivocal places where they could elbow brutal vice and taste the delights of remaining incognito. When they furtively returned to the house, worn out with fatigue, they fell asleep in each other's arms, sleeping off the drunkenness of obscene Paris, with snatches of smutty verses still ringing in their ears. On the morrow Maxime imitated the actors, and Renée, accompanying herself on the piano of the little drawing-room, tried to recall the hoarse voice and the wriggling of Blanche Müller in her part of the *Belle Hélène*. The music lessons she had taken at the convent now only served her to murder the verses of the new burlesques. She had a religious horror of serious airs. Maxime poked fun at German music with her, and he thought it his duty to go and hiss *Tannhauser*, both by conviction and to defend his stepmother's sprightly refrains.

One of their great enjoyments was skating; it was fashionable that winter, the Emperor having been one of the first to try the ice on the lake in the Bois de Boulogne. Renée ordered a complete Polish costume, velvet and fur, of Worms; and insisted upon Maxime wearing high boots and a foxskin cap. They reached the Bois in the intense cold which made their noses and lips tingle as if the wind had blown fine sand into their faces. It amused them to feel cold. The Bois was quite grey, with threads of snow, like narrow lace, along the branches of the trees. And under the pale sky, above the congealed and bedimmed lake, only the pines of the islands still displayed on the edge of the horizon their theatrical drapery, on which the snow had also sewn broad bands of lace. The lovers darted along together in the frozen air, with the rapid flight of swallows skimming just above the ground. Setting one hand behind their backs, and placing one upon each other's shoulder, they went off, erect, smiling, side by side, and revolving round the broad space, marked out by thick ropes. Loungers looked on at them from the roadway. From time to time they came to warm themselves at the braziers lighted at the edge of the lake, and then they started off again. They enlarged the course of their flight, with their eyes watering both with pleasure and with cold.

Then when the spring came Renée remembered her old elegiac fancy. She insisted upon Maxime strolling with her in the Parc Monceaux at night time by moonlight. They went into the grotto and sat down on the grass, in front of the colonnade. But when she expressed a desire to row on the little lake they found that there were no oars in the boat, which could be seen from the house, moored at the edge of a pathway. They were evidently removed every evening. This was a disappointment. Besides the vast shadows of the park made the lovers nervous. They would have liked to have had a Venetian fête given there, with red lanterns and an orchestra. They preferred it during the day-time, of an afternoon, and they then often stationed themselves at one of the windows of the mansion to watch the equipages following the graceful curve of the main avenue. They enjoyed themselves in gazing upon this charming corner of new Paris, this clean smiling bit of nature, these lawns looking like stripes of velvet, dotted with flower beds and choice shrubs, and edged with magnificent white roses. Carriages passed by each other, as numerous as on the Boulevard; lady promenaders carelessly trailed their skirts as if they had not ceased treading the carpets of their drawing-rooms. And athwart the foliage, Renée and Maxime criticised the dresses and pointed out the equipages to each other, deriving real enjoyment from the soft tints of this large garden. A scrap of gilded railing shone between two trees, a party of ducks passed over the lake, the little renaissance bridge looked white and new amid the green stuff, whilst on either side of the main avenue, mammas seated on yellow chairs forgot, in their chatter, the little boys and girls who looked at one another with a pretty air, and pouted like precocious children.

The lovers had a great liking for new Paris. They often rambled through the city in their carriage, going out of their way so as to pass along certain Boulevards for which they had a personal affection. The lofty houses adorned with large carved doors, loaded with balconies, whereon names and callings glittered in large gold letters, delighted them. While the brougham darted along, they followed with a friendly glance the grey bands of interminable footways, with their seats, their variegated columns and their scrubby trees. This bright gap which extended to the limits of the horizon, growing narrower, and opening upon a bluey parallelogram of space, the uninterrupted double row of large shops, where shopmen smiled at female customers, the currents of the stamping swarming crowd, filled them little by little with a feeling of absolute and complete satisfaction, they realised that they beheld the perfection of street life. They were enamoured even of the jets of the watering hose, which passed like white smoke before their houses and then spread out and fell in a fine rain under the wheels of the brougham, darkening the ground and raising a slight cloud of dust. They still went on, and it seemed to them that the vehicle was rolling over carpets along the straight endless highway, which had been pierced solely so that they might not have to pass through dark alleys. Each Boulevard became some passage of their mansion. The gay sunshine smiled upon the house fronts, lit up the window panes, fell upon the verandahs of the shops and cafés and heated the asphalt under the busy tread of the crowd. And when they returned home, somewhat dazed by the bright confusion of these long bazaars, they found enjoyment in the Parc Monceaux, which was like the complementary plat-band of the new Paris which displayed its luxury amid the first warmth of spring.

When the exigencies of fashionable life absolutely compelled them to leave Paris, they went to the seaside, regretfully however, and thinking of the Boulevardian side-walks while on the shores of the ocean. Then love itself grew dull there. It was a hot-house flower which needed the spacious grey and pink bed; the naked fleshy aspect of the dressing-room and the gilded dawn of the little drawing-room. Alone of an evening, in front of the sea, they no longer found anything to say to each other. Renée tried to sing the airs she had heard at the Variety Theatre, accompanying herself on an old piano which was agonising in a corner of her room at the hotel, but the instrument, damp with the breezes from the open, had the dreary voice of the great waters. *La Belle Hélène* seemed lugubrious and fantastic. To console herself Renée astonished the people on the sands by her prodigious costumes. The whole band of fashionable women there was yawning while waiting for the advent of winter, and trying despairingly to invent some bathing dress which would not make them look too ugly. Renée was never able to prevail upon Maxime to bathe. He had an atrocious fear of water, he turned quite pale when the tide reached his boots, and for nothing in the world would he have approached the edge of a cliff; he kept away from all pits, and made a long circuit to avoid any steep part of the shore.

Saccard came to see "the children" on two or three occasions. He was overwhelmed with worry, he said. It was only about October, when they all three found themselves again in Paris, that he seriously thought of drawing nearer his wife. The Charonne affair was ripening. His plan was a simple and brutal one. He relied upon capturing Renée by the same devices that he would have employed with a harlot. She lived on amid an increasing need of money, and out of pride she only applied to her husband at the last extremity. The latter resolved to profit by her first request to shew his gallantry, and, in the delight occasioned by the payment of some heavy debt, to resume relations which had so long been severed.

Some terrible embarrassments awaited Renée and Maxime in Paris. Several of the promissory notes drawn to Larsonneau's order had fallen due; but as Saccard naturally left them slumbering at the lawyer's, they did not cause the young wife much worry. She was far more alarmed by her debts as regards Worms, whose bill now amounted to nearly two hundred thousand francs. The tailor demanded something on account, and threatened to suspend all credit. Renée felt sudden shudders when she thought of the scandal of a law-suit, and especially of a quarrel with the illustrious man milliner. Moreover, she needed pocket money. She and Maxime would feel bored to death if they did not have a few louis a-day to spend. The dear boy was quite stumped since he had vainly rummaged through his father's drawers. His fidelity and exemplary behaviour during the last seven or eight months were largely due to the absolute emptiness of his purse. He did not always have twenty francs in his pocket to invite some street-walker to supper, and so he philosophically returned to the house. At each of their freaks the young woman handed him her purse so that he might defray the expenses in the restaurants, the balls and petty theatres. She continued treating him maternally, and, indeed, it was she who, with the tips of her gloved fingers, settled at the pastry-cook's, where they stopped almost every afternoon to eat little oyster patties. Of a morning he often found in his waistcoat some louis which he had not known to be there, and which she had placed there like a mother filling a schoolboy's pocket. And to think that this delightful life of snacks, satisfied fancies and facile pleasure was about to end! But a yet more grievous worry came to alarm them. Sylvia's jeweller, to whom Maxime owed ten thousand francs, grew angry and talked about Clichy, the debtors' prison. Such costs had accumulated on the notes of hand which he held, and had long since protested, that the debt had increased by some three or four thousand francs. Saccard plainly declared that he could do nothing in the matter. The imprisonment of his son at Clichy would increase his notoriety, and when he secured the young fellow's release he would make a great noise over his paternal liberality. Renée was in despair; she saw her dear child in prison—in a perfect dungeon, sleeping on damp straw. One evening, she seriously proposed to him not to leave her rooms, but to live there unknown to everyone, and sheltered from the bailiffs. Then she swore that she would procure the money. She never referred to the origin of the debt, of that woman Sylvia, who confided the secret of her affections to the mirrors of private rooms. Some fifty thousand francs—that was what she needed; fifteen thousand for Maxime, thirty thousand for Worms, and five thousand as pocket money. They would then have a fortnight's happiness before them. She embarked on the campaign.

Her first idea was to ask her husband for these fifty thousand francs, but it was only with a feeling of repugnance that she decided to do so. On the last occasions that he had entered her room to bring her some money he had printed fresh kisses on her neck, taking hold of her hands and talking about his affection. Women have acute powers of perception which enable them to guess men's feelings. So she expected some demand on his side, some tacit bargain concluded with a smile. And, indeed, when she asked him for the fifty thousand francs, he cried out, declared that Larsonneau would never lend such a sum, and that he himself was still too embarrassed. Then changing his tone, as if conquered and seized with sudden emotion:

"One cannot refuse you anything," he murmured; "I will run about Paris and accomplish the impossible. I want you to be pleased, my dear."

And setting his lips to her ear and kissing her hair, he added, in a slightly trembling voice—

"I will bring you the money to-morrow evening, here in your room—without any note to sign."

But she hastily said that she was not in a hurry, that she did not wish to trouble him so much. He, who had just set all his heart in that dangerous, "without any note," which had escaped him and which he regretted, did not appear to have encountered a disagreeable refusal. He rose up saying:

"Very well, I am at your disposal. I will find you the sum when the moment arrives. Larsonneau will be for nothing in it, you understand. It is a present which I mean to make you." He smiled with a good natured air. She remained in a state of cruel anguish. She felt she would lose the little equilibrium left her, if she surrendered herself to her husband. It was her last pride to be married to the father and to be only the son's wife. Often, when Maxime seemed to her to be cold, she tried to make him understand the situation by very transparent allusions; it is true that the young man, whom she expected to see fall at her feet after this revelation, remained altogether indifferent, imagining, no doubt, that she merely wished to reassure him as to the possibility of a meeting between his father and himself in the grey silk room.

When Saccard had left her, she hastily dressed herself and had the horses put to. While her brougham was conveying her towards the Île Saint-Louis, she prepared the manner in which she would ask her father for the fifty thousand francs. She flung herself into this sudden idea, without consenting to discuss it, feeling very cowardly at the bottom of her heart and seized with invincible fright at the thought of such a step. When she arrived, the courtyard of the Béraud mansion froze her with its mournful, cloister-like dampness, and it was with a desire to run away that she mounted the broad stone staircase on which her little high-heeled boots resounded terribly. She had been foolish enough in her haste to choose a costume of dead-leaf tinted silk, with long flounces of white lace trimmed with bows of ribbon and cut athwart by a plaited sash. This toilet, which was completed by a little hat with a large white veil, set such a singular note in the dark gloom of the staircase, that she herself became conscious of how strange she looked there. She trembled as she crossed the austere suite of spacious rooms, where the personages vaguely visible on the tapestry seemed surprised to see this stream of skirts pass by in the semi-daylight of their solitude.

She found her father in a drawing-room looking on to the courtyard, where he habitually remained. He was reading a large book placed on a desk adapted to the arms of his chair. In front of one of the windows Aunt Élisabeth sat knitting with long wooden needles; and in the silence of the room the tick-tack of these needles was the only sound one heard.

ÉMILE ZOLA

Renée sat down, ill at ease, unable to make a movement without disturbing the severity of the lofty ceiling by a noise of rustling silk. Her laces looked crudely white against the dark background of tapestry and old furniture. Monsieur Béraud Du Châtel gazed at her with his hands resting on the edge of the desk. Aunt Élisabeth talked about the approaching wedding of Christine who was to marry the son of a very rich attorney; the young girl had gone to a tradesman's with an old family servant; and the good aunt talked on alone, in her placid voice, without ceasing to knit, gossiping about household affairs, and casting smiling glances at Renée from above her spectacles.

But, the young woman became more and more disturbed. All the silence of the house weighed upon her shoulders, and she would have given a great deal for the lace of her dress to have been black. Her father's gaze embarrassed her to such a point that she considered Worms really ridiculous to have imagined such high flounces.

"How smart you are, my girl!" suddenly said Aunt Élisabeth, who had not yet even noticed her niece's lace.

She stopped knitting and settled her spectacles to see the better. Monsieur Béraud Du Châtel gave a faint smile.

"It is rather white," said he. "A woman must be greatly embarrassed with that on the side-walks."

"But one doesn't go out on foot, father!" cried Renée, who immediately afterwards regretted these words from her heart.

The old gentleman seemed about to reply. Then he rose up, straightened his high stature and began walking slowly, without again looking at his daughter. The latter remained quite pale with emotion. Each time that she exhorted herself to take courage, and that she tried to find a transition that would lead up to the request for money, she experienced a shooting pain at the heart.

"We never see you now, father," she murmured.

"Oh!" replied her aunt, "your father hardly ever goes out except at long intervals to stroll in the Jardin des Plantes. And I even have to get angry to make him do that! He pretends that he loses himself in Paris, that the city is no longer made for him. Ah! you do right to scold him!"

"My husband would be so happy to see you at our Thursdays, from time to time," continued the young woman.

Monsieur Béraud Du Châtel took a few steps in silence. Then in a quiet voice: "You must thank your husband for me," he said. "He is an active fellow, it appears, and I hope, for your sake, that he conducts his enterprises honestly. But we haven't the same ideas, and I feel ill at ease in your fine house in the Parc Monceaux."

Aunt Élisabeth seemed vexed by this reply.

"How wicked men are with their politics!" she said. "Would you like to know the truth? Your father is furious with you because you go to the Tuileries."

But the old gentleman shrugged his shoulders, as if to say that his dissatisfaction had far more grievous causes. He began slowly walking again, with a dreamy air. Renée remained for a moment silent, with the request for the fifty thousand francs on the tip of her tongue. But seized with even greater cowardice than before, she kissed her father and went off.

Aunt Élisabeth insisted upon accompanying her to the staircase. As they crossed the suite of rooms, she continued chattering in her old woman's squeaky voice:

"You are happy, my dear child. It pleases me very much to see you looking beautiful and well; for if your marriage had turned out badly I should have thought myself guilty! Your husband loves you, you have all you need, haven't you?"

"Of course," replied Renée compelling herself to smile though feeling sick at heart.

Her aunt still detained her, with her hand on the balustrade of the staircase.

"Do you see, I have only one fear, that you may become intoxicated with all your happiness. Be prudent, and above all don't sell anything. If you had a child some day, you would have a little fortune all ready for him."

When Renée was in her brougham again she heaved a sigh of relief. She had drops of cold perspiration on her forehead; she wiped them off, thinking of the icy dampness of the Béraud mansion. Then as the brougham rolled along amid the clear sunlight of the Quai Saint-Paul she remembered the fifty thousand francs, and all her suffering was revived again, acuter than before. She, whom people thought so bold, how cowardly she had just been! And yet it was a question of Maxime, of his liberty, of their joint delights. Amid the bitter reproaches which she addressed to herself, an idea suddenly sprung up which brought her despair to a climax; she ought to have spoken about the fifty thousand francs to Aunt Élisabeth on the stairs. What had she been thinking about? The worthy woman would perhaps have lent her the amount, or at all events have helped her. She was already leaning forward to tell her coachman to drive back to the Rue Saint-Louis-en-l'Île, when she thought she again beheld her father slowly crossing the solemn darkness of the grand drawing-room. She would never have the courage to return at once to that room. What could she say to explain this second visit? And in the depth of her heart she no longer even found the courage to speak of the affair to Aunt Élisabeth. So she told her coachman to drive her to the Rue du Faubourg-Poissonnière.

Madame Sidonie uttered a cry of delight when she saw her opening the discreetly curtained door of the shop. She was there by chance, she was about to hasten to the magistrate's, where she had summoned a customer. But she would not put in an appearance, she could do so some other day; she was so happy that her sister-in-law had at length had the amiability to pay her a little visit. Renée smiled with an embarrassed air. Madame Sidonie would not by any means allow her to remain downstairs; she made her go up into her room, by the little staircase, after removing the brass knob from the shop door. She removed and refixed this knob, which was secured by a simple nail, at least twenty times a day.

"There, my beauty," she said, making Renée sit down on a couch, "we shall be able to chat nicely. Do you know that you come in the very nick of time—I meant to go and see you this evening."

Renée, who knew the room, experienced that vague feeling of uneasiness, which a promenader feels on finding that a strip of forest has been cut down in a favourite landscape.

"Ah!" she said at last, "you have changed the position of the bed, haven't you?"

"Yes," quietly replied the lace-dealer, "one of my customers thought it would be much better in front of the mantelpiece. She also advised me to have red curtains."

"That's what I was thinking, the curtains used not to be of that colour. Red is a very common colour."

She put on her eye-glasses, and looked at this room which displayed the kind of luxury one finds in a large hotel. On the mantelshelf she saw some long hair-pins which certainly did not come from Madame Sidonie's meagre chignon. The paper of that part of the wall, against which the bed had formerly stood, was all torn, discoloured and dirtied by the mattresses. The agent had certainly tried to hide this sore with the backs of two arm chairs, but these backs were rather low, and Renée's glance remained fixed on this worn strip of paper.

"You have something to say to me?" she asked at last.

"Yes, it's quite a story," said Madame Sidonie, joining her hands and assuming the expression of a glutton who is about to relate what she has eaten at dinner. "Just fancy, Monsieur de Saffré is in love with the beautiful Madame Saccard. Yes, with yourself, my pretty one."

Renée did not vouchsafe even a gesture of coquetry.

"Indeed!" she remarked, "but you said he was so smitten with Madame Michelin."

"Oh! that's finished, quite finished—I can prove it to you if you like. Don't you know then that little Michelin has pleased Baron Gouraud? It's incredible. Every one who knows the baron is amazed. And now she's on the way to obtaining the red ribbon for her husband! Ah, she's a woman of spirit. She isn't faint-hearted, she doesn't need any one to steer her boat."

Madame Sidonie said this with an air of some little regret mingled with admiration.

"But to return to Monsieur de Saffré—It would seem that he met you at an actresses' ball, muffled up in a domino, and he even accuses himself of having somewhat cavalierly offered you a supper. Is it true?"

The young woman was quite surprised.

"Perfectly true," murmured she; "but who could have told him?"

"Wait a bit, he pretends that he recognised you later on, when you were no longer in the room, and that he remembered having seen you leave on Maxime's arm. Since then he has been madly in love. It has grown in his heart, you understand, been a sudden fancy. He came to see me to beg me to make you his apologies—"

"Well, tell him that I forgive him," interrupted Renée negligently.

And again assailed by all her worries, she continued:

"Ah! my good Sidonie, I am awfully bothered. It is absolutely necessary that I should have fifty thousand francs to-morrow morning. I came to speak to you about the matter. You know some money-lenders, you told me."

The agent, vexed by the abrupt manner in which her sister-in-law had interrupted her story, made her wait some time for an answer.

"Yes, certainly; only, I advise you, first of all to try and obtain the money from a friend. If I were in your place I know very well what I should do. I should simply apply to Monsieur de Saffré."

Renée smiled in a constrained manner.

"But it would hardly be proper," she answered, "since you pretend that he is so much in love."

ÉMILE ZOLA

The old woman looked at her with a fixed stare; then her flabby face gently softened into a smile of tender pity.

"Poor dear," she muttered, "you have been crying; don't deny it, I can see it by your eyes. You must be strong and accept life. Come, let me arrange the little matter in question."

Renée rose up, twisting her fingers, and making her gloves crack. And she remained standing, quite shaken by a cruel internal struggle. She was opening her mouth, to accept perhaps, when a gentle ring at the bell resounded in the next room. Madame Sidonie hastily went out, leaving the door ajar, so that a double row of pianos could be seen. The young woman then heard a man's step, and the stifled sound of a conversation carried on in an undertone. She mechanically went to examine more closely the yellowish stain with which the mattresses had streaked the wall. This stain disturbed her, made her ill at ease. Forgetting everything, Maxime, the fifty thousand francs, and Monsieur de Saffré, she stepped back to the front of the bed, reflecting; this bed had been much better placed, as it had formerly stood; some women were really wanting in taste; of a certainty when one lay down one must have the light in one's eyes. And in the depths of her memory she vaguely saw the figure of the stranger of the Quai Saint-Paul rise up, her novel in two assignations, that chance amour which she had partaken of, there, at that other place. The wearing away of the wall paper was all that remained of it. Then the room filled her with uneasiness, and the hum of voices which continued in the next apartment made her feel impatient.

When Madame Sidonie returned, opening and closing the door with due precaution, she made repeated signs with the tips of her fingers, to recommend Renée to speak low. Then, she whispered in her ear:

"You don't know, the adventure's a good one: it's Monsieur de Saffré who's there."

"You didn't tell him though that I was here?" asked the young woman anxiously.

The agent seemed surprised, and with an air of great simplicity answered:

"But I did—He is waiting for me to tell him to come in. Of course I didn't speak about the fifty thousand francs—"

Renée, who was quite pale, had drawn herself up as if she had been struck with a whip. A great pride again rose to her heart. That creaking of boots, which she heard growing louder in the next room, exasperated her:

"I am going," she said curtly. "Come and open the door for me."

Madame Sidonie tried to smile.

"Don't be childish," she said. "I can't be left with that fellow on my hands, since I have told him you are here—You really compromise me—"

But the young woman had already descended the little staircase. She repeated, in front of the closed shop door:

"Open it, open it."

When the lace-dealer withdrew the brass knob, she had the habit of putting it in her pocket. She wished to continue parleying. Finally seized with anger herself, and displaying in the depths of her grey eyes the tart acridity of her nature, she cried: "But come, what shall I say to the man?"

"That I'm not for sale," replied Renée, who already had one foot on the side-walk.

And it seemed to her that she could hear Madame Sidonie muttering as she banged the door: "Eh! get off, you jade! you shall pay me for this!"

"By heavens," thought Renée as she again entered her brougham, "I prefer my husband to that."

She returned straight home. In the evening she told Maxime not to come; she was poorly, she needed repose. And, on the morrow, when she handed him the fifteen thousand francs for Sylvia's jeweller, she remained embarrassed in presence of his surprise and his questions. Her husband, she said, had done a good stroke of business. From that day forth, however, she became more capricious, she often changed the hour of the appointments which she gave the young fellow, and even she frequently watched for him in the conservatory to send him away. He did not worry himself much about these changes of humour; it pleased him to be an obedient thing in women's hands. What bored him a great deal more was the moral turn which their lovers' meetings took at times. She became quite sad; and it even happened that she had big tears in her eyes. She left off singing the refrain about the "handsome young man" in the *Belle Hélène*, she played the hymns she had learnt at school and asked her lover if he did not think that sin was always punished, sooner or later.

"She's decidedly growing old," he thought. "It will be the utmost if she's funny for another year or two."

The truth was that she suffered cruelly. She would now have preferred to deceive Maxime with Monsieur de Saffré. She had revolted at Madame Sidonie's, she had given way to instinctive pride, to disgust for such a low bargain. But on the following days, when she endured the anguish of adultery, everything in her foundered; and she felt herself so despicable that she would have surrendered herself to the first man who pushed open the door of the room containing the pianos. The thought of her husband had, at times, formerly passed before her, amid her incest, like a touch of voluptuous horror; but henceforth the husband, the man himself, entered into it with a brutality that transformed her most delicate sensations into intolerable sufferings. She, who had enjoyed the refinement of her sin, and had willingly dreamt of a corner of a superhuman paradise where the gods partook of their amours together, was now descending to vulgar debauchery, to being shared by two men. In vain did she try to derive enjoyment from her infamy. Her lips were still warm with Saccard's kisses when she offered them to Maxime's. Her inquisitiveness descended to the depths of these accursed pleasures. She went as far as to mingle the two affections, and to seek for the son amid the father's hugs. And she emerged yet more alarmed and more bruised from this journey into unknown evil, from this ardent darkness in which she confounded the person of her double lover, with a terror which was like the death-rattle of her enjoyment.

She kept this drama to herself alone, and increased the suffering it occasioned by the feverishness of her imagination. She would have preferred to die rather than own the truth to Maxime. She had an inward fear that the young man might revolt and leave her; she had such an absolute belief in the monstrosity of her sin and in eternal damnation, that she would have more willingly crossed the Parc Monceaux naked than have confessed her shame aloud. On the other hand, she still remained the madcap who astonished Paris by her extravagant conduct. Nervous gaiety seized hold of her, prodigious caprices which the newspapers talked about, designating her by her initials. It was at this period that she seriously wished to fight a duel with pistols with the Duchess de Sternich who had, intentionally, so she said, upset a glass of punch over her dress. To calm her, it was necessary for her brother-in-law, the minister, to get angry. On another occasion she bet with Madame de Lauwerens that she would make the round of the Longchamps racecourse in less than ten minutes, and it was only a question of costume that deterred her from doing so. Maxime himself began to feel afraid of this head, in which madness lurked; and on the pillow at night-time he thought he could hear all the hubbub of a city bent on enjoying itself.

One evening they went together to the Théâtre-Italien. They had not even looked at the bill. They wished to see the great Italian tragedian,

Ristori, who then attracted all Paris, and in whom, by the command of fashion, they were bound to interest themselves. The play was *Phèdre*. Maxime remembered his classical repertory sufficiently, and Renée knew enough Italian to follow the performance. And indeed they derived an especial emotion from this drama, performed in a foreign language, the sonority of which seemed to them at times to be a simple orchestral accompaniment supporting the pantomime of the actors. Hippolytos was a tall, pale fellow, a very poor actor, who whimpered his part.

"What a ninny!" muttered Maxime.

However, Ristori, with her broad shoulders shaken by her sobs, with her tragical face and fat arms, moved Renée deeply. Phædra was of Pasiphae's blood, and she asked herself of what blood she was, the incestuous stepmother of modern times. She saw nought of the piece save this tall woman drawing the ancient crime over the stage. When Phædra confides her criminal tenderness to Œnone in the first act; when, all on fire, she declares herself to Hippolytos in the second; and later on, in the fourth act, when the return of Theseus overwhelms her and she curses herself, in a crisis of gloomy fury, she filled the house with such a cry of savage passion, with such a yearning for superhuman voluptuousness, that the young woman felt every shudder of her desire and remorse pass through her own flesh.

"Wait," murmured Maxime in her ears, "you are going to hear Theramene's narrative. The old fellow has a funny head!"

And he muttered in a hollow voice:

"Scarce had we passed the gates of Trezene, He on his chariot mounted—"

But while the old fellow spoke, Renée neither looked nor listened any more. The light blinded her, and stifling heat came to her from all the pale faces stretched out towards the stage. The monologue continued, interminable. She imagined herself in the conservatory under the ardent foliage, and she dreamt that her husband came in and surprised her in the arms of his son. She suffered horribly, she was losing consciousness, when the death-rattle of Phædra, repentant and dying in the convulsions caused by the poison, made her open her eyes again. The curtain fell. Would she have the strength to poison herself some day? How petty and shameful her drama was beside the ancient epopœia! And while Maxime fastened her opera cloak under her chin, she still heard, growling behind her, Ristori's rough voice to which Œnone's complacent murmur replied.

In the brougham, the young fellow talked on alone. He considered tragedies sickening as a rule, and preferred the pieces performed at the Bouffes. However, *Phèdre* was spicy. He had taken an interest in it, because—And he pressed Renée's hand to complete his meaning. Then a funny idea darted through his head, and he gave way to an impulse to say something witty.

"It was I," he murmured, "who did right not to approach the sea at Trouville."

Renée, lost in the depths of her painful dream, remained silent. It was necessary for him to repeat his phrase.

"Why?" asked she, astonished and failing to understand.

"But the monster—"

And he gave vent to a little titter. This joke froze the young woman. Everything was upset in her head. Ristori was no longer aught, but a big puppet who tucked up her peplum and poked out her tongue to the public like Blanche Müller in the third act of the *Belle Hélène*; Theramene danced the cancan, and Hippolytos eat bread and jam while stuffing his fingers into his nose.

When a more galling remorse made Renée shudder, she evinced superb revolt. What was her crime after all, and why should she blush? Did she not every day tread upon greater infamies? Did she not elbow at the ministers', at the Tuileries, everywhere in fact, wretches like herself who had millions on their flesh, and who were adored on both knees! And she thought of the shameful friendship of Adeline d'Espanet and Suzanne Haffner, at which one smiled, at times, at the Empress's Mondays. And she recalled to herself the traffic of Madame de Lauwerens, whom husbands celebrated for her good conduct, her order, and her exactitude in settling her tradesmen's bills. She named Madame Daste, Madame Teissière, the Baroness de Meinhold, those creatures whose luxury was paid for by their lovers, and who were quoted in society like shares are quoted upon change. Madame de Guende was so stupid and so well formed, that she had three superior officers for her lovers at the same time, and was unable to distinguish them from each other on account of their uniforms. This made that demon of a Louise say that she first of all made them strip to their shifts so as to know which of the three she was talking to. As for the Countess Vanska, she remembered the courtyards in which she had sung, the side-walks on which people pretended they had again seen her, dressed in printed calico, and prowling about like a she-wolf. Each of these women had her shame, her triumphant, displayed sore. And, overtopping them all, the Duchess de Sternich rose up, ugly, old, worn out, with the glory of having passed a night in the Imperial bed; she typified official vice, from which she derived the majesty of debauchery and a kind of sovereignty over this band of illustrious hussies.

The incestuous stepmother accustomed herself to her sin, as to a gala robe the stiffness of which might at first have inconvenienced her. She followed the fashions of the period, she dressed and undressed herself in the style of others. She ended by believing that she lived amid a circle above common morality, in which the senses became more acute and developed, and in which one was allowed to strip oneself naked for the joy of all Olympus. Sin became a luxury, a flower set in the hair, a diamond fastened on the brow. And she again saw, like a justification and redemption, the Emperor passing on the general's arm, between two rows of inclined shoulders.

Only one man, Baptiste, her husband's valet, continued to disturb her. Since Saccard showed himself gallant, this tall, pale, dignified valet, seemed to walk around her with the solemnity of mute censure. He did not look at her, his cold glances passed higher, above her chignon, with the modesty of a beadle who refuses to defile his eyes by letting them rest on a hair of a sinner. She imagined that he knew everything, and she would have purchased his silence had she dared. Then feelings of uneasiness took possession of her, she experienced a kind of confused respect when she met Baptiste, and said to herself that all the honesty of her household had withdrawn and hidden itself under this lackey's dress-coat.

One day she asked Céleste:

"Does Baptiste joke in the servants' hall? Do you know if he has had any adventure, if he has any mistress?"

"What a question!" was all the maid replied.

"Come, he must have paid you some attentions?"

"Why! he never looks at women. We barely see him. He is always in master's rooms or in the stables. He says that he is very fond of horses."

Renée was irritated by this respectability, for she would have liked to be able to despise her servants. Although she had taken a liking to Céleste, she would have rejoiced to learn that she was someone's mistress.

"But you, Céleste," she continued, "don't you think that Baptiste is a good-looking fellow?"

ÉMILE ZOLA

"I, madame!" cried the chambermaid with the stupefied air of a person who has just heard something prodigious. "Oh! I've very different ideas in my head. I don't want a man. I've my plan. You will see later on. I'm not a fool, no."

Renée could not draw anything more precise from her. Moreover, her worries were growing. Her noisy life, her mad rambles, met with numerous obstacles which she had to overcome, and against which she at times bruised herself. It was thus that Louise de Mareuil rose up one day between herself and Maxime. Renée was not jealous of the "hunchback," as she disdainfully called her; she knew her to be condemned by the doctors, and could not believe that Maxime would ever marry such an ugly chit, even at the price of a dowry of a million. In her fall she had retained a middle-class naivete respecting the people around her; although she despised herself, she readily believed that they were superior and very estimable. But whilst rejecting the possibility of a marriage which would have seemed to her a piece of sinister debauchery and a theft, she suffered from the young folks' familiarities and friendliness. When she spoke of Louise to Maxime, he laughed with satisfaction, he repeated the child's sayings to her, and said:

"The urchin calls me her little man, you know."

And he displayed such freedom of mind that she did not dare to tell him that this urchin was seventeen, and that their playfulness with their hands, and their eagerness when they met in drawing-rooms to find out some shady corner to poke fun at everybody, grieved her and spoilt her most pleasant evenings.

An incident occurred which imparted a strange character to the situation. Renée often felt the need of acting boastingly, and she had whims of brutal boldness. She dragged Maxime behind a curtain, behind a door, and kissed him at the risk of being seen. One Thursday evening, when the buttercup drawing-room was full of people, she was seized with the fine idea of calling the young fellow who was talking with Louise, she advanced from the depths of the conservatory where she was to meet him, and abruptly kissed him on the mouth between two clumps of shrubbery, thinking that she was sufficiently concealed. But Louise had followed Maxime, and when the lovers raised their heads, they saw her a few paces off, looking at them with a strange smile, without the least blush or astonishment, but with the quiet friendly air of a companion in vice, who is learned enough to understand and appreciate such a kiss.

Maxime felt really frightened that day, and it was Renée who showed herself indifferent and almost joyful. It was all over. It was now impossible for the hunchback to take her lover from her. She thought:

"I ought to have done it on purpose. She now knows that her 'little man' belongs to me."

Maxime felt reassured when he again found Louise as gay and as funny as before. He considered her to be "very acute and a very good-natured girl." And that was all.

There was good reason, however, for Renée to be disturbed. For some little time past Saccard had been thinking of his son's marriage with Mademoiselle de Mareuil. There was a dowry of a million francs to be had, which he did not wish to let escape, meaning to get his hands into this money later on. As Louise remained in bed during nearly three weeks at the beginning of the winter, he was so afraid of seeing her die before the projected union was accomplished, that he decided the children should marry at once. He certainly thought them rather young; but the doctors feared the month of March for the consumptive girl. Monsieur de Mareuil on his side was in a delicate position. He had eventually succeeded in getting himself returned as a deputy at the last poll. Only the Corps Législatif had just quashed his election, which had provoked a great scandal when the Chamber deliberated on the validity of the returns. This election was quite a heroi-comical poem, on which the newspapers lived for a whole month. Monsieur Hupel de la Noue, the prefect of the department, had displayed such vigour that the other candidates had not even been able either to placard their addresses to the electors, or to distribute their voting papers. At his advice, Monsieur de Mareuil covered the constituency with tables at which the peasants ate and drank for a week. He, moreover, promised a railway line, the erection of a bridge and three churches, and on the eve of the poll he forwarded to the influential electors the portraits of the Emperor and Empress, two large engravings covered with glass and set in gold frames. This gift met with tremendous success, and the majority in Monsieur de Mareuil's favour was overwhelming. But when the Chamber, in presence of the bursts of laughter which came from all France, found itself compelled to send Monsieur de Mareuil back to his electors, the minister flew into a terrible passion with the prefect and the unfortunate candidate who had really shown themselves too "zealous." He even spoke of choosing someone else as the official candidate. Monsieur de Mareuil was terrified, he had spent three hundred thousand francs in the department, he owned there some large estates where he felt bored, and which he would have to sell at a loss. So he came to beg his dear colleague to appease his brother, and to promise him in his name a most properly conducted election. It was on this occasion that Saccard again spoke of the children's marriage and that the two fathers finally decided upon it.

When Maxime was sounded on the subject he felt embarrassed. Louise amused him, and the dowry tempted him still more. He said yes, he accepted all the dates that Saccard named to avoid the worry of a discussion. But, at heart, he owned to himself that matters would unfortunately not be arranged with such charming facility. Renée would never consent, she would cry, she would upbraid him, she was capable of provoking some great scandal to astonish Paris. It was very disagreeable. She now frightened him. She watched him with alarming eyes, and she possessed him so despotically that he thought he could feel claws digging into his shoulder whenever she laid her white hand on it. Her turbulence became roughness, and there was a cracked sound in the depths of her laughter. He really feared that she would go mad one night in his arms. With her, remorse, fear of being surprised, the cruel joys of adultery did not manifest themselves as with other women, by tears and dejection, but by greater extravagance, and a more irresistible longing for noise. And amid her growing affrightment one began to hear a rattling, the derangement of this adorable, astonishing machine which was breaking up.

Maxime passively awaited an occasion which would rid him of this troublesome mistress. He again said that they had been very stupid. If their comradeship had at first lent additional voluptuousness to their love, it now prevented him from breaking off as he would certainly have done from any other woman. He would not have returned; that was his mode of bringing his amours to a finish so as to avoid any effort or any quarrel. But he felt himself incapable of a row, and he still even willingly forgot himself in Renée's embraces; she behaved maternally, she paid his expenses, and she would pull him out of embarrassment if any creditors became angry. Then the thought of Louise, the thought of the dowry of a million of francs returned to him, and made him reflect—even amid the young woman's kisses—"that it was all very charming and nice, but that it wasn't serious and must come to an end."

One night Maxime was so rapidly stumped at the house of a woman where one often gambled till daylight, that he experienced one of those mute attacks of anger familiar to the gamester whose pockets are empty. He would have given everything in the world to have been able to fling a few more louis on the table. He took up his hat, and with the mechanical step of a man who is impelled by a fixed idea, he repaired to the Parc Monceaux, opened the little gate, and found himself in the conservatory. It was past midnight. Renée had forbidden him to come that night. When she now closed her door to him she did not even try to invent an explanation, while he merely thought of profiting of his holiday. He only clearly remembered the young woman's prohibition when he was in front of the glass door of the little drawing-room which was closed. As a rule when he was to come, Renée undid the fastening of this door in advance.

"Bah!" said he on seeing that the window of the dressing-room was lighted up, "I will whistle and she will come down. I sha'n't disturb her; if she has a few louis, I will go off at once."

And he whistled gently. He indeed often employed this signal to announce his arrival. But that evening he fruitlessly whistled several times. He grew obstinate, raising the key, and unwilling to abandon his idea of an immediate loan. At last he saw the glass door opened with infinite precaution and without his having heard the least sound of footsteps. In the dim light of the conservatory Renée appeared to him, with her hair down, and scarcely dressed, as if she were going to bed. She was barefooted. She pushed him towards one of the arbours, descending the steps and walking over the gravel of the pathways, without seeming to feel the cold or the roughness of the ground.

"It's stupid to whistle as loud as that," she muttered with restrained anger. "I told you not to come. What do you want with me?"

"Eh? Let's go up," said Maxime, surprised by this reception. "I will tell you upstairs. You will catch cold here."

But as he stepped forward she held him back and he then perceived that she was horribly pale. Mute fright bent her form. Her clothes, the lace of her linen, hung down like tragic shreds upon her shuddering skin.

He examined her with growing astonishment:

"What is the matter with you? You are ill?"

And instinctively he raised his eyes and looked through the glass panes of the conservatory at the window of the dressing-room where he had seen a light.

"But there's a man in your room," he said suddenly.

"No, no, it isn't true," she stammered, supplicating, distracted.

"Pooh, my dear, I see his shadow."

Then, for a minute they remained there face to face, not knowing what to say to each other. Renée's teeth chattered with terror, and it seemed to her as if some one were throwing bucketsful of iced water over her bare feet. Maxime experienced more irritation than he would have believed; but he still remained sufficiently possessed to reflect, and say to himself that the occasion was a good one, and that he would now break off the connection.

"You won't make me believe that Céleste wears a coat," he continued. "If the glass panes of the conservatory were not so thick I should perhaps recognize the gentleman."

She pushed him deeper into the shadow of the foliage, saying, with her hands clasped, and seized with growing terror:

"I beg of you, Maxime—"

But all the young fellow's teasing faculties were aroused, a ferocious malice which sought for vengeance. He was too weak to ease himself by anger. Spite compressed his lips; and, instead of striking her, as he had at first had the impulse of doing, he sharpened his voice and rejoined:

"You ought to have told me of it, I shouldn't have come to disturb you—It happens every day that one no longer cares for one another. I myself was beginning to have enough of it—Come, don't be impatient. I will let you go up again; but not before you have told me the gentleman's name—"

"Never, never!" murmured the young woman, forcing back her tears.

"It isn't to call him out, it's to know—The name, tell me the name, quick, and off I go."

He had caught hold of her wrists and he looked at her, laughing his wicked laugh. She struggled, distracted, bent upon not opening her lips again, so that the name he asked for might not escape from them.

"We shall make a noise, you will be nicely placed then. Why are you frightened? Aren't we good friends? I want to know who replaces me, it's legitimate—Come, I will help you—It's Monsieur de Mussy whose grief has touched you."

She did not answer. She bowed her head beneath such an interrogatory.

"It isn't Monsieur de Mussy? The Duke de Rozan, then? Really, nor he either? Perhaps the Count de Chibray? Not even he?"

He stopped short, he reflected.

"The devil, I can't think of any one else. It can't be my father after what you told me—"

Renée quivered as if she had been burnt, and said huskily:

"No. You know very well that he no longer comes. I shouldn't accept, it would be ignoble."

"Then who is it?"

And he pressed her wrists still more tightly. The poor woman struggled for a few moments longer.

"Oh, Maxime, if you knew! I can't, however, tell you—"

Then conquered, crushed, looking with affright at the lighted window: "It is Monsieur de Saffré," she stammered in a very low voice.

Maxime, whom the cruel game had amused, turned extremely pale on hearing this confession which he had asked for so persistently. He was irritated by the unexpected pain which this man's name caused him. He violently threw back Renée's wrists, drawing near to her, and saying to her full in the face, and with clinched teeth:

"Well, do you want to know you are a—!"

He said the word. And he was going off, when she hastened to him, sobbing, taking him in her arms, murmuring tender things, requests for pardon, swearing that she still adored him, and that she would explain everything to him on the morrow. But he disengaged himself, and banged the door of the conservatory, replying:

"No! all's over, I've had quite enough of it."

She remained crushed. She watched him crossing the garden. It seemed to her that the trees of the conservatory revolved round her. Then she slowly dragged her bare feet over the gravel of the pathways, she reascended the steps, her skin discoloured by the cold, and more tragical than ever amid the disorder of her lace. Upstairs she answered, in reply to the questions of her husband who was waiting for her, that she had thought she could recollect where she had dropped a little note-book she had lost since the morning. And when she was in bed, she suddenly felt immense despair on reflecting that she ought to have told Maxime that his father, after returning home with her, had followed her into her room to talk to her about some money matter.

It was on the morrow that Saccard decided to hasten the finish of the Charonne matter. His wife belonged to him; he had just felt her, soft and inert in his hands, like something that surrenders itself. On the other hand, the line which the Boulevard du Prince Eugène was to follow was about to be decided upon, and it was necessary that Renée should be despoiled before the approaching expropriation was noised about. Saccard displayed an artist's love in all this affair; it was with devotion that he watched his plan ripen, and he set his traps with the refinement of a sportsman who prides himself on capturing his game in skilful fashion. He felt the satisfaction of an expert gamester, of a man who derives a special enjoyment from stolen gain; he wished to obtain the ground for a crust of bread, and then to give his wife a hundred thousand francs' worth of jewellery, amid the joy of the triumph. The simplest operations grew complicated, became black dramas, as soon as he dealt with them; he became impassioned, he would have beaten his father for five francs. But afterwards he scattered gold in regal fashion. However, before obtaining from Renée the cession of her share in the property, he prudently went to probe Larsonneau as to the black-mailing intentions which he had scented in him. His instinct saved him on this occasion. The expropriation agent had imagined, on his side, that the fruit was ripe and that he could pluck it. When Saccard entered the office in the Rue de Rivoli he found his compeer overcome, and showing signs of the most violent despair.

"Ah! my friend," murmured Larsonneau, taking hold of his hands, "we are lost. I was about to hasten to your place so that we might consult together and get out of this horrible scrape."

While he wrung his arms and tried to sob, Saccard noticed that he had been engaged in signing letters prior to his arrival, and that the signatures were penned with admirable precision. He accordingly looked at him quietly, saying:

"Bah! what has befallen us then?"

But the agent did not reply at once; he had thrown himself into his arm-chair in front of his writing table, and there, with his elbows on the blotting pad and his brow between his hands, he furiously shook his head. Finally in a husky voice:

"I have been robbed of the ledger containing the inventory, you know."

And he related that one of his clerks, a scamp worthy of the galleys, had abstracted a large number of papers among which the famous inventory figured. The worst was that the thief had realized to what use he might turn the document in question, and he wished to sell it back for a hundred thousand francs.

Saccard reflected. The story seemed to him altogether too clumsy. Plainly enough Larsonneau did not much care at heart whether he was believed or not. He sought for a simple pretext to make Saccard understand that he wanted a hundred thousand francs in the Charonne affair; and indeed, that he would, on this condition, return the compromising papers which were in his possession. The bargain seemed too onerous to Saccard. He would willingly have allowed his ex-colleague a share, but he was irritated by the setting of this snare, by this pretension to make a dupe of him. On the other hand he was not without his apprehensions; he knew the personage he had to deal with, he knew that he was quite capable of taking the documents to his brother, the minister, who would certainly have paid a price for them so as to stifle any scandal.

"The devil!" he muttered, sitting down in his turn, "this is a nasty story. And can one see the scamp in question?"

"I will have him sent for," said Larsonneau. "He lives close by, in the Rue Jean-Lantier."

Ten minutes had not elapsed when a little young fellow with a squint, light hair, and a face covered with freckles, stepped softly into the room, taking care that the door should not make a noise. He wore an old black frock coat, too large for him and horribly threadbare. He remained standing at a respectful distance, quietly looking at Saccard out of the corner of his eye. Larsonneau, who called him Baptistin, made him undergo an interrogatory, to which he replied in monosyllables without humbling himself the least in the world; indeed he accepted with the utmost indifference the epithets of thief, swindler and scoundrel, which his master thought fit to adjoin to each of his questions.

Saccard admired this wretched fellow's coolness. At one moment the expropriation agent sprang from his arm-chair as if to strike him; and he contented himself with retreating a step, squinting with still more humility.

"That will do, leave him alone," said the financier. "And so, sir, you demand a hundred thousand francs for the papers."

"Yes, a hundred thousand francs," replied the young man.

And he went off. Larsonneau seemed unable to calm himself.

"What a blackguard, eh?" he stammered. "Did you see his underhand looks? Fellows of that stamp have a timid air, but they would murder a man for twenty francs."

Saccard however interrupted him, saying:

"Pooh! he isn't terrible. I think one will be able to arrange matters with him—I came to see you about a much more worrying affair—You were right in mistrusting my wife, my dear friend. Just fancy, she's going to sell her share of the property to Monsieur Haffner. She needs money, she says. Her friend Suzanne must have influenced her."

ÉMILE ZOLA

The other abruptly ceased despairing; he listened, rather pale, readjusting his stick-up collar, which had become bent during his fit of anger.

"This sale," continued Saccard, "means the ruin of our hopes. If Monsieur Haffner becomes your fellow-partner, not only will our profits be compromised, but I am dreadfully afraid that we shall find ourselves in a most disagreeable position towards that over-scrupulous fellow, who will want to go over the accounts."

The expropriation agent began walking about with an agitated step, his patent leather boots creaking on the carpet.

"You see," muttered he, "in what a position one puts oneself to oblige people! But, my dear fellow, if I were in your place, I should absolutely prevent my wife from doing anything so foolish. I would beat her sooner."

"Ah! my friend!" said the financier with a wily smile, "I have no more power over my wife than you seem to have over that blackguard of a Baptistin."

Larsonneau stopped short in front of Saccard, who was still smiling, and gazed at him with a profound air. Then he resumed walking up and down, but with a slow measured step. He approached a looking glass, pulled up the bow of his necktie, and then walked on again, regaining his usual elegant manner. And suddenly:

"Baptistin!" he cried.

The little young fellow who squinted came in, but by another door. He no longer carried his hat, but twisted a pen between his fingers.

"Go and fetch the ledger," said Larsonneau to him.

And when the clerk was no longer there, the agent discussed the sum that was to be given him.

"Do it for me," he ended by plainly saying.

Thereupon Saccard consented to give thirty thousand francs out of the future profits of the Charonne affair. He considered that he still escaped cheaply from the usurer's gloved hand. The latter had the promise made out in his name, prolonging the comedy to the end, and stating that he would be accountable to the young man for the thirty thousand francs. It was with a laugh of relief that Saccard burnt the ledger page by page at the fire flaming in the grate. Then, this operation over, he exchanged vigorous hand shakes with Larsonneau, and left him saying:

"You are going to Laure's this evening, aren't you? Wait for me there. I shall have arranged everything with my wife, I we will decide on our final plans."

Laure d'Aurigny, who often moved, then resided in a large apartment on the Boulevard Haussmann, in front of the Expiatory Chapel. She had just fixed one day a week to be at home, like a lady of real society. It was a manner of assembling on the same occasion, the men who saw her, one by one, during the week. Aristide Saccard triumphed on Tuesday evenings; he was the acknowledged protector; and he turned his head with a vague laugh whenever the mistress of the house betrayed him between two doors, by giving one of the gentlemen an appointment for the same night. When he remained there, the last of the set, he lit another cigar, talked business, and joked about the gentleman who was dancing attendance in the street, waiting until he left; then after calling Laure his "dear child," and giving her a little pat on the cheek, he quietly went off by one door while the gentleman came in by another. The secret treaty of alliance which had consolidated Saccard's credit and procured the d'Aurigny two sets of furniture in a month, still continued to amuse them. But Laure wanted a finish to the comedy. This finish, a predetermined one, was to consist in a public rupture, to the profit of some fool who would pay dearly for the right of being the serious protector, known as such to all Paris. The fool was found. The Duke de Rozan, tired of uselessly boring the women of the same social standing as himself, dreamt of acquiring the reputation of a debauchee, so as to lend some relief to his insipid personality. He was very assiduous at the Tuesday at homes of Laure, whom he had conquered by his absolute simplicity. Unfortunately, although thirty-five years old, he was still dependent upon his mother, to such a point that he could at the most dispose of merely ten louis at a time. On the evenings when Laure deigned to take his ten louis, pitying herself, and talking of the hundred thousand francs she needed, he sighed, and promised her the amount on the day when he would be the master. It was then that she had the idea of putting him on friendly terms with Larsonneau, who was one of her good friends. The two men went to lunch together at Tortoni's; and at dessert Larsonneau, while relating his amours with a delicious Spanish beauty, pretended that he knew some money-lenders; but he strongly advised Rozan never to let himself pass into their hands. This confidential announcement inflamed the duke, who ended by wringing from his dear friend a promise that he would occupy himself about his "little affair." He occupied himself about it so well that he was to bring the money on the very evening that Saccard was to meet him at Laure's.

　　　　　　　　　　　　　　　　　　ÉMILE ZOLA

When Larsonneau arrived, the d'Aurigny's large white and gold drawing-room only contained some five or six women, who took hold of his hands, and clung to his neck with a furious outburst of affection. They called him "that big Lar!" a caressing nickname which Laure had invented. And he in a fluty voice exclaimed:

"There, that'll do, my little kittens; you will crush my hat."

They calmed down, and gathered close around him on a couch, while he told them about an attack of indigestion which had befallen Sylvia, with whom he had supped the night before. Then drawing a sweetmeat box from the pocket of his dress-coat he offered them some burnt almonds. Meanwhile, Laure came out of her bedroom, and as several gentlemen arrived, she drew Larsonneau into a boudoir situated at one end of the drawing-room, from which it was separated by double hangings.

"Have you got the money?" she asked him when they were alone.

Larsonneau, without replying, bowed in a jocular manner and tapped the inner pocket of his coat.

"Oh! you big Lar!" murmured the delighted young woman.

She took him round the waist and kissed him.

"Wait a bit," she said, "I want the flimsies—Rozan is in my room, I will go and fetch him."

But he detained her, and, in his turn, kissing her shoulders:

"You know what commission I asked of *you*."

"Why, yes, you big stupid, it's agreed."

She came back bringing Rozan. Larsonneau was dressed more correctly than the duke, with better fitting gloves, and a more artistic bow to his necktie. They negligently touched hands, and talked about the races of two days before, at which one of their friends had had a horse beaten. Laure stamped impatiently.

"Come, never mind all that, my darling," said she to Rozan. "Big Lar has the money, you know. The affair had better be settled."

Larsonneau pretended to remember.

"Ah, yes, it's true," he said, "I have the amount—But how much better you would have done had you listened to me, my dear fellow! To think that these rogues demanded fifty per cent of me. However I agreed to it all the same, as you told me that it didn't matter."

Laure d'Aurigny had procured some bill stamps during the day. But when it was a question of a pen and an inkstand, she looked at the two men with an air of consternation, doubting whether these objects would be found in the place. She wanted to go and look in the kitchen, when Larsonneau drew from his pocket, the pocket containing the sweetmeat box, two marvels, a silver pen-holder which lengthened by means of a screw, and a steel and ebony inkstand, of jewel-like finish and delicacy. And as Rozan sat down:

"Draw the notes to my name," the agent said. "I didn't wish to compromise you, you understand? We will arrange matters together. Six notes of twenty-five thousand francs each, eh?"

Laure counted the flimsies on a corner of the table. Rozan did not even see them. When he had signed and raised his head, they had already disappeared in the young woman's pocket. However she came to him and kissed him on both cheeks, which appeared to delight him. Larsonneau looked at them philosophically while folding the promissory notes, and replacing the inkstand and pen-holder in his pocket.

The young woman still had her arms round Rozan's neck, when Aristide Saccard raised a corner of the door-hanging.

"Well, don't disturb yourselves," he said, laughing.

The duke blushed. But Laure went to shake the financier's hand, exchanging a wink of intelligence with him. She was radiant.

"It's done, my dear," said she. "I warned you of it. You are not too angry with me?"

Saccard shrugged his shoulders with a good-natured air. He pulled back the hanging, and drawing aside to allow Laure and the duke to pass, he cried out in an usher's yelping voice:

"The duke, the duchess!"

This witticism met with tremendous success. On the morrow the newspapers repeated it, plainly naming Laure d'Aurigny, and designating the two men, by extremely transparent initials. The rupture between Aristide Saccard and fat Laure, caused even more of a stir than their pretended amours had done.

Saccard had let the door curtain fall again amid the burst of gaiety which his jocularity had occasioned in the drawing-room.

"Ah! what a good girl!" said he, turning towards Larsonneau. "She is vicious! It's you, you scamp, who no doubt profits by all this. What are you to have?"

But the agent protested, with smiles, and pulled down his shirt-cuffs, which had caught up under the sleeves of his coat. At last he went and sat down near the door, on a couch to which Saccard motioned him:

　　　　　　　　　　　　　　　　　　　　　　　　　ÉMILE ZOLA

"Come here, I don't want to confess you, dash it all! Let us now deal with serious matters, my dear fellow. I have had a long talk with my wife this evening. Everything is decided."

"She consents to cede her share in the property?" asked Larsonneau.

"Yes, but it wasn't without trouble on my part—Women are so obstinate! My wife, you know, had promised an old aunt not to sell the ground. There was no end to her scruples. Luckily, however, I had prepared quite a decisive story."

He rose up to light a cigar at the candelabrum which Laure had left on the table, and returning and stretching himself languidly on the couch:

"I told my wife," he continued, "that you were completely ruined—You had gambled at the Bourse, spent your money with harlots, dabbled in bad speculations; in fact you are on the point of ending by a frightful bankruptcy—I even let it be understood that I did not consider you perfectly honest—Then I explained to her that the Charonne affair would be wrecked in your fall, and that the best course would be for her to accept the proposal you had made to me to disengage her, by buying her share, for a crust of bread, it's true."

"It isn't an able story," muttered the expropriation agent. "Do you fancy your wife will believe such trash?"

Saccard smiled. He was in a disposition to be communicative.

"You are simple, my dear fellow," he resumed. "The basis of the story is of little consequence; the details, gestures and tone of voice are everything. Call Rozan and I bet I will persuade him that it is broad daylight. My wife has scarcely any more brains than Rozan—I let her have a glimpse of a precipice. She hasn't the least idea of the coming expropriation. As she was astonished, that in the midst of a catastrophe, you could think of taking a still heavier burden on your shoulders, I told her that no doubt she hampered you in dealing some ugly blow intended for your creditors. Finally, I advised the transaction as the only means of avoiding being mixed up in interminable law suits, and of deriving some money from the ground."

Larsonneau still considered the story somewhat brutal. His method was less dramatic; each of his operations was concocted and unravelled with the elegance of a drawing-room comedy.

"I should have imagined something different," he said. "However, everyone his own system. So all we have to do now is to pay—"

"It is on this point," replied Saccard, "that I want to make arrangements with you. To-morrow I will take the deed of sale to my wife, and she will simply have to send you this deed to receive the stipulated amount. I prefer to avoid any interview."

He had indeed never allowed Larsonneau to visit them on a footing of intimacy. He did not invite him to his entertainments, and he accompanied him to Renée's on the days when it was absolutely necessary that they should meet; this had happened on three occasions at the utmost. He almost always transacted matters with a power of attorney from his wife, not wishing to let her see too closely into his affairs.

He now opened his pocket-book, adding:

"Here are the two hundred thousand francs' worth of bills accepted by my wife; you will give them her in payment, and you will add to them a hundred thousand francs which I will bring you to-morrow morning. I am bleeding myself, my dear friend. This business will cost me a fortune."

"But that will only make three hundred thousand francs," remarked the expropriation agent. "Will the receipt be for that amount?"

"A receipt for three hundred thousand francs!" rejoined Saccard, laughing. "Ah! in that case we should be nicely placed later on! According to our inventories, the property must now be estimated at two millions five hundred thousand francs. The receipt will naturally be for half that amount."

"Your wife will never sign it."

"Yes, she will. I tell you that it is all agreed. Why, dash it all! I told her that that was your first condition. You present a pistol at our heads with your bankruptcy, do you understand? And it was for that reason that I appeared to doubt your honesty, and accused you of wanting to dupe your creditors. Do you think my wife understands anything of all that?"

Larsonneau shook his head, muttering:

"No matter, you ought to have devised something simpler."

"But my story is simplicity itself!" said Saccard, very much astonished. "How the devil do you find it complicated?"

He was not conscious of the incredible number of devices which he tacked on to the most ordinary transaction. He derived real enjoyment from the cock-and-bull story which he had just told Renée; and what delighted him was the impudence of the lie, the piling up of impossibilities, the astonishing complicacy of the plot. He would long since have had the ground if he had not imagined all this drama; but he would have experienced less enjoyment had he obtained it easily. Besides, he displayed the utmost simplicity in making the Charonne speculation quite a financial melodrama.

He rose up, and taking Larsonneau's arm, walked towards the drawing-room:

"You have perfectly understood me, eh?" he said. "Content yourself with following my instructions, and you will applaud me later on. Do you know, my dear fellow, you do wrong to wear yellow gloves, they quite spoil your hands."

The expropriation agent contented himself with smiling and murmuring:

"Oh! gloves have their value, dear master: one can touch anything without dirtying oneself."

As they returned into the drawing-room, Saccard was surprised and somewhat alarmed to find Maxime on the other side of the door curtains. He was seated on a couch beside a fair-haired woman, who was telling him, in a monotonous voice, a long story, no doubt her own. The young fellow had, in point of fact, overheard the conversation between his father and Larsonneau. The two accomplices seemed to him to be a pair of sharp blades. Still vexed by Renée's betrayal, he tasted a cowardly enjoyment in learning the theft of which she was about to be the victim. It avenged him a little. His father came and shook his hand with a suspicious air; but Maxime, showing him the fair-haired woman, whispered in his ear:

"She isn't bad looking, is she? I mean to have her this evening."

Thereupon Saccard attitudinized, and showed himself gallant. Laure d'Aurigny came and joined them for a moment. She complained that Maxime scarcely paid her one visit a month. But he pretended that he had been very much occupied, which statement made everybody laugh. He added that in future he should be here, there and everywhere.

"I have written a tragedy," said he, "and I only hit on the fifth act last night—I now mean to rest myself at the abodes of all the pretty women in Paris."

He laughed and enjoyed his allusions which he alone could understand. However, the only other persons now remaining in the drawing-room were Rozan and Larsonneau, on either corner of the mantelpiece. The Saccards rose up, as well as the fair-haired woman who lived in the house. The d'Aurigny then went to speak in a low tone to the duke. He seemed surprised and vexed. Seeing that he did not make up his mind to leave his arm-chair:

"No, really, not this evening," she said in an undertone, "I've a headache! To-morrow evening, I promise you."

Rozan had to obey. Laure waited till he was on the landing and then said quickly in Larsonneau's ear:

"Eh! big Lar, I keep my word. Shove him into his carriage."

When the fair-haired woman took leave of the gentlemen to return to her rooms on the floor above, Saccard was surprised that Maxime did not follow her.

"Well?" he asked him.

"Well, no," replied the young fellow. "I've reflected—"

And he had an idea which he thought a very funny one:

"I abandon my rights to you, if you like. Make haste, she hasn't yet shut her door."

But his father gently shrugged his shoulders, saying: "Thanks, youngster, I've something better than that for the time being."

The four men went down. Outside, the duke absolutely wished to take Larsonneau with him in his carriage. His mother lived in the Marais, and he would have dropped the expropriation agent at his door in the Rue de Rivoli. The latter refused, however, shut the carriage door himself, and told the coachman to drive off. And he then lingered on the side-walk of the Boulevard Haussmann, talking with the two others instead of going away.

"Ah, poor Rozan!" said Saccard, who suddenly understood the truth.

Larsonneau swore that it was not so, that he didn't care a fig for all that, that he was a practical man. And as the other two continued joking, and the cold was very keen, he finished by exclaiming:

"'Pon my word, so much the worse; I'm going to ring! You are indiscreet, gentlemen."

"Good night!" called Maxime, as the door closed again.

And taking his father's arm he went up the Boulevard with him. It was one of those clear, frosty nights when it is so agreeable to walk on the hard ground, in the icy atmosphere. Saccard remarked that Larsonneau was wrong, that it was preferable to be simply the d'Aurigny's comrade. He started from this point to declare that the love of these women was really pernicious. He showed himself moral, and hit upon sentences and advice of astonishing wisdom.

"You see," said he to his son, "all that only lasts for a time, my good fellow. A man loses his health at it, and doesn't taste real happiness. You know that I'm not a puritan. All the same, I've had quite enough of it; I'm going to settle down."

Maxime chuckled; he stopped his father and gazed at him by the moonlight, declaring that he had a fine head. But Saccard became still more grave.

"Joke as much as you like. I repeat to you that there is nothing like married life to preserve a man and make him happy."

Thereupon he spoke of Louise. And he began walking more slowly so as to settle that matter, he said, since they were talking of it. Everything was fully arranged. He even informed Maxime that he and Monsieur de Mareuil had fixed the signing of the contract for the Sunday following the Mid-Lent Thursday. On that Thursday there was to be a grand party at the mansion in the Parc Monceaux, and he could profit by the occasion to make a public announcement of the marriage. Maxime considered all this to be very satisfactory. He had rid himself of Renée, he saw no more obstacles, and he surrendered himself to his father, as he had surrendered himself to his stepmother.

"Well, it's understood," said he. "Only don't talk about it to Renée. Her friends would twit and tease me, and I prefer that they should know the news at the same time as everyone else."

Saccard promised him to keep silent. Then, as they approached the top of the Boulevard Malesherbes he again gave him a quantity of excellent advice. He told him how he ought to act to make his home a paradise.

"Above everything never break off with your wife. It's folly. A wife with whom you no longer have connection costs you a fortune. In the first place a man has to pay some harlot, hasn't he? Then the expenditure is much greater at home: there are dresses, madame's private pleasures, her dear friends, the devil and all his train."

He was in a moment of extraordinary virtue. The success of his Charonne affair had set idyllic tenderness in his heart.

"I," he continued, "was born to live happy and ignored in the depths of some village with all my family around me. People don't know me, my little fellow. I seem to be very flighty. But in reality not at all, I should adore remaining near my wife, I would willingly abandon my affairs for a modest income which would enable me to retire to Plassans. You are about to become rich, make yourself a home with Louise in which you will live like two turtle-doves. It's so nice! I will go to see you. It will do me good."

He ended by having sobs in his voice. Meanwhile they had reached the iron gate of the mansion, and stood talking on the curb of the sidewalk. A sharp north-east wind swept over these Parisian heights. Not a sound arose in the pale night, white with frost. Maxime, surprised by his father's sentimentality, had for a moment past had a question on his lips.

"But you," he said at last, "it seems to me—"

"What?"

"As regards your wife!"

Saccard shrugged his shoulders.

"Eh! quite so! I was a fool. That's why I speak to you by experience—However we have become husband and wife again, oh! quite so. It happened nearly six weeks ago. I go and join her of an evening when I don't return home too late. To-night however the poor ducky must dispense with me; I have to work till daylight. She has such an awfully fine figure!"

As Maxime held out his hand to his father the latter detained him, and added in a lower key, in a confidential tone:

"You know Blanche Müller's figure, well, it's that, but ten times more supple. And such hips! They have a curve, a delicacy—"

And then he concluded by saying to the young fellow who was going off:

"You are like me, you have a heart, your wife will be happy. Good-bye youngster!"

When Maxime had at last rid himself of his father, he went rapidly round the park. What he had just heard surprised him so much, that he experienced an irresistible desire to see Renée. He wished to ask her forgiveness for his brutality, to find out why she had lied to him in naming Monsieur de Saffré, and to learn the story of her husband's tenderness. He thought of all this confusedly, however, with but the one distinct wish to smoke a cigar in her room and renew their comradeship. Providing she were well disposed he would even announce his marriage to her, so as to make her understand that their amours must remain dead and buried. When he had opened the little door, the key of which he had fortunately retained, he ended by saying to himself that after his father's confidential revelations, his visit was necessary and quite proper.

In the conservatory he whistled as he had done the night before; but he did not have to wait. Renée came to open the glass door of the little drawing-room, and went upstairs before him without speaking a word.

ÉMILE ZOLA

She still wore a dress of white tulle forming puffs and covered with satin bows; the tails of the satin body were edged with a broad band of white jet which the light of the candelabra tinged with blue and pink. When Maxime looked at her upstairs he was touched by her pallor and the deep emotion which deprived her of her voice. She could not have been expecting him, she still quivered all over at seeing him arrive as quietly as usual, with his coaxing air. Céleste returned from the wardrobe, where she had gone to fetch a night-gown, and the lovers remained silent, deferring their explanation until the girl had withdrawn. As a rule they did not inconvenience themselves in her presence; but the things which they felt upon their lips filled them with a kind of shame. Renée would have Céleste undress her in the bedroom, where there was a large fire. The chambermaid removed the pins, took off each article of finery, one by one, without hurrying herself. And Maxime, feeling bored, mechanically took up the chemise which was lying on a chair beside him, and warmed it in front of the flames, leaning forward with his arms apart. It was he who used to render Renée this little service in happy times and she felt moved when she saw him delicately holding the gown to the fire. Then as Céleste showed no signs of finishing the young fellow asked:

"Did you enjoy yourself at the ball?"

"Oh! no, it's always the same thing you know," answered Renée. "A great deal too many people, a perfect crush."

Maxime turned the night-gown, which was now warm on one side.

"What did Adeline wear?" he asked.

"A mauve dress, rather awkwardly devised. Although she is short she is mad on flounces."

They then talked about the other women. Maxime was now burning his fingers with the gown.

"But you will scorch it," said Renée whose voice was maternally caressing.

Céleste took the gown from the young fellow's hands. He rose up, and went to look at the large pink and grey bed, fixing his eyes upon one of the bouquets embroidered on the curtains, so as to be able to turn his head, and not see Renée's bare bosom. It was instinctive. He no longer considered himself her lover, so he no longer had the right to look. Then he drew a cigar from his pocket and lighted it. Renée had given him permission to smoke in her apartments. At last Céleste retired, leaving the young woman by the fireside, quite white in her night attire.

Maxime walked about for a few moments longer, silent, and looking out of the corner of his eye at Renée who seemed to be again seized with a shudder. Then stationing himself in front of the mantelpiece with his cigar between his teeth, he asked in a curt voice:

"Why didn't you tell me that it was my father who was with you last night?"

She raised her head, his eyes dilated with supreme anguish; then a rush of blood crimsoned her face, and, overwhelmed with shame, she hid it with her hands and stammered:

"You know that? you know that?"

Regaining her self-possession she tried to lie:

"It's not true—Who told it you?"

Maxime shrugged his shoulders.

"Why my father himself, who considers you nicely formed, and talked to me about your hips."

He had allowed a little vexation to show itself while saying this; but he now began walking about again, continuing in a chiding but friendly voice, between two puffs of smoke:

"Really now I don't understand you. You are a singular woman. It was your fault if I was rude yesterday. If you had told me that it was my father, I should have gone off quietly, you understand? I have no right—But you go and name Monsieur de Saffré to me!"

She was sobbing, with her hands over her face. He drew near, knelt down before her, and forcibly drew her hands aside.

"Come, tell me why you named Monsieur de Saffré?" he said.

Then, still averting her head, she answered in a low tone, amid her tears:

"I thought that you would leave me, if you knew that your father—"

He rose to his feet, took up his cigar which he had laid on a corner of the mantelshelf, and contented himself with muttering: "You are very funny, really!"

She no longer cried. The flames of the grate and the fire of her cheeks were drying her tears. Her astonishment at seeing Maxime so calm in presence of a revelation which, she had thought, was bound to crush him, made her forget her shame. She looked at him as he walked about; she listened to him speaking, as if she had been in a dream. Without abandoning his cigar, he repeated to her that she was unreasonable, that it was quite natural she should have connection with her husband, and that he really could not think of resenting it. But to go and confess that she had a lover when it was not true! And he constantly returned to that point, which he could not understand, and which seemed really monstrous to him. He talked about women's "mad imaginations."

"You are a little bit cracked, my dear," he said, "you must take care."

Then he ended by asking inquisitively:

"But why Monsieur de Saffré rather than anyone else?"

"He courts me," said Renée.

Maxime restrained an impertinent remark; he had been on the point of saying that she had fancied herself a month older on owning that Monsieur de Saffré was her lover. However, he merely gave expression to the evil smile which this spiteful idea prompted, and throwing his cigar into the fire, he went and sat down on the other side of the mantelshelf. There he talked reason, and gave Renée to understand that they ought to remain good friends. The young woman's fixed gaze certainly embarrassed him somewhat; he did not dare to announce his marriage to her. She contemplated him for a long time, her eyes still swollen by her tears. She found him petty, narrow-minded, despicable, but she still loved him with the same tenderness that she felt for her lace. He looked pretty in the light of the candelabra placed on the corner of the mantelshelf beside him. As he threw his head back, the light of the candles gilded his hair and glided over his face, amid the soft down of his cheeks, with a charming aurulent effect.

"All the same I must be off," said he several times.

He had quite decided not to stop. Besides, Renée would not have allowed it. They both thought it, and said it: they were now nothing more than two friends. When Maxime had at last pressed the young woman's hand, and was on the point of leaving the room, she detained him for another moment by speaking to him about his father, upon whom she bestowed great praise.

"You see, I felt too much remorse," she said. "I prefer that this should have happened. You don't know your father; I was astonished to find him so kind, so disinterested. The poor fellow has such great worries just now!"

Maxime looked at the tips of his boots without replying, and with an embarrassed air. She dwelt on the subject.

"As long as he did not come into this room, it was all the same to me. But afterwards—When I saw him here so affectionate, bringing me money which he must have picked up in all the corners of Paris, ruining himself for me without a murmur, I felt ill—If you knew how carefully he has watched over my interests!"

The young fellow returned softly to the mantelpiece, and leant against it. He remained embarrassed, with bowed head and a smile gradually rising to his lips.

"Yes," muttered he, "my father is very skilful in watching over people's interests."

His tone of voice astonished Renée. She looked at him, and he, as if to defend himself, added:

"Oh! I know nothing. I only say that my father is a skilful man."

"You would do wrong to speak ill of him," she rejoined. "You must judge him rather superficially. If I acquainted you with all his worries, if I repeated to you what he confided to me again this evening, you would see how mistaken people are, when they think he cares for money."

Maxime could not restrain a shrug of the shoulders. He interrupted his stepmother with an ironical laugh.

"Ah, I know him, I know him well," he said. "He must have told you some very pretty things. Relate them to me."

This tone of raillery wounded her. She then enlarged upon her praises; she considered her husband quite a great man; she talked about the Charonne affair, that piece of jobbery of which she had understood nothing, as about a catastrophe in which Saccard's intelligence and kindness had been revealed to her. She added that she should sign the deed of cession on the morrow, and that if this affair were really a disaster, she accepted it in punishment for her sins. Maxime let her go on, sneering and looking at her slyly; then he said, in an undertone:

"That's it; that's just it."

And raising his voice, and settling his hand on Renée's shoulder:

"Thanks, my dear, but I already know the story. You are of nice composition!"

He again seemed to be on the point of leaving, but he felt a furious itching to tell Renée everything. She had exasperated him with her praises of her husband, and he forgot that he had promised himself not to speak, so as to avoid anything disagreeable.

"What! what do you mean?" she asked.

"Why, that my father has 'done' you in the prettiest way in the world. I really pity you—you are too much of a simpleton!"

And he then cowardly, craftily, related to her what he had heard at Laure's—tasting a secret delight in descending into these infamies. It seemed to him that he was taking his revenge for a vague insult which

ÉMILE ZOLA

some one had just addressed to him. With his harlot's temperament he lingered beatifically over this denunciation, over this cruel chatter of what he had overheard behind a door. He spared Renée nothing, neither the money which her husband had lent her usuriously nor that which he meant to steal from her, with the help of ridiculous stories fit to send children to sleep. The young woman listened to him, very pale and with clinched teeth. Standing in front of the chimney-piece, she slightly lowered her head, and looked at the fire. Her night dress, the gown which Maxime had warmed, spread out, revealing the motionless, statue-like whiteness of her limbs.

"I tell all this," continued the young man, "so that you may not seem to be a fool. But you would do wrong to get angry with my father. He isn't wicked. He has his failings like every one. Till to-morrow, eh?"

He still advanced towards the door. But Renée stopped him with a sudden gesture:

"Stay!" she cried, imperiously.

And taking hold of him, drawing him to her, almost seating him on her knees in front of the fire, she kissed him on the lips, saying:

"Ah, well! it would be too stupid to put ourselves to inconvenience now. Don't you know that my head has no longer seemed to belong to me since yesterday, since you wanted to break off? I am like an idiot. At the ball to-night I had a fog before my eyes. It is because I cannot now live quite without you. When you leave me I shall be done for. Don't laugh; I tell you what I feel."

She looked at him with infinite tenderness, as if she had not seen him for a long time.

"You found the word," she continued. "I was a simpleton. Your father would have made me see stars in broad daylight. Did I know anything about it? While he was telling me his story, I only heard a loud buzzing, and I was so crushed that, if he had chosen, he could have made me go down on my knees to sign his papers. And I fancied to myself that I felt remorseful—I was really as stupid as that!"

She burst out laughing, and gleams of folly shone in her eyes. Pressing her lover still more tightly, she went on:

"Do we sin, we two? We love each other, we amuse ourselves as it pleases us. Everyone has come to that, eh? You see your father doesn't put himself out. He likes money, and he takes it wherever he finds it. He's right, it sets me at my ease. In the first place, I sha'n't sign anything, and then, you will come here every evening. I was afraid that you wouldn't, you know, on account of what I told you. But as you don't mind it—Besides, I shall close my door to him now, you understand?"

She rose up and lighted the night-light. Maxime hesitated in despair. He realised what a piece of folly he had perpetrated, and he harshly reproached himself for having said too much. How could he announce his marriage now? It was his fault. The rupture had been accomplished, there had been no need for him to go up into that room again, or especially to prove to the young woman that her husband deceived her. Maxime's anger with himself was increased, as he no longer knew what feeling he had first obeyed. But if for a moment he thought of being brutal a second time, of going away, the sight of Renée, who was letting her slippers fall, lent him invincible cowardice. He felt frightened. He remained.

On the morrow, when Saccard came to his wife's apartments to make her sign the deed of cession, she quietly answered him that she should not do so, that she had reflected. She did not, however, allow herself even an allusion to the truth; she had sworn that she would be discreet, for she did not want to create worries for herself, but rather wished to taste the renewal of her amours in peace. The Charonne affair would finish as it could; her refusal to sign was merely an act of vengeance; she did not care a fig for the rest. Saccard was on the point of flying into a passion. All his dream crumbled. His other affairs were going from bad to worse. He found himself at the end of his resources, and merely sustained himself by performing miraculous feats of equilibrity; that very morning he had been unable to pay his baker's bill. This did not prevent him, however, from preparing a splendid entertainment for the Mid-Lent Thursday. In presence of Renée's refusal he experienced the white rage of a vigorous man impeded in his work by a child's whim. With the deed of cession once in his pocket, he had relied upon raising funds pending the award of the indemnity. When he had slightly calmed down, and his intelligence had become clear again, his wife's sudden change astonished him; she must, undoubtedly, have been advised. He scented a lover. This was so clear a presentiment, that he hastened to his sister's to question her, to ask her if she did not know anything about Renée's private life. Sidonie showed herself very bitter. She had not forgiven her sister-in-law for the affront she had given her by refusing to see Monsieur de Saffré. So when, by her brother's questions, she understood that the latter accused his wife of having a lover, she cried out that she was certain of it. And of her own accord she offered to spy upon "the turtle doves." In that way, the haughty thing would see who it was she had to deal with. Saccard did not habitually seek after disagreeable truths; his interest alone compelled him to open his eyes, which, as a rule, he wisely kept closed. He accepted his sister's offer.

"Oh! be easy, I shall learn everything," said she to him in a voice full of compassion. "Ah! my poor brother! Angèle would never have betrayed you! So good, so generous a husband! These Parisian dolls have no hearts. And to think that I never cease giving her good advice!"

VI

There was a fancy dress ball at the Saccards' on the Mid-Lent Thursday. The great curiosity, however, was the poem of the "Amours of handsome Narcissus and the nymph Echo" in three *tableaux*, which the ladies were to perform. For more than a month the author of this poem, Monsieur Hupel de la Noue, had been travelling from his Prefecture to the mansion of the Parc Monceaux, so as to superintend the rehearsals, and give his opinion on the costumes. He had at first thought of writing his work in verse, but later on he had decided in favour of *tableaux vivants*; it was more noble, he said, nearer to antique beauty.

The ladies no longer slept. Some of them changed their costumes no fewer than three times. There were some interminable conferences, over which the prefect presided. The personage of Narcissus was at first discussed at length. Should a man or a woman personate him? At last, at the instance of Renée, it was decided that the part should be confided to Maxime, but he was to be the only man in the *tableaux*; and, indeed, Madame de Lauwerens declared that she would never have consented to it if "little Maxime had not been so like a real girl." Renée was to be the nymph Echo. The question of the costumes was far more complicated. Maxime gave a good lift up to the prefect, who was quite tired out amid nine women, whose mad imaginations threatened to grievously impair his conception's purity of lines. If he had listened to them, his Olympus would have worn powder. Madame d'Espanet absolutely wished a dress with a long skirt to hide her somewhat large feet, while Madame Haffner dreamt of dressing herself in a wild beast's skin. Monsieur Hupel de la Noue was energetic, and he even turned angry on one occasion; he was convinced, and he said that if he had renounced versification it was to write his poem "in cleverly combined stuffs and attitudes selected among the best."

"The harmony, ladies," repeated he at each fresh exigency, "you forget the harmony. I can't, however, sacrifice the entire work to the flounces you ask me for."

The conferences took place in the buttercup drawing-room. Entire afternoons were spent there, deciding on the cut of a skirt. Worms was summoned several times. At last everything was settled, the costumes decided on, the positions learnt, and Monsieur Hupel de la Noue

ÉMILE ZOLA

declared himself satisfied. The election of Monsieur de Mareuil had given him less trouble.

The performance of the "Amours of handsome Narcissus and the nymph Echo," was to begin at eleven o'clock. The large drawing-room was already full at half-past ten, and as there was to be a ball afterwards, the ladies were there in costumes, seated in arm-chairs ranged in a semi-circle in front of the improvised stage—a platform, hidden by two broad curtains of red velvet with golden fringe, running on iron rods. The gentlemen stood behind, or moved to and fro. At ten o'clock, the upholsterers had struck the last nails home. The platform rose up at the end of the drawing-room, occupying a portion of this long gallery. Access to the stage was obtained by the smoking-room, converted into a green-room for the artistes. In addition, the ladies had at their disposal several apartments on the first floor, where an army of maids prepared the costumes of the different *tableaux*.

It was half-past eleven, and the curtains were not yet drawn aside. A loud buzz filled the drawing-room. The rows of arm-chairs were occupied by a most astonishing crowd of marchionesses, noble dames, milk-maids, Spanish beauties, shepherdesses, and sultanas; while the compact mass of dress-coats set a large dark stain beside the glistening of light stuffs and bare shoulders, glowing with the bright sparkle of jewellery. The women alone were in costume. It was already warm. The three chandeliers lit up the golden sheen of the drawing-room.

At last Monsieur Hupel de la Noue was seen to emerge from an opening on the left hand side of the platform. He had been assisting the ladies since eight o'clock in the evening. His dress-coat bore on the left sleeve the mark of three white fingers—a woman's little hand which had rested there after dabbling in a box of rice powder. But the prefect had something else than the mishaps of his attire to think about! He had huge eyes, and a swollen and somewhat pale face. He did not seem to see anyone. And advancing towards Saccard, whom he recognised among a group of grave-looking men, he said to him in an undertone:

"Dash it all! Your wife has lost her girdle of foliage. We are in a pretty pickle!"

He swore, and felt inclined to beat the people around him. Then, without waiting for a reply, without looking at anything, he turned his back, plunged under the draperies again and disappeared. The singular apparition of this gentleman made the ladies smile.

The group amid which Saccard found himself had gathered behind the last row of seats. One arm-chair had even been drawn out of the row for Baron Gouraud whose legs had for some time begun to swell. Monsieur Toutin-Laroche, whom the Emperor had just raised to the Senate, was there with Monsieur de Mareuil, whose second election the Chamber had deigned to accept, and Monsieur Michelin, decorated the day before; and a little in the rear were Mignon and Charrier, one of whom had a large diamond on his cravat, while the other displayed a still larger one on his finger. The gentlemen chatted together. Saccard left them for a moment to go and exchange a few words with his sister, who had just come in and seated herself between Louise de Mareuil and Madame Michelin. Madame Sidonie was dressed as a sorceress; Louise jauntily wore a page's costume which gave her the air of an urchin; little Michelin, made up as an alme, smiled in a love-sick manner amid her veils embroidered with golden threads.

"Do you know anything?" Saccard softly asked his sister.

"No, nothing as yet," she replied. "But the swain must be here. I will catch them to-night, you may be sure."

"Inform me at once, eh?"

And then Saccard, turning to the right and to the left, complimented Louise and Madame Michelin. He compared the latter to one of Mahomet's houris and the former to a mignon of Henri III. His Provençal accent seemed to make the whole of his spare strident figure sing with delight. When he returned to the group of grave-looking men, Monsieur de Mareuil drew him on one side and spoke to him about the marriage of their children. Nothing was altered, the contract was still to be signed on the following Sunday.

"Quite so," said Saccard. "I even mean to announce the marriage to our friends this evening, if you see no impediment—I am only waiting for my brother, the minister, who has promised to come."

The new deputy was delighted. However, Monsieur Toutin-Laroche was raising his voice as if he were a prey to lively indignation.

"Yes, gentlemen," he was saying to Monsieur Michelin and the two contractors who drew nearer, "I was simple enough to let my name be mixed up in such an affair."

And as Saccard and De Mareuil joined the group, he added:

"I was telling the gentlemen about the deplorable adventure of the Société Générale of the ports of Morocco, you know, Saccard?"

The latter did not flinch. The company in question had just collapsed amid a frightful scandal. Over-inquisitive shareholders had wished to know what progress had been made with the establishment of the famous commercial stations on the shores of the Mediterranean, and a judicial inquiry had demonstrated that the ports of Morocco only existed on the plans of the engineers, very handsome plans, hung on the walls of the company's offices. Since then, Monsieur Toutin-Laroche cried out even louder than the shareholders, growing indignant and demanding that his name should be restored to him spotless. And he made so much noise, that the government, to calm and rehabilitate this useful man in the eye of public opinion, had decided to send him to the Senate. It was thus that he fished up the much-coveted seat, in an affair which had almost brought him to the police court.

"You are really too good to occupy yourself about that," said Saccard. "You can show your great work, the Crédit Viticole, an establishment which has come victorious out of every crisis."

"Yes," murmured De Mareuil, "that is an answer to everything."

Indeed the Crédit Viticole had just emerged from great and skilfully concealed embarrassments. A minister who was very kindly disposed towards this financial institution which held the city of Paris by the throat, had brought about a rise on 'change, which Monsieur Toutin-Laroche had turned to advantage marvellously well. Nothing titillated him more than the praise bestowed on the prosperity of the Crédit Viticole. He usually provoked it. He thanked Monsieur de Mareuil with a glance, and leaning towards Baron Gouraud, on whose arm-chair he was familiarly leaning, he asked him:

"You are all right? You are not too warm?"

The baron gave a slight grunt.

"He is breaking up, he breaks up more every day," added Monsieur Toutin-Laroche turning towards the other gentlemen.

Monsieur Michelin smiled, and from time to time gently lowered his eyelids to look at his red ribbon. Mignon and Charrier, firmly planted on their large feet, seemed much more at ease in their dress-coats since they wore diamonds. However, it was nearly midnight, and the assemblage was growing impatient; it did not venture to murmur; but the fans fluttered more nervously, and the noise of conversation increased.

At length, Monsieur Hupel de la Noue reappeared. He had just passed one shoulder through the narrow opening when he perceived Madame d'Espanet at length mounting on to the stage; the other ladies already in position for the first *tableau* had only been waiting for her.

The prefect turned round, showing the spectators his back, and he could be seen talking with the marchioness whom the curtains concealed. He lowered his voice, and making complimentary gestures with the tips of his fingers, said:

"My congratulations, marchioness, your costume is delicious."

"I have a much prettier one underneath!" cavalierly rejoined the young woman, who laughed in his face, so funny did she find him, buried in this manner, among the draperies.

The audacity of this witticism momentarily astonished the gallant Monsieur Hupel de la Noue; but he recovered himself, and enjoying the repartee more and more as he gradually fathomed its depths:

"Ah! charming! charming!" he murmured with a delighted air.

He let the corner of the curtain fall, and went to join the group of grave looking men, wishing to enjoy his work. He was no longer the scared man running after the nymph Echo's girdle of foliage. He was radiant and panting, wiping his forehead. He still had the little white hand marked on the sleeve of his coat; and in addition the glove of his right hand was stained with red at the tip of the thumb; he had no doubt dipped his thumb into one of the ladies' pots of colour. He smiled, fanned himself with his handkerchief and stammered:

"She is adorable, lavishing, stupefying—"

"Who?" asked Saccard.

"The marchioness. Fancy, she just said to me—"

And he repeated the witticism. It was considered extremely smart. The gentlemen repeated it to one another. Even worthy Monsieur Haffner, who had approached, could not prevent himself from applauding. However, a piano which few people had seen, began to play a waltz. There was then deep silence. The waltz had a capricious, interminable roll; and a very soft phrase ever ascended the keyboard, finishing in a nightingale's trill; then deeper notes resounded more slowly. It was very voluptuous. The ladies smiled with their heads slightly inclined. The piano had, however, suddenly put a stop to Monsieur Hupel de la Noue's gaiety. He looked at the red velvet curtains with an anxious air, he said to himself that he ought to have placed Madame d'Espanet in position as he had placed the others.

The curtains slowly opened, the piano again began the sensual waltz in a minor key. A murmur sped through the drawing-room, the ladies leaned forward, the gentlemen stretched out their necks, whilst admiration displayed itself here and there by a remark, made in too loud a voice, by a spontaneous sigh, or a stifled laugh. This lasted for five long minutes, beneath the blaze of the three chandeliers.

Monsieur Hupel de la Noue, now reassured, smiled beatifically at his poem. He could not resist the temptation of repeating to the people around him, what he had already been saying for a month past:

"I thought of doing it in verse. But the lines are more noble, eh?"

Then, while the waltz came and went in an endless lullaby, he gave some explanations. Mignon and Charrier had drawn near and were listening attentively.

"You know the subject of course? Handsome Narcissus, son of the river Cephise and the nymph Liriope, scorns the love of the nymph Echo—Echo belonging to the suite of Juno whom she amused with her speeches while Jupiter visited the world—Echo, daughter of the Air and the Earth, as you know—"

And he went into transports over the poetry of mythology. Then in a more confidential tone:

"I thought I might give rein to my imagination. The nymph Echo leads handsome Narcissus before Venus, in a marine grotto, so that the goddess may inflame him with her fire. But the goddess remains powerless. The young man indicates by his attitude that he is not touched."

The explanation was not out of place, for few of the spectators in the drawing-room understood the real meaning of the groups. When the prefect had named the personages in an undertone, the admiration increased. Mignon and Charrier continued staring with wide open eyes. They had not understood.

A grotto was shown on the platform, between the red velvet curtains. The scenery was formed of silk with large irregular plaits imitating rocky anfractuosities on which shells, fish and large sea plants were painted. The broken ground rose up like a hillock, covered with the same silk, on which the scene painter had depicted fine sand constellated with pearls and silver spangles. It was a fitting retreat for a goddess. On the summit of the hillock stood Madame de Lauwerens figuring Venus; somewhat stout, wearing her pink tights with the dignity of a duchess of Olympus, she depicted the sovereign of love with large severe, all devouring eyes. Behind her, showing merely her malicious face, her wings and quiver, little Madame Daste lent her smile to that amiable personage Cupid. Then, on one side of the hillock, the three Graces, Mesdames de Guende, Teissière, and de Meinhold, all in muslin, smiled and entwined each other as in Pradier's group; whilst on the other side the Marchioness d'Espanet and Madame Haffner, enveloped in the same flow of lace, their arms round each other's waists and their hair mingled, lent something suggestive to the *tableau*, a souvenir of Lesbos which Monsieur Hupel de la Noue explained in a lower voice and for the gentlemen only, saying that he had wished by this to show the full extent of the power of Venus. Below the mound the Countess Vanska personated Voluptuousness; she stretched herself out, twisted by a last spasm, with her eyes half closed and languishing, as if weary; very dark, she had unloosened her black hair, and her tunic, spotted with tawny flames, was cut so as to allow glimpses of her glowing skin. The scale of colour which the costumes furnished, from the snowy whiteness of Venus's veil to the dark red of Voluptuousness's tunic, was soft, generally pink, and of a fleshy tinge. And under the electric ray, ingeniously cast upon the stage from one of the garden windows, the gauze, the lace, all the light transparent stuffs mingled so well with the shoulders and the lights, that these pinky whitenesses seemed alive, and one no longer knew whether the ladies had not carried plastic accuracy to the point of stripping themselves naked. This was but the apotheosis; the drama was enacted in the foreground. On the left side, Renée, the nymph Echo, stretched out her arms towards the great goddess, her head half turned in supplicating fashion in the direction of Narcissus, as if to invite him to look at Venus, the mere sight of whom kindles terrible fires; but Narcissus, on the right, made a gesture of refusal, hid his eyes with his hand and remained icily cold. The costumes of these two personages, especially had cost Monsieur Hupel de la Noue's imagination infinite trouble. Narcissus, as a wandering demi-god of the forests, wore the attire of an ideal huntsman: greenish tights, a short close-fitting jacket, and a branch of oak in his hair. The dress of the nymph Echo was a complete allegory in itself alone; it partook of the high trees and lofty mountains, of the resounding spots where the voices of the Earth and Air reply to each other; it was a rock by the white satin of the skirt, a thicket by the foliage of the girdle, a pure sky by the cloud of blue gauze forming the body. And the groups retained the stillness of statues, the carnal note of Olympus resounded in the blaze of the broad ray, while the piano continued its complaint of acute love.

It was generally considered that Maxime was admirably formed. In making his gesture of refusal he developed his left hip, which was much remarked. But all the praises were for Renée's expression of face. As Monsieur Hupel de la Noue remarked, it typified "the pangs of unsatisfied desire." Her face; wore an acute smile which tried to become humble, she begged her prey with the supplication of a hungry she-wolf who half hides her teeth. The first *tableau* went off very well, save that that madcap of an Adeline moved, and only with difficulty restrained an intense desire to laugh. At last the curtains closed again and the piano became silent.

Then the audience applauded discreetly and the conversation was resumed. A great breath of love, of restrained desire, had come from the nudities of the platform, and darted about the drawing-room where the women leaned more languidly on their seats, while the men spoke in low voices in each other's ears, and smiled. There was a whispering as in an alcove, a semi-silence as suited to good society, a longing for voluptuousness, barely expressed by a quiver of lips; and in the mute looks exchanged amid this well-mannered delight, there was the brutal boldness of love offered and accepted with a glance.

There was no end to the judgments passed on the perfections of the ladies. Their costumes acquired almost as great importance as their shoulders. When Mignon and Charrier wished to question Monsieur Hupel de la Noue, they were greatly surprised to see him no longer beside them; he had already plunged behind the platform again.

"I was telling you then, my beauty," said Madame Sidonie, resuming a conversation which the first *tableau* had interrupted, "that I had received a letter from London, you know, about the affair of the three milliards. The person whom I had charged to make inquiries writes to me that she thinks she has discovered the banker's receipt. England must have paid in that case. It has made me feel ill all day."

She was indeed more yellow than usual, in her sorceress's robe dotted with stars. And as Madame Michelin did not listen to her, she continued in a lower voice, muttering that it was impossible that England could have paid, and that she should decidedly go to London herself.

"Narcissus's costume is very pretty, isn't it?" said Louise to Madame Michelin.

The latter smiled. She looked at Baron Gouraud, who seemed quite cheerful again in his arm-chair. Madame Sidonie, perceiving the direction of her glance, leant forward and whispered in her ear, so that the child might not hear:

"Has he kept his engagement?"

"Yes," replied the young woman, languishing, playing the part of an alme delightfully. "I have chosen the house at Louveciennes, and I have received the title deeds of it from his man of business. But we have broken off, I no longer see him."

Louise had particularly sharp ears to catch what one wanted to hide from her. She looked at Baron Gouraud with a page's boldness, and said quietly to Madame Michelin:

"Don't you think that the baron is frightful?"

Then bursting out laughing she added:

"I say, he ought to have been entrusted with the part of Narcissus. He would be delicious in apple-green tights!"

The sight of Venus, of this voluptuous corner of Olympus, had indeed revived the old senator. He rolled his eyes with delight and turned half round to compliment Saccard. Amid the buzz which filled the drawing-room the group of grave-looking men continued talking business and politics. Monsieur Haffner said that he had just been named president of a jury charged with settling questions of indemnities. Then the conversation turned upon the works of Paris, on the Boulevard du Prince-Eugène, of which the public was beginning to talk seriously. Saccard seized the opportunity and spoke of a person he knew, a proprietor who would no doubt be expropriated. The baron softly wagged his head. Monsieur Toutin-Laroche went so far as to declare that there was nothing so disagreeable as to be expropriated; Monsieur Michelin assented, and squinted still more in looking at his decoration.

"The indemnities can never be too high," sententiously concluded Monsieur de Mareuil who wished to please Saccard.

They had understood each other. But Mignon and Charrier now brought their private affairs forward. They meant to retire soon, no doubt to Langres, they said, keeping an occasional lodging in Paris. They made the gentlemen smile when they related that after completing the building of their magnificent mansion on the Boulevard Malesherbes, they had found it so handsome that they had not been able to resist the desire to sell it. Their diamonds must have been a consolation which they had offered themselves. Saccard laughed with a bad grace; his old partners had just realized enormous profits from an affair in which he had played the part of a dupe. And as the interval between the *tableau* grew longer, phrases of praise about Venus's bosom, and the nymph Echo's dress, were heard amid the conversation of the grave-looking men.

At the end of a long half hour Monsieur Hupel de la Noue reappeared. He was on the high road of success and the disorder of his attire increased. As he regained his seat he met Monsieur de Mussy. He shook hands with him in passing; and then he retraced his steps to ask him:

"You don't know the marchioness's remark?"

And he related it to him, without waiting for his reply. It penetrated him more and more; he criticised it, he ended by finding that it was of exquisite naivete. "I have a much prettier one underneath." It was a cry from the heart!

But Monsieur de Mussy was not of this opinion. He considered the remark indecent. He had just been attached to the embassy in England, where, so the minister had told him, the greatest propriety was necessary. He refused to lead the cotillon any more, made himself old, and no longer spoke of his love for Renée, to whom he bowed gravely when he met her.

Monsieur Hupel de la Noue was again joining the group, formed behind the baron's arm-chair, when the piano struck up a triumphal march. A loud burst of harmony, produced by bold strokes on the keys, preluded a melody of great amplitude, amid which a metallic clang resounded at intervals. Each phrase as soon as finished was repeated in a louder strain, accentuating the rhythm. It was at once brutal and joyous.

"You will see," muttered Monsieur Hupel de la Noue. "I have, perhaps, carried poetical licence rather far; but I think that my audacity has answered. The nymph Echo, seeing that Venus is powerless over the handsome Narcissus, conducts him to Plutus, the god of wealth and precious metals. After the temptation of the flesh, the temptation of gold."

"That's classical," replied the lean Monsieur Toutin-Laroche with an amiable smile. "You are well acquainted with your period, my dear prefect."

The curtains parted, the piano played louder. The effect was dazzling. The electric ray fell upon a flaming splendour, which the spectators at first thought was a brazier in which bars of gold and precious stones seemingly melted. A new grotto was presented, but this one was not the cool retreat of Venus, bathed by the waters which eddied on fine pearl besprinkled sand; it must have been situated in the bowels of the earth, in some deep fiery stratum, it seemed a fissure of the ancient Hades, a crevice amid a mine of liquescent metals inhabited by Plutus. The silk, simulating the rock, displayed broad metallic lodes, layers which looked like the veins of the old world, teeming with incalculable wealth and the eternal life of the soil. On the ground, by a bold anachronism, which Monsieur Hupel de la Noue had decided on, there was an avalanche of twenty-franc pieces, louis spread out, louis piled up, a pullulation of ascending louis. On the summit of this heap of gold sat Madame de Guende as Plutus, a female Plutus, a Plutus showing her bosom, amid the broad streaks of her dress imitating all the metals. Around the god, erect or reclining, united in bunches, or blooming apart, were grouped the fairy-like efflorescences of this grotto into which the caliphs of the "Arabian Nights" had seemingly emptied their treasure. There was Madame Haffner as Gold, with a stiff skirt as resplendent as the robes of a bishop; Madame d'Espanet as Silver, shining like moonlight; Madame de Lauwerens in warm blue as a Sapphire, having beside her little Madame Daste, a smiling Turquoise, of a tender shade of blue; then were spread out the Emerald, Madame de Meinhold, and the Topaz, Madame Teissière; and lower down, Countess Vanska, lending her dark ardour to Coral, was stretched out with her arms raised and loaded with red drops, similar to some monstrous and adorable polype, which displayed a woman's flesh amid the pink and pearly openings of her shell. These ladies wore necklaces, bracelets, complete sets of jewels formed of the precious stone they represented.

The audience particularly noticed the original jewellery of Mesdames Haffner and d'Espanet, exclusively composed of little gold and little silver coins, fresh from the mint. In the foreground the drama remained the same: the nymph Echo tempted handsome Narcissus who again refused with a gesture. And the eyes of the spectators grew accustomed with delight to this yawning cavity opening amid the inflamed entrails of the earth, to this pile of gold on which the wealth of a world was wallowing.

This second *tableau* met with still more success than the first one. The idea appeared particularly ingenious. The boldness of the twenty-franc pieces, this stream from some modern safe, which had fallen into a corner of Grecian mythology, delighted the minds of the ladies and the financiers who were present. The words, "What a number of coins! what a quantity of gold!" sped by, amid smiles and long quivers of satisfaction; and assuredly, each of the ladies, each of the gentlemen dreamt of having all this money to her or himself, in a cellar.

"England has paid, those are your milliards," maliciously murmured Louise in Madame Sidonie's ear.

And Madame Michelin, her mouth slightly parted by delighted desire, threw back her alme's veil and fondled the gold with a sparkling glance, while the group of grave-looking men went into transports. Monsieur Toutin-Laroche, beaming, murmured a few words in the ear of the baron whose face was becoming spotted with yellow stains. But Mignon and Charrier, less discreet, said with brutal simplicity:

"Dash it all! there would be enough there to demolish all Paris and rebuild it."

The remark seemed a profound one to Saccard, who was beginning to think that Mignon and Charrier trifled with people in passing themselves off as fools. When the curtains closed again and the piano finished the triumphal march with a loud noise of notes thrown one upon the other, like final shovelfuls of crowns, the applause burst forth, louder and more prolonged.

However, in the middle of the *tableau*, the minister accompanied by his secretary, Monsieur de Saffré, had appeared at the door of the drawing-room. Saccard, who was impatiently watching for his brother, wished to dart to meet him. But the latter requested him by a gesture not to stir. And he softly approached the group of grave-looking men. When the curtains had closed again, and people had perceived him, a long whisper travelled through the drawing-room and all heads were turned round. The minister counterbalanced the success of the "Amours of handsome Narcissus and the nymph Echo."

"You are a poet, my dear prefect," he said, smiling to Monsieur Hupel de la Noue. "You once published a volume of verse, 'The Convolvuli,' I believe? I see that the cares of office have not exhausted your imagination."

The prefect detected the point of an epigram in this compliment. The sudden advent of his superior put him out of countenance, the more as, on giving himself a glance to see if his attire were correct, he perceived on his coat sleeve the little white hand which he did not dare to rub off. He bowed and stammered.

"Really," continued the minister, addressing himself to Monsieur Toutin-Laroche, Baron Gouraud, and the other personages who were there, "all that gold was a marvellous spectacle. We should do great things if Monsieur Hupel de la Noue coined money for us."

In ministerial language, this was the same remark as Mignon's and Charrier's. Thereupon Monsieur Toutin-Laroche and the others paid their court, and played on the minister's last phrase: the Empire had already accomplished marvels; there was no lack of gold, thanks to the great experience of those in power; France had never occupied such a splendid position in the eyes of Europe; and the gentlemen ended by becoming so servile, that the minister himself changed the conversation. He listened to them with his head erect and the corners of his mouth slightly raised, whereby an expression of doubt and smiling disdain was imparted to his fat, carefully shaven, white face.

Saccard, who wished to bring about the announcement of the marriage of Maxime and Louise, manœuvred so as to find a skilful transition. He affected great familiarity, and his brother played the good-natured, and consented to do him the service of seeming to be very fond of him. He was really a superior man, with his clear look, his evident contempt of petty rascalities, his broad shoulders which could have overturned all these folks with a mere shrug. When the marriage at last came into question he showed himself charming, he let it be understood that he had his wedding gift ready; he spoke of Maxime's appointment as an auditor of the Council of State. He went so far as to repeat twice to his brother, in a tone of good fellowship:

"Tell your son that I wish to be his witness."

Monsieur de Mareuil blushed with delight. Saccard was congratulated. Monsieur Toutin-Laroche offered himself as a second witness. Then the group abruptly began talking about divorce. A member of the opposition had just had "the sad courage," said Monsieur Haffner, to defend this social shame. And every one protested. Their sense of propriety furnished them with profound remarks. Monsieur Michelin smiled delicately at the minister, while Mignon and Charrier observed with astonishment that the collar of his dress-coat was worn.

In the meantime Monsieur Hupel de la Noue remained embarrassed, leaning on the arm-chair of Baron Gouraud, who had contented himself with exchanging a silent hand-shake with the minister. The poet did not dare to leave the spot. An indefinable feeling, the fear of appearing ridiculous, the fear of losing the good-will of his superior, detained him despite his furious desire to go and set the ladies in position on the stage for the last *tableau*. He waited for some happy remark to occur to him and reinstate him in favour; but he could think of nothing, and he was feeling more and more ill at ease when he perceived Monsieur de Saffré; he took his arm and clung to him as to a saving plank. The young man had just arrived, he was quite a fresh victim.

"You don't know the marchioness's remark?" the prefect asked him.

Monsieur Hupel de la Noue was so disturbed, however, that he no longer knew how to present the anecdote in a spicy manner; he floundered:

"I said to her: 'You have a charming costume,' and she answered—"

"'I have a much prettier one underneath,'" quietly added Monsieur de Saffré. "It's old, my dear fellow, very old."

Monsieur Hupel de la Noue looked at him in consternation. The remark was old, and he had meant to sift his commentary on the naivete of this cry from the heart!

"Old, as old as the world," repeated the secretary. "Madame d'Espanet has said it twice already at the Tuileries."

This was the last blow. After that the prefect no longer cared a fig for the minister or the whole drawing-room. He was proceeding towards the platform when the piano began a prelude, in a saddened tone, with trembling notes which seemed to weep; then the complaint expanded, dragged on at length, and the curtains parted. Monsieur Hupel de la Noue, who had already half disappeared, returned into the drawing-room on hearing the slight grating of the rings. He was pale, exasperated; he made a violent effort to restrain himself from apostrophizing the ladies. What! they had taken up their positions unassisted! It must be that little d'Espanet who had fomented a plot to hasten the change of costume and dispense with him. That wasn't it, that was worth nothing at all!

He returned, mumbling indistinct words. He looked on to the platform, shrugging his shoulders, and murmuring:

"The nymph Echo is too near the edge—And that leg of handsome Narcissus, nothing noble in its attitude, nothing noble at all."

Mignon and Charrier, who had approached him to hear "the explanation," ventured to ask "what the young man and the young woman were doing there, lying on the ground." But he did not answer, he refused to explain any more of his poem; and as the contractors insisted:

"Why," he said, "it no longer concerns me, since the ladies set themselves in position without me!"

The piano softly sobbed. On the platform a clearing, on which the electric ray set a stretch of sunlight, revealed a vista of leaves. It was an ideal glade with blue trees, and large red and yellow flowers which rose as high as the oaks. Venus and Plutus stood on a grassy mound side by side, and surrounded by nymphs who had hastened from the neighbouring thickets to serve as their escort. There were the daughters of the trees, the daughters of the springs, the daughters of the heights, all the laughing naked divinities of the forest. And the god and the goddess triumphed, and punished the apathy of the proud young fellow who had scorned them, while the group of nymphs looked inquisitively and with religious fright at the vengeance of Olympus displayed in the foreground. The drama was there being unravelled. Handsome Narcissus, lying on the margin of a brook which came down from the back of the stage, was looking at himself in the clear mirror; and exactitude had been carried to the point of placing a strip of looking-glass, at the bottom of the brook. But he was no longer the free young fellow, the forest wanderer; death surprised him amid his delighted admiration of his own figure, death enervated him, and Venus with her outstretched finger, like a fairy in a transformation scene, consigned him to his deadly fate. He was becoming a flower. His limbs became verdant and longer, in his tight-fitting costume of green satin; the flexible stalk, figured by his slightly bent legs, sank into the ground to take root there, while his bust, decked with broad lappets of white satin, expanded into a marvellous corolla. Maxime's fair hair completed the illusion, and set, with its long curls, yellow pistils amid the whiteness of the petals. And the large, nascent flower, still human, inclined its head towards the spring, with its eyes bedimmed, and smiling with voluptuous ecstasy, as if handsome Narcissus had at length satisfied in death the passion which he had felt for himself. A few paces off the nymph Echo was dying also, dying of unquenched desires; she found herself gradually caught in the rigidity of the soil, she felt her burning limbs congeal and harden. She was not a vulgar rock, soiled by moss, but white marble, by her shoulders and arms, by her long snowy robe from which the girdle of foliage and the blue drapery had glided. Sunk down amid the satin of her skirt, which formed large plaits, similar to a block of Paros, she threw herself back, with nought alive, in her statue-like congealed body, save her woman's eyes, eyes which glistened as they remained fixed on the flower of the waters, languidly leaning above the mirror of the spring. And it already seemed as if all the love sounds of the forest, the prolonged noises of the thickets, the mysterious quivers of the leaves, the deep sighs of the old oaks, came and beat upon the marble flesh of the nymph Echo, whose heart, still bleeding amid the block, resounded protractedly, repeating afar the slightest complaints of the Earth and of the Air.

"Oh! how they have muffled up poor Maxime!" murmured Louise. "And Madame Saccard, you would say a dead woman!"

"She is covered with rice powder," said Madame Michelin.

Other scarcely complimentary remarks circulated. This third *tableau* did not meet with the same unqualified success as the two others. And yet it was this tragical ending which made Monsieur Hupel de la Noue enthusiastic about his own talent. He admired himself in it, as his Narcissus did in his strip of looking-glass. He had set a number of poetical and philosophical allusions in it. When the curtains had closed again for the last time, and the spectators had applauded like people of good breeding, he experienced mental regret at having given way to anger and not having explained the last page of his poem. He then wished to give the people around him the key to the charming, grand, or simply suggestive things which handsome Narcissus and the nymph Echo represented, and he even tried to say what Venus and Plutus were doing in the depths of the clearing; but the gentlemen and ladies, whose clear practical minds had understood the grotto of flesh and the grotto of gold, had no inclination to descend into the prefect's mythological complications. Only Mignon and Charrier, who absolutely wished to inform themselves, were good-natured enough to question him. He took possession of them, and kept them during nearly two hours, standing in the embrasure of a window, relating to them the "Metamorphoses" of Ovid.

The minister now withdrew. He apologised for not being able to wait for the beautiful Madame Saccard to compliment her on the perfect gracefulness of the nymph Echo. He had just been three or four times round the drawing-room on the arm of his brother, giving a few shakes of the hand and bowing to the ladies. He had never before compromised himself so much for Saccard. He left him radiant, when, on the threshold, he said to him in a loud voice:

"I shall expect you to-morrow morning. Come and breakfast with me."

The ball was about to begin. The servants had ranged the ladies' arm-chairs along the walls. The large drawing-room now displayed from the little yellow room to the platform, its bare carpet the large purple flowers of which opened under the dripping light which fell from the crystal of the chandeliers. The heat was increasing; the reflection of the red hangings brightened the gilding of the furniture and the ceiling. To open the ball one waited until the ladies, the nymph Echo, Venus, Plutus, and the others, had changed their costumes.

Madame d'Espanet and Madame Haffner appeared the first. They had reassumed their costumes of the second *tableau*; the first as gold, the other as silver. They were surrounded and congratulated; and they recounted their emotions.

"As for me I nearly burst out," said the marchioness, "when I saw Monsieur Toutin-Laroche's big nose looking at me in the distance!"

"I think that I have a stiff neck," languidly remarked the fair-haired Suzanne. "No, really, if it had lasted a minute longer I should have replaced my head in a natural position, my neck hurt me so much."

From the embrasure into which Monsieur Hupel de la Noue had pushed Mignon and Charrier, he cast nervous glances at the group formed around the two young women; he was afraid that people were poking fun at him. The other nymphs arrived one after the other; they had all resumed their costumes as precious stones; the Countess Vanska, as coral, met with prodigious success when one was able to closely examine the ingenious details of her dress. Then Maxime entered, correct in his dress coat and with a smiling air; and a flow of women enveloped him, he was placed in the centre of the circle, he was joked about his part as a flower, and his passion for looking-glasses. Without any embarrassment, as if delighted with his part, he continued smiling, answered the jokes, confessed that he adored himself, and that he was sufficiently cured of women to prefer himself to them. People laughed the louder at this, the group grew larger, and took possession of the whole centre of the drawing-room, while the young man, drowned amid this people of shoulders, this medley of bright costumes, retained his perfume of monstrous love, his vicious fair flower's gentleness.

When Renée, however, at last came down, there was semi-silence. She had attired herself in a new costume of such original grace and such audacity that the gentlemen and the ladies, although accustomed to the young woman's eccentricities, at first gave a movement of surprise. She was dressed as an Otaheitian. This costume, it appears, is most primitive: as she wore it, it comprised soft tinted tights which rose from her feet to her bosom, leaving her shoulders and arms bare; and over these tights a simple muslin blouse, short and trimmed with two flounces so as to slightly hide the hips. In her hair a wreath of wild flowers; and gold rings round her ankles and her wrists. Nothing more. She was naked. The tights had the suppleness of flesh under the paleness of the blouse; the pure line of her nudity could be detected from her knees to her arm-pits, vaguely bedimmed by the flounces, but reappearing at the slightest movement, and becoming more distinct between the threads of the lace. She was an adorable savage, a barbarous, voluptuous girl scarcely hidden by a white vapour, a patch of sea fog, amid which her whole body could be divined.

With rosy cheeks Renée advanced at a rapid step. Céleste had made the first tights burst; but the young woman had fortunately foreseen the eventuality and taken her precautions. These torn tights had delayed her. She seemed to care little about her triumph. She smiled, however, and briefly answered the men who stopped and complimented her on the purity of her attitudes in the *tableaux vivants*. Behind her she left a trail of dress coats astonished and charmed by the transparency of her muslin blouse. When she had reached the group of women who surrounded Maxime, she gave rise to curt exclamations, and the marchioness began to look at her from head to foot, with a tender air, and murmuring:

"She is adorably formed."

Madame Michelin, whose alme's costume became horribly heavy beside this simple veil, pursed her lips, while Madame Sidonie, shrivelled up in her black sorceress's dress, murmured in her ear:

"It's the height of indecency, isn't it, my beauty?"

"Ah! yes indeed," said the pretty brunette at last, "Monsieur Michelin *would* be angry if I undressed myself like that."

"And he would be quite right," concluded the agent.

The band of serious men were not of this opinion. It went into ecstacies at a distance. Monsieur Michelin, whom his wife so inappropriately brought into question, showed himself transported so as to please Monsieur Toutin-Laroche and Baron Gouraud whom the sight of Renée enraptured. Saccard was greatly complimented on the perfection of his wife's figure. He bowed and professed to be very touched. The evening was a good one for him, and but for a preoccupation which darted from his eyes at moments when he cast a rapid glance at his sister, he would have been supremely happy.

"I say, she has never shown us so much," jokingly said Louise in Maxime's ear, and indicating Renée by a glance.

She paused, and then with an undefinable smile:

"At least, to me."

The young fellow looked at her with a nervous air; but she continued smiling, strangely, like a schoolboy delighted with some bit of fun rather too strong.

The ball began. The platform of the *tableaux vivants* had been utilized to accommodate a little orchestra in which brass instruments predominated, and the bugles and the cornets-à-piston launched forth their clear notes, amid the ideal forest with blue trees. First came a quadrille, "Ah! he has boots, he has boots, Bastien!" which then constituted the delight of public balls. The ladies danced. Polkas, waltzes, mazurkas alternated with quadrilles. The swinging couples came and went, filled the long gallery, leaping under the lash of the brass instruments, swaying amid the lullaby of the violins. The costumes, this flood of women of all countries and all periods, displayed a swarming medley of bright stuffs. After mingling the colours and carrying them off in cadenced confusion, the rhythm at certain touches of the bows abruptly brought back the same tunic of pink satin, the same dress body of blue velvet beside the same black coat. Then another touch of the bows, a blast of the cornets, pushed the couples on, made them travel in files around the drawing-room, with the swinging motion of a bark floating away under a gust of wind which had severed the fast that moored it. And so on, always, endlessly, for hours together. At times, between two dances, a lady approached a window, stifling, inhaling a little icy air; a couple rested on a couch in the little buttercup drawing-room, or descended into the conservatory, going slowly round the paths. Skirts, only the edges of which could be seen, seemed to laugh languidly under the arbours of tropical creepers, in the depths of the tepid shade, where the loud notes of the cornets were wafted during the quadrilles of "Hallo! the little lambs," and "I've a foot on the move."

When the servants opened the door of the dining-room, transformed into a refectory with sideboards against the walls, and a long table laden with cold meats in the centre, there was a shove, a crush. A tall handsome man, who had timidly kept his hat in his hand, was so violently flattened against the wall that the unfortunate hat burst with a dull moan. This made people laugh. The guests rushed upon the pastry and the truffled poultry, brutally digging their elbows into one another's ribs. It was a pillage, hands met amid the viands, and the lackeys did not know whom to answer, in the midst of this band of well-bred men whose extended arms expressed the sole fear of arriving too late and finding the dishes empty. An old gentleman became angry because there was no Bordeaux wine, and champagne, so he affirmed, prevented him from sleeping.

"Softly, gentlemen," said Baptiste in his grave voice. "There will be enough for everyone."

But he was not listened to. The dining-room was already full, and yet more anxious dress-coats rose up at the door. In front of the sideboards, stood groups eating quickly and pressing closely together. A good many swallowed without drinking, not having been able to set their hands on a glass. Others, on the contrary, drank after fruitlessly running about for a morsel of bread.

"Listen," said Monsieur Hupel de la Noue, whom Mignon and Charrier, weary of mythology, had led to the buffet, "we sha'n't get anything if we don't help each other. It's much worse at the Tuileries, and I have acquired some experience there. You look after the wine, and I'll see to the meat."

The prefect was watching a leg of mutton. He stretched out his hand, at the right moment, through a break in the surrounding shoulders, and quietly carried it off, after filling his pockets with little rolls. The contractors returned from their side, Mignon with one bottle, and Charrier with two bottles of champagne; but they had only been able to secure two glasses; they said, however, that it did not matter, that they would drink out of the same. And the party supped on the corner of a flowerstand at the end of the room. They did not even take off their gloves, but put the slices of mutton already cut between their bread, and kept the bottles under their arms. And standing up, they talked with their mouths full, stretching out their chins in advance of their waistcoats so that the gravy might fall on to the carpet.

Charrier, having finished his wine before his bread, asked a servant if he could not have a glass of champagne.

"You must wait, sir," angrily replied the scared servant, losing his head and forgetting he was no longer in the kitchen. "Three hundred bottles have already been drunk."

However, one could hear the notes of the orchestra swelling with sudden gusts. Couples were footing the polka called "The Kisses," famous at public balls, and the rhythm of which each dancer had to mark by kissing his partner. Madame d'Espanet appeared at the door of the dining-room, flushed, her hair slightly disordered, and trailing her silver robe with charming lassitude. People barely drew aside, and she had to shove with her elbows to obtain a passage. She made the round of the table, hesitating, a pout on her lips. Then she went straight to Monsieur Hupel de la Noue who had finished, and, who was wiping his mouth with his pocket-handkerchief.

"You would be very amiable, sir," she said to him with an adorable smile, "if you would find me a chair! I have been round the table fruitlessly—"

The prefect had a spite against the marchioness but his gallantry did not hesitate; he hastened, found a chair, installed Madame d'Espanet and remained behind her, serving her. She would only take a few shrimps with a little butter and two thimblefuls of champagne. She eat in a delicate manner amid the gluttony of the men. The table and the chairs were exclusively reserved for the ladies. However an exception was always made in favour of Baron Gouraud. He was there seated at ease, in front of a bit of pastry the crust of which he crunched with his jaws. The marchioness re-conquered the prefect by telling him that she should never forget her emotions as an artiste in the "Amours of handsome Narcissus and the nymph Echo." She even explained to him why they had not waited for him at the last *tableau* in a manner which completely consoled him: the ladies on learning that the minister was there had thought that it would hardly be proper to prolong the interval. She ended by begging him to go in search of Madame Haffner who was dancing with Monsieur Simpson, a brute of a man who displeased her, she said. And when Suzanne was there she no longer looked at Monsieur Hupel de la Noue.

Saccard, followed by Messieurs Toutin-Laroche, De Mareuil and Haffner, had taken possession of a sideboard. As there was no room at the table and Monsieur de Saffré passed by with Madame Michelin on his arm he detained them, and insisted that the pretty brunette should share with his party. She nibbled some pastry, smiling, raising her clear eyes on the five men who surrounded her. They leaned towards her, touched her alme's veils embroidered with threads of gold, brought her to bay between themselves and the sideboard, against which she ended by leaning, taking cakes from every hand, very gentle and very caressing, and showing the loving docility of a slave amid her masters. All by himself, at the other end of the room, Monsieur Michelin was finishing a terreen of goose's liver which he had succeeded in capturing.

Madame Sidonie, who had been prowling about the ball since the first bow strokes, now entered the dining-room and summoned Saccard with a glance.

"She isn't dancing," she said to him in a low voice. "She seems anxious. I think she is meditating some bit of folly. But I have not yet been able to discover the swain. I am going to eat something and then return to the watch."

And standing like a man, she eat a chicken's wing, which she procured, thanks to Monsieur Michelin who had finished his terreen. She poured herself out some Malaga in a large champagne glass; then, after wiping her mouth with the tips of her fingers, she returned to the drawing-room. The train of her sorceress's robe already seemed to have gathered up all the dust of the carpets.

The ball was languishing, and the orchestra gave signs of being blown, when a murmur sped about: "The cotillon! the cotillon!" and revived the dancers and the brass instruments alike. Couples came from all the clumps of plants in the conservatory; the large drawing-room grew as full as when the first quadrille was danced; and there was a discussion among the awakened crowd. It was the last flash of the ball. The men who did not dance looked with sluggish good nature out of the depths of the embrasures at the talkative group swelling in the middle of the room; while the supper-eaters at the sideboards stretched out their necks to see, but without letting go of their bread.

"Monsieur de Mussy won't," said one lady. "He swears that he no longer leads it. Come, once more, Monsieur de Mussy, only this once. Do it for us."

But the young embassy attaché remained stiff in his high collar turned down at the points. It was really impossible, he had sworn. There was a disappointment. Maxime also refused, saying that he couldn't, that he was tired out. Monsieur Hupel de la Noue did not dare to offer himself; he only descended as far as poetry. On a lady speaking of Monsieur Simpson she was silenced; Monsieur Simpson was the strangest cotillon leader one ever saw; he gave himself up to fantastic and malicious devices; it was related that in one drawing-room where the guests had been so imprudent as to choose him, he had compelled the ladies to jump over the chairs, and one of his favourite figures was to make everyone go round the room on all fours.

"Has Monsieur de Saffré left?" asked a childish voice.

He was leaving, he was saying good-bye to the beautiful Madame Saccard with whom he was on the best possible terms, since she would not have him. This amiable sceptic admired other people's caprices. He was triumphantly brought back from the hall. He tried to escape, and said with a smile that he was being compromised, that he was a serious man. Then, in presence of all the white hands that were stretched out towards him:

"Well," said he, "take your places. But I warn you that I'm classical. I haven't a copper's worth of imagination."

The couples sat down round the drawing-room, on all the seats that could be gathered together; some young fellows even went to fetch the iron chairs of the conservatory. It was a monster cotillon, Monsieur de Saffré, who had the solemn air of an officiating priest, chose, as his partner, the Countess Vanska, whose costume as Coral preoccupied him. When everyone was in position, he cast a long glance at this circular row of skirts, each flanked by a dress-coat. And he made a sign to the orchestra, the brass instruments of which resounded. Heads leaned forward along the smiling band of faces.

Renée had refused to take part in the cotillon. She had been nervously gay since the beginning of the ball, scarcely dancing, but mingling with the groups, unable to remain still. Her friends found her strange. During the evening she had talked of making a balloon journey with a celebrated aeronaut with whom all Paris was occupied. When the cotillon began she was vexed not to be able to walk about at her ease, so she stationed herself at the hall-door, shaking hands with the gentlemen who left and talking with her husband's intimate friends. Baron Gouraud, whom a lackey carried off in his fur cloak, paid a final eulogium to her Otaheitian's costume.

Meanwhile Monsieur Toutin-Laroche shook hands with Saccard.

"Maxime relies on you," said the latter.

"Quite so," replied the new senator.

And turning towards Renée:

"I haven't congratulated you, madame. So the dear boy is now settled!"

And as she gave an astonished smile:

"My wife doesn't yet know," observed Saccard, "We have decided this evening on Mademoiselle de Mareuil's marriage with Maxime."

She continued smiling, bowing to Monsieur Toutin-Laroche who went off saying:

"You sign the contract on Sunday, eh? I am going to Nevers about a mining affair, but I shall be back in time."

Renée remained for a moment alone in the middle of the hall. She no longer smiled, and as she gradually dived into what she had just learnt, she was seized with a great shudder. She looked at the red velvet hangings, the rare plants, the pots of majolica with a fixed stare. Then she said aloud:

"I must speak to him."

And she returned to the drawing-room. But she had to remain near the entry. A figure of the cotillon barred the way. The orchestra was playing a waltz air in a low key. The ladies, holding each other hands, formed a circle, one of those circles that are formed by little girls singing, "Giroflé girofla," and they spun round as quickly as possible, pulling one another's arms, laughing and sliding. In the centre, a gentleman—it was the malicious Monsieur Simpson—held a long pink scarf in his hand; he raised it with the gesture of a fisherman who is about to cast a net; but he did not hurry, he no doubt thought it funny to let these ladies turn round and tire themselves. They breathed hard and asked for mercy. Then he threw the scarf, and he threw it with such skill that it went and wound around the shoulders of Madame d'Espanet and Madame Haffner who were turning side by side. It was one of the Yankee's bits of fun. He then wished to waltz with both ladies at once, and he had already taken them both by the waist, one with his left arm and the other with his right, when Monsieur de Saffré, in the severe tone of the king of the cotillon, said:

"You can't dance with two ladies."

But Monsieur Simpson would not let go of the two waists. Adeline and Suzanne threw themselves back in his arms laughing. The point was argued, the ladies grew angry, the hubbub was prolonged, and the dress-coats in the embrasures of the windows asked themselves how Saffré would extricate himself from this delicate dilemma to his glory. He, indeed, seemed perplexed for a moment, seeking by what refinement of gracefulness he might win the laughers over to his side. Then he smiled, he took Madame d'Espanet and Madame Haffner by the hand, whispered a question in their ears, received their replies, and afterwards addressing himself to Monsieur Simpson:

"Do you pluck the verbena, or do you pluck the periwinkle?" he asked.

Monsieur Simpson, looking rather foolish, said that he plucked the verbena, whereupon Monsieur de Saffré gave him the marchioness saying:

"Here is the verbena."

There was discreet applause. It was found very pretty. Monsieur de Saffré was a cotillon leader "who never remained embarrassed," such was the ladies' remark. In the meanwhile the orchestra had resumed the waltz air with all its instruments, and Monsieur Simpson, after making the round of the room, waltzing with Madame d'Espanet, reconducted her to her seat.

Renée was able to pass. She had bit her lips till they bled at sight of all this foolishness. She considered these women and men stupid to throw scarfs and take the names of flowers. Her ears rung, a furious impatience lent her a brusque desire to throw herself forward, head first, and open a passage. She crossed the drawing-room with a rapid step, jostling the belated couples who were regaining their seats. She went straight to the conservatory. She had not seen either Louise or Maxime among the dancers, and she said to herself that they must be there, in some nook formed by the foliage, united by that partiality for drollery and impropriety which made them seek out little corners as soon as they found themselves anywhere together. But she fruitlessly explored the dimness of the conservatory. She only perceived, in the depths of an arbour, a tall young fellow who was devoutly kissing the hands of little Madame Daste and murmuring:

"Madame de Lauwerens told me right: you are an angel."

This declaration in her house, in her conservatory, shocked Renée. Madame de Lauwerens ought really to have taken her traffic elsewhere! And Renée would have felt relieved could she have chased all these people who bawled so loud out of her apartments. Standing in front of the basin, she looked at the water and asked herself where Louise and Maxime could well have hidden themselves. The orchestra still played that waltz, the slow undulation of which made her feel sick. It was insupportable, one could no longer reflect in one's own abode. She became confused. She forgot that the young folks were not yet married, and she said to herself that it was simple enough, that they had gone to bed. Then she thought of the dining-room, and quickly reascended the conservatory staircase. But at the door of the drawing-room she was stopped for the second time by a figure of the cotillon.

"These are the 'black specks,' ladies," gallantly said Monsieur de Saffré. "This is an invention of mine, and I inaugurate it for you."

There was a great deal of laughter. The gentlemen explained the allusion to the young women. The Emperor had just delivered a speech, which recorded the presence of certain "black specks" on the political horizon. These black specks had met with great success, no one knew why. Parisian wits had appropriated the expression, and to such a point that for a week past the black specks had been introduced into everything. Monsieur de Saffré placed the masculine dancers at one end of the drawing-room, making them turn their backs to the ladies who were left at the other end. Then he ordered the men to turn up their coats in such a way as to hide the backs of their heads. This operation was accomplished amid tremendous merriment. Hump-backed, with their shoulders hidden by the tails of their coats which now only fell to their waists the gentlemen looked really frightful.

"Don't laugh, ladies," cried Monsieur de Saffré with most comical gravity, "or I shall make you put your lace flounces on your heads."

The merriment increased. And the leader energetically availed himself of his sovereignty over some of the gentlemen who would not hide the napes of their necks.

"You are the 'black specks,'" said he; "hide your heads, only show your backs, it is necessary that the ladies should only see so much black. Now, walk, mingle together, so that you may not be recognized."

The hilarity was at its height. The "black specks" went to and fro on their skinny legs with the undulatory motion of headless ravens. One gentleman's shirt was seen with a bit of braces. Then the ladies begged for mercy, they were stifling, and Monsieur de Saffré was pleased to order them to go and fetch the "black specks." They went off like a covey of young partridges amid a loud rustle of skirts. Then, each of them, at the end of her trip, seized hold of the gentleman who came within her grasp. It was an undescribable medley. And the improvised couples disengaged themselves in a file, and made the round of the drawing-room, waltzing, amid the louder strains of the orchestra.

Renée had leant against the wall. Pale, and with compressed lips, she looked on. An old gentleman came and asked her gallantly why she was not dancing. She had to smile and give some kind of answer. Escaping at last, she entered the dining-room. It looked empty, but amid the pillaged sideboards and the trailing bottles and plates, Maxime and Louise, seated side by side, were quietly supping at one end of the table, on a napkin which they had spread out. They seemed to be at their ease, they laughed amid the disorder, the dirty glasses, the dishes soiled with grease, the remnants, which testified to the gluttony of the supper-eaters with white gloves. They had contented themselves with brushing off the crumbs around them. Baptiste gravely walked round the table without a glance for the room, through which a band of wolves seemed to have passed; he was waiting for the other servants to come and set the sideboards in a little order.

Maxime had still been able to gather a very fair supper together. Louise adored hardbake with pistachio nuts, a plateful of which had remained on the top of a sideboard. They had three partially emptied bottles of champagne before them.

"Papa has perhaps gone off," said the young girl.

"So much the better," replied Maxime, "I will see you home."

And as she laughed:

"You know that they really want me to marry you," he added. "It's no longer a joke, it's serious. But what shall we do with ourselves when we are married?"

"Why, we'll do what others do, of course."

This repartee escaped her rather quickly, and as if to withdraw it, she hastily added:

"We will go to Italy. It will do my chest good. I am very ill. Ah! my poor Maxime, what a sorry wife you will have! I am not bigger than two sous of butter."

She smiled, with a shade of sadness, in her page's costume. A dry cough brought red gleams to her cheeks.

"It's the hardbake," said she. "At home I'm forbidden to eat it. Pass me the plate, I will put the rest in my pocket."

And she was emptying the plate when Renée entered the room. She went straight to Maxime, making unheard-of efforts not to swear, not to beat the hunchback whom she found there at table with her lover.

"I wish to speak to you," she stammered in a husky voice.

He hesitated, frightened, dreading to be with her.

"To you alone, at once," repeated Renée.

"Go then, Maxime," said Louise, with her undefinable look. "At the same time you might try to find my father. I lose him at every party."

He rose up, he tried to stop the young woman in the middle of the dining-room by asking her what she could have of so urgent a nature to say to him. But she resumed between her teeth:

"Follow me, or I shall speak out before every one!"

He turned very pale and followed her with the docility of a beaten animal. She thought that Baptiste was looking at her; but at this moment she cared nought for the valet's clear gaze! At the door, the cotillon detained her for the third time.

"Wait," she murmured. "These fools will never have done."

Monsieur de Saffré was placing the Duke de Rozan with his back against the wall, in one corner of the drawing-room, beside he dining-room door. He stationed a lady in front of him, then a gentleman back to back with the lady, then another lady in front of the gentleman, and this in a line, couple by couple, forming as it were a long serpent. As the dancers talked together and tarried behind:

"Come, ladies," he cried, "to your places for the 'columns.'"

They came, and "the columns" were formed. The indecency of finding oneself thus caught, pressed between two men, leaning against the back of one of them, with the chest of the other in front of one, made the ladies very gay. The tips of the women's bosoms touched the facings of the men's dress-coats, the gentlemen's legs disappeared amid the ladies' skirts; and whenever any sudden merriment made a woman's head lean forward, the moustaches in front were obliged to draw back, so as not to carry matters as far as kissing. At one moment a joker must

ÉMILE ZOLA

have given a slight push, for the line closed up, the dress-coats plunged deeper into the skirts, there were little cries and laughs, coughs which did not end. The Baroness de Meinhold was heard saying, "But you are stifling me, sir; don't squeeze me so hard!" this seemed so funny, and gave the whole line such an attack of hilarity, that the shaken "columns" staggered, clashed together and leaned upon one another to avoid falling. Monsieur de Saffré waited with his hands raised ready to clap. Then he clapped. At this signal every one abruptly turned round. The couples who were face to face took each other by the waist, and the file dispersed waltzing round the room. The only one left was the poor Duke de Rozan, who on turning round found his nose against the wall. He was derided by everybody.

"Come," said Renée to Maxime.

The orchestra was still playing the waltz. This soft music, the monotonous rhythm of which at last became insipid, increased the young woman's exasperation. She gained the little drawing-room holding Maxime by the hand; and pushing him to the staircase which led to the dressing-room:

"Go up," she ordered.

She followed him. At this moment Madame Sidonie, who, throughout the evening, had been prowling round about her sister-in-law, astonished by her continual promenades through the rooms, just reached the conservatory steps. She saw a man's leg disappear amid the darkness of the little staircase. A pale smile lit up her waxen face, and catching up her sorceress's skirt to walk the quicker, she sought her brother, upsetting a figure of the cotillon and questioning all the servants she met. She at last found Saccard with Monsieur de Mareuil in an apartment which adjoined the dining-room, and which had been turned provisionally into a smoking-room. The two fathers were talking about the dowry and the contract. But when Saccard's sister had said a word in his ear, he rose up, apologised, and disappeared.

Upstairs, the dressing-room was in complete disorder. Over the chairs trailed the costume of the nymph Echo, the torn tights, bits of crumpled lace, under-garments thrown aside in a bundle, everything that a woman, expected elsewhere, leaves in her haste behind her. The little ivory and silver tools lay about a little bit everywhere; there were brushes and files fallen on the carpet; and the towels still damp, the soap forgotten on the marble slab, the scent bottles left open, emitted a strong penetrating perfume in the flesh-tinted tent. To take the white off her arms and shoulders the young woman had dipped herself in the pink marble bath after the *tableaux vivants*. Iridescent scales expanded on the sheet of water now grown cold.

Maxime stepped on some stays, narrowly missed falling, and tried to laugh. But he shivered at sight of Renée's stern face. She approached him, pushing him, and saying in a low voice:

"So you are going to marry the hunchback?"

"Not a bit of it," he murmured. "Who told you so?"

"Oh! don't lie. It's useless."

He was prompted to rebel. She alarmed him, he wished to finish matters with her.

"Well, yes, I am to marry her. What of it? Am I not the master?"

She came towards him, with her head somewhat lowered, and with an evil laugh, and taking hold of his wrists:

"The master! you, the master! You know very well it isn't so. It is I who am the master. I could break your arms if I were cruel; you have no more strength than a girl."

And as he struggled, she twisted his arms, with all the nervous violence that anger imparted to her. He uttered a slight cry, and she then let go of him, resuming:

"Don't let us fight, I should prove the stronger."

He remained pale, with the shame of the pain which he felt at his wrists. He watched her coming and going about the room. She pushed back the furniture, reflecting, deciding on the plan which had been revolving in her head since her husband had apprized her of the marriage.

"I am going to shut you up here," she said at last; "and when it is daylight we will start for Havre."

He grew still paler with alarm and stupor.

"But this is madness!" he cried. "We can't go off together. You are going crazy—"

"Perhaps so. At all events it's you and your father who are making me so. I need you and I take you. So much the worse for fools!"

Red gleams shone in her eyes. Again approaching Maxime and scorching his face with her breath, she continued:

"What would become of me if you married the hunchback? You would deride me, and I should perhaps be forced to take back that big simpleton De Mussy, who would not even warm my feet—When people have done what we have done they remain together. Besides, it's

ÉMILE ZOLA

clear enough, I feel bored when you are not there, and as I'm going off, I take you with me. You can tell Céleste what you want her to go and fetch at your place."

The unfortunate fellow held out his hands and supplicated.

"Come, my little Renée, don't commit such folly. Become yourself again. Think a little of the scandal."

"I don't care a fig for the scandal! If you refuse, I shall go down into the drawing-room and cry out that I have slept with you, and that you are now cowardly enough to want to marry the hunchback."

He bowed his head and listened to her, already giving way, and accepting this will so roughly imposed upon him.

"We will go to Havre," she resumed in a lower tone, caressing her dream, "and from there we can reach England. No one will bother us any more. If we are not far enough off, we will start for America. I, who always feel cold, I shall be comfortable there. I have often envied creoles."

But while she enlarged the scope of her project, terror again seized hold of Maxime. To leave Paris, to go so far away with this woman who was certainly mad, to leave behind him a story the shameful character of which would exile him for ever! it was like some atrocious nightmare stifling him. He sought in despair for a means of escaping from this dressing-room, this pink retreat where the bell of the lunatic asylum of Charenton seemed to toll. At last he thought he had found an expedient.

"But I have no money," he said gently, so as not to exasperate her. "If you shut me up I cannot procure any."

"I have some money, though," she replied with an air of triumph. "I have a hundred thousand francs. Everything tallies perfectly well—"

She took out of the wardrobe the deed of cession which her husband had left with her in the vague hope that she might change her mind. She laid it on the toilet table, compelled Maxime to give her a pen and an inkstand which were in the bedroom, and pushing back the soap, and signing the act:

"There," she said, "the folly's done. If I'm robbed it is because I choose to be. We will call on Larsonneau before going to the station. Now, my little Maxime, I am going to shut you up, and we will escape by way of the garden, when I have turned all these people out of the house. We don't even need to take any luggage."

She became gay again. This wild freak delighted her. It was a piece of supreme eccentricity, a finish which, amid her fever, seemed to her mind altogether original. It surpassed her desire to make a balloon journey by a great deal. She went and took Maxime in her arms, murmuring:

"I hurt you a little while ago, my poor darling! But then you refused. You will see how nice it will be. Would your hunchback ever love you as I do? That little blackamoor isn't a woman!"

She was laughing—she was drawing him to her and kissing him on the lips, when a sound made them both turn their heads. Saccard was standing on the threshold of the room.

Terrible silence followed. Renée slowly withdrew her arm from Maxime's neck, but she did not lower her brow, she continued gazing at her husband with her big eyes, which stared fixedly like those of a corpse; while the young fellow, overwhelmed and terrified, staggered, with bowed head, now that he was no longer sustained by her embrace. Saccard, stunned by this supreme blow which, at last, made the husband and the father cry out within him, did not advance, but, livid, he scorched them from afar with the fire of his glances. In the moist, odoriferous atmosphere of the room, the three tapers flared very high, their flames erect, with the stillness of fiery tears. And, alone breaking the silence, the terrible silence, a breath of music ascended the narrow staircase; the waltz, with its snake-like undulations, glided, coiled, and died away on the snowy carpet, amid the split tights and the fallen skirts.

Then the husband advanced. The impulse which he felt to resort to brutality brought blotches to his face; he clinched his fists to knock down the guilty pair. Anger, in this restless little man, burst forth like the report of fire-arms. He gave a strangled titter, and, still advancing:

"You were announcing your marriage to her, eh?"

Maxime retreated and leant against the wall.

"Listen," he stammered, "it was she—"

He was about to accuse her like a coward, to cast the odium of the crime upon her, to say that she wanted to carry him off, to defend himself with the humility and the shudders of a child detected in fault. But he did not have the strength, the words expired in his throat. Renée retained her statue-like rigidity, her air of mute defiance. Then Saccard, no doubt in view of finding a weapon, gave a rapid glance around him. And, on the corner of the toilet table, among the combs and nail-brushes, he perceived the deed of cession, the stamped paper of which set a yellow stain on the marble. He looked at the deed; he looked at the guilty pair. Then, on leaning forward, he saw that the deed was signed. His eyes went from the open inkstand to the pen still wet, which had been left on the foot of the candelabrum. He remained erect in front of this signature, reflecting.

The silence seemed to increase, the flames of the candles shot up higher, the waltz resounded in a softer lullaby along the hangings. Saccard gave an imperceptible shrug of the shoulders. He again looked at his wife and his son with a profound air, as if to wring from their faces an explanation which he could not divine. Then he slowly folded up the deed and placed it in the pocket of his dress-coat. His cheeks had become extremely pale.

"You have done well to sign, my dear," he said gently to his wife. "You gain a hundred thousand francs by doing so. I will give you the money this evening."

He almost smiled, and his hands alone, retained a trembling. He took a few steps, adding—

"It's stifling in here! What an idea to come and plot one of your jokes in this vapour bath!"

And then addressing himself to Maxime, who had raised his head, surprised by his father's appeased voice:

"Here come with me," he resumed: "I saw you go up, and I came to fetch you so that you might wish Monsieur de Mareuil and his daughter good night."

The two men went down talking together. Renée remained alone, standing in the middle of the dressing-room, looking at the yawning cavity of the little staircase, in which she had just seen the shoulders of the father and the son disappear. She could not take her eyes off this cavity. What, they had gone off, quietly, amicably! These two men had not murdered each other. She lent an ear; she listened to ascertain if some atrocious struggle did not make their bodies roll down the stairs. Nothing! In the tepid darkness, nothing but a noise of dancing—a long lullaby. She thought she could hear in the distance the marchioness's laughter and Monsieur de Saffré's clear voice. Then the drama was ended? Her crime, the kisses in the large grey and pink bed, the wild nights in the conservatory, all the accursed love that had consumed her during months, had led to this mean, ignoble ending! Her husband knew all and did not even beat her. And the silence around her—this silence through which trailed the endless waltz—terrified her even more than the sound of murder. She felt afraid of this peacefulness, afraid of this soft-tinted, discreet dressing-room, full of the scent of love.

She perceived herself in the high glass-door of the wardrobe. She approached, astonished to see herself, forgetting her husband, forgetting Maxime, and altogether preoccupied by the strange woman whom she beheld before her. Madness was rising to her brain. Her yellow hair, caught up off the temples and the neck, seemed to her a nudity—an obscenity. The wrinkle of her forehead, deepened to such a degree that it set a dark bar above her eyes, the thin bluish scar of a lash with a whip. Who had marked her like that? Her husband had certainly not raised his hand. And her lips astonished her by their pallor, her myops' eyes seemed dead to her. How old she looked! She inclined her brow, and when she beheld herself in her tights, in her slight gauze blouse, she gazed at herself with lowered eyelashes and sudden blushes. Who had stripped her naked? What was she doing there, bare-breasted, like a harlot who uncovers herself down to the belly? She no longer knew. She looked at her thighs which the tights rounded, at her hips, the supple lines of which she discerned under the gauze, at her bust broadly displayed; and she was ashamed of herself, and contempt for her flesh filled her with inflexible anger against those who had left her thus, with simple circlets of gold round her ankles and wrists to hide her skin.

Then trying, with the fixed idea of drowning intelligence, to remember what she was doing there, quite naked in front of that glass, she went back by a sudden leap to her childhood. She again saw herself, as she had been when seven years old, in the solemn gloom of the Béraud mansion. She remembered a day when Aunt Élisabeth had dressed them—herself and Christine—in woollen dresses, with a little red check pattern on a grey ground. It was Christmas-time. How pleased they were with those two dresses exactly alike! Their aunt spoiled them, and she carried matters so far as to give each of them a bracelet and a necklace of coral. The sleeves were long, the dress-bodies rose up to their chins, the jewellery displayed itself on the stuff, and this seemed very pretty to them. Renée also remembered that her father was there, and that he smiled with his sad air. That day, instead of playing, her sister and herself had walked about the nursery like grown-up persons for fear of soiling themselves. Then at the Convent of the Visitation her schoolfellows had joked her about "her clown's dress," which came down to her finger tips and rose up over her ears. She had begun to cry during lessons; and when play-time came she turned up her sleeves, and tucked in her neckband, so that she might not be derided any longer. And the coral necklace and bracelet seemed to her much prettier on the skin of her neck and arm. Was it on that day that she had begun to strip herself?

Her life unrolled itself before her. She recalled her long bewilderment, the hubbub of gold and flesh which had risen within her, which had mounted first to her knees, then to her stomach, then to her lips, and the flood of which she now felt sweeping over her head, striking her skull, with swiftly repeated blows. It was like a bad sap; it had wearied her limbs, set excrescences of shameful affection in her heart, and made whims, fit for a sick person or an animal, sprout in her brain. This sap had impregnated the soles of her feet while they rested on her carriage rug and on other carpets too, on all the silk and all the velvet over which she had walked since her marriage. The footsteps of others must have left these seeds of poison, now yielding fruit in her blood, and circulating in her veins. She well remembered her childhood. She had merely been inquisitive when she was little. Later on even, after that rape which had cast evil into her, she had not wished for so much shame. She would certainly have become better had she remained knitting beside Aunt Élisabeth. And while she gazed fixedly into the looking-glass to read therein the peaceful future she had missed, she could hear the regular tick tick of her aunt's needles. But she only saw her own pink thighs, her pink hips, the strange woman of pink silk whom she had before her, and whose skin of fine stuff, of close texture, seemed made for the amours of puppets and dolls. She had come to that—to be a big doll from whose torn bosom but a thread of sound escaped. Then, at thought of the enormities of her life, the blood of her father, that middle-class blood which tormented her during hours of crisis, cried out within her and revolted. She who had always trembled at the thought of hell, she ought to have lived in the depths of the black severity of the Béraud mansion. Who was it then that had stripped her naked?

And, in the bluish shade of the glass, she thought she could see the figures of Saccard and Maxime rise up. Saccard, black and sneering, with a hue of iron, and pincer-like laughter, standing on his skinny legs. That man was a will. For ten years she had seen him at the forge, amid the shivers of the reddened metal, with his flesh burnt, breathless, but still striking, raising hammers twenty times too heavy for his arms, at the risk of crushing himself. She understood him now; he seemed to her to have been made taller by this superhuman effort, this huge rascality, this fixed idea of an immense, immediate fortune. She remembered him springing over obstacles, rolling in the mud, and not taking the time to wipe himself, so bent was he upon arriving early at the goal, not even tarrying to enjoy himself on the road, but munching his gold pieces while he ran. Then Maxime's fair, pretty head appeared behind his father's rough shoulders; he had his clear harlot's smile, his empty strumpet's eyes which were never lowered, his parting in the middle of his hair showing the whiteness of his skull. He derided Saccard, he considered him vulgar to give himself so much trouble to earn money, which he, Maxime, expended with such adorable laziness. He was kept. His long soft hands testified to his vices. His hairless body had the wearied attitude of a satisfied woman. Not even a flash of curiosity as to sin shone in all his cowardly, sluggish being, through which vice gently coursed like so much warm water. He did not initiate, he underwent. And Renée, looking at the two apparitions emerge from the slight shade of the mirror, retreated a step, and saw that Saccard had thrown her like a stake, like an investment, and that Maxime had chanced to be there to pick up this louis fallen from the speculator's pocket. She had been an asset in her husband's pocket-book; he had urged her on to the toilettes of a night, to the lovers of a season; he had twisted her in the flames of his forge, employing her, as though she had been a precious metal, to gild the iron of his hands. Little by little the father had thus rendered her mad enough, depraved enough for the kisses of the son. If Maxime were Saccard's impoverished blood, she felt that she herself was the product, the worm-eaten fruit of these two men, the pit of infamy which they had dug together, and into which they both rolled.

She knew it now it was these men who had stripped her naked. Saccard had unhooked her dress-body, and Maxime had loosened her skirt. Then, between them, they had just torn off her chemise. At present she was without a rag, merely with golden rings, like a slave. They had looked at her a little while before, but they had not said to her, "You are naked." The son had trembled like a coward, had shuddered at the thought of carrying his crime to the end, had refused to follow her in her passion. The father, instead of killing her, had robbed her; this man punished people by emptying their pockets; a signature fell like a sunray amid the brutality of his anger, and, by way of vengeance, he carried the signature off. Then she had seen their shoulders retreat into the darkness. No blood upon the carpet, not a cry, not a moan. They were cowards. They had stripped her naked.

And she said to herself that on one sole occasion she had read the future—on the day when, in sight of the murmuring shadows of the

ÉMILE ZOLA

Parc Monceaux, the thought that her husband would soil her, and bring her one day to madness, had come and frightened her growing desires. Ah! how her poor head suffered! how she realised now the fallacy of the idea which had made her believe that she lived in a happy sphere of divine enjoyment and impunity! She had lived in the land of shame, and she was chastised by the abandonment of her whole body, by the death of her agonizing being. She wept that she had not listened to the loud voices of the trees.

Her nudity irritated her. She turned her head, she looked around her. The dressing-room retained its musky heaviness, its warm silence, whither still came the phrases of the waltz, like the last expiring circles on a sheet of water. This low laughter of distant voluptuousness passed over her with intolerable raillery. She stopped up her ears, so as to hear it no longer. Then she beheld the luxury in the room. She raised her eyes to the pink tent, even to the silver crown, within which one perceived a Cupid preparing his arrows; she dwelt on the furniture, on the marble slab of the toilet-table, encumbered with pots and tools which she no longer recognised; she went to the bath, still full of slumbering water; she pushed back with her foot the stuffs trailing over the white satin of the arm-chairs, the costume of the nymph Echo, the petticoats, the forgotten towels. And from all these things voices of shame arose: the robe of the nymph Echo spoke to her of the pastime she had shared because she had thought it original to offer herself to Maxime in public; the bath exhaled the scent of her body, the water in which she had dipped herself filled the room with the feverishness of a sick woman; the table, with its soaps and oils, the furniture, with its bed-like roundnesses, reminded her brutally of her flesh, her amours, all the filth that she wished to forget. She returned into the middle of the room, her face purple, not knowing where to fly from this alcove perfume, this luxury which bared itself with a harlot's immodesty, which displayed all this pink. The room was naked like herself; the pink bath, the rosy skin of the hangings, the pink marble of the two tables became animated, stretched themselves, coiled themselves up, and surrounded her with such a display of living voluptuousness that she closed her eyes, lowering her forehead, overwhelmed amid the lace of the ceiling and the walls which crushed her.

But in the blackness she again saw that flesh-tinted spot the dressing-room, and she also beheld the grey softness of the bedroom, the soft aurulent lustre of the little drawing-room, the crude greenness of the conservatory, all the wealth that had been her accomplice. It was there that her feet had become impregnated with the evil sap. She would not have slept with Maxime on a pallet in the depth of a garret. It would have been too ignoble! The silk around her had made her crime coquettish. And she dreamt of tearing down this lace, of spitting upon this silk, of breaking her large bed to pieces with kicks, of dragging her luxury into some gutter, whence it would emerge worn-out and dirtied like herself.

When she re-opened her eyes she approached the mirror, looked at herself again, and examined herself closely. She was done for. She saw herself dead. Her whole face told her that the cerebral cracking was being completed. Maxime, that last perversion of her senses, had finished his work, exhausted her flesh, and unhinged her intelligence. She had no more joys to taste, no hope of an awakening. At this thought a savage rage was rekindled within her, and in a last crisis of desire she dreamt of retaking possession of her prey, of agonizing in Maxime's arms, and carrying him off with her. Louise could not marry him; Louise knew very well that he did not belong to her, since she had seen them kissing each other on the lips. Then she threw a fur mantle over her shoulders, so as not to pass naked through the ball, and she went downstairs.

In the little drawing-room she came face to face with Madame Sidonie. The latter, in view of enjoying the drama, had again stationed herself on the steps of the conservatory. But she no longer knew what to think when Saccard reappeared with Maxime, and brutally replied to her whispered questions that she was dreaming, that there was "nothing whatever." Then she scented the truth. Her yellow face grew pale, she considered this really too strong. And she softly went and placed her ear against the staircase door, hoping that she would be able to hear Renée crying upstairs. When the young woman opened the door, it almost smacked her sister-in-law in the face.

"You are playing the spy on me!" Renée angrily said.

But Madame Sidonie replied with fine disdain:

"Do I occupy myself with your filth?"

And catching up her sorceress's dress, and retiring with a majestic look:

"It isn't my fault, little one, if accidents befall you. But I have no spite, do you hear? And understand that you would have found, and would still find, a second mother in me. I shall expect you at my place whenever you please."

Renée did not listen to her. She entered the large drawing-room, and passed through a very complicated figure of the cotillon without even remarking the surprise which her fur mantle occasioned. In the middle of the room there were groups of ladies and gentlemen who mingled waving bandrols, and Monsieur de Saffré's fluty voice called out:

"Come, ladies, 'the Mexican War.' The ladies who figure the bushes must spread their skirts out around them and remain on the ground—Now, the gentlemen must turn round the bushes—Then when I clap my hands each of them must waltz with his bush."

He clapped his hands. The brass instruments resounded, the waltz once more sent the couples revolving round the room. The figure had not been very successful. Two ladies had remained on the carpet entangled in their dresses. Madame Daste declared that the only thing that amused her in the "Mexican War," was making a "cheese" of her dress, as she had done at school.

Renée on reaching the hall found Louise and her father, whom Saccard and Maxime were accompanying. Baron Gouraud had left. Madame Sidonie withdrew with Mignon and Charrier, while Monsieur Hupel de la Noue escorted Madame Michelin, whom her husband followed discreetly. The prefect had spent the rest of the evening courting the pretty brunette. He had just persuaded her to spend a month of the fine weather in the chief town of his department where "some really curious antiquities were to be seen."

Louise, who was nibbling on the sly the hardbake which she had in her pocket, was seized with a fit of coughing at the moment of leaving the house.

"Cover yourself up well," said her father.

And Maxime hastened to tighten the strings of the hood of her opera-cloak. She raised her chin and let herself be swaddled. But when Madame Saccard appeared, Monsieur de Mareuil retraced his steps and bid her good-bye. For a moment they all remained there together talking. Renée, wishing to explain her pallor and her shudders, said that she had felt cold, and had gone upstairs to throw the fur over her shoulders. And she watched for the moment when she might speak in a low voice to Louise, who was looking at her with inquisitive tranquillity. While the gentlemen again shook hands she leant forward and murmured:

"You won't marry him, will you? It isn't possible. You know very well—"

But the child interrupted her, rising on tip-toe and speaking in her ear:

"Oh! be easy, I shall take him off—It is of no consequence since we are going to Italy."

And she smiled with the vague smile of a vicious sphinx. Renée remained stammering. She did not understand, she fancied that the hunchback was deriding her. Then when the Mareuils had gone off, repeating several times: "Till Sunday!" she looked at her husband and at Maxime with her frightened eyes, and on beholding them, with quiet flesh and satisfied attitudes, she hid her face in her hands, fled, and sought a refuge in the depths of the conservatory.

The pathways were deserted. The large leaves were asleep, and on the heavy sheet of water of the basin two budding Nymphæa slowly unfolded. Renée would have liked to cry; but the damp warmth, the strong perfume which she recognised, caught her at the throat and strangled her despair. She looked at her feet, at the edge of the basin, at the spot of yellow sand where she had stretched the bearskin the winter before. And when she raised her eyes she again saw between the two open doors a figure of the cotillon being danced right away in the background.

There was a deafening noise, a confused mass in which she at first only distinguished flying skirts and black legs, footing and turning. Monsieur de Saffré's voice cried out: "Change your ladies! change your ladies!" And the couples passed by amid a fine yellow dust; each gentleman, after three or four turns in the waltz, threw his partner into the arms of his neighbour, who, in turn, threw him his. Baroness de Meinhold, in her costume as the Emerald, fell from the hands of the Count de Chibray into the hands of Monsieur Simpson; he caught her as he could by a shoulder, while the tip of his gloves glided under her dress body. Countess Vanska, very red and making her coral drops jingle, went with a bound from the chest of Monsieur de Saffré on to the chest of the Duke de Rozan, whom she entwined and compelled to pirouette for five turns, when she hung herself on the hips of Monsieur Simpson who had just thrown the Emerald to the leader of the cotillon. And Madame Teissière, Madame Daste, Madame de Lauwerens, shining like large living jewels, with the fair pallor of the Topaz, the soft blue of the Turquoise, the fiery blue of the Sapphire, abandoned themselves for a minute, vaulted under the extended wrist of a waltzer, then started off again, came frontwards or backwards into a fresh embrace, visiting one after the other all the masculine embraces of the drawing-room. However Madame d'Espanet had, in full view of the orchestra, succeeded in catching hold of Madame Haffner as she passed by, and now waltzed with her, refusing to let go her hold. Gold and Silver danced lovingly together.

Renée then understood this whirling of skirts, this stamping of legs. Standing on a lower surface she could see the fury of the feet, the patent-leather boots and white ankles mingling pell-mell. At intervals it seemed to her as if a gust of wind were about to blow off the dresses. The bare shoulders, the bare arms, the bare heads which flew past and revolved, now seized hold of, now thrown off, and again caught at the end of the gallery where the waltz of the orchestra grew madder, where the red hangings seemed thrown into a transport amid the final fever of the ball, appeared to her like the tumultuous image of her own life, of her nudities and abandonments. And she experienced such a pang, at the thought that Maxime, to take the hunchback in his arms, had just cast her there, on the spot where they had loved each other, that she dreamt of plucking a stalk of the Tanghinia which grazed her cheek, and of chewing it till the sap was exhausted. But she was cowardly, and she remained in front of the plant shivering under the fur which her hands drew over her with a tight clutch, and a great gesture of terrified shame.

VII

Three months later, on one of those gloomy spring mornings which bring back into Paris the dimness and dirty dampness of winter, Aristide Saccard alighted from his carriage at the Place du Château-d'Eau, and turned with four other gentlemen into the gorge of demolitions opened by the future Boulevard du Prince-Eugène. The party formed a committee of inquiry which the expropriation jury had despatched to the spot to estimate the value of certain property, the owners of which had not come to an amicable arrangement with the city of Paris.

Saccard was renewing his Rue de la Pépinière stroke of fortune. So that his wife's name might completely disappear from the affair, he had at first devised a mock sale of the ground and the music-hall. Larsonneau relinquished the whole to a supposed creditor. The deed of sale enunciated the colossal figure of three millions of francs. The sum was so exorbitant, that when the expropriation agent, in the name of the imaginary owner, claimed the amount of the purchase money as an indemnity, the commission of the Hôtel-de-Ville would not grant more than two millions five hundred thousand francs, despite the underhand endeavours of Monsieur Michelin, and the speeches of Monsieur Toutin-Laroche and Baron Gouraud. Saccard had expected this repulse; he refused the offer, and let the case go before the expropriation jury, of which he happened to be a member, together with Monsieur de Mareuil, by a chance he had no doubt assisted. And it was thus that, with four of his colleagues, he found himself deputed to make an inquiry respecting his own ground.

Monsieur de Mareuil accompanied him. Of the three remaining jurors one was a doctor, who smoked a cigar without caring the least in the world for the stones and mortar he climbed over, and the others, two commercial men, one of whom, a manufacturer of surgical instruments, had once turned a grindstone in the streets.

The path which the gentlemen took was in a frightful state. It had rained all night. The soaked ground was becoming a river of mud between the fallen houses, beside this road, traced out over loose soil, wherein the transport carts sank up to the naves of their wheels. On either side fragments of the walls, shattered with pick-axes, remained standing; lofty eviscerated buildings, displaying their pallid entrails, opened in mid-air their empty staircase frames, their suspended gaping rooms, which appeared like the broken drawers of some great ugly piece of furniture. Nothing could look more lamentable than the wall-papers of these rooms, blue or yellow squares, falling in tatters, and indicating, at the height of a fifth or sixth floor, just under the roofs, the place occupied by some poor little garrets, narrow holes, in which perhaps a man's whole life had been confined. The ribbons of the chimney flues rose side by side on the bare walls, lugubriously black and with abrupt bends. A forgotten weathercock grated at the edge of a roof, whilst some half-detached water-spouts hung down like rags. And the gap still deepened amid these ruins, like a breach opened by cannon; under the grey sky, amid the sinister pallidity of the falling plaster dust, the roadway, barely marked out, covered with refuse, with piles of earth and deep pools of water, stretched away, edged with the black marks of chimney flues, as with a mourning border.

The gentlemen, with their well-blackened boots, their frock-coats, and their tall silk hats, set a singular note in this muddy landscape, of a dirty yellow tint, and across which there only passed some pale workmen, some horses splashed to the chine, and some carts, the woodwork of which disappeared beneath a coat of dust. The jurors followed each other in Indian file, jumping from stone to stone, avoiding the pools of flowing filth, at times sinking in up to their heels, and then shaking their feet, and swearing. Saccard had talked about taking the Rue de Charonne, by which they would have avoided this promenade over broken ground, but they unfortunately had several bits of property to visit on the long line of the Boulevard, and, impelled by curiosity, they had decided to pass right through the works. Besides, the sight greatly interested them. At times they stopped, balancing themselves on some bit of plaster which had fallen into a rut, raising their noses, and calling each other to point out some perforated floor, some chimney-pot which had remained in the air, some joist which had fallen on to a neighbouring roof. This bit of a destroyed city, seen on leaving the Rue du Temple, seemed altogether funny to them.

"It is really curious," said Monsieur de Mareuil. "Look there, Saccard, look at that kitchen up there. An old frying-pan has remained hanging over the stove. I can distinguish it perfectly."

However, the doctor, with his cigar between his teeth, had set himself in front of a demolished house, of which there only remained the rooms of the ground floor, filled with the remnants of the other storeys. A single fragment of wall rose up above the pile of materials; and to overthrow it at one effort, it had been girt round with a rope, at which several workmen were tugging.

"They won't manage it," muttered the doctor. "They are pulling too much to the left."

The four other jurors had retraced their steps to see the wall tumble. And all five of them, with their eyes stretched out, and with bated breath, waited for the fall with a quiver of delight. The workmen, giving way, and then suddenly stiffening themselves, cried out, "Oh! heave oh!"

"They won't manage it," repeated the doctor.

Then after a few seconds of anxiety:

"It is moving, it is moving," joyfully cried one of the commercial men.

And when the wall gave way at last, and fell with a frightful crash, raising a cloud of plaster, the gentlemen looked at each other with smiles. They were delighted. Their frock-coats became covered with a fine dust, which whitened their arms and shoulders.

Resuming their prudent march amid the puddles, they now began to talk about the workmen. There were not many good ones. They were all idle fellows, prodigals, and withal most obstinate, only dreaming of their masters' ruin. Monsieur de Mareuil, who for a moment had been looking with a shudder at two poor devils perched on the corner of a roof demolishing a wall with their pick-axes, expressed, however, the opinion that, all the same, these men really possessed great courage. The other jurors again paused and raised their eyes to the workmen who balanced themselves, leaning and striking with all their strength; they pushed the stones down with their feet, and quietly looked at them shattering below. If the pick-axes had missed striking, the mere impulsion of the men's arms would have precipitated them into space.

"Bah! it's habit," said the doctor, setting his cigar in his mouth again. "They are brutes!"

The jurors had now reached one of the houses which they had to visit. They finished their work in a quarter of an hour, and then resumed their walk. By degrees they no longer felt so much disgust for the mud; they walked in the middle of the pools, abandoning the hope of keeping their boots clean. When they had passed the Rue Ménilmontant one of the commercial men, the ex-knife-grinder, became nervous. He examined the ruins about him, and no longer recognised the neighbourhood. He said that he had lived in that part, on his arrival in Paris more than thirty years previously, and that he should be very pleased to find the house again. He continued searching with his eyes, when suddenly the sight of a house which the workmen's picks had already cut in twain, made him stop short in the middle of the road. He studied the door and the windows. Then, pointing upward with his finger to a corner of the partially demolished building:

"There it is," he cried; "I recognise it!"

"What, pray?" asked the doctor.

"My room, of course! That's it!"

It was a little room, situated on the fifth floor, and it must have formerly overlooked a courtyard. A breach in the wall showed it, quite bare, already demolished on one side, with a broad torn band of its wall paper, of a large yellow flowery pattern, trembling in the wind. On the left hand, one could still see the recess of a cupboard, lined with blue paper, and beside it was an aperture for a stove-pipe, with a bit of piping in it.

The ex-workman was seized with emotion:

"I spent five years in there," muttered he. "My means were small in those times, but no matter, I was young. You see the cupboard; it was there that I put by three hundred francs, copper by copper. And the hole for the stove-pipe, I can still remember the day when I made it. The room had no fire-place, and it was bitter cold, all the more so as we were not often two together."

"Come, come," interrupted the doctor, joking, "we don't ask you for your secrets. You played your games like every one else."

"That's true," naively resumed the worthy man. "I still remember an ironing girl who lived over the way. You see the bed was over there, on the right hand side near the window. Ah! my poor room, how they've knocked it about."

He was really very sad.

"Come," said Saccard, "no harm's done by throwing those old cabins down. Handsome houses in freestone will be built in place of them. Would you still live in such a den while you might very well lodge yourself on the new Boulevard?"

"That's true," again replied the manufacturer, who seemed quite consoled.

The commission of inquiry halted again at the two other houses. The doctor remained at the door smoking and looking at the sky. When they reached the Rue des Amandiers the houses became fewer; they now passed through large inclosures and over uncultivated land, where some half fallen buildings straggled. Saccard seemed delighted with this promenade through ruins. He had just remembered the dinner he had once shared with his first wife on the heights of Montmartre, and he well recollected having indicated with his hand the cut across Paris from the Place du Château-d'Eau to the Barrière du Trône. The realisation of this far distant prediction delighted him. He followed the cut, with the secret joys of authorship, as if he himself had with his iron fingers struck the first blows with a pickaxe. And he jumped over the puddles, reflecting that three millions awaited him under building materials, at the end of this river of greasy filth.

Meanwhile the gentlemen fancied themselves in the country. The road passed through some gardens, the walls of which had been felled. There were large clumps of budding lilac, with foliage of a very delicate light green. Each of these gardens, looking like a retreat hung with the leaves of the shrubs, displayed a narrow basin or a miniature cascade, with bits of wall on which to deceive the eye, arbours, in perspective and bluish landscape backgrounds had been painted. The buildings, scattered and discreetly hidden, resembled Italian pavilions and Grecian temples, and moss was wearing away the feet of the plaster columns, whilst weeds had loosened the mortar of the pediments.

"Those are *petites maisons*," said the doctor, with a wink.

But as he saw that the gentlemen did not understand what he meant, he explained that under Louis XV the nobility had retreats of this kind for their pleasure parties. It was then the fashion. And he added:

"They were called *petites maisons* (little houses). This neighbourhood was full of them. Some stiff things took place in them, and no mistake!"

The commission of inquiry had become very attentive. The two commercial men's eyes were shining, and they smiled and looked with great interest at these gardens and pavilions, on which they had not bestowed a glance prior to their colleague's explanations. A grotto detained them for a long time. But when the doctor, seeing a house already attacked by the pick, said that he recognised it as the Count de Savigny's *petite maison*, well known on account of that nobleman's orgies, the whole commission left the Boulevard to go and visit the ruins. They climbed on to the fallen materials, entered the ground floor rooms by the windows, and as the workmen were away at their mid-day meal, they were able to linger there quite at their ease. They indeed remained there for a good half hour, examining the rosettes of the ceilings, the paintings above the doors, the strained mouldings of the plaster grown yellow with age. The doctor reconstructed the building.

"Do you see," said he, "this room must be the banqueting hall. There was certainly an immense divan in that recess of the wall. And, indeed, I'm sure that a looking-glass surmounted the divan. See, there are the holdfasts of the glass. Oh! those fellows were scamps who knew deucedly well how to enjoy themselves!"

The jurors would never have left these old stones which tickled their curiosity, if Aristide Saccard, growing impatient, had not said to them, laughing:

"You may look as much as you like, the ladies are no longer here. Let's get to our business."

Before leaving, however, the doctor climbed on to a mantelshelf, to delicately detach, with one blow of a pick, a little painted head of Cupid, which he slipped into the pocket of his frock-coat.

They at length reached the end of their journey. The land which had formerly belonged to Madame Aubertot was very vast; the music-hall and the garden occupied barely more than half of the surface; a few unimportant houses were scattered about the rest of it. The new Boulevard cut obliquely across this large parallelogram, and this circumstance had quieted one of Saccard's fears; he had long imagined that only a corner of the music-hall would be removed by the new thoroughfare. Larsonneau therefore had received orders to open his mouth, as the bordering plots ought to at least quintuple in value. He was already threatening the city of Paris to avail himself of a recent decree authorising landowners to deliver up only the ground necessary for works of public utility.

It was the expropriation agent who received the jurors. He took them over the garden, made them visit the music-hall and showed them a huge pile of papers. But the two commercial men had gone down again accompanied by the doctor, whom they were still questioning about Count de Savigny's *petite maison*, of which their minds were full. They listened to him with gaping mouths, standing all three beside a *jeu de tonneau*. And he talked to them about La Pompadour, and related the amours of Louis XV, while Monsieur de Mareuil and Saccard continued the inquiry alone.

"It's all finished," said the latter on returning into the garden. "If you will allow me, gentlemen, I will myself draw up the report."

The surgical-instrument maker did not even hear. He was deep in the Regency.

"What funny times, all the same!" he muttered.

Then they found a cab in the Rue de Charonne and they went off, muddy to the knees, but as satisfied with their promenade as with a pleasure trip in the country. In the cab the conversation changed—they talked politics, they said that the Emperor did great things. The like of what they had just seen had never been witnessed before. This long, perfectly straight street would be superb when the houses were erected.

It was Saccard who drew up the report and the jury granted the three millions. The speculator was at the end of his tether, he could not have waited a month longer. This money saved him from ruin, and even a little from the assize court. He gave five hundred thousand francs on the million which he owed to his upholsterer and his contractor for the mansion in the Parc Monceaux. He stopped up other holes, rushed into new companies, and deafened Paris with the noise of the real crowns which he flung by the shovelful on to the shelves of his iron safe. The golden river had a source at last. But this was not yet a solid, entrenched fortune flowing with a regular, continuous gush. Saccard, saved from a crisis, thought himself pitiful with the crumbs of his three millions, and naively said that he was still too poor, and could not stop there. And soon the ground again cracked beneath his feet.

Larsonneau had behaved so admirably in the Charonne affair that Saccard, after a slight hesitation, carried honesty to the point of giving him his ten per cent, and his bonus of thirty thousand francs. The expropriation agent thereupon opened a banking-house. When his accomplice accused him in a snappish tone of being richer than himself, the coxcomb with yellow gloves replied, laughing:

"You see, dear master, you are very clever in making money rain down, but you don't know how to pick it up."

Madame Sidonie profited by her brother's stroke of fortune to borrow ten thousand francs from him, with which she went to spend a couple of months in England. She returned without a copper, and it was never known what had become of the ten thousand francs.

"Well, it costs," she replied when she was questioned. "I ransacked all the libraries. I had three secretaries to assist me in my researches."

And when she was asked if she at length had any positive information about her three milliards, she at first smiled with a mysterious air, and then ended by muttering:

"You are all incredulous. I have found nothing, but no matter. You will see, you will see some day."

She had not, however, lost all the time she spent in England. Her

ÉMILE ZOLA

brother the minister profited by her journey to entrust her with a delicate commission. When she returned she obtained large orders from the ministry. It was a fresh incarnation. She made contracts with the government, and charged herself with supplying it every imaginable thing. She sold it provisions and arms for the troops, furniture for the prefectures and public departments, fire wood for the offices and the museums. The money she made did not induce her to set aside her eternal black dresses, and she retained her yellow, doleful face. Saccard then reflected that it was really she whom he had seen once long ago furtively leaving their brother Eugène's house. She must at all times have kept up a secret connection with him, for matters with which no one was acquainted.

Renée was agonizing amid these interests, these ardent thirsts which could not satisfy themselves. Aunt Élisabeth was dead; Christine had married and left the Béraud mansion, where her father alone remained erect in the gloomy shade of the large rooms. Renée exhausted what she inherited from her aunt in one season. She gambled now. She had found a drawing-room where ladies sat at table till three o'clock in the morning, losing hundreds of thousands of francs in a night. She tried to drink, but she could not, she experienced invincible qualms of disgust. Since she had found herself alone again, abandoned to the worldly flood which carried her off, she surrendered herself all the more, not knowing how to kill time. She ended by tasting of everything. And nothing touched her amid the immense boredom which was crushing her. She grew older, blue circles appeared round her eyes, her nose became thinner, her pouting lips parted in sudden and causeless laughter. It was the end of a woman.

When Maxime had married Louise, and the young folks had started for Italy, she no longer troubled herself about her lover; she even seemed to forget him completely. And when Maxime returned alone six months later, having buried the "hunchback" in the cemetery of a little town in Lombardy, it was hatred that she displayed towards him. She remembered Phèdre, she no doubt recollected that poisoned love to which she had heard Ristori lend her sobs. Then, so as never more to meet the young fellow in her home, to dig an abyss of shame between the father and the son for ever, she compelled her husband to take cognisance of the incest, she told him that on the day when he had surprised her with Maxime, the latter, who had long pursued her, was seeking to assault her. Saccard was horribly worried by the insistence she evinced in wishing to open his eyes. He was obliged to quarrel with his son and cease to see him. The young widower, rich with his wife's dowry, went to live a bachelor's life in a little house of the Avenue de l'Impératrice. He had renounced the Council of State, and kept a racing stable. Renée derived one of her last satisfactions from this rupture. She revenged herself, she flung the infamy which these two men had set on her back in their own faces, and she said to herself that now she would never more see them making game of her, arm-in-arm, like a couple of comrades.

Amid the crumbling of Renée's affections there came a moment when she had no one left to love her but her maid. She had by degrees been taken with a maternal affection for Céleste. Perhaps this girl, who was all that remained near her of Maxime's love, reminded her of the hours of enjoyment forever dead. Perhaps Renée was simply touched by the fidelity of this servant, of this brave heart the quiet solicitude of which nothing seemed to shake. From the depth of her remorse she thanked Céleste for having witnessed her shame without leaving her in disgust; and she pictured all kinds of abnegation, a whole life of renunciation to arrive at understanding the calmness of the chambermaid in the presence of incest, her icy hands, her respectful, quiet attentions. And the girl's devotion made Renée all the happier as she knew her to be honest and economical, without a lover, without a vice.

At times in her sad moments she would say to her:

"Ah! my girl, it is you who will close my eyes."

Céleste never answered, but she gave a singular smile. One morning she quietly informed her mistress that she was going to leave, that she meant to return into the country. Renée remained trembling all over on hearing this, as if some great misfortune had befallen her. She cried out, and plied Céleste with questions. Why would she leave her when they got on so well together? And she offered to double her wages.

But the maid, in answer to all her kind words, made a gesture meaning no, in a quiet, obstinate manner.

"You see, madame," she ended by replying, "you might offer me all the gold of Peru, but I could not remain a week longer. Ah! you don't know me—I've been with you for eight years, haven't I? Well, on the very first day I said to myself: 'As soon as I have collected five thousand francs together, I will return to my village; I will buy Lagache's house, and I shall live very happily!' It's a promise I made to myself, you understand. And the five thousand francs were completed yesterday, when you paid me my wages."

Renée felt a chill at her heart. She saw Céleste passing behind her and Maxime while they were kissing each other, and she saw her with her indifference, in a perfect state of abstraction, dreaming of her five thousand francs. However, she still tried to retain her, frightened by the void in which she would have to live, longing, despite everything, to keep near her this obstinate animal whom she had thought devoted, and who was merely egotistical. The girl smiled, still shaking her head and muttering:

"No, no, it isn't possible. Even if it were my mother I should refuse. I shall buy two cows. I shall perhaps start a little haberdasher's business. It is very pretty down our way. Oh! for the matter of that, I am willing you should come and see me. It is near Caen. I will leave you the address."

Renée then no longer insisted. She shed hot tears when she was alone. On the morrow, with a sick person's whimsicality, she decided to accompany Céleste to the Western Railway station, in her own brougham. She gave her one of her travelling rugs and made her a present in money, and showed her the attentions of a mother whose daughter is about to start upon some long difficult journey. In the brougham she looked at her with moist eyes. Céleste chatted and said how pleased she was to go away. Then emboldened, she spoke out and gave some advice to her mistress.

"I shouldn't have understood life like you, madame. I often said to myself when I found you with Monsieur Maxime: 'Is it possible one can be so foolish for men!' It always ends badly—Ah! for my part I always mistrusted them!"

She laughed and threw herself back in the corner of the brougham:

"My money would have danced!" she continued, "and now-a-days I should be destroying my eyes with crying. So whenever I saw a man I took up a broomstick—I never dared to tell you all that. Besides, it didn't concern me. You were free to do as you liked, and I only had to earn my money honestly."

At the railway station Renée insisted upon paying her fare and took her a first class ticket. As they had arrived before the time, she detained her, pressing her hands and repeating:

"And take good care of yourself, don't neglect your health, my good Céleste."

The latter allowed herself to be caressed. She stood looking happy, with a fresh smiling face, before her mistress's tearful eyes. Renée again spoke of the past, and the maid abruptly exclaimed:

"I was forgetting: I didn't tell you the story of Baptiste, master's valet. Probably no one has liked to tell you."

The young woman owned that she indeed knew nothing.

"Well, you remember his grand dignified airs, his disdainful glances, you yourself spoke to me about them. It was all so much acting. He didn't care for women, he never came down to the servants' hall when we were there; I can repeat it now, he even pretended that it was disgusting in the drawing-room, on account of all the low-neck dresses. I well believe that he didn't care for women!"

And she leant towards Renée's ear, and made her blush, though she herself retained all her honest placidity.

"When the new stable boy," she continued, "told everything to master, master preferred to dismiss Baptiste rather than send him to jail. It seems that these disgusting things had been going on for years in the stables. And to think that the big scamp pretended he was fond of horses! It was the grooms that he liked!"

The bell interrupted her. She hastily took up the eight or ten packages which she had not wished to part with. She let herself be kissed; and then she went off, without looking round.

Renée remained in the station until the engine whistled. And when the train had gone off, she was overcome with despair, she no longer knew what to do; her days seemed to stretch before her as empty as the vast waiting hall where she had been left alone. She again entered her brougham and told the coachman to drive her home. But on the way she changed her mind, she was afraid of her room, of the boredom awaiting her there. She no longer felt the necessary courage to return home and change her dress for her usual drive round the lake. She felt a longing for sunlight, a longing to mingle with the crowd.

She ordered the coachman to drive to the Bois.

It was four o'clock. The Bois was awakening from the drowsiness of a warm afternoon. Clouds of dust flew along the Avenue de l'Impératrice, and one could see, spread out afar, the expanse of verdure which the slopes of Saint-Cloud and Suresnes, crowned by the grey walls of Mont Valérien, limited. High above the horizon the sun shed its rays, filling the recesses of the foliage with golden dust, lighting up the tall branches, and changing the ocean of leaves into an ocean of light. Past the fortifications, in the avenue of the Bois leading to the lake, the ground had just been watered; and the vehicles rolled over the brown soil as over a carpet, amid a rising freshness and an odour of damp earth. Mingled with the low bushes on either side, the little trees of the copses reared their crowd of young trunks, growing indistinct in the greenish dimness which flashes of light pierced here and there with yellow glades; and, by degrees, as one approached the lake, the chairs on the side-walks became more numerous, families sat, gazing with quiet silent faces at the interminable procession of wheels. Then, on reaching the open space in front of the lake, there was a dazzlement, the oblique sun transformed the round expanse of water into a huge mirror of polished silver reflecting the brilliant disk of the planet. All eyes blinked, one could only distinguish the dark form of the pleasure boat on the left hand side near the bank. The parasols in the vehicles were inclined with a gentle and uniform movement towards this splendour, and only rose erect again on reaching the roadway skirting the sheet of water, which, from the summit of the bank, now assumed a metallic blackness, streaked with golden burnishings. On the right hand side the clumps of fir trees lined the road with their colonnades of straight slender stems, the soft violet tinge of which was reddened by the flames of the sky; on the left the lawns, bathed in light and similar to fields of emeralds, stretched away as far as the distant lace-like ironwork of the gate of La Muette. And on approaching the cascade, while the dimness of the copses again presented itself on one side, the islands at the end of the lake rose up into the blue air, with the sunshine playing over their banks, and bold shadows darting from their pines, at the feet of which the chalet looked like some child's plaything lost in a corner of a virgin forest. The whole wood laughed and quivered in the sunshine.

The weather was so magnificent that Renée felt ashamed of her closed brougham and her costume of flea-tinted silk. She drew back a little, and, with the windows open, looked at this flow of light stretching over the water and the verdure. At the bends of the avenues she perceived the line of wheels revolving like golden stars amid a long train of blinding gleams. The varnished panels, the flashing steel and brass mountings, the bright colours of the dresses passed on, at the even trot of the horses, and set against the background of the wood a long moving bar, a ray fallen from the sky, stretching out and following the bends of the roadway. And in this ray, as the young woman blinked her eyes, she saw every now and then the light chignon of a woman, the black back of a footman, the white mane of a horse, stand out. The arched parasols of watered silk shone like moons of metal.

Then, in presence of this broad daylight, this expanse of sunshine, Renée thought of the fine dust of twilight which she had seen one evening falling on the tawny foliage. Maxime had been with her. It was at the period when her desires for that child were dawning in her. And she again saw the lawns dampened by the evening air, the darkened underwood, the deserted pathways. The line of vehicles had gone by with a sad sound past the unoccupied chairs, whilst now the rumble of the wheels, the trot of the horses, resounded with the joyfulness of a flourish of trumpets. Then the recollection of all her drives in the Bois returned to her. She had lived there. Maxime had grown up there, at her side, on the cushion of her carriage. It had been their garden. Rain had surprised them there, sunshine had brought them back, the fall of night had not always driven them away. They had been there in every kind of weather, they had there tasted the worries and the joy of their life. Amid the emptiness of her being, the melancholy imparted by Celeste's departure, these memories gave Renée bitter joy. Her heart said: "Never again! never again!" and she was like frozen when she evoked the image of the winter landscape, the congealed, dull-tinted lake on which they had skated; the sky then was of a sooty colour, the snow had set white lace on the trees, the wind had thrown fine sand in their eyes and on their lips.

However, on the left hand side, on the side reserved to equestrians, she had already recognised the Duke de Rozan, Monsieur de Mussy, and Monsieur de Saffré. Larsonneau had killed the duke's mother by presenting her the hundred and fifty thousand francs' worth of bills accepted by her son, and the duke was devouring his second half million with Blanche Müller, after leaving the first five hundred thousand francs in the hands of Laure d'Aurigny. Monsieur de Mussy, who had left the embassy in England for the embassy in Italy, had become gallant again; and he led cotillons with newly acquired gracefulness. As for Monsieur de Saffré, he remained the most amiable sceptic and fast-liver in the world. Renée saw him urging his horse towards the carriage of the Countess Vanska, with whom he was said to be madly in love since the evening when he had seen her as Coral at the Saccards'.

All the ladies were there, moreover; the Duchess de Sternich, in her sempiternal eight-springed carriage; Madame de Lauwerens in a landau, with the Baroness de Meinhold and little Madame Daste seated in front of her; Madame de Teissière and Madame de Guende in a victoria. Amid these ladies, Sylvia and Laure d'Aurigny displayed themselves on the cushions of a magnificent calash. Madame Michelin even passed by

ÉMILE ZOLA

in the depths of a brougham; the pretty brunette had been to visit the chief town of Monsieur Hupel de la Noue's department; and on her return she had made her appearance in the Bois in this brougham, to which she hoped to soon add an open carriage. Renée also perceived the Marchioness d'Espanet and Madame Haffner, the inseparables hidden under their parasols, stretched out side by side, laughing tenderly, and gazing into each other's eyes.

Then the gentlemen passed by: Monsieur de Chibray driving a mail-coach; Monsieur Simpson in a dog-cart; Messieurs Mignon and Charrier, more eager than ever for work, despite their dream of approaching retirement, in a brougham which they left at the corner of an avenue, to go a bit of the way on foot; Monsieur de Mareuil, still in mourning for his daughter, seeking bows for his first interruption launched forth the day before at the Corps Législatif, and airing his political importance in the carriage of Monsieur Toutin-Laroche, who had once more saved the Crédit Viticole, after placing it within two fingers' length of ruin, and whom the Senate made thinner and more influential than ever.

And, to close the procession, like a final majesty, Baron Gouraud showed his inert heaviness in the sunlight, on the pillows with which his carriage was provided. Renée felt surprised and disgusted on recognising Baptiste seated, with a white face and solemn air, beside the coachman. The tall flunky had entered the baron's service.

The copses continued to stretch away, the water of the lake grew iridescent under the sunrays now become more oblique, the line of carriages spread out its dancing gleams. And the young woman, herself seized and carried away by this enjoyment, vaguely divined all the appetites rolling, along in the midst of the sunlight. She did not feel indignant with these sharers of the spoil. But she hated them for their joy, for this triumphal march, which showed them to her full in the golden dust from the sky. They were superb and smiling; the women displayed themselves white and plump, the men had the rapid glances, the delighted deportment of favoured lovers. And she, in the depth of her empty heart, found nothing more than lassitude and covert envy. Was she better than the others, then, that she thus bent under the weight of pleasure? or was it the others who were praiseworthy for having stronger loins than her own. She did not know, she was just longing for new desires with which to begin life anew, when, on turning her head, she perceived beside her, on the footway bordering the underwood, a sight which rent her heart like a supreme blow.

Saccard and Maxime were walking along slowly, arm-in-arm. The father must have paid a visit to the son, and they had both come down from the Avenue de l'Impératrice to the lake chatting.

"Listen to me," repeated Saccard, "you are a simpleton. When a man has money like you have, he doesn't let it slumber at the bottom of a drawer. There is a hundred per cent to be gained in the affair I mention. It is a safe investment. You know very well that I wouldn't let you in!"

However, the young fellow seemed bored by his father's insistence. He smiled with his pretty air, and looked at the carriages.

"Do you see that little woman over there, the one in mauve," he suddenly said. "She's a washerwoman, whom that beast De Mussy has brought out."

They looked at the woman in mauve; after which Saccard drew a cigar from his pocket, and addressing himself to Maxime who was smoking:

"Give me a light," he said.

Then they stopped for a moment in front of each other, drawing their faces near together. When the cigar was lighted:

"You see," continued the father, again taking his son's arm, and pressing it tightly under his own; "you would be a fool if you didn't listen to me. Is it agreed, eh? Will you bring me the hundred thousand francs to-morrow?"

"You know very well that I no longer go to your house," replied Maxime, compressing his lips.

"Pooh! A lot of bosh! It's time there was an end to all that."

And while they took a few steps in silence, just at the moment when Renée, feeling as though she would swoon, hid her head in the padding of the brougham, so as not to be seen, a growing buzz swept along the line of vehicles. The pedestrians on the footways halted, and turned round with gaping mouths, watching something that approached. There was a louder rumble of wheels, the equipages respectfully drew aside, and two postilions appeared, clad in green, with round caps, on which golden tassels jolted with their cords spread out. Leaning slightly forward, they hastened on at the trot of their tall bay horses. Behind them they left an empty space; and, then, in this empty space, the Emperor appeared.

He occupied alone the back seat of a landau. Dressed in black, with his frock-coat buttoned up to his chin, he wore, slightly on one side, a very tall hat, the silk of which glistened. In front of him, on the other seat, two gentlemen, dressed with that correct elegance which was favourably looked upon at the Tuileries, remained grave, with their hands on their knees, and the silent air of two wedding guests promenaded amid the curiosity of a crowd.

Renée found the Emperor aged. His mouth was parted more languidly under his thick waxed moustaches. His eyelids had grown heavy to the point that they half covered his dim eyes, the yellow greyness of which had become yet more cloudy. And his nose alone still looked like a dry bone set in his vague face.

Meantime, while the ladies in the carriages smiled discreetly, the people on foot pointed the sovereign out to one another. A fat man declared that the Emperor was the gentleman who turned his back to the coachman on the left side. Some hands were raised to salute. But Saccard, who had taken off his hat, even before the postilions had passed, waited till the imperial carriage was exactly in front of him, and then he cried out in his thick Provençal voice:

"Long live the Emperor!"

The Emperor, surprised, turned, recognised the enthusiast, no doubt, and returned the bow smiling. And everything then disappeared in the sunlight, the equipages closed up, and Renée could only perceive, above the manes of the horses, and between the backs of the footmen, the postilions caps jolting with their golden tassels.

She remained for a moment with her eyes wide open, full of this apparition, which reminded her of another hour of her life. It seemed to her as if the Emperor, by mingling with the line of carriages, had set the last necessary ray therein, and given a meaning to this triumphal march. Now, it was a glory. All these wheels, all these decorated men, all these women languidly stretched out, disappeared amid the flash and the rumble of the imperial landau. This sensation became so acute and so painful that the young woman experienced an imperious need of escaping from this triumph, from Saccard's cry, which was still ringing in her ears, from the sight of the father and the son slowly walking along, and chatting with their arms linked. She reflected, with her hands on her breast, as if burnt by an internal fire: and it was with a sudden hope of relief and salutary coolness that she leant forward, and said to the coachman:

"To the Béraud mansion."

The courtyard retained its cloister-like coldness. Renée went round the arcades, made happy by the dampness which fell upon her shoulders. She approached the fountain, green with moss, and polished by wear at the edges; she looked at the lion's head, now half effaced, which, with parted jaws emitted a gush of water by an iron pipe. How many times had she and Christine taken this head between their girlish arms to lean forward to reach the stream of water, the icy flow of which they liked to feel upon their little hands. Then she mounted the great silent staircase; she perceived her father at the end of the suite of spacious rooms; he drew up his tall figure, and silently went deeper into the shade of the old residence, of the haughty solitude in which he had absolutely cloistered himself since his sister's death; and Renée thought of the men of the Bois, of that other old man, Baron Gouraud, who had his flesh rolled about on pillows in the sunlight. She went up higher, she followed the passages, the servants' stairs, she was bound for the nursery. When she reached the top landing she found the key hanging on the usual nail; a large rusty key it was, on which spiders had woven webs. The lock gave a plaintive cry. How sad the nursery was! She felt a pang at her heart of finding it so empty, so grey, so silent. She closed the open door of the abandoned aviary, with the vague idea that it must have been by that door that the joys of her childhood had flown away. In front of the flower-boxes, still full of soil hardened and cracked all over like dry mud, she stopped and broke off a rhododendron stem; this skeleton of a plant, shrivelled and white with dust, was all that remained of their living clumps of verdure. And the matting, the matting itself, faded, gnawed by rats, displayed itself with the melancholy aspect of a shroud which has for years awaited a promised corpse. In one corner amid this mute despair, this silent weeping abandonment, Renée found one of her old dolls; all the bran had flowed out of it by a hole, but its porcelain head continued smiling with its enamelled lips, above the tabid body, which a doll's follies seemed to have exhausted.

Renée felt stifled in the tainted atmosphere of the abode of her childhood. She opened the window and gazed on the immense view. Nothing there was soiled. She again found the eternal delights, the eternal juvenescence of the open air. The sun must have been sinking behind her; but she only saw the rays of the setting planet, as they lent, with infinite softness, a yellowish tinge to this corner of the city which she knew so well. It was like the last lay of daylight, a gay refrain, which slowly subsided on all things. There were gleams of tawny fire about the boom below, while the lace-work of the iron cables of the Pont de Constantine stood out above the whiteness of the pillars. Then, on the right hand, the umbrage of the Halle aux Vins and the Jardin des Plantes seemed like a great mere with stagnant, mossy water, the greenish surface of which blended in the distance with the mist of the sky. On the left, the Quai Henri IV and the Quai de la Rapée were lined with the same rows of houses, those houses which, as girls, twenty years before, they had seen there, with the same brown patches of sheds, the same ruddy factory chimneys. And, above the trees, the slate roof of the Salpêtrière hospital, made blue by the sun's good-bye, suddenly appeared to her like an old friend.

But what calmed her, and imparted coolness to her bosom, were the long grey banks, and especially the Seine, the giantess, which she saw coming from the limits of the horizon straight towards her, just as in those happy times when she had feared to see it well and rise up to the very window. She remembered their affection for the river, their love for its colossal flow, for this quivering of noisy water, spreading out in a sheet at their feet, parting around and behind them in two arms, the ends of which they could not see, though they still felt the great pure caress. They were then already coquettish, and on the days when the sky was clear they said that the Seine had put on her beautiful dress of green silk, flecked with white flames; and the eddies where the water curled set frills of satin on the dress, while afar off, beyond the belt of bridges, a play of light spread strips of stuff the colour of the sun.

And Renée, raising her eyes, looked at the vast expanse of soaring sky of a pale blue, fading little by little in the obliteration of twilight. She thought of the accomplice city, of the blazing nights of the Boulevard, of the hot afternoons of the Bois, of the pallid, crude day, of the grand new mansions. Then, when she lowered her head, when she again saw at a glance the peaceful horizon of her childhood, this corner of a city, inhabited by the middle and working classes, where she had dreamt of a life of peace, a final bitterness mounted to her lips. With her hands clasped, she sobbed in the gathering night.

The following winter, when Renée died of acute meningitis, it was her father who paid her debts. Worms's bill amounted to two hundred and fifty-seven thousand francs.

THE END

A Note About the Author

Émile Zola (1840–1902) was a French novelist, journalist, and playwright. Born in Paris to a French mother and Italian father, Zola was raised in Aix-en-Provence. At 18, Zola moved back to Paris, where he befriended Paul Cézanne and began his writing career. During this early period, Zola worked as a clerk for a publisher while writing literary and art reviews as well as political journalism for local newspapers. Following the success of his novel *Thérèse Raquin* (1867), Zola began a series of twenty novels known as *Les Rougon-Macquart*, a sprawling collection following the fates of a single family living under the Second Empire of Napoleon III. Zola's work earned him a reputation as a leading figure in literary naturalism, a style noted for its rejection of Romanticism in favor of detachment, rationalism, and social commentary. Following the infamous Dreyfus affair of 1894, in which a French-Jewish artillery officer was falsely convicted of spying for the German Embassy, Zola wrote a scathing open letter to French President Félix Faure accusing the government and military of antisemitism and obstruction of justice. Having sacrificed his reputation as a writer and intellectual, Zola helped reverse public opinion on the affair, placing pressure on the government that led to Dreyfus' full exoneration in 1906. Nominated for the Nobel Prize in Literature in 1901 and 1902, Zola is considered one of the most influential and talented writers in French history.

A Note from the Publisher

Spanning many genres, from non-fiction essays to literature classics to children's books and lyric poetry, Mint Edition books showcase the master works of our time in a modern new package. The text is freshly typeset, is clean and easy to read, and features a new note about the author in each volume. Many books also include exclusive new introductory material. Every book boasts a striking new cover, which makes it as appropriate for collecting as it is for gift giving. Mint Edition books are only printed when a reader orders them, so natural resources are not wasted. We're proud that our books are never manufactured in excess and exist only in the exact quantity they need to be read and enjoyed.